The Harlot's Heart

The Harlot's Heart

By Brenda Richardson-McGhee

XULON PRESS

Xulon Press
2301 Lucien Way #415
Maitland, FL 32751
407.339.4217
www.xulonpress.com

PRESS

Unless otherwise indicated, Scripture quotations taken from the King
James Version (KJV) – *public domain*.

Printed in the United States of America

Paperback ISBN-13: 978-1-6322-1886-5
Ebook ISBN-13: 978-1-6322-1887-2

To Judy Hale- you stood by me (as my critic) through the process and waited patiently for each new chapter as I created it.

To Theresa Wysocki Burbridge- as always, my friend the artist, you were there with me and took my book to another level with your cover design. I can never thank you enough.

To Gina Stephens-You prayed and said it was in me- I had to let it out. Well, I did.

To those that told me "You should write a book", I thank you for your encouragement way back when I never thought I could.

To the memories of what it was to be loved, forgiven, and held when you felt nothing but pain.

Thank God for His grace, mercy, and second chances to redeem us from a harlot's heart.

I love you all.

Prologue

April 28, 2019

Lithia looked over the treetops at the full moon rising. How beautiful was the sky with all its shimmering stars crowning the regal pines behind the apartment? She had to admit, the view from her bedroom was amazing. To watch the sunset was breathtaking, and sipping coffee on the balcony each morning for sunrise was mesmerizing. But it was the stillness of the night heavens that she could get lost. Her thoughts would meander through the stars and lights, wondering how she had missed this wonderful creation God had made. The vastness of the heavens was beyond her comprehension. She knew the creation story and didn't doubt it, but it was so large. Could God see her in the tiny portion she took up in His great world?

Her mind flittered to the past. When she was little, she would stand on her bed, looking out her bedroom window, and she wished and prayed so hard-little girl fantasies of unicorns and fairies, and a little sister-things that were just dreams. Lithia believed in fairytales, happily ever afters, and prayer changes things. But now, she wasn't so sure.

"Oh, ye of little faith?" Lithia could hear her grandmother say in her head.

Grandmother was gone, along with Lithia's hopes of anymore happiness. She was always welcome at her grandparents' home, sitting on her grandmother's lap as they rocked in the big green rocking chair by the window. During the day, they studied the rose bushes Grandmother treasured. She could tell Lithia about each one and when she had gotten it. See, everyone gave Grandmother a rose bush for Mother's Day or her birthday. She knew exactly who and when. Lithia had helped prune, plant, fertilize, and water from the time she was in kindergarten. The pink tea roses were her favorite, but Grandmother liked the red grandiflora roses that Uncle Clyde had given her when he left for the Army, or the white English rosebush Uncle Larry gave her when he married Aunt Jeannie. Whenever Lithia would ask why Grandmother liked them best, it was because they came from her sons. Grandmother would go into the story of how white represented the purity of a heart after Christ had cleaned a person of sin. The red symbolized the blood of Jesus that made the person pure. Aunt Sue would laugh under her breath, "Larry was just trying to get you to believe Jeannie was still a virgin at the wedding." At the time, Lithia had no idea, but by the time she was seventeen, she understood Aunt Jeannie's red face and why her parents would leave.

Sitting in that rocker was also the place Grandmother taught her to speak to God. She would tell Lithia how He made a garden to place the first people, so they could come and talk with Him there. It was looking out into the sky at night Grandmother explained how God was up there in the heavens. He knew everything happening to us on earth. He cared. It looked so big at six years old; it wasn't any smaller at twenty-four. Did He know about her now? Did He still care? She wasn't what she was back then, small and safe in her grandmother's arms. White roses didn't, well, they weren't the flowers for her. Lithia needed black. Nothing was innocent or pure; it would never be again.

Jolting to the sound of her phone ringing, Lithia gasped, realizing she had been holding her breath as she watched the stars slowly begin to shine in the sky. Reaching over her pile of clean clothes she was supposed to be putting away, she grabbed the cell phone. Quickly, she glanced at the caller ID. Not him again.

Her boss, Daniel Armstrong III. There were times she said "The Turd" in her mind, but today she said it aloud. No one could hear her anyway. She was alone. "Yes, Mr. Armstrong, what do you need from me on my day off?" Lithia shouldn't be so catty, but he was so demanding all the time. He held her past over her head. But she had needed a job at the time and she'd learn to deal with it.

"There's a client coming in from out of town tomorrow. I need you to pick him up at the airport at 7 am, check him into the company suite, and make sure he has breakfast. Can you do that? Oh, send a car for him at 9 to bring him to the office." Daniel knew Lithia would do it, but how would she react to this client? Polite and interested in whatever he might say, or like the last client? Rude and outright sarcastic? Daniel's guess was as good as anyone's.

"Fine, who is it? What airline and flight number?" Lithia wrote the information down as Daniel told her, but she was pretty sure the name sounded familiar. "Okay, Southwest Airlines, Gate 8, on Flight 74 from Raleigh, North Carolina. Craig O'Shay. I got it." Daniel went on and on about how she needed to be polite and cater to Mr. O'Shay's every whim. All she comprehended was "blah, blah, blah."

Finally, Lithia was able to put the phone down. She was going to have to put it on charge after that one-sided conversation. She glanced down at the notepad she had been writing on. She had rewritten over and over Craig O'Shay's name. She even placed a heart for the dot over the "i" in Craig. Why did that name seem intriguing? One percent battery left. When would she ever remember to turn off her phone on her days not at work? Sticking her feet into her slippers, she wandered into the kitchen looking for her charger. It had to be on the granite counter; she was sure she had it on charge yesterday morning while fixing a bagel for breakfast. As she plugged in the cord, she tried to decide if she was hungry or not.

Her stomach rumbled, and Lithia opened the refrigerator door. Hmm, a sandwich and salad, or should she eat a bowl of soup and crackers? Exactly, not a very exciting meal, but she couldn't gain any weight back, it would just be another mark against her at work. *Who cares! I'll order a pizza anyway.* She picked up her cell and called the neighborhood Domino's and ordered a gluten-free ten-inch veggie pizza to be delivered. *Daniel, be damned! I don't have to eat it all tonight.*

Lithia took a water bottle out of the case sitting by the pantry. So many things she should have done today. Gotten dressed might have been the first step, but pajama day was it. Cozy cotton t-shirt and shorts with four-leaf clovers on them made her look about twelve years old than in her twenties. She liked the shirt with the pot of gold under the rainbow with "Follow My Lucky Charms" written on the front.

They were comfortable, and she had no one to impress at all. She had completed her laundry, though the clean clothes still lay on her bed. Maybe she could get those put away before the pizza came. The kitchen had been cleaned up after breakfast, and there were the bills she paid online at some point earlier. Yep, she should have taken her car to get the oil changed, and she needed groceries. But that required clothes other than her jammie shorts. Nope, she would wait until after work tomorrow.

"So, what's on the boob tube tonight?" Lithia spoke out loud. Sometimes she craved another person in the apartment with her, but at what cost could a roommate bring? She had been there, done that before. Solitude was her friend. The news and weather showed thunderstorms in the surrounding area of Tampa. That would tamper with her view of the full moon later in her bedroom. Lithia channel-surfed until she was sure there was nothing on that was interesting, until she heard the name Craig O'Shay. She jumped back and heard the last bit from the anchorman, "Craig O'Shay is speaking at a charity ball for domestic violence victims on Saturday, May 4, at the Teco Hall in the Tampa Bay History Center."

Lithia turned off the television. Interesting, that's what he is doing here. But how does he know Daniel and what is Daniel's interest in Mr. O'Shay? "What is wrong with me? I'm trying to figure out what Daniel wants in this guy and I don't even know who he is. Maybe he is just as shady as Daniel. They could be two peas in a pod. God knows I have met my share of Daniels in the world." Lithia shook her head. *I'm losing my mind talking to myself. I need to worry about me and not other people's business. My problem is I don't trust men, especially men like Daniel Armstrong III. If O'Shay is anything like Daniel, I need to do my job tomorrow and hope that is the end of that.*

The buzzer rang, and she let the pizza delivery guy come up. She gave him a twenty and said he could keep the change. The kid was probably about seventeen. He had given her that look when she answered the door. He tried to step through the threshold, but she had the money in her hand too fast for him to get more than a foot inside. Lithia had seen those looks before with delivery guys and maintenance men. She tried not to be alone when there was maintenance to be done, or she had the landlord deal with it when she was gone. Delivery guys were harder. There were some places she asked specifically for a female to deliver.

The aroma of the pizza was to die for as Lithia opened the hot box. She pulled a green pepper off the top and popped it into her mouth. It burned her tongue, but the mix of tomato sauce, cheese, and garlic was lethal. She scooped up the biggest slice, placing it on a paper plate, and snatched a water bottle from the fridge. Curling on the sofa, she took the first bite of pizza she had eaten in a year. One slice of pizza wasn't going to kill her. She would put the rest up for later, or take the rest to work. She could put it in the refrigerator, and someone was bound to eat it for lunch. No one had to know she had brought it.

Channel surfing again, she skimmed over the news and The Big Bang Theory. Why would she want to watch depressing channels or reruns? Some game shows were on, but she would start getting annoyed when someone yelled or missed the easiest questions. She stopped on a station with a commercial. She'd wait to see what this channel had to offer. Maybe a comedy is what she needed- a good laugh to relieve the stress. Then she heard a voice she recognized.

But the woman didn't look like ...Lithia moved to the edge of the sofa. "Go back to the woman, cameraman! Give me a close-up!"

The hair was cut differently, and the clothes were classy. She was wearing a nice beige suit with a knee-length skirt, a rose-colored blouse and brown pumps. Her makeup was natural, and she was only wearing a single gold wedding band and small pearl stud earrings. Her hands didn't have the long red acrylic nails, but the average length and painted light pink. The woman's face showed she had aged, but the tired worn look she once wore was gone.

No, it can't be her! Lithia heard the voice; the camera revealed the scar on the corner of her lip. No one else could have the same mark. Lithia was there when she got it. But this wasn't the same girl. She had changed. Her face glowed, and she smiled. She turned up the volume to try to hear. Lithia kept thinking, *"What changed her? How did this happen?"* It was like the woman could hear what Lithia was thinking.

"One day, when I didn't think I had the strength to go on, I wanted to end my life. I hated myself and what I had become, what I had allowed myself to do. I couldn't look in the mirror anymore. My friends were gone or deeper in trouble than me. My family had disowned me; to get away meant death, or worse. I had no one. Then I heard a song. It was coming from the inside of the building I had been hiding in the dumpster. The words came to me like a soothing hand on my brow. 'What a friend we have in Jesus. All our sins and griefs to bear. What a privilege to carry, everything to God in prayer. Oh, what peace we often forfeit, Oh, what needless pain we bear. All because we do not carry everything to God in prayer. Have we trials and temptations? Is there trouble everywhere? We should never be discouraged, Take it to the Lord in prayer.'"

Lithia clicked the button quick. She didn't believe it was the same person. It couldn't be. But the words of the song kept going over and over in Lithia's mind all night. She could hear her grandmother singing them to her as she stared out the bedroom window, looking at the full moon.

Chapter 1

February 2010

*E*ver since Lithia could remember, she was in the *friend zone*. Just once could she have one guy find her attractive and enticing? She had plenty of friends, guys and girls. She got invited to parties and events, and many times was in the spotlight, but dates were not the same. Guys didn't ask her out; they asked her friends out. Oh, they called her and could talk for hours, but it was about Carrie, or Leslie, or Renee. "How do you think they would like me in this shirt?" or "Do you think she would go with me to prom or the Friday night football game?"

She was everyone's couple's counselor as well. Like she knew anything about relationships. The closest thing she every came to a date was being forced to ask a guy to a church Sadie Hawkins dinner. He was a LOT older than she, and she was not interested.

If another one of her friends told her how much they liked Leo, she was going to scream. Let her mention she even the thought that a guy was cute, Leslie was all over him. By the following week, they were "going together." All that meant, they sat together in church and talked on the phone for five minutes if Leslie was lucky enough to get one that called. It was taboo for a girl to call a guy, Grandmother said. Boys were to be the pursuer. That might be in Grandmother's day or for her mom, but no way, not now. She tried to call one guy, but all she could hear in her ear was, *"You are going to be labeled a Jezebel if you start calling boys."* God forbid that happen. It would be the unpardonable sin in her families' eyes.

See, Lithia had "blossomed" long before her other friends. Most people thought she was sixteen or seventeen when she was only twelve. She would be out mowing the yard or sitting out under the tree in the front, and grown men would whistle or holler at her. They didn't want her dad to hear them. He would come out so fast from the shed. He would tell them to keep walking or driving. She was only twelve. Thank God, he didn't have the shotgun near him any time it happened. Her mom made her start playing in the backyard or told her to not be so conspicuous.

She got her first kiss at twelve. It wasn't what she thought it would be. He was older than her. A friend's big brother. He was cute and sixteen. He knew how old she really was and said all the right things. Barry told her she was mature for her age, that's what he liked about her. The other girls were so giggly and immature, even girls in high school. Lithia could show them what a man wanted in a woman. Then Barry showed her what he wanted anyway.

It was a Monday after school, and she had ridden her bike to hang out with Barry's three younger sisters. Their mom was at work, and so they were sitting around in the carport talking about school, boys, music, and movie stars. Tina had even brought out a disc player and some CDs to listen to. While they were making up silly dance moves, Barry begins to clap. Lithia turns beat red when she swirls around to see him staring right at her though his sisters tell him to go play basketball with his friends at the park or finish his homework. He ignores everyone but Lithia. Lithia is out of breath, from Barry's looks or from the dancing? She's not sure.

Barry kept moving closer to her; Lithia can feel her pulse racing in her chest. As her breasts noticeably move up and down, she realizes where Barry's eyes are drawn. Since he was so tall, looking at her, she knew he could see down her shirt. He turns to Tina and tells her to take the younger sisters inside and make some lemonade for everyone. He insists they do it together so they could bring a glass back for all five of us when they return. He would keep me company and could show me a dance move for one of the songs we had been singing.

Lithia didn't have much space to move. He had backed her into the wall of the house, away from doors or windows so his sisters couldn't see what was going on in the carport. Tilting her head back with one hand and placing the other around Lithia's waist, he pulled her tight against him. She felt the heat of his body and the pressure on her lower abdomen. She was glued against him as he bought his mouth over her lips, he moved his hand from her chin, slowly down her neck to cup her breast. Lithia couldn't speak as he tried to spread her legs apart and press his leg between.

What could she do? Her hands were pinned down, she was against the wall. He was stronger and bigger than she was. She couldn't cry out or hit him. She was doing everything to keep her legs together. She wasn't sure where that one hand was going, but it wasn't on her breast anymore, and it kept getting lower. Would his sisters ever come back out? Surely, it didn't take that long to make lemonade unless they were squeezing the lemons. Finally, she bit down. Hard. He grabbed his mouth and acted like he was going to strike her, but stopped. She spit at him over and over. All Lithia could taste was Barry. She wanted to throw up. On him. Then he started laughing at her. She jumped on her bike and rode home.

Lithia was humiliated. She had acted like a stupid baby. All that hogwash about her being all grown up and mature; she just showed him how elementary school she was. And he laughed at her. Running into the house, she went straight to the bathroom and grabbed her toothbrush. She didn't remember how long she was in there, but she scrubbed her teeth with peroxide and toothpaste for a long time. She was spitting into the sink and gagging when her mom came knocking at the bathroom door.

"What in the world are you doing? Hold on, don't you put that peroxide in your mouth. Spit that out! Why are you crying and so angry? Did a bug fly in your mouth and you swallowed it?" Why was her daughter so hard to talk to her? Lola stared to walk away. Why should she try to understand Lithia?

Finally, Lithia began to cry. It was hard to understand her at first, but Lola got the gist of what happened. Barry had kissed her and made her open her mouth. It was disgusting. Lola bent over laughing at Lithia. That was not the reaction Lithia expected at all. Well, there was no reason to tell her what else he did. She would be rolling on the floor, laughing even more if Lithia did. When her mom stopped laughing, Lithia was told to go right back over there to Tina's house and apologize for being so rude. "What? I was rude!

4

For what? Hating him touching me or that nasty-tasting kiss?" Lithia was furious. Lola asked her if she told the girls bye and did she know spitting on someone was very disrespectful. She was to ride her bike over to Barry's and apologize for being so disrespectful when he was just trying to show her how he felt about her. She also had to tell Tina and her sisters how sorry she was for leaving so abruptly. Lithia thought about just riding her bike around the neighborhood instead and make her mom think she went over there. Until Lola told her she was going to call Tina's mom in a couple of hours after dinner and tell her what happened. She would find out if Lithia came and apologized.

Longest bike ride ever. Of course, no one was outside anymore, and Lithia had to knock on the door. Barry totally ignored her and acted like he was into the show on television. She knew better than that. He had told his sisters Lithia had realized it was time to go home and was afraid she would get in trouble for being late. Coming back messed his lie up; he wasn't too happy when Tina knew what really happened. Lithia stayed for a while, hanging with the girls.

It wasn't until their mom came home that Barry finally stepped out in the carport to talk to Lithia alone. She quietly apologized for spitting in his face and biting his tongue. She just had never been kissed before and didn't know what it would be like. He told her fine, but the next time she wanted to flirt with him, he wasn't going to stop. Girls that tease would get what they wanted. Lithia wasn't too sure how she "teased" him. But when he pushed her back against the wall and pressed his groin on her, she got worried. He grabbed her hands above her, tilted her head so she had to look at him, and leaned where his lips were almost touching hers. Lithia gasped; he was going to do it again. Her heart was beating out of her chest; she couldn't breathe. His words were hot on her face, on her neck. He promised if she ever was kissed by him again, his mouth would leave marks all over her body. Lithia never told anyone his promise. Ever.

Why, after three years, did this memory come up so vividly? Lithia didn't know, she just wanted to be kissed by someone who cared about her. She wanted the *forever after*. At fifteen, she knew that wasn't going to happen anytime soon, but she did want a "do-over" on that first kiss. But with whom? Leo would be a good start; however, Leslie had already put her claws into him, and no one else was even a contender. Even at church, the guys were only interested in the slutty girls. Lithia was doomed to be a nun.

By sixteen, high school boys were nice to Lithia, but she still was always in the friend's zone. She would hang with Leslie, and just because Leslie let the boys go a lot farther than most, guys would talk to Lithia. But as soon as they realized she wasn't going to let them touch, see, or do whatever they wanted, she was made fun of, called names, and horrible rumors were passed throughout the campus. One of Leslie's boyfriends even had told Lithia he would love to see her model. She had the body for it. Curves in all the right places. Lithia was flattered, until he wanted to have her model nude and take photos. She didn't come around anymore when he was at Leslie's. Nevertheless, how do you stay clear of him when he sat by you in Biology and English class? She made up lies to get her schedule changed, but the administration refused to let her. So, she did the next best thing.

Lithia quit high school and started to prepare to just take her GED. She looked older anyway; she'd get a job. Lola and Peter were frustrated with Lithia. Her older brother never gave them these issues. It had to be the female hormones that made her so hard to make friends or get depressed about boys. She started to gain weight and tell lies. She didn't want to go to school. Church was okay, or her grandmother's house, but school wasn't going to happen. So, her parents compromised. The GED wasn't happening. Her parents said no, but she could go to night school. That's when things really turned around. Some could say for the good; others may say for the bad. Depends on your point of view.

Chapter 2

April 29, 2019

Sleep had not come well after seeing the interview last night. All these old memories had poured out of her soul, where she had buried them ages ago. Lithia had been tormented with them the entire night. She just wished they would go back from where they came. When she was younger, there were ways to forget, but she had been striving to make better choices the past eighteen months. Daniel didn't make that elementary with his constant snide remarks in the office.

What would she wear today? Pants or skirt? Maybe a nice suit or spring dress? Mulling in her wardrobe, the phone rang; Daniel's face darkened her phone screen. *Already? It's only 6:30 in the morning. Can't I have my first cup of coffee before the madness begins?* "Yes, Daniel, what do you need from me this morning?" Lithia placed him on speaker so she could try to finish dressing.

"Lithia, don't forget to pick up Craig O'Shay at the airport. You do remember the flight number?" Daniel seemed uptight, not like normal uptight, but extremely wound up. She was glad he called, for she had totally forgotten Mr. O'Shay's chauffeur service.

"I was headed out the door, when you called. I had to lay my purse and briefcase down to find my phone. Now I am going to be late." She knew she had lied, but right now, she did not care. Did he realize how much later she was going to be if she didn't off the phone with him?

"Don't you dare wear some grandma-looking dress either. Show off your figure and some cleavage. I want him to know we are a trend-setting company, not some old-fashioned, conservative, closed-minded business." Lithia could hear him mumbling under his breath about hand-me-downs from Goodwill. Hmm, she'd show him. *I'll wear this light blue sleeveless dress with the billowy cut. No cleavage, and you can't see the waist at all. It comes to the knee. I can accessorize with the pastel earrings, bracelet, and necklace I got from my brother on my 18th birthday. Oh, and white sandals will finish the outfit.* She would put her hair up in a messy bun. Daniel wasn't going to be loving her look today. He was still talking when she pulled into the parking lot of the airport.

"Look, Daniel, I can't really look for the man if you keep talking to me. Send me his number so I can tell him where I am. I will be at the office as soon as I drop him off at the hotel. Thank you, bye, Mr. Armstrong." She knew he didn't like it when she went formal on him. He couldn't get her to bend whenever she called him *mister.* Click. If he wasn't going to hang up, Lithia would. Ok, it would make this so much easier if she had a photo of this O'Shay guy. She was not going to do like some did, a big poster with his name over her head. That wasn't happening.

The strap of her sandal slipped down off her ankle. *I must have not tightened it enough, thanks to Daniel giving me such a headache while I was dressing.* Lithia stepped out of the walkway so she could lean over and fix her shoe, when two ten-year-old boys came barreling by and bumped her. She would have fallen face-first into the tile if a gentleman hadn't grabbed her elbow at just the right time. He placed her hand on his shoulder and got on one knee in front of her. As he reached down, lifting her foot on his extended knee, "I saw you trying to fix your strap and knew those boys were destined to hit into you. I'm glad I caught you in time. Here, I think that is tight enough not to fall down again." The man's hands were strong, and quickly unbuckled the strap and pulled it snug around her ankle. Then he slowly placed his hand on her calf as he set her foot down on the floor. His hand was warm and gentle, and did not go any farther up her leg then needed. So many other guys would have completely taken advantage of the situation.

Lithia couldn't tell much about the businessman since she really didn't get a look at his face. With steadying herself and gripping her purse, she could only see his broad shoulders and his auburn hair. He had placed his briefcase and baggage down beside him, draping his suit jacket over them. The shirt was pulled taunt, showing the muscles in his arms and chest, though she tried to look at his face as he stood up, it was his hands that also drew her attention. It was certain they were gentle and warm; she knew from his touch on her foot. Lithia expected some well-manicured smooth hands, but was surprised to see hands bearing scars and calluses. The stranger might dress like a CEO, but his hands cried blue-collar worker.

As he collected his things, the stranger asked, "Will you be all right? I am to meet my ride and I know I'm late. If you need me, I can stay with you until your party arrives." That's when Lithia saw his face. His eyes were so kind, they were the eyes her grandmother said smiled. She stammered, "No, no, I... I am fine. I am meeting someone as well. I...I...I am late as well. Thank you, for my shoe." *Oh, my goodness, did I really say, 'thank you for my shoe'? I have got to look so stupid to this man. He is probably some rich company president and thinks I am some country bumpkin.* "I meant thank you for fixing my shoe and keeping me from crashing face-first. I do appreciate your kindness."

"I am glad to be there for the damsel in distress, but my steed awaits me to my dreary life of knighthood. Till we meet again, fair maiden. I bid you adieu." He took her hand, and bowing, he kissed it. Then turned and began to walk toward the exit.

She would never wash this hand again.

A lady walked by with a screaming baby in her arms, and Lithia came to her senses. She rummaged through her purse to find her cell and pulled up the text from Daniel that had Craig O'Shay's number. She immediately hit dial. She knew her cheeks were flushed from the stranger's kiss as she turned toward the wall. Lithia didn't want to seem disheveled when she met Mr. O'Shay. She almost hung up after the fifth ring, when a man answered, "O'Shay here." *So far so good, he didn't sound angry, yet.*

"Yes, Mr. O'Shay, this is Miss Murphy, Mr. Armstrong's personal secretary. I am here at the airport to give you transportation to the hotel and prepare you for the next few days' schedule. If you tell me where you are located, I will come right to you. I am sorry for any inconvenience I have caused with my tardiness." Silence on the other end of the phone. "Mr. O'Shay, did we lose connection?" *I spoke too soon; he is not happy I am late. The man is probably used to*

*prompt employees and thinks we are idiots here. What was
it her grandmother use to tell her to do, "Ask God for favor"
whenever she needed help? She hadn't prayed in years, but
made a quick one.*

"I apologize, Miss Murphy. I didn't expect someone so
charming to be coming for me. I figured some hard-nosed
executive who wanted to begin pounding me with proposals
all the way to the office without a chance for breakfast and
time to dispose of my luggage. I am standing outside of the
main exit to the left of the door. Will you be coming from the
parking garage or from inside the airport? I can come to you."

*If this man will be this nice in person, maybe this isn't
too bad of an assignment.* "I am near the exit myself. I will
step out the door within a minute or two. Could you tell me
what you are wearing? Maybe the color of your suit or shirt?"

"Blue shirt and grey pants."

"I believe I see you, sir." Lithia ended the call as the
stranger turned toward her. He was wearing a blue shirt
and grey pants.

Craig could not speak. The beautiful damsel in distress
was Miss Murphy, his ride? *God does answer prayers. And
fast, too. What was it, five, ten minutes ago I asked if I could
see her again before I left Tampa, and boom, God, you
are awesome!*

Lithia was stunned. Her assignment was none other than
the auburn-haired stranger. *Asking for favors does work.
Chop one up for Grandmother.*

"Long time no see. This is a pleasant surprise. Let me
introduce myself. I am Craig O'Shay, founder of Saoirse's
Heart of Hope. That's pronounced *"ser-sha,"* which means,
"freedom" or "liberty." I am assuming you know this is a place
for domestic violence victims. We have safe housing for up

to a month, and counseling, daycare, job training, a nurse and doctor available when necessary. There are even lawyers that work pro bono for the women. That's why I am here. To gain donations to open another home in the Tampa area."

"Wow, that is phenomenal, Mr. O'Shay! Mr. Armstrong had not told me anything about you other than to pick you up and where to drive you this week. I do know you are old acquaintances from childhood or college. And I saw where you are speaking Friday night for a huge charity ball, but I found that out on the news last night."

Dead silence. They still hadn't moved from outside the airport door.

"Do you mind if I ask, but where did you get the name, "Saoirse" for the safe house?" Lithia looked in his eyes, and she saw a sadness that overtook him. She wished she hadn't said a word, but it was too late.

"Saoirse was my mother's name." Without another word, Craig picked up his baggage and followed Lithia to her car.

The drive to the hotel was in total silence. Lithia knew there were things she was to discuss with Mr. O'Shay, but she didn't think it was proper. She had brought up his mom; he must have loved her deeply. She wondered if his mom was still alive. Lithia's intuition told her no, Mrs. O'Shay passed away. Her son still grieved; could it have been recent?

The bellboy saw to Craig's bags as Lithia went to the front desk to let the attendee know Mr. Armstrong's guest would be in the executive suite for the next week. She collected the extra key and stepped into the elevator with the bellboy and Craig. The bellboy tried to make small talk, but it was futile. Craig tipped the bellboy automatically, nodded his head, stepping onto the balcony. Lithia was still standing right inside the doorway as the bellboy closed the door behind him.

Craig's stomach growled; it wasn't quiet either. He realized he hadn't eaten since yesterday morning. He probably should see about room service before his 9 o'clock meeting with Daniel. "God, help me today. I miss her so much. Let her know how much I love her. Mom would have wanted to hear everything about the trip and the damsel in distress I rescued. However, she would call me Prince Charming with the Cinderella shoe thing."

Wow, he talks to God like a friend. She hadn't heard anyone do that in so long. Her grandparents, parents, Pastor Johnson, it had just been a long time since she was home or in a place where someone prayed like that. Then when he mentioned her 'damsel in distress' 'Prince Charming' event, she didn't mean to, but she laughed out loud.

"What are you doing here?" Craig thought the bellboy was still hanging around wanting a bigger tip. He didn't realize Miss Murphy had come up with them. Her face was hurt. It was his words that scared her. He had yelled when he heard someone laugh at his private prayer, but he didn't know it was his Cinderella. She looked as if she was going to bolt out the door, but hesitated. He knew they were to review the schedule for the week prior to the morning meeting, and neither had said a word on the drive to the hotel. Miss Murphy wanted to leave; she was forced to stay.

"I am so ashamed of the way I spoke to you. I have no right to talk to you that way. Please accept my apology, Miss Murphy. It's just, well, I didn't think anyone was in my room with me. I thought you had left and so had the bellboy. It threw me off guard when you laughed at my prayer." Craig bowed his head and sat on the bed. He had been so strong

14

lately; he hadn't cried over his mom's death in months. *Why now, in front of her? She will go back, telling Daniel, and it will be high school all over again. Odd, she's not laughing; it looks like a tear running down her cheek. No, God, please don't let me have hurt her feelings. I never intended to do any of that.*

Lithia was embarrassed more than he was. She had stayed, even when she knew he was praying, then she laughed at him. Well, not at him, but the thought of him telling his mom about his valiant act of chivalry with her sandal. Priceless. She willed herself to walk to his side and sit in the chair facing him. Lithia took his hand, "Don't be ashamed. I should have left when I realized you were praying. I was wrong. I just haven't heard anyone pray like that in years, and to be described as Cinderella, to God, well, I am honored. Shall we get breakfast before it is too late? I did hear your stomach rumble and I think mine is harmonizing with yours. Would you like to go down to the dining area, or we could just walk across the street to IHOP?"

"IHOP, I could go for a big stack of chocolate chip pancakes with a side order of bacon. Oh, plus orange juice and coffee. What will you have?" *It was like having a sixteen-year-old with her. Mr. O'Shay sure could switch directions fast. Maybe he wanted to make her comfortable after that fiasco.* "Biscuits and gravy, and fruit salad. Coffee black." He let go of her hand long enough to pick the room card off the dresser, look in the mirror, and half drag her out the door. "Lead the way, Your Majesty."

They dodged traffic crossing the intersection to get to IHOP, and jumped into the first booth they saw vacant and waited for the middle-aged waitress with a tattoo of a butterfly on her wrist to hand them menus. Since they knew what they wanted, it didn't take long to get their food. They used the time wisely, eating and reviewing the schedule Daniel had for Craig. Lithia saw time was getting away from them, she started to text for Daniel to send a car to pick up Craig in front of the hotel. Craig stopped her. "Aren't you going to the office, too? No need to take two cars to the same place. Just let me run up to my room and get my jacket and briefcase. Have the valet bring the car around. I will meet you out front."

Lithia didn't want the morning to end. He was so delightful to talk to and polite. He even prayed over their breakfast. She hadn't prayed over a meal since probably five years ago this Thanksgiving, or was it her father's funeral? She hadn't been home since then. *Nope, I am not thinking sad and morose anymore today. I am going to have an amazing Monday.*

Walking into the office, several of the women gazed at Craig as he walked to the conference room behind Lithia. He was easy on the eyes as Grandmother would say. She stuck her head in to tell Daniel she was depositing Mr. O'Shay as directed, then turned to go to her own small office down the hall.

Craig didn't want the time with this Cinderella to end either, but it must for now. He leaned out the conference room door, "Thanks for breakfast, Cinderella." Daniel was staring at him when he sat at the table. "Who is Cinderella?"

"Why, your secretary, Miss Murphy. She has been a wonderful change in who normally picks me up at the airport. Will she be my driver and tour guide this week? I would really like that. Cinderella was quite satisfying to start my day." Craig leaned back in his chair and closed his eyes. The grin on his face gave Daniel a bit of excitement. *Great, Lithia did her job and handled Craig. She can do this all week if he wants her, and I'll give her a bonus after he is gone. If she does this right, Craig will sign the contract, and I will have a two-million-dollar bonus check of my own.*

"I would be happy to clear 'Cinderella's' calendar for the week to be your personal escort. She can work in the office whenever you are in meetings, and when you leave, she can accompany you wherever you would like. If you want to use her car, or I can have a company car available, which-ever you prefer. I can make sure she is your date at the charity ball as well."

"Daniel, I think I can get my own date for the ball. Just get me the ticket for her. I can ask her myself. Let's go with the company car. She won't have to waste her gas or wear and tear on me. Do you think she will be available to sightsee tomorrow? No matter, I'll step over to her office after this meeting. Daniel, I think I'm going to enjoy myself more than I have in a long time."

When Lithia's lunchtime came, she left the office to walk the few blocks to pick up a salad. She grabbed a diet coke, heading back to the company. She found a note on her desk; it was from Daniel. Mr. O'Shay had raved about her all morning and would like for her to be his personal tour guide all week. Daniel was giving her the job. However, when Craig was in meetings, Lithia had to be at the office. A company car would be assigned to her and Mr. O'Shay the entire week. Tomorrow she would need to be ready to go wherever Craig wanted to go. Lithia would be receiving a hefty check when Mr. O'Shay returned to North Carolina. And if the contract was signed, Daniel would double the amount. The last thing on the note: GIVE HIM ANYTHING HE WANTS!!!!! (P.S. I know you brought in the pizza.)

All Lithia could do was let the tears come. Daniel had sold her again.

Chapter 3

April 2010

School started; boy, was it different than public high school. She had to be the youngest person in attendance. Most were old people or middle aged that had dropped out for one reason or another. Some twenty-year-old girls who had gotten pregnant in high school were now trying to go back since their babies were in kindergarten now. Lithia had nothing in common with these people. She was naive and clueless.

Not only was the atmosphere completely weird from her old high school, but rules were quite liberal. For starters, cursing was allowed. The first time Lithia heard the teacher use a few four-letter words to describe a political figure from history, she literally jumped in her seat. Being from a home where profanity was never spoken nor encouraged, her virgin ears were stunned. Then to hear a student openly verbalize his feelings toward the grade he earned on an essay in earshot of the teacher, she turned pale. *"Whatever is in a man's heart, the mouth speaks."* She could just hear her grandmother's words echo in her head. Good thing

Grandmother was not here; somebody would be getting his mouth washed out with soap.

Lola was not impressed with the "school atmosphere" for Lithia during the evenings with all the "worldly people" in the classroom. After a long discussion with Peter late one evening, the decision was made for Lithia to go to the daytime classes where most students were her age or a little older. That worked out much better; consequently, the language of her fellow peers did not change much. It seemed to get worse. The disrespect for the teachers was even nastier. Because she never cursed or spoke sarcastically to her teachers, they started calling her *the Angel*.

By the second semester, Lithia was doing very well with her classes and had met a new friend, Marisol Esposito. Her looks were as different as night and day with Lithia's porcelain skin. Her hair was long and almost black, falling in waves down to her bottom. The olive skin tone was every Hollywood actress's dream. In contrast, Lithia with her fair skin and freckles. Sure, their hairs were the same in length, but strawberry blonde curls surrounded Lithia's face, and her eyes changed colors from light brown to green, depending on her clothes and mood. Marisol's were always walnut brown. Voluptuous in all the right places, the guys were head over heels over the extra curves on either one, if they could see down their shirts. While most girls their age called them fat.

Marisol was the only other sixteen-year-old in the class. Two babies in the midst of everyone else. When others heard Marisol was Catholic, she ended up with the nickname of the Virgin Mary. So now you had two inseparable girls, one an Italian Catholic, the other an Irish Methodist. Walking across campus with guys calling out, "Oh, watch your mouths. Here comes the Virgin Mary and the Angel," it could get annoying fast. The peer pressure was tremendous from peers and even faculty.

Luckily, Marisol's mom worked at another portion of the school. After classes, the girls would walk over to her mom's culinary class to hang out, and hopefully get a sample of what the class made earlier in the day. Yep, it kept them out of trouble, but then the afternoon snacks began to show in places more than either of them wanted. Mrs. Esposito would tell them to make salads instead of eating the pastries or fried foods.

"Why don't you girls go work out at the gym today or walk the entire campus for exercise? You can even drive to the springs and go swimming; that's a great way to take off the pounds you two have been adding on those plump thighs." Mrs. Esposito couldn't have been more than a hundred and ten pounds soaking wet. What did she know about two girls with self-esteem issues and all the peer pressure?

The following term, both girls started taking dance classes and aerobics. They went swimming at the springs at least once a week, and would listen to music and dance in the living room to get their heart rates up and drop pounds. A couple pounds would fall off, until one of their mothers made dessert. *"Why are you being so rude and not try the cheesecake? You are so picky! No wonder you don't have a boyfriend."* Then two weeks later, *"No man is going to want a chunky girl like you. That's why you'll never get a date. Such a great personality, but a full figure at seventeen is ridiculous."* Self-esteem fell deeper and deeper into the pit of each girl's heart. *If our own moms don't even think we are pretty, how will a guy ever like us?* Lithia didn't want to think like this, but she knew Marisol felt the same way.

If they could just look like their moms did at sixteen, seventeen, slender and graceful, petite, with all those adoring Kurt Cameron, bad-boy Johnny Depp, Christian Slater, or Leonardo DeCaprio wannabe guys following them. Instead, they looked like Gilbert Grapes' mom.

Grandmother saw Lithia's pain. "Jesus loves you no matter what you look like. Just like me, I have a full-figure, and Thomas still thinks I look good. Don't you, honey?"

Granddaddy was so funny. He looked up from his newspaper, pulled his glasses down, giving her a wink, "Men want meat; the bones are for the dogs. I like a hearty meal. Isn't that right, Rosa?" That's when Grandmother would send a magazine hurling over the living room straight at Granddaddy. Most of the time, he could dodge them, but this time, there was a direct impact. The book hit with a thud, right into Granddaddy's lap.

"And there's *Good Housekeeping* with some great recipes for supper. Get to cooking your own hearty meal tonight." She chuckled as she stood up, but as she passed by him, she leaned down and kissed his forehead. If Lithia could just one day find a man like that; she wanted this type of relationship.

Chapter 4

April 29, 2019

*L*ithia had stayed to herself as much as possible the rest of the day. She went to the staff bathrooms upstairs just so she never encountered Craig near the ones on this floor. She walked all the way on the other side of the offices to bypass the conference room. Even when she ordered the catering for lunch, she had another secretary set up the food while she ran some copies to the mail room three levels down. Every time Daniel texted her to come into the conference room, she had an excuse. *I'm running to the restroom*; *copy machine jammed, trying to fix it*; *on the phone with another company about a problem*; *ran an errand down, not in the building right now*. When he called her to complain, she told him if he expected her to be at Mr. O'Shay's beck and call the rest of the week, she had too much to do to be his gopher all day. That seemed to get Daniel to stop nagging her, and she relaxed.

Right before five o'clock, a single yellow rose in a crystal vase was delivered to Miss "Cinderella" Murphy. A card was attached. *"A beautiful rose for an equally beautiful woman.*

I truly enjoyed our morning together and can't wait until tomorrow. Be ready at eight am for breakfast. Wear comfortable clothes; we're going to Busch Gardens. Have a good evening. Your friend, Craig aka Prince Charming (yellow rose = friendship-here's to new friends)."

Well, Mr. O'Shay doesn't seem to want her the way Daniel was implying. Of course, Daniel is Daniel. Then Mr. O'Shay prayed and talked about God. He never gave one hint that he wanted anything but a respectable interaction with Lithia. But she had known church guys too. Christians on Sunday or in front of the pastor, but behind closed doors, they were anything but Christ-like. *By their fruit you will know them.* Grandmother's motto. Lithia heard it once again.

Tonight, Mr. O'Shay was on his own. The driver was to take him to the hotel, and he had told Daniel he was going to order room service. He might take advantage of the gym and hot tub downstairs if he felt like it. Who knows, he might even go for a swim in the pool. Daniel didn't need to worry about him. He was a big boy and could take care of himself.

Craig just hoped he wouldn't get tongue-tied tomorrow with Cinderella. She seemed to be a lovely girl and had such a sweet spirit. *"There was, I don't know, something..."* His mind ran the morning over in his mind. Every minute of the time he was with Miss Murphy, his damsel in distress, played like a recording. Her smile, the bashful flitter of her eyelashes when he complemented her, even the clothes she wore did not show arrogance, no immodesty, classy, and a little old-fashion reserve in her dress. Yes, this woman was a natural beauty; Cinderella had no reason for makeup; God had been her sculptor.

At 1 AM, Craig hadn't fallen asleep, Cinderella was not leaving his thoughts. He decided to go down to the gym. It would be open and empty; there he could work out his anxiety, get tired, and pass out when he came back to his room. After an hour of treadmill, cross-trainer, and even a few laps in the pool, she was still dominant in his mind. His mother always told him, *"Honey, if you can't sleep, God just wants you to talk to him. And if there is someone running through your head, pray for them."*

So Craig lay in his bed and spoke to his Heavenly Father on "Cinderella's" behalf. "Lord, I don't know what to do. I never expected to meet someone who could knock me off my feet like this woman did to me today. It's been so long since I even questioned my single life." He let out a deep sigh. "There isn't time for me to pursue a relationship. What am I doing now? I don't know, but the connection I felt was automatic as soon as I touched her."

Craig did not want to be one of those Christians who lost their way off the path God intended because of a love interest. He remembered an old friend from years ago, how his entire world turned upside down because of a girl. "I'm asking for your love to shine through me tomorrow. Give me the opportunity to share the Gospel with Miss Murphy this week. I don't even know if she has a relationship with you, Father, but if not, give me the chance to introduce her to salvation through Jesus. Give her grace and mercy; let her sleep peacefully tonight; may any problems she is facing be swept away. Let her know the miracle is from you. I ask in Jesus' name. Amen." Craig exhaled one long sigh, turned over, and fell asleep. The hotel alarm clock read 3:15 in the morning.

This has got to be insane. I cannot go to sleep. The minute hand is moving so slow. I have got to go to sleep, and it is 3 AM!!!!! How am I going to function with a couple of hours of shuteye, especially at Busch Gardens? I would do better in the office then walk around a theme park all day long. He is probably sleeping like a baby in those satin sheets. Mr. O'Shay is going to be bright-eyed and bushy-tailed, raring to go until the park closes. Or will he want to find other ways of entertainment all day? Gosh, I haven't been to Busch Gardens since I was like sixteen. It was right after her brother Sean graduated from high school. The month before she met...what is my problem? I can't forget that summer; the summer everything would change.

Lithia looked at her cell phone, 3:15 in the morning. Tears ran down her face, but sleep came, a restful slumber.

Chapter 5

June 2010

*P*eter woke the kids up at 7 AM. He had taken the next couple of days off so they could have a family-long weekend. Lola had said they didn't know how many more the Murphys would have before Sean would be away for college, and Lithia too. "Peter, you aren't getting any younger, and the way you work, I'm always worried you're a heart attack waiting to happen." Lithia hated it when her mom made comments like that.

"Just because your dad worked himself to death, Lola, doesn't mean I will. I'm healthy as a horse. Doctor Smith tells me all the time I'll live to be 100." He kissed her full on the mouth and stuck a slice of bacon in his mouth.

"Eating all that bacon doesn't help keep you healthy."

"Well, you could always stop cooking it or buying it. I mean, if you were so concerned."

"And hear you complain, Peter? Not in this lifetime."

Her parents were something else. Twenty years and two kids. Peter was the rock that stood on the solid foundation of Christ; Lola struggled. She would worry and not use faith. Lola complained instead of being grateful for what she did have. Grandmother said her daughter-in-law was like Martha in the Bible, she worked for the Lord diligently, but sometimes she just needed to sit at the feet of Jesus and let him work on her.

Sean came into the kitchen in his PJs, hair a mess, and no shirt. "Geesh, Dad, why do we have to get up so early? I didn't get home from Leo's until one this morning. Remember you gave me permission to ride with him to Orlando yesterday?" The look on Peter's face let Sean know his dad had completely forgotten. "We took all those donations from Pastor Johnson and the church to the pastor who lost everything in a house fire."

"I can't believe the police haven't found anything yet on the arson of the parsonage. It's a miracle those hoodlums didn't burn the church while they were at it, instead of just breaking all the windows and stealing all the sound equipment." Lola shook her head as she placed a waffle on Sean's plate and passed him the syrup. "Eat up! We won't be eating again until lunch. Food at Busch Gardens is too expensive to buy snacks throughout the day. Lithia, I looked online and you should be able to stick to your diet today. Most of the restaurants have salad options or lettuce wraps for sandwiches."

Lithia couldn't get a break from dieting. Mom always had her on one, and she would lose a few pounds, then gain it back and more. Lola didn't know the stress she put Lithia under, so whenever she could, Lithia broke the meal plan. She would eat whatever she wanted at her friends' homes, at her grandmother's, at school. It was at home that she never wavered.

Peter looked up from his bacon and waffle. "Really? Can she just have one day of cheating? This is a family FUN trip. How can you have fun eating rabbit food unless you are a rabbit?" Peter thought Lola carried this diet thing way too far and could see Lithia had no self-esteem when it came to her weight, mainly because of her own mother.

"Peter, you have no idea what it is like being a teen girl. Hormones scrambling your head up and your digestive system. Acne, peer pressure, and, of course, the dreaded boys. It is horrible being in high school without a boyfriend! I mean, I won't know personally, but I saw how other girls were treated, and I can't let my daughter be treated like that. She will thank me later when she's married and happy."

Her dad said no more, finished his breakfast, and told them the car was leaving at 8:30. Everyone better be locked and loaded when he backed out of the garage.

Later that day, when Lola was on a rollercoaster with Sean, Peter bought his daughter an ice cream cone and a soda; that he recollected Lithia had only eaten an apple for breakfast and been drinking water all day. Her lunch was a Caesar salad. Florida heat was doing his baby girl in, and he wasn't going to let it happen on his watch. It bothered him Lola thought their daughter was fat. She even had told Lithia there would be rides she would have to miss because she was over the weight limit. Peter hadn't seen anything Lithia couldn't ride, and he was sure she didn't weigh more than he did. Guess he was going to have to pray harder; Lithia had to lose some weight and Lola had to back off. But something had to give and soon.

Lithia's favorite part of the day was the Serengeti Safari. She loved feeding the giraffes and seeing the animals in as normal habitat as possible. She wondered the splendor of God's creation, how each creature was special in God's heart. He knew exactly what they needed, so how could he not know her heart as well? She turned toward her mother, *if you would love me no matter how I look. I want to be accepted.*

When they got off the safari tour, Peter decided it was time for dinner. They wouldn't be at the park much longer, so he wanted to eat and then catch the up-close encounter with the sloths before the park closed. Once again, Lola ordered Lithia a salad; however, this time it did come with grilled chicken. She had just taken the last bite of lettuce when Peter slid a piece of chocolate cake over to his daughter. "I bought that for you. I know it's your favorite."

She was able to take two bites, but right when she was opening her mouth for bite number three...

"HOW DARE YOU! SPIT THAT OUT NOW!"

Lithia put down the fork and slid the saucer of cake back to her dad. Peter mouthed he was sorry as he verbally tried to calm Lola down. He missed the sloth encounter; the family fun day was over. The tension driving home could have been cut by a knife. Peter silently prayed for both wife and daughter. Sean stuck in his ear buds to listen to iTunes, Lola complained, and Lithia let the tears fall onto her lap as she sat in the corner of the back seat.

That was the last family-fun day the Murphy family ever had.

Chapter 6

April 30, 2019

That had to be the best night sleep Craig had in months. He had looked at the clock once more, then closed his eyes. He didn't remember anything else until the alarm rang. Jumping up, he turned on the shower to get the water temperature perfect, as he pulled out a shirt and shorts to wear. He was going to be comfortable. A quick shower was all he needed to feel fresh and ready to start the day. Craig brushed his teeth, combed his hair, decided to leave the razor stubble, and dressed. He still had forty-five minutes before the car would be downstairs waiting for him.

Sitting on the edge of the bed, Craig leaned over to tie his Jordans. He was going to Busch Gardens with Cinderella. *I am in such shock. I always wanted to go when I was a kid and never had the money. Then, never had the time or someone I wanted to go with me. It's going to be like a birthday present. Happy Birthday to me!* Looking at him, some one would think he was a kid. Craig was singing "Happy Birthday to Me" while dancing around the room.

Craig walked out on the balcony, scooping up his Bible off the desk. The sun wasn't completely up yet, but the variations of colors in blues, pinks, and oranges were art from God. The mixture of clouds of white causing a mist of purple in His palette were breathing-taking. *What a wonderful view to speak to God this morning!* Then taking it all in, he opened his Bible to have morning devotions. *Let's see what Proverbs has for me, Lord. 'Let marriage be held in honor among all, and let the marriage bed be undefiled, for God will judge the sexually immoral and adulterous.' And what are you trying to tell me, Father? Is this a warning? Since my life was changed by you, I've never allowed myself to be one with a woman. I will stay celibate until my wedding night. Please send me the right one who will not condemn me for my past faults. I want to be worthy of the woman you have for me.* He closed his Bible and looked at his watch. The car would be coming at any minute. *Lord, if Cinderella is for me, give me some sign.*

The balcony door shut behind Craig as he stepped back into the room. He was checking his hair as the phone rang, letting him know the car was ready. He was going to have the best birthday ever. The smile on his face radiated from ear to ear as he came out of the elevator and headed to the car.

Lithia had woken up with a song on her mind that she hadn't thought of since she sang in the praise team at church. It was a contemporary Christian song, "East to West." The lyrics came clear, as if it was on the radio in the bedroom.

I can't bear to see the man I've been...
In the arms of your mercy I find rest...
From one scarred hand to the other.

She had no idea what had triggered this song in her head. It was weird how in twenty-four hours, things from her old life had been peeping up to confuse her. Good and bad memories. This was a good one when she had felt clean and whole in Christ. Oh, if only she could believe these words were for her. But she had gone too far.

Busch Gardens. Lithia stood in the middle of her walk-in closet. *Hmmm, what should I wear? Comfortable and cool are a must. Not sure about a tank top. It would be cool, but I could get sunburnt by noon. Need to take sunscreen. I'll wear the lilac and pink tank with the white denim shorts. Sandals or sneakers? Sneakers with pink socks. Let's see, what I look like in the mirror. Okay, my heart earrings and the gold heart pendant necklace are sufficient. I don't want to wear something I might lose.* She French-braided her chestnut hair for the final look, then stepped in front of the full-length mirror. *"You look like a twelve-year-old!"* She thought maybe the child look would reduce the chances of Mr. O'Shay wanting anything else from her today. She said a little prayer that he wouldn't. *If only he would just want the same camaraderie they had the prior morning; today would be perfect.*

The car was to pick Mr. O'Shay up first, then come for her. Lithia thought this way he would have the time to discuss the day's agenda with the driver before she was picked up. It also gave her more time to get ready. She pulled a small backpack out of the closet and switched her sunglasses, wallet, keys, and lipstick from her purse into it. She added the sunscreen and a pack of gum and tic tacs. Under the cabinet was a Thermos, she filled it with cold Gatorade. Later, she would be able to fill it with water at a fountain around the theme park. With that tucked in the side pocket of the backpack, she headed to the lobby of the apartment building.

Her stomach was growling, and they were supposed to get breakfast first. Lithia rubbed her belly as it made an awful roar right when a young couple joined her in the elevator. She blushed. They laughed, "Guess you're headed to the same place we are, the direction of food." Lithia's face turned back to the normal shade and nodded in agreement. She didn't know what today would bring, but she wished Mr. Craig "Prince Charming" O'Shay would be the perfect gentleman from the day before.

The door opened and immediately she saw him getting out of the company car. He looked so...excited. It's the only word she could think of to describe his actions. Craig's face had a smile that made everyone at ease. She watched him speak to the young couple as they walked by him, he held the door for an elderly neighbor who was coming in from walking her poodle, then their eyes met. If Lithia thought his smile was big before, nothing compared to the grin when he saw her.

Craig bowed, "At your service, m' lady. Your chariot awaits." Lithia giggled, taking his outstretched hand. When she sat down in the car, he pointed to a coffee cup that was still steaming with black coffee. Then he handed her a box of Krispy Kreme donuts and a napkin. "Thought we could get our sugar fix in before we got to the park. Gets our adrenaline pumping."

She hesitated. Oh, how she wanted to eat the whole half dozen. Then she heard her mother's warning on donuts and any other sugary food. She pulled her hand away, placing it her lap. "The coffee is enough, thank you." But her stomach snitched on her as it growled.

"You don't like donuts? You're un-American! If you are worried about your figure, I don't think a donut or two is going to kill you. As much walking we are going to do at the park, plus the heat and all the sweating, you will drop off any calories you'll intake." He picked one up with a napkin and handed it to Lithia. "See, they're still warm. I got them when the HOT sign was on."

The sadness in his face softened her, and she accepted the pastry. He was right; it was warm. She took a bite of the glazed treat. She closed her eyes and her moan said it all. "Well, Miss Murphy, I didn't expect that reaction to a donut. I'm glad you found my favorite breakfast satisfactory."

Oh, dear God, help me! I just moaned like a common slut, over a donut for that matter. How could I be so stupid? She squeezed her eyes tight afraid to open them and see him staring at her

It was then that she heard him, "Ohh, yes, this is sooo delicious! Mmmmm, yummy sweetness to my tummy!"

She opened her eyes just a tiny fraction; he had his eyes closed with his head leaned back on the headrest. His left hand held a donut over his face. He would take a bite, moan, rub the rest of the donut on his lips, and sigh. He grinned as he opened one eye, "Finger-licking good!" Craig looked ridiculous. Lithia ate the rest of the donut.

Craig told the driver not to come back until 9 PM. He said if we want to leave before that, he would text. He scanned the tickets he had purchased on his phone at the kiosk, and they entered the park.

"So, Cinderella, have you been here before? I haven't and always wanted to as a kid. Today is a fulfillment of a bucket list wish. Where do you suggest we go first?" He couldn't keep still. He was bobbing his head every which way. He pointed at a sign for giraffes and another one for elephants. He wanted to know which way to the gorillas. What animals were they allowed to touch? Feed?

Here I was worried he wanted to have sex with me; instead, I'm going to be babysitting a six-year-old. Here is this twenty-eight, maybe thirty-year-old executive, dressed like some teenage boy, going out to play basketball. Then he is acting like a little kid on his birthday, not knowing which present to open first.

Lithia grabbed a map and a pamphlet of all the attractions. "Ok, let's make a plan. What animals are your favorite? Those are the must-see. If there are rides you want to go on, we need to do those first because the lines will get long later this morning. Any water rides, those are best when it is scorching hot, then we have time to dry off before we get back in the company car. When we start to get tired, I loved the Serengeti Safari. It was my dad's and my favorite. You go on this forty-five-minute ride into the "plains of Africa." You see the animals in their natural environment. It's really cool."

Craig went to a gift stand and purchased a pen with a lion's head on it. They sat down on a bench, and he circled everything he wanted to do. Lithia prioritized the attractions by times and distances on the map, or she was trying to, when he jerked her arm, pulling her into the line for the Montu. *What a waste of time on planning. This little boy is going to run me ragged.*

It dawned on Lithia why they were getting on the rides so quickly, Craig had bought the fast pass. They made it through Montu, Tigris, Kumba, and Cobra's Curse in less than two hours. She was trying to catch her breath. She got him to slow down and see the sloths, but their exhibit was near Falcon's Fiery and SheiKra; he pulled her on both rollercoasters. She expected him to have a full out temper tantrum when she put her foot down to stop for lunch. He literally was pouting, the lip and the puppy eyes.

Her respite was short-lived. Craig gulped his food down and was pacing behind Lithia while she finished her chicken salad sandwich. No matter how Lithia tried to get Craig to look at animals while his stomach settled, he refused. He dragged her onto the Scorpion and then the Wild Surge.

Then it happened. On the second loop of the Cheetah Hunt, lunch was revisited. Craig gave the wide-eyed grey look to Lithia and leaned over the side as best he could before his double burger exploded into the crowd below. Thank God they were on the last row of seats. However, Lithia wasn't spared the disgust. Her cute little shirt got spattered. She was glad nothing got on her white shorts. He bought them t-shirts to match; the dirty shirts went in a bag to be washed as soon as Lithia got home.

After both water rides, Lithia talked him into the Serengeti Safari, where they both took tons of photos. She even got an up-close picture when a giraffe walked up to the truck and ate a leaf out of Craig's hand. By the time the safari was over, their clothes were almost dry.

She didn't notice when Craig had started holding her hand until he let go to get his wallet from his pocket and buy them lemonade. Now she was restless. Would he take her hand again? Was it a friendly jester? Her palms were sweating; she kept wiping them on her shorts.

By 7:30, they were progressing slowly to the exit gate. They needed to eat dinner. Craig had vomited up everything he had eaten except the ice cream cone with the lemonade; and it had been two hours since then. Craig wanted a steak. Today was special, and he could eat wherever he wanted. There wasn't anything like that at the park, so it was time to go.

Texting the driver to come and get them within the hour, he began strolling the shops. He bought a beach towel with Busch Gardens Tampa on it and a big stuffed giraffe. He chose a picture frame for his Cobra Curse action photo, and a hanging three-toe stuffed sloth that could wrap around you like a hug. Craig immediately flipped it over Lithia's head. He purchased a couple of magnets and key chains, then asked if Lithia had a beach towel.

"Yes, or no? I want you to pick one out, if you don't, there is a very pretty one of a white Bengal tiger you might like." She shook her head. "I don't care; I'm getting it anyway. You're going to need it tomorrow where we are going. Bathing suit and flip flops, oh, and a sunhat. You need all of those." She tried to protest, but he bought the towel and a big straw hat for her anyway.

The driver placed the packages in the trunk while they settled into the backseat. The air condition felt so good. The humidity had been horrible. Within a few minutes, they pulled up to Ruth's Steakhouse. She figured Craig had told the driver to get them reservations. They were taken to the table as soon as they entered the restaurant, and salads were bought to them. Shortly after, a steak and huge baked potato was set before Lithia.

"I can't eat all of this, Mr. O'Shay. This is more than I eat in two days." It looked and smelled scrumptious; she was going to gain ten pounds in one day.

Craig took her hand and bowed his head, "Lord, I want to thank you for this food and the company you have allowed me to have for the day. Bless Miss Murphy and give her the desires of her heart as she grows in your love and mercy.

Thank you for an amazing day and granting me a wish I had since a boy. May this food be nourishing to our bodies." He paused and opened his eyes.

Lithia was looking at him with such tenderness. She even tightened her grasp on his hand. Craig looked deep into her face. "Thank you for answering my prayer for the best birthday ever. Amen." A tear rolled from his eye as he dropped his head, refusing to let more fall.

Lithia's heart went out to him; she only wanted him to know she cared. She reached over and wiped his cheek with her thumb. Her hand cupped his chin and she tilted it up to look in his eyes. "Happy birthday, Craig O'Shay. I'm pleased I could be a part of your special day. I hope all your birthdays to come keep getting better." Not even thinking twice, Lithia leaned over and kissed the tear rolling down Craig's cheek.

His heart overflowed with such happiness at her caress. Craig didn't break the eye contact as he took her face in his hands, slightly rubbing his index finger over her lips. She was holding her breath; Lithia knew he was going to kiss her. She wanted him to, but then what?

Craig sensed the confusion in Lithia's skin, though her eyes surged with a passion he had never seen before. It was up to him-the Christian man-to harness self-control. His mouth wanted to taste her lips, and his body yearned to devour her. Instead, he gritted his teeth with every power within him, he kissed the tip of her nose and released her face.

Dinner finished in silence, along with the coconut cake for dessert. Lithia couldn't eat everything, so the waiter boxed up over half the steak and some of the baked potato. She had eaten her slice of cake. *When did I have cake last? At Dad's funeral, I ate a slice of sweet potato pie and a huge piece of German chocolate cake. Then Mom yelled at me in front of First Lady Johnson how I should leave the sweets alone and eat a Weight Watcher's cookie. Well, I showed her. If I couldn't have it, neither could anyone else.* The crash of the plate was audible in Lithia's ear as she remembered flinging the cake into the dining room wall.

Helping with the packages Craig purchased at Busch Gardens, the driver held them as Craig sorted through what he wanted Lithia to have and what he was going to keep. He placed a magnet in with the tiger beach towel, draped the sloth back over her neck, and tucked the gigantic giraffe under his arm. "After you, Cinderella." Calling over his shoulder to the driver, "I'll be back down in a jiffy."

Lithia fumbled with the key to open her apartment door. Craig went in ahead of her and laid the packages on the sofa. "Nice place you got." He looked around at the house décor. His eyes stopped at a photo in a small frame on a bookshelf on the other side of the sofa. It looked odd in this apartment full of sophisticated design to see a macaroni-glued popsicle-made frame around a group of teens standing in a gazebo. He figured it was something a younger sibling must have made her or a niece or nephew.

Turning around he caught Lithia putting her leftovers in the refrigerator and retrieving a cold bottle of water. "Would you like a water bottle to take with you? I am a little thirsty, are you?" He nodded as she leaned over the bar, passing him the bottle, then opened the refrigerator and pulled out one for herself.

He took a small sip, "Now about tomorrow's plans. Towel, bathing suit, flip flops, and the hat I got you. You will need the sunscreen again, too. We will be going on a boat exertion at Tampa Bay. I figured you might need some time at the office, so I will be here for you at noon. Do not eat lunch. We will have a picnic meal on the boat and a seafood dinner while watching the sunset." He headed for the front door.

"Thank you for the day and the souvenirs. I do hope you had a wonderful birthday. I'm honored to have been a part of it. I'll be ready at 12. I'm looking forward to sunset on the bay."

He bowed at the waist, "Until tomorrow, m' lady" and was gone.

Lithia closed the door and locked the deadbolt. Resting her head on the door, she exhaled a slow breath. She touched her lips. His finger had caressed them; his lips had kissed her nose. It was romantic and sweet, like some Hallmark movie on Saturday night. Not what she was used to at all, but something she had always wanted.

Then it dawned on her-*I'm to wear a bathing suit tomorrow in front of him, so like, he will see most of my body. Terrific! How can I get out of that? If I tell him I don't own one, he will buy one in the morning. Mom had me be modest and wear a one piece most of my life; then when I didn't, Daniel has made me put on itsy-bitsy bikinis. It's all I have. What am I going to do? I just don't feel comfortable wearing them, never have. Mr. O'Shay doesn't seem like he would respect me if I was wearing one of those skimpy things. Of course, you could be wearing a sweatshirt and jogging pants, and a nasty guy could still have only one thing on his mind. I have no choice. I'll go in to work at 7 AM and leave at 11. The mall is right by the office; if I run in quick, I can get a suit and be home by the time he arrives at 12 if I can find one that fits.*

Chapter 7

July 2010

S ummer came to Hopewell, Florida. Tourists were not really a big deal since the biggest city near them was Tampa. However, there were some people who did like to stay in small towns to relax, to get away from all the noise. Visitors would say it had the perfect name, "It gave us hope that life was good, and the community reminds us to be grateful. We felt like family."

Hopewell was the kind of town where most everyone knew the other. You were born there, and you died there. If you hadn't been born there, your car must have broken down and the mechanic couldn't get the part fast enough because you found love waiting in Hopewell; you just stayed. People knew their kin. Generations after generations of O'Leary, Randall, and Donaldson families lived in Hopewell, giving you four or five generations' worth of ancestry documentations. No one needed any DNA testing from an ancestry website to tell you if they were Irish stock from Sheffield, Ireland, or Seminole Native American Indians. When the Christmas parade was held, every culture was presented, somehow or another. From the Indian natives on horseback in full headdress to "Feliz Navidad" played by a mariachi band, sombreros and all to the Odi Dance by the Abara family whose ancestors came from Kenya. Color of skin didn't matter, for at one time or another, the town would have never made it without everyone working together. It was a place grandparents still sat on the porch in the evening, taking in the breeze, drinking iced tea. It reminded Lithia of the novel she read in ninth grade called *To Kill a Mockingbird*. The author could have described the street she lived on just like the one Scout lived on in the novel. Unfortunately, Maycomb had secrets Scout learned, which made it not as perfect as it seemed in chapter one. Lithia wondered how many secrets Hopewell could have too.

And summer brought youth camp.

Every summer since Lithia could remember, Hopewell Methodist Church sent the kids to youth camp up in Central Florida at Wekiva Springs. Several other Methodist churches in the state sent kids too. It was like the best thing all summer long. For the entire month of July, well, after Independence Day, each week was dedicated to a certain age group of kids. Lithia's brother Sean had gone his entire life. Since first grade, Sean went. After he turned sixteen, Sean would go and help in the concession stand for the elementary and middle school kids for two weeks, then he just stayed the last week for high school as a camper. If he worked the first weeks, he didn't have to pay for his week of fun.

When Lithia finally wasn't scared to go to camp, she loved it. By then, she was in middle school, but she enjoyed the crafts and swimming; Bible study for an hour each morning with the rest of the day to do fun activities. At night when dinner was over, there was always a passionate young preacher to speak to all the campers and encourage them in Christ. The message was the same: "Don't be a follower of man, but of Jesus. Show others, when you go back to school, a Christ-like spirit. Be bold for the Gospel."

Lithia was always pumped up when she returned home; but her courage fell as soon as a bullying remark was thrust at her. She could be bold and proud of being a Christian at home or church, but at school she didn't have the guts. If she couldn't speak up for herself, how could she speak up for Christ?

Peter was not as excited about Lithia going to camp this summer. He didn't want to pay for her to attend camp when she could have been at camp for two weeks already, helping. Why couldn't she just ride with Sean and Leo Randall, Sean's best friend, to Wekiva Springs, when they left two weeks ago? Now Peter had to leave right after church on Sunday to drive Lithia up to camp. He was going to miss the baseball game for the two-hour drive there. Lola couldn't do it; she would be making food for the Barnes family who lost their son in a car accident Thursday night. Lola and a few other ladies from the church were going over to serve supper because of the funeral on Monday. Peter would be the only choice.

"Mom, I leave in two days for camp and I need a new bathing suit. When are we going to go buy one? Leslie is going to the mall tonight to grab a couple from Dillard's; they're having a sale. Buy one full-price and the second one is only fifty percent. You know it would be better to have two anyway. If you can't go, I'll hitch a ride with her." Lithia waited for thirty seconds, then she spoke into her phone, "She didn't say no, Leslie. Can you pick me up on the way? I have my own money, and if I can get two cheap, I might as well. Fifteen minutes? Ok, I'll come down when you flash your headlights."

Lola hadn't heard a thing. The dishwasher was on, Peter had on the news, and Mom was on her cell, talking to her mother-in-law. "Yes, Mother Murphy, Lithia is very excited to go to camp this year. She's had almost everything packed for a week." Pause. Her mother-in-law was going on and on about when Peter used to go as a teen, how much he enjoyed it, meeting new people, and growing in the Lord. She couldn't believe this would be Sean's last time unless he went as a full counselor whenever he was home from college each summer. Then she said something about only two years and Lithia would be the same.

"How is Papa Murphy doing? His shingles any better since Monday?"

Mother Murphy went into the meds, the oatmeal baths, and Papa sleeping in the spare room because he was afraid she was going to catch it. "I told him over and over, if the Lord was going to let me get them, he would do it without me having to sleep alone. Well, if we aren't at church Sunday, or Lithia doesn't get to come over before she goes, tell her to have a good time."

By the time Lola hung up from talking to Rosa Murphy, Lithia was on the way to the mall with Leslie, buying two bikinis, a white one and a blue one. Dad and Mom would never have approved.

Saturday morning came, and Lola had been out early to the store, getting some small toiletries for Lithia to take to camp. When she placed the items on her daughter's bed, she noticed the Dillard's shopping bag on top of the partial-ly-packed luggage. Being a nosy momma, and not knowing

Lithia had been anywhere near the mall, she dumped out the contents.

Taking two steps at a time, Lola was downstairs, waving the string bikinis as she walked into the kitchen. Peter was sipping his coffee while checking his email on the laptop when Lola dropped the material on the keyboard. "Look at this! Our daughter has the audacity to think she is going to take THESE to camp! Well, that girl has another thing coming." She put her hands on her hips as she blew air out her mouth like she was in the middle of a Lamaze class. Her eyes were wide, and her face was heated.

Peter could see her veins in her neck, and they were bulging. He didn't even want to know what she was raging about now. He picked up the strings, turning them over in his hand. "Excuse me, but what is this?" Looking at his wife, he was almost afraid her eyes were going to pop out of her head.

"Are you kidding me? I found that in YOUR daughter's room, laying in her suitcase to go to camp with her." She could see Peter was still unsure of what he was holding; men could be so clueless. Lola took the bottom half of the white bikini and put it to her hips, then to her backside, turning around, letting him see how much it was going to cover of HIS daughter's bottom.

"OVER MY DEAD BODY!!! LITHIA!!!"

Lithia had just turned off the shower when she heard her dad screaming her name from downstairs. She stuck her head out the bathroom door, "I'm just getting out of the shower, Dad. Give me a minute, and I'll be down there." Now, what did she do? Wrapping her hair in a towel, she darted across the hallway to her room to throw on a pair of shorts and a t-shirt. She held the towel balanced on her head as she bounced down the stairs.

"Yep, Dad, what's up?" Her cheeks flushed crimson when her dad picked up the blue bikini and dangled it in front of her. She glanced at her mom from the corner of her eye, Lola had her arms crossed and was tapping her foot on the ceramic tile. The scowl on her mom's face let her know there would be no help from her.

Peter shook the strings in her face, "Explain yourself? And it better be very good."

It was the look of disappointment in her dad's face that made Lithia begin to cry. "But all the girls wear them. Leslie, Carrie has a two-piece; well, even Sunshine Johnson has a two-piece bathing suit. I don't know why you want me to be embarrassed, looking like some little girl."

"Lithia, I do not care what everyone else is allowing or not allowing their daughter to wear. That is not my concern; you are. I refuse to have you represent yourself and this family in some ungodly clothing. As a Christian, I would think you would know better as well. I want you to go upstairs, get the receipt, and your mother will be taking you to exchange these into a decent, body-covering, MODEST, one-piece suit. Is that clear?"

Her mouth opened as she thought about arguing with her father, but the death stare from her mom and the hurt look in her dad's eyes...she closed her mouth.

Within twenty minutes, Lola and Lithia were on their way to exchange the "trashy" clothing; however, the scolding would continue.

"Not only are those not going to cover your boobs or your bottom, everyone is going to laugh at you. Even if your father and I would allow you to wear that whorish bathing suit, you would look like that character in the movie "Norbit." No one could see the bottom half of the suit cause your belly would hang over it. I don't want you to go through that humiliation. I don't want to see you hurt."

Lithia tried to interrupt, but that wasn't going to help. She tried to explain, but that wasn't working either. Not only did her mom tell the cashier how ridiculous Lithia would look in the bikini, but how only a harlot would wear something like it. Her mother bought her two one-piece bathing suits. A solid black one with a skirt and a floral print, which looked like her grandmother's tablecloth. Lithia was going to be the laughingstock of camp for sure this year. Good grief, even her grandmother's bathing suit had less material then hers.

Chapter 8

May 1, 2019

$\mathcal{L}$ithia changed her calendar on the desk. May 1, 2019. *"May Day, Play Day,"* her grandmother used to call it. Something about how they played games all day at school. She could imagine her grandmother running around the school football field or on the playground at the elementary school. Things had changed since then.

Dressed in business attire, she gathered her briefcase and purse for a quick retreat, but went back into her closet to pick out what to wear later with Mr. O'Shay. She laid out red capris and a navy blue and white cotton blouse. Her white tennis shoes would finalize her sailor suit.

Emptying her backpack from yesterday's Busch Gardens' trip, she folded her new towel and stuck flip flops, lip balm, and sunscreen inside. Her black cover-up would have to work, so she placed it in as well. Her sunglasses were in the side pocket, and she laid her new straw hat on top of the pack. All she needed to do is change clothes and stick a bathing suit into the compartment. *If I can even find one in thirty minutes, I will be surprised.*

Even as nervous as she was about today's outing, she had fallen asleep quickly and dreamt of Craig's kiss on her nose, wondering what a full kiss on the mouth would be like from a man like him. *I have got to be nuts thinking about a man kissing me. Like I have never been kissed before, more times then I wished.* She thought of how yesterday could have turned out. She could have never designed it any better.

Piled on her desk were four numbers she had to return calls, a list of letters she needed to type and send for Daniel, and all of Daniel's physical mail from yesterday to read and sort through. Lithia was glad she came in an hour early. It was quiet, and she should be able to get the letters finished before anyone else came in. She knew Daniel wouldn't show up until nine, so the more she completed by then, the earlier she should be able to leave. It really had to do with what Daniel would expect her to accomplish after he came.

Letters, call backs, and most of the mail had been handled when Daniel waltzed in her office. "I have the letters you wanted typed and emails sent out, I responded to the phone calls too. You need to call Mr. Radcliffe from State Farm about the insurance claim. I put his number on your desk. There is a stack of mail you will need to review. It's in order of importance in your bin. I have around fifteen more pieces of mail to sort through, and whatever it is you need me to do...well, I must leave here no later than eleven to meet Mr. O'Shay. You are now all caught up. What do you want?"

Daniel was taken back. Lithia hadn't been this bold in a while, but since Craig had come to town, something had changed in her. He had gotten a text a couple of times during the day before from Craig. He had said that "Cinderella" was "amazing," "Better than expected trip," "Best day ever." The last one from last night: "She made me feel things I haven't felt before." Lithia could be as curt as she wanted. Craig wasn't complaining, so she must be taking care of all his needs. Well, Lithia had always been the top-dollar girl he had.

"I do have a couple more emails I need you to send, and set up a meeting with Brooks Sterling for Thursday morning. Call the newspapers and all the radio stations in the area to remind them to advertise the charity ball on Friday. I want to see if I can get Craig on a radio show to tell about his House of Hope thing. It could pull in those last few donations before the ball. If you can get that done, you're free to leave."

He turned to walk out; she was relieved. Then he stopped, "Seems you haven't lost your touch. Craig said you were making him feel good. I believe the word he used was 'amazing.' Don't give all your secrets out yet. String him along. After the ball, you can let him see why you are so expensive."

"What do you mean by that?" Lithia questioned.

But Daniel laughed as he shut her door.

Great! Something else to ponder. What was Daniel saying? Craig was paying for me. She had thought after yesterday, how polite Craig was, maybe the implications of being purchased were all Daniel. That he was willing to have Lithia to do whatever it took for Craig to sign over the property to the company. Even if it meant Lithia should give herself to this man.

But in the past, the other men had already made their moves, whether it was on her or whoever Daniel had placed as the client's escort. Out on the boat today, if Craig wanted to take this to another level, one she had been forced to go for Daniel before, she didn't think she would hate it. Months had passed from the last time her job was to entertain a client. It hadn't gone very well; she had some scars to prove it.

She walked out of the office with an extra twenty minutes to find a swimsuit. She purchased a hollow back high-neck one piece. It was black with the bodice white-checkered. It dropped low in the back and tied at the neck. Nothing could fall out the top, nor were any cheeks falling out the bottom. It accentuated all the right spots with a modest appeal. She felt sexy, but not "trashy." Her mom would be pleased.

Lithia had enough time to shave her legs and vacuum her apartment before Craig knocked on her door at noon. He handed her a yellow rose, then walked over the threshold.

"My Cinderella turned Sailor Moon on me, huh? Cute outfit. Here I am with swim trunks and flip flops. I think my t-shirt matches my trunks." He turned himself around as if to model his clothes for her. She laughed. The trunks had surf boards all over it and the base color was orange. The t-shirt read "In God We Trust" and it was printed like a dollar bill. Nope, the man didn't match at all.

She put the rose in the vase with the other one he had given her. Craig picked up her backpack, and she locked the door behind them after they walked out. Lithia was hungry; she had only had a cup of coffee since she woke up. The picnic he promised better be tasty.

Craig wasn't too sure how to take Cinderella this morning. He knew there had been chemistry between them the day before, but did he imagine it? He glanced toward her, she lowered her head and started to pick at her fingernails. He wondered if she had been a nail biter when she was younger, could be why the fake nails now? He noticed a scar on the palm of her hand and another on her wrist. It looked old, but not far enough back to be when she was a kid. Probably dropped a glass washing dishes or something similar.

The drive was not a great distance, only forty-five minutes, and they were parked at the marina. Craig asked for assistance from a man stepping off a boat, and then quickly spotted the sailboat with "Angel's Wings" painted on the side.

It was a thirty-eight foot, two-mast sailboat, painted white and red. *This is amazing, now to be able to steer the boat properly and not look like a fool.* Craig was worried he would not be able to manage by himself; it had been a few years since he had been sailing. Relief filled his face when a grey-haired gentleman with an authoritarian look on his face came up from the cabin below as Craig helped Lithia step down onto the deck of the ship.

"Greetings shipmates, I'm Captain Fred, and welcome to the Angel's Wings. You must be Craig O'Shay." He reached out and gave a hearty handshake to Craig and a gentler one to Lithia. "I understand you are friends of my son and daughter-in-law. From college, I believe?" He tipped his head to one side as if trying to remember. Now young'uns make yourself at home. We will be sailing shortly. I'm just waiting for the cook to return with the ingredients for the supper you requested."

Lithia had never been on a boat like this before, and she was enthralled. She had figured Craig had rented some little speedboat. If she would have to go to the bathroom, she would have to get in the water to relieve herself. Was she wrong? This had a galley and a couple of bedrooms and a full bathroom below. Craig must have some rich friends, and nice, too, for him to get this treatment.

When Lithia came back up to the deck, an older lady was struggling with a couple of paper sacks of groceries. She couldn't see over the bags to place them on the table. Lithia took one bag from her and sat it on a chair. The lady placed her bag on the table and plopped down on a lounge chair, putting up her feet.

"Thank you, sweetie. I was about to drop both bags if you hadn't rescued me. I'm plum out of breath, toting them all the way from the car. I couldn't find a parking space any closer, and Lord knows my husband can't answer the cell phone when I need him to do it." She had a strain of hair that kept falling into her face as she spoke with Lithia. No matter how many times she tried to attach to the bun, it came tumbling down again. Her bleached-out jeans had a rip at the knee, and her shirt said Margaritaville Jimmy Buffet with a big parrot on the back.

"So, what's your name, honey? I'm LeeAnn, Captain Fred's better half."

Before Lithia could introduce herself, Craig and Captain Fred came from the hull. "Well, I see you met the cook, Cinderella. This is my wife, LeeAnn, and the best darn cook to sail the seven seas." He then saw the packages of groceries. "Why didn't you call me, Lee? I'd come out to the car to help you carry the food to the boat."

"I don't know what got into me, but I thought I would work on my muscles." LeeAnn begin to stand up and gather the bags to go down into the galley. "And if you look at your phone, I bet you have a couple of missed calls. It was nice to meet you, Cinderella?" She looked at Craig, "And the same Prince Charming to you?" She gave a death glare to Fred and headed down with Captain Fred right behind her, trying to get her to let him help with at least one bag. Craig and Lithia only heard LeeAnn's husband's voice until, "I love you anyway," and LeeAnn replied, "You better if you know what's good for you."

Captain Fred returned five minutes later with a big grin on his face and lipstick print on his cheek. "The old bat drives me crazy."

"In more ways than one," Craig whispered under his breath and nudged Lithia. "This day is going to be entertaining to say the least." With a grin, he took her hand and walked to the bow of the boat.

"I'm going to help Captain Fred get us under way. I haven't been sailing for three years, but I can lend a hand getting us out of port. You won't be unattended for long periods of time. Why don't you go down and change into your bathing suit? I know once we get out into the water, I plan on jumping overboard for a swim. There is also the cooler on the table with potato salad, ham sandwiches, and watermelon slices to eat."

Lithia was hungry, very hungry, and cold watermelon did sound divine. If she ate more of the watermelon than the sandwich and potato salad, maybe she wouldn't gain weight on this meal. She was also getting extra hot with the capris and cotton top. The bathing suit would be cooler to have on, then she wouldn't mind dipping in the water. "Okay, Mr. O'Shay, no more tempting me, I'll change and get the picnic lunch ready."

LeeAnn was putting a couple of sandwiches and a big pickle on a plate for Fred as Lithia came out of the bathroom, wearing her suit and cover-up. "My, you look lovely. I'm happy to see some young ladies don't parade all the goods God gave them to the world. 'Modesty is sexy' is what

I always told my son. He listened to his momma and got a good girl too. Sunny is the daughter I never had."

"Thank you. I had parents that were strict when it came to the types of clothing I wore. There have been times, well, I didn't always share their views, but I know now why they were like that." Lithia felt better about her purchase of the black and white swimsuit. She was hesitating on disrobing in the presence of Craig. All she could think of was his reaction. No, it wasn't like she was getting naked or such, but a bathing suit was only hiding the private areas.

Craig was loving this. He hadn't been sailing in three years. The wind had picked up and caught the sail almost the minute they had reached thirty yards off the coastline. He had already grabbed a ham sandwich from the cooler and had eaten a slice of watermelon before Miss Murphy had come back from changing.

His anticipation on what Cinderella would look like in a swimsuit was gnawing at him. He hoped he could keep his reserve if her taste in swimsuits was not as modest as the rest of her wardrobe had been. He didn't know if that would make his feelings change or cause other impulses. Craig had a dilemma. If she is dressed modestly, he would be thrilled, and could still see the curves. All in the right places. But, if she wore something flimsy and covering a little of nothing, would he be repulsed, or would his body have a mind of its own? *God, keep my thoughts pure. Don't let my body lose control.*

"WOW!" *Did I say that out loud? How could I be so dumb! She looks so beautiful. Adorable swimsuit, enough, but not too much to lose my salvation over. Now just keep the thoughts on things of God, not how smooth her skin is or how soft it would be to kiss. Or the freckles on the backs of her thigh and her shoulder blades.*

Oh my God, he took off his shirt! Lithia watched his muscles tighten as he pulled the robes for the mast. The wind tousled his auburn curls. Her eyes followed down his chest to the small patch of hair in the center of his chest. Lithia wished she could lie her head on his chest for just one night.

Sensations flowed warmly inside her as she raised her eyes to Craig's. He was watching her. She knew he observed every part of her. In a way, she felt intruded, but that never stopped a guy before that she could remember.

Lithia looked away self-consciously.

"Did you eat anything yet? I have, though I'll have some potato salad with you." Lithia shook her head. "Come, let's get some food. I want to get in the water as soon as we can."

He placed a sandwich and a big spoonful of potato salad on a plate and handed it to Lithia. She took the plastic fork next to the bowl of salad and sat on a crate near the opening of the hatch below. Craig dumped a gigantic mound of potato salad on his plate, snatched a fork, then leaned back on the table. He seemed to shovel in the salad. She told him to go slow before they had a relapse of yesterday's rollercoaster upchuck. He slowed down. By the time Lithia had cleaned her plate, Craig was on his second piece of watermelon.

"You better leave me some watermelon."

Craig tried to hand Lithia the rest of his slice. He had watermelon juice running down his face onto his chest. She watched the slow move of the juice get closer and closer to the waistband of Craig's trunks. Heat shot through her body as she saw he had followed her glaze. "You need a paper towel to clean the juices off your belly," she managed to gasp, breathless.

"Oh, I'll clean that off when I dive in the water. We are about to put down anchor in thirty minutes. Why don't you relax and get some sun while you wait to go swimming? I can apply sunscreen on your back, if you would do the same for me." He turned around and handed her a bottle of sunscreen.

Wishing her heart would stop pounding so hard, her eyes were wide. *How am I going to handle this one? I'm already trembling; he will notice and ask me questions. Craig was watching again.* She felt nervous beneath his interested scrutiny.

Nervous was exactly what she felt. She put lotion in her hands and placed her hands on his biceps. Intensely aware of his masculinity, threatened by her own stirred emotions, fear of what Daniel had told him about her and what he could do with her, didn't help.

He cautiously turned on his stomach in the lounge chair for Lithia to get his back. He couldn't dare let her touch his chest; the closer her hands would move to the top of his shorts, he would lose all control on certain body parts. That would be a disaster. Even now, he could feel the discomfort. Oh, but her hands glided over his back with such tender-ness. She'd stop to add more lotion to her hands, then begin again. His shoulders, biceps, his sides even, it seemed she deliberately was avoiding his lower back.

When he thought she wouldn't venture farther down his back, the tickle came. She massaged with her thumbs in the center of the dip before his waistband. Shivers shot up his spine. Her hands backed away; Craig almost caught his breath. Warmth crept up his legs as she began to rub lotion into his calf muscles and thighs. "Oh, Cinderella," he tried to suppress the moan.

The last thing Lithia expected was the warmth going through her veins as she touched him. *He is expecting to rub lotion on me next. How am I going to be still? I was shaking the whole time, but it was weird how he was too.* Lithia could see her touch had made an impact on Craig as well; nevertheless, *what will happen when he touches me? My resistance is wilting, and I can't give in.*

Craig wasn't moving; he seemed to be trying to "will" himself to calm down. He needed a cold shower or to just dive overboard. Think pure thoughts. *Jesus loves me. He died for my sins. He heals the sick. The son of God at the right hand of the Father. Heaven. Do not sin, Craig. You can't think about her as anything but a child of God. How will you put lotion on her?*

Splash!!! Craig jumped up from the lounge to see water coming over the side of the boat. He looked around; Cinderella was nowhere in sight. Captain Fred laughed, "About peed yourself there now? The young lady dived in right after you fell asleep. Guess she figured you weren't going to finish the bargain."

Sure, enough there was Cinderella treading water on his left. She must have swum a little after she hit water. She wasn't far away, but not right by the boat. His first thought was to jump in after her, nope, he needed a minute to get his hormones in check. I'll go to the galley, get a cold bottle of Coke and drink it, then go in.

He got his head together and dove in the warm water. As he was coming up to the surface, he looked for Cinderella's legs under the water, but didn't see them. His head popped up, taking a breath, he turned his body all around in the water. She wasn't there. He would have to swim farther out to be able to see up onto the boat. He had been down below with time for her to have come back on board without him realizing it.

No need to panic. The boat was anchored, furthermore, he needed to cool off and fast. Cinderella was probably on the boat or had swam to the other side of the ship. He submerged to look for her just in case.

Lithia had seen Captain Fred observing the lotion event, and she shrugged her shoulders when Craig just laid there. She took the cue and pulled off her cover-up and dived over. The water washing over her body made her feel clean again. It was a wake-up call.

So far, he hadn't seen her without the cover-up, and he hadn't massaged lotion into her body. Those were prayers answered. But they still had hours on the boat. She didn't know Captain Fred and LeeAnn. Maybe they didn't care what happened on deck or down in a cabin below. And with the sensations that were busting from her inner core, it wouldn't take much to give him what Daniel had already commanded her to give.

Swimming out a few yards from the sailboat gave her some sense of privacy. She knew Captain Fred could still see her, and she would be okay. Craig would be bouncing over the rail any moment, but at least she could get a minute to organize her thoughts. There he was, speak of the devil. Craig O'Shay leaning over the rail, eyeing her. It surprised her when he didn't jump right in, but turned, and she could see him enter the hatch to go below.

Taking the opportunity, Lithia began to swim towards the stern. She swam rapidly, so when Craig came back on deck, Lithia was hidden from him. She heard him jump in, but knew he would swim towards the point he had seen her last, not the opposite of the boat. She wasn't sure how long it would last; alone time was needed for her to get ready for whatever was to come. The ladder was on this side anyway, if she wanted to get back on the boat, all she had to do was climb.

Craig swim away from the sailboat fifty yards. He looked back at the ship, but nothing. He saw no one at all, anywhere in the water or near the ship. He prayed she was okay. He would feel terrible if she'd drown. Occasionally, he would allow himself to go under, trying to see if she was playing some game with him and holding her breath. Finally, he headed for the boat. Captain Fred saw him and waved. Then he pointed his finger to the other side of the ship and made a woman's shape with his hands in the air. He had been worried, and all she did was swim to the other side of the ship. He couldn't believe how he didn't think of that.

Lithia could feel the sun burning her shoulders and nose. She hadn't put any sunscreen on her body, and any more time without it, she couldn't risk. She swam to the side of the boat and was climbing over the railing when Craig's auburn head peeked the top of the opposite side. She had to get to her cover-up before he made it over the railing.

Three feet was all she needed to reach her cover-up and towel. *I can do this; he hasn't turned around yet. If I can get it over my head, he won't see me in just the suit.*

Thump! Clang! She had taken her eyes off where she was going and tripped over Craig's flip flops laying between her and the chair. At the same time, Craig had made it over the rail and slipped as he placed his foot the deck. They both flanked, stumbling into the lounge chair, and fell. *Plop!* Craig landed flat on his back as Lithia came down on top.

Wet bodies entangled, with Lithia's long hair, her hair all in her face, she couldn't see what she was doing. Craig was looking quite pleased with himself. He wasn't even trying to get up or help her. The more Lithia tried to get a grip, she'd slip and fall right back down on him. She was doing her best not to use his chest to push up on to stand, and if she went up on her knees, she wasn't sure if Craig could survive.

"Why don't you let me help you? Roll off my body, and I will stand up first. Then I'll get your towel and lend you a hand to get you to your feet." She did as he requested, though she could feel his eyes undressing her as he stood. But when she got the courage to look at him, he wasn't looking at her at all, but even had his back to her as he handed her the towel. He gave her a moment to drape the towel around her, before he went behind her, then taking her by the elbows, he lifted her to her feet. Craig even held her until she was stable, standing on her own.

"For a man today, it's a nice change to find a woman who has morals and modesty. And beautiful as well." He took his own towel and began to dry her hair with it. "Why don't you go below and dry off? LeeAnn has a blow-dryer for your hair. When you are dressed, I'll come down and switch clothes as well." Before he took his towel, he leaned in close to her ear, "God made you in His image; don't believe what someone has told you in the past; you are desirable for your beauty and brains."

Craig took his towel as he wildly rubbed his hair dry, and began heading toward Captain Fred.

Lithia stood, looking at his features. His walk with shoulders back, confident but not arrogant, like some men from her past. He had a swagger that came naturally. Since he scrubbed his head with the towel, his hair was sticking up on all directions. Craig O'Shay was a man she would not easily erase from her mind when he leaves.

After a shower, dry clothes and hair, Lithia could feel the sting on her shoulders and face. Unfortunately, she hadn't brought soothing gel if this had happened. So she went to the galley to find LeeAnn prepping for the dinner meal.

"Excuse me, LeeAnn, but do you have any aloe lotion or soothing gel for sunburn? I didn't put any sunscreen on earlier, and I'm already feeling the pain for my mistake."

"Here, this works for me. The smell isn't bad either. I don't think you got too much sun. On your face seems to be the worst," LeeAnn gave her motherly advice to Lithia. She rubbed some of the ointment on Lithia's shoulders, letting Lithia applied the medicine on her own face. She felt the coolness in seconds.

"Can I help you with dinner? It looks like you still have a lot to do." Lithia loved to help her grandmother and mother cook. However, it wasn't the only reason to stay below. She didn't want to face Craig yet, it was postponing the inevitable, but so be it.

LeeAnn was happy for another pair of hands, setting Lithia to cut up tomatoes, onions, carrots, and lettuce. She shredded cheese and peeled two boiled eggs. Adding all the ingredients in a large bowl, Lithia mixed a salad fit for all four of them. LeeAnn had lobster boiling on the range as she melted butter. There was rice pilaf and cheese biscuits. Lithia opened the refrigerator to replace the unused vegetables to find a dish of cold shrimp cocktail ready to be served.

"Why don't you check on the men and see if they are going to be ready to eat in thirty minutes? I'm sure Fred is starving. He always is. You'll have to ask your Prince Charming, I'm not sure about him. Nevertheless, he is a man, and I would bet he says he is too."

She started to argue with LeeAnn that Craig was NOT her Prince Charming, but she figured there was no point. It wasn't like she would ever see this woman again, though there was something vaguely familiar about her. Lithia just couldn't put her head on it.

As Lithia came out of the hull below, her eyes had to adjust to the light. The sun had started setting. The peaches and blues were mingled like they had been whisked in the kitchen. Some reds and purples twisted in the middle, with a touch of yellows. "Another watercolor painting made by God just for His children; don't you think, Cinderella?" Captain Fred crossed his arms and smiled, "This is why I told the honey I wanted to spend time on the water more. I like to see these types of beginnings and endings each day."

"Oh, yes, it is so lovely. I have a view from my bedroom window that is very similar, but not as spectacular as this one. Too many streetlights and car horns to distract you from the display of the heavens."

"You wait until the stars begin coming out. That's going to make today worthwhile. I hope LeeAnn fixes dinner soon; we can have a starlight dinner on deck." Captain Fred grinned at Lithia. "That boy sure is taken with you. I hope you know that. I don't know him personally, but I do know him through my son. He has been a godsend to my boy since college. My son told me he is asking Craig to be the twins' godfather. Now don't go telling him that yet. He doesn't know."

"No, I won't tell him. Are these your first grandkids? I'm sure you're going to make a great granddaddy." Fred was nodding his head and wiping his eyes. "LeeAnn has dinner almost ready to put on the table in less than thirty minutes."

She didn't see Craig anywhere, so she began to ascend below through the hatch. Hands came around her waist before she was able to place her foot off the last rung. Craig's arms held her slowly turning Lithia to face him. She had to look up to see his face. Her hands were on his forearms. Pulling her close, his arms engulfed her. His face went into her hair. "Cinderella, I'm so glad I let Daniel talked me into having you as my tour guide. I couldn't have asked for a better escort; I hope more than that when the week is over."

Her body fit perfect in his arms and he couldn't help himself. He had to hold her against him. She tensed at first when he caught her waist, but as he pulled her close, he felt their hearts beat as one. She seemed to lean her head onto his chest when he placed his face in her hair. He only wanted to speak in her ear so LeeAnn didn't hear him in the galley. But at the mention of Daniel, Cinderella held her breath; he wasn't expecting that reaction to his words.

Lobster dinner was delightful under the stars. Craig and Captain Fred spoke of past ships, hundreds of years ago, using the stars for navigation. How God made the constellations to help wandering travelers find Him. It was far from romantic, but there was an intimacy Lithia couldn't describe as they spoke of God and His ultimate plan for creation. It reminded her of long ago.

Before Lithia debarked, she stood at the bow of the boat alone, looking up to the heavens. "God, if you still love me, help me get away from my old life. Let me go home."

The company car was waiting at the marina to take Lithia home and Craig to his hotel. Lithia fell asleep not long from leaving the marina. She was leaning to the left, and with each turn, she leaned even more. Craig took her so she curled up into his arms, lying her head in his lap. He liked having her close. He wanted to take care of her, protect her. She looked so innocent with her hand under her face.

She was still sound asleep when they reached her apartment. He couldn't bear to wake her. He had the driver get her things and open the door. Craig carried her upstairs and into her apartment. He laid her on her bed, took off her shoes, and pulled the covers around her. Finding her phone charger, he plugged in her phone. Then he looked for paper and pen. He wrote her a quick note:

Cinderella,
I couldn't bear to wake you up, so I carried you to bed.
Your purse and backpack are on the kitchen counter.
Your wet swimsuit and towel were hung in the bathroom.
Tomorrow, I have lots of work, but I will see you for dinner
at 6pm. Until then,
Prince Charming

Stretching her legs, Lithia woke to find herself in bed. Confused on what bed, she began to panic, until she realized no one was with her. She was in her apartment, clothed, wrapped in her favorite green blanket.

Getting her bearings, she tried to remember what was the last thing she did. Craig had her on the sailboat with LeeAnn and Captain Fred. They had eaten lobster, and she even washed dishes with LeeAnn in the galley. The stars were beautiful over their heads as they had sat on the deck, even after tying in at the marina.

"Let's see, I was exhausted from the sun. LeeAnn put more aloe lotion on my shoulders. Mr. O'Shay said it was time to go, and we got into the company car. I wanted to go to sleep for the drive home, so I closed my... I fell asleep! On him! In the backseat! It wasn't a dream. I was cuddled up with my head in Craig O'Shay's lap." She put her head in her hands. *How could I have ever let myself...couldn't you have leaned towards the window?*

Lithia was an over-thinker. Her teachers told her, bosses told her, even her parents. To get things on a level to survive, she coped with talking to herself...aloud. She began pacing in her bedroom, trying to make sense of how and what he might have done to her while she was asleep.

"Okay, he isn't in the bed with me, and my clothes are on. There're my shoes by the closet. Phone? Not in my pocket, or on the bed. Did I put it on...yes, it's on charge? I don't remember doing it. I didn't even drink, it's like I was drunk without the hangover."

Walking into her bathroom, she found her Bengal tiger towel and her swimsuit hanging on the shower rod. Nope, she didn't remember doing that either. She started to undress and take a hot shower, then halted. *What if he is in the living room? Sleeping on her sofa or in the kitchen?*

Tiptoeing around the corner, Lithia peered into the living room. Nothing out of the ordinary that she could tell. No tall, intriguing man hanging around that she could see, unless he was in the kitchen. She took a few tiny steps closer to get a better view...

Nope, I'm alone. But what is this?

"*Cinderella, I couldn't bear to wake you up, so I carried you to bed.*"

He did what? Carried...from the car? Downstairs? There are my bag and purse, and I know how my suit and towel got placed in the bathroom. This is a first. Maybe this guy is a "real" Christian. I don't know what man wouldn't have taken liberties last night with me. He is not Daniel, that's for sure.

As she took her shower and got ready to go into the office, Craig was on her mind. It wasn't the hard-toned abs she'd admired when he took his shirt off, or the legs that shook when she rubbed sunscreen higher and higher on his thigh. No, she admired his values and kindness to those around him. He wasn't rude to the driver or order Captain Fred around, nor her. Craig was generous. He left a hundred-dollar bill in the galley for LeeAnn with a thank-you note for dinner. She was sure he stuck another one in Captain Fred's jacket pocket hanging on the hook by the table. Mr. O'Shay was not looking for a bedfellow, not that Lithia could tell. If she did her job, he would have scored three different nights.

Her day consisted of normal office events, meetings, letters, phone calls, emails, one big blog of existence. But her mind was fixed and determined on one thing, who is Craig O'Shay and how in the world does he know Daniel? Tonight, at dinner, game on.

Chapter 9

November 2000

"Craig O'Shay? Craig Jenson O'Shay? Please raise your hand or say 'here.'"

Mrs. Carter was starting to get aggravated. Every day, the little O'Shay boy was either sleeping in class or absent. Fourth grade was getting away from him too. Without the knowledge she was teaching, he wouldn't get promoted to fifth grade.

His mother wasn't any help. If Mrs. Carter called, she didn't answer. Mr. O'Shay? Well, the social worker said there wasn't a father's name on the birth certificate. Saoirse O'Shay was only listed on the school emergency card. There was a mobile number and a work number. When someone from the school ever called the work number, a burly sounding man answered, clueless to who Saoirse O'Shay even was.

One day after almost two weeks of absences, Mrs. Carter took it upon herself to drive to Craig's home. It really wasn't what she would call a home at all.

The street was lined with grey derelict buildings. Trash cans were up and down the sidewalk, most with the garbage on the pavement, not in the cans. In the easement of one building sat a homeless person protecting a rickety Wal-Mart shopping cart full of his possessions. The smell of urine and rotting foods filled the air. Window air conditioners or box fans were in any windows capable of holding it in place. Even during the fall and winter, heat would permeate through Miami Beach.

Businesses and apartments were mixed on both sides of the street. The only way to tell them apart was the name signs on the windows or the front of the doors. The one in the center had the number 506, with the 6-hanging upside down. Windows were boarded up or covered with cardboard. Shutters had fallen off years ago. The bright yellow paint had faded to a pasty sour milk color, and the white trim looked molded. The porch on the front had ripped screens, and the storm door was attached by the bottom hinge. This was the apartment the O'Shays lived in.

When Mrs. Carter walked up the three flights of stairs, she found apartment 34D in the back corner. There was a black garbage bag sitting outside to be taken to the dumpster. The odor told how many days it had been sitting outside the door. She could hear a baby crying in an upstairs apartment and a television on in the apartment. The volume wasn't very high, and she heard a child talking.

Knock, knock, knock! Ten-year-old Craig didn't know what to do. His mom was asleep until seven pm, when he was to wake her for work. If the person decided to knock again, like the old landlord would do, she would wake up and be angry. So he took a chair and put it up to the peephole to see who it was.

Oh, no, Mrs. Carter. She's going to upset Momma. I got to do something where Momma doesn't know she came by.

He put the chair back and opened the door just a bit. "Why hello, Craig. I came to speak to your mother for a few minutes. Is it all right that I came inside?" She was smiling, but didn't want to be standing in the hallway for long. A wine-o had made some nasty comments as she was coming upstairs, and she wasn't waiting for him to get the chance again.

Craig didn't want her to come inside. Their apartment wasn't very big, and the furniture had been taken from an old lady's apartment after she died. It even kinda smelled like death. His mom was in the only bedroom; he slept on the mattress in the corner by the window, but that was only when it was hot. Momma said he would stay cooler that way; when it got cold, his mattress moved to the other side of the room. Mrs. Carter wouldn't like his home.

"Come on, Craig. I'm tired from teaching all day. Let me come inside. Don't you want me to meet your momma? I'm sure she would love to hear me tell her how sweet you are and always caring about others." She knew he was hesitant to let her in. Red flags had already been waving in her head, and now the negative scenarios were playing a production in her mind. Somehow, she had to get into that apartment to see for herself.

"My momma is sleeping right now, and I ain't to wake her up until the clock says seven. She has to go to work after I eat my dinner." He turned and looked back at the bedroom door. "I'm not to let people inside without Momma being awake."

Mrs. Carter was not going to be deterred. "Do you have a kitchen chair I could sit in, Craig? I'm sure your momma would be okay if you let me sit in a chair right here at the doorway. I'll sit out here, and you can be inside the apartment. We'll just leave the door open so we can talk. That way, you haven't broken your promise to your momma, and we can be quiet to not wake her up."

His teacher was nice. She made school fun. Her class was always inviting, and she hugged everyone every day at least once, even if their clothes were dirty, and they didn't always take a bath. Craig didn't think she had any children of her own, for she always told them God had given her too many children to count.

Shutting the door, he gently picked up the chair he had stood on and placed it beside the door. *I hope Momma doesn't get mad at me.*

Mrs. Carter didn't know what was going to happen when he closed the door, but she knew he hadn't locked it. She was about to grab the knob when the door opened wide, and Craig, holding a chair out to her, he grinned.

"Now we can't be too loud cause Momma won't be too happy if we are. What would you like to talk about with my momma and me, Mrs. Carter?"

Oh, dear Lord, this poor baby. He must sleep on that mattress over there by the window. Paint's peeling off the walls, and there's a crack in one and a hole in another. Her eyes darted to and fro in the dim light coming from the dirty window. She didn't see any lamp, and it looked like the ceiling fixture was without a bulb. The television set was an old box TV and reception didn't look good. It was sitting on a cardboard box. A table that could seat four was between the living area and the few cabinets, refrigerator, and a stove. Another window was over the sink, but it was covered by plywood.

Craig patted her knee and she came to her senses. "Oh, I apologize. I didn't hear what you were saying, dear. Can you tell me again?" She took his hand in hers.

"I liked the story you're reading to us in class, *The Boxcar Children*. I hope it ends happily for the kids. I only like stories with happy endings." Craig thought about the story. Sometimes in class when she was reading, he wasn't asleep, but would cover his face so he could cry.

He knew Mrs. Carter could see his house wasn't the best. But she never said anything. The whole time she was there, he was happy. She told him she loved his drawings and stories he wrote for her. How she knew he was very intelligent, but she knew there were days he was tired. She asked him if he had a bedtime and did he obey when told to go to bed?

He thought about these questions. Momma had told him what he was to say if he was asked at school. "Oh, Momma has me go to bed by eight-thirty every evening, Mrs. Carter. But sometimes I can't sleep until Momma comes home." He had his hands behind his back, crossing his fingers as he lied. He never went to bed until his momma got home; he couldn't, for she might need him when she came in.

Mrs. Carter hugged him before she left. He thought she smelled like roses and was soft and squishy like old Señora Corona downstairs. His momma wasn't squishy, but she was soft, and when she went to work, smelled pretty. He promised to be a good boy for his mother, and he would do his best for her in class. Craig would always think of Mrs. Carter as the nicest teacher in the world.

Chapter 10

May 2, 2019

Craig had thought of work and contracts and the charity ball. This one and that needed him for something. He had spoken to his secretary in Raleigh with changes he wanted to an advertisement in the newspaper, and rearranged meetings he expected to attend next week.

Daniel had taken him to lunch with some important city commissioner and bragged how good friends they were back in high school. But Craig wasn't the same as he was back then. A lot changed when he became an adult. He didn't forget people; he wasn't the man he was today without the history of the past. However, he hadn't gone in the same direction as Daniel, at least he hoped what he heard wasn't how Daniel had made his money.

Any blank moment and he thought on Cinderella. She smelled like flowers, and her skin was soft like velvet. Her body was perfect in his arms, with her head on his chest, he could have stayed forever. It took all the strength within him to keep his composure when she slumped down in the car, then slid her head into his lap.

Her hair had fallen over her face. Craig had brushed it back and played with it as he stroked her back and laid his arm around her protectively. He watched her breast move up and down as she sighed in her sleep. His thoughts weren't as holy when he closed his eyes and thought of her on top of him when they fell. He never wanted to let her up.

Tonight, he had to concentrate on tonight. He was going to tell her, his Cinderella, his Miss Murphy, about his relationship with God. Everything within him was telling Craig he could not leave Tampa without telling her Jesus loved her. No matter what. He couldn't leave that piece out. His mind could hear it, "Tell her I love her, no matter what. Remember, I love her, no matter her past and present; I can change her future." Each night, he promised God he would if He just presented him the opportunity.

Lithia had been downstairs in the mailroom when the red and white roses were delivered to her office. They were gorgeous, with baby breaths in a crystal vase. The card read: *See you tonight at seven. Always, Craig.* It took her by surprise the red and white since he had been giving her yellow and only one. What did these dozen roses mean? She flashed back to her grandmother's meanings and wondered if he believed these flowers meant the same. Well, she had about three hours, and maybe she would find out.

Not knowing where or exactly what Mr. O'Shay's plans were for dinner, Lithia wasn't sure how to dress. Jeans and a cute shirt might be too casual, while heels and an evening gown may be too much. However, the way Craig seemed to be so spontaneous, she had no clue. She decided on a mid-calf length off-the-shoulder dress. *At least I don't have to worry about bra straps on my sunburn. Strapless bras are awesome.* The solid lavender dress was made of gauze-like fabric, so it wasn't too thick or too thin on a steamy Florida evening. A robe belt with sandals made her look like a model for a romance movie, all she needed was an open field of grass.

Lithia was ready with minutes to spare, so she sat down at the counter with pad and pencil. On the top of the page she wrote: *What I know about Craig O'Shay*, and underlined it.

<u>What I know about Craig O'Shay</u>
Knew Daniel in high school in Miami College degree-from? Polite
Lives in Raleigh, NC 28-29 years old Scars –how?
Not married-never married? Divorced? Mother deceased
Soul-searching eyes
No mention of father or siblings Pets? Birthday-April 30
Talks about God/prays-Christian? Nice body and muscles
Generous/charitable work Home for women who were abused

I will learn more tonight. I wish I had notecards I could reference, but that might not go over well. But I am going to find out about the friendship of Daniel and Craig. That's gotta be juicy. Then there's the scars on his lower back and on his right thigh, how did he get those? She circled scars and the one of Daniel in high school, then folded the page up and stuck it in her purse. If she needed to write something down, or if she wanted to think about another question to probe, she could try and sneak a peek.

Instead of coming up to the apartment to get her, Craig called Lithia on the phone and told her he was waiting out front of her apartment. She didn't really think twice about it, until she opened the outer door and saw him. He had rented a horse-drawn carriage. He took her hand, and holding her elbow, guided her into the carriage. She found a yellow long-stemmed rose on the seat waiting for her. Craig climbed in and sat across from her.

Leaning with his elbows on his knees, "Where would you like to go? If you are hungry, we can get dinner first, or we can enjoy the carriage ride."

She was drawn to this man and she just didn't know why. Those eyes cut right to her soul. "Could we eat and ride? I don't mind a street vendor or food truck, and this way, we can have dinner while enjoying this treat. I was looking forward to talking with you. We would be interrupted by waiters at a typical restaurant."

Okay, God, I'm taking this as a sign. I see this as a door opening for me to speak to her about you. I'm going to need a little courage.

"Sounds enchanting, Cinderella. Coachman, my good sir, find us some food trucks with delectable dishes." The horses began to trot slowly away from Lithia's apartment building.

"I have a confession to make, Miss Murphy, I, too, wanted the opportunity for us to chat. I even prayed God would open the door for us to be more trusting to each other's hearts and feelings this evening." He saw her eyes squint up and a frown on her face. "Maybe I am not expressing myself very well. See, I want to get to know you. Like your family, your hobbies, what are things that interest you? How did you begin working with Daniel? It's a question I wanted to ask you since Monday."

Why did her smile vanish as soon as I mentioned Daniel? I noticed that yesterday. Her mood completely changes when his name comes up in conversation. It is as if I trigger something; it's not a good sign.

Turning the corner, the horses pulled the carriage into a street full of street-side vendors with pastries and other desserts. Food trucks lined the block on both sides with offerings from tacos to Greek gyros. Even ice cream and corn dogs were represented in the maze of trucks. Lithia saw a 12-inch corn dogs with chips sign. She opted for a Diet Coke to drink with her Doritos and corn dog. Craig chose a chili dog and French fries with a large, sweet tea. Napkins, they needed lots of napkins.

There was some wind, but not too gusty to get dirt in their food, but enough to help with the heat of the evening. Craig spilled chili down his shirt when the coachman had to stop the horses abruptly when a dog ran out in front of them. Thank God for napkins. The rest of their dinner made it to their stomachs and no other spills occurred. He had the driver stop, and Craig jumped down to throw their trash away, but when he returned to the carriage, he sat beside Lithia, not across from her like before.

Time for the interrogation. "How old did you turn Monday for your birthday? I'm twenty-four, turning twenty-five at the end of the month. Your turn."

"I'm twenty-nine, though I acted six on my birthday, wouldn't you say?" He laughed at himself. She laughed with him. His eyes were twinkling again.

"Where did you grow up, Cinderella? Tampa always been your home?" Craig saw her eyes begin to moisten. She shook her head no.

"Tampa isn't the place I grew up, no, it's a tiny town about an hour away, depending on traffic. More rural than most cities close by. You know the type, everyone knew everyone's business, sometimes before the people in the same house knew it." *Yep, like Sister Brown at church.*

"Sounds nice, you had rural and city in close distance, so you got the best of both worlds. Small towns like from shows I watched as a kid; those were the kind I wanted my children to grow up in. Miami wasn't anything at all like Mayberry or Walton's Mountain, nor any other old mom and pop television show." He looked off into the night sky and drifted to another world for a moment.

Chapter 11

April 30, 2002

Twelve was an important birthday. Craig hoped his mom would do something special this year. Maybe this year, he'll get a cake. The last one he could remember was on his eighth birthday when the neighbor lady made him a chocolate cake with sprinkles. His mom was at work and missed it. She cried every year when she couldn't give him one.

This year, it was different. His mom had a boyfriend that gave her money. She had gotten some new furniture and clothes. They even moved to a two-bedroom apartment. He had his own bed. If he ever had friends, now he wouldn't be ashamed for them to come inside and hang out.

School was over and it was the weekend. He was thinking his mom wouldn't work, not this Friday, not this birthday. She could take one weekend for her son. The movies, the go-carts, putt-putt, he would be happy with going to the beach for the day. He'd have to wear a shirt or get sunburned, but he hadn't been in so long. He might even see some friends from school there.

But unfortunately, his mom wasn't missing work for his birthday. "Uncle Jim," as her boyfriend was to be called, said Craig would grow up and realize one day that life wasn't fair, and people had to work. Even on birthdays and holidays.

"Am I a getting a cake, Mom? Could we go to MacDonald's for supper before you go to work? Can I open my presents now?" he begged.

Craig was sure there was going to be something this year. His mom was wearing a new dress and had makeup on. She must be doing something extra nice. That's not the type of clothes for a waitress to wear. Her hair was all fancy and hanging down her back. He couldn't remember Momma ever going to work with her hair like that. He was all excited.

Momma looked gloomy to Craig. She was putting up a front. He had seen those looks before when she was worried about money, or she was tired. But he thought things were good, finally. Momma glanced at "Uncle Jim," "Don't you think it would be okay if we waited to go for an hour or two? I would like to spend some time with my son for his birthday. We could go to the buffet restaurant that you always wanted to try. You could stuff yourself silly, or Denny's has free birthday meals." *I knew Momma added that because of the nasty glare from "Uncle Jim."*

"A cake? Do I get one this time?" His eyes pleaded and hoped.

"I didn't make you one or buy one. I thought we could get dessert at the restaurant. That would be nice. Don't you think we could do that, Jim?" *Momma gave him the best puppy eyes I had ever seen. I just knew he would be okay with everything.*

"Seriously, See See, he isn't a six-year-old."

Momma had been sitting by me on the sofa with her arm around me. I felt so happy and content; if only her boyfriend would just go away, even for a couple of hours. Or come back after she got off work. I was thinking Denny's would be cheaper on her if I could eat free for my birthday. Plus, a lot of restaurants, I heard, gave free dessert to the birthday boy. Sounded like a win-win to me.

Jim snatched Momma's wrist and yanked her to her feet. "You're going to work. I'm not having my money wasted on some punk kid who is too selfish to see how important my time is with you." *He looked over at me and told me I could eat a frozen pizza from the freezer.*

I let him know he wasn't my father and to let go of my momma. I wasn't as big as him, but I was almost as tall. I wasn't too sure of where I was going with this, but he did seem to hesitate; then he grinned.

"Kid, you're a bastard; no one knows who your daddy is anyway. And I'll treat your mother any way I want to while she's working for me. Go on now and fix your damn pizza. Let's go, See See."

I didn't move from where I stood, and I stared the man down as hard as I could. My hands were in fists at my side, but I wanted to knock him to the ground so bad it hurt. I could tell he was gripping my mom's wrist extra rough. She had tears in her eyes, and I could see her hand turning blue from no blood flowing to it. Then I got the courage to step up and grab his arm. The arm he was holding my momma.

I must have taken him by surprise when I did it; he let go of Momma. She got behind me, but pulled me away from her boyfriend. It was a close call; he swung at me, hitting me in the shoulder. I think it hurt him more than me.

"You better control that boy of yours."

Momma got between us. She was protecting me, though I think it should have been the other way around. "I have control of my son; you should do the same with yourself. We are going to Denny's for Craig's birthday. You can either come with us, or not, I don't care." *She snatched her purse off the couch and took my hand heading for the door.*

Jim seemed to be in shock, but it didn't last. "You work for me."

"We will be back in two hours. It's only 4pm. I can go with you when we return. I believe that gives all of us what we want. Of course, the longer we argue about this, the later I go to work." *Momma put her foot down. I didn't know then what that night would cost us. For Momma, more than I would ever know.*

We walked to the Denny's closest to our apartment building. It was still a twenty-block distance. I kept turning around to see if Jim was following us; he was, but two or three blocks back. When we stopped to cross the street, a car pulled up, rolled down the window, and asked how much to my mother. She ignored it. Another man came up to us on the sidewalk, told her to ditch the kid, so he could have a good time. Then it dawned on me what these guys were saying to my momma. My blood boiled.

Sitting in the booth at Denny's, I had not a care in the world. Jim had crept in behind us, but he didn't sit at our booth. He took a seat at the counter so he could watch us. Momma couldn't get my meal for free, but I was allowed a free dessert. She said I could get whatever I wanted from the menu. I was in hog heaven. It didn't matter I hadn't received any presents so far, but time with my momma was precious.

When the waitress brought the ice cream brownie dessert, Craig was stuffed from his Grand Slam meal. "I'm still going to eat it all," he announced. He was so busy feeding his face, he didn't see the note the waitress handed his mother. Craig just thought it was the bill, but his mother didn't pull any money out of her purse. Instead, she placed the note in her bra.

Jim walked by their table and tapped his watch, just a little reminder on how much longer she had with her two hours. It was when he stepped into the bathroom, his mother handed Craig $20. "This is for your birthday, son. I want you to know how proud I am of you. Don't spend it on junk, maybe save it up for something important. I love you."

Craig had slipped the bill into his front pocket right before Jim came out of the bathroom. He stopped at their table. "Well, you about done with the birthday boy?" He was sarcastic, but Craig didn't care. His mother told Jim to go on and she would be at the apartment in a few minutes. She was walking back with her son. He didn't look happy, but he left, and Craig could see he was headed back toward the apartment.

His mother got up to leave, but Craig wanted to get a take-home coke. He went to ask the waitress for one, that's when he saw another man come up to his mother. He watched, trying to be the protector, giving the evil eye to the man even from a distance. The guy didn't seem to be rude or anything. Maybe his mother knew him from work.

"Momma, you haven't paid the bill yet or leave a tip." He thought this would get the man to leave them and help the situation with Jim if he got irritated they weren't home yet.

Patting Craig on the shoulder, "Don't worry about it; I took care of the bill for your mom. She was telling me it was your birthday today. How are old you, young man?" *I told him I was twelve, but I think he was just trying to get rid of me when he handed me a whole fifty-dollar bill. It did make me feel special. I was just about to tell him thank you when...*

"You owe me tonight. I expect you by ten o'clock at the address on the paper. Since you have already received part of your payment, I want you at your best later. Take Sonny Boy home and tuck him in. You will be playing house with me later."

He slapped my momma on the rear-end hard she almost stumbled. I wanted to tell him to apologize, but Momma took my arm, briskly walking to the door. He told her not to forget 10 o'clock. Momma nodded, but didn't stop walking away. I wish we could go home and get in pajamas and watch a movie on television. Jim would be there, and Momma had work.

"Don't let Jim see that money. Keep it hidden, especially the money from the nice man."

"I will. Who was that?" *I cringed when Momma replied,* "A Client." *My twelfth birthday-the day I found out my momma was a harlot.*

Chapter 12

May 2, 2019

Though it was only a minute or two, Craig was lost in his own thoughts. Lithia wasn't sure where he went, but the feeling she sensed was eerie. She had to get the atmosphere to change somehow or she might never get to ask the important question of how he and Daniel became friends. *I'll just ask another question to see where it takes me.* "Do you have any hobbies Mr. O'Shay? Play golf, collect antiques? What about siblings?"

"Huh, Oh, I'm so sorry. I didn't notice I went silent on you. Let's see, siblings, no biological ones, though your boss is the closest to a brother I have, him and Leonard, Captain Fred's son." Craig was more at ease now. "Funny you should pick golf, no, I don't know the difference between a putter and a driver, but I can play a mean game of putt-putt. I'm not your football kind of guy; I will watch the Super Bowl. I do like to play baseball, and I love to swim. What about you? Do you like sports?"

"Me? No, never been into sports other than volleyball or softball as a kid. Normally, I would strike out or was all net. I didn't have the athletic build or skill most sports take. Music was my thing. I was the band nerd." *Yep, let's tell him how dorky I looked, all hundred and fifty pounds of me back then while all the other girls my age weighed one ten or so.*

If Craig noticed her change in voice for the seconds she spoke of her "athletic build," he didn't say anything. "I play the piano. A neighbor, Señora Corona, had a piano in her apartment. I would sometimes stay with her when my mom was at work. She said I had talent and was a natural." His tone changed with a respect and solemn touch. "When she moved away to a nursing home, she gave me her keyboard. I still have it. She insisted I get lessons, but I couldn't afford them. It wasn't until college I was able to take real lessons. She passed away when I was gone. I saw her the day before I left for my third year of college; she never heard me play again. She was like the grandmother I never had."

Lithia took Craig's hand and held it between her own. "I was very close to my grandmother. I don't know what I would have done without her in my life. No matter what was going on, I could talk to her. I felt safe and loved at her house. She's the one who got me to love roses, so I think of her each time you have given me one. I can't remember a time I left her house without a hug and kiss and a big 'I love you' from her and Granddaddy. That was a pair. Granddaddy called her his 'Proverbs 31 wife.' If I ever find a relation-ship like the two of them had, I will be the happiest girl in the world."

Craig had lifted his head as she began to talk. He laid his other hand over hers. Even though Señora Corona wasn't his real grandmother, her house was a safe place, a loving place; he understood exactly what Cinderella felt. "She sounds like a wonderful lady. When was the last time you visited with her?" He regretted that question as soon as he spit it out his mouth.

Lithia looked at Craig and with a sorrowful face, "My grandmother passed away when I was a senior in high school. She and granddaddy had driven up to visit my aunt and uncle in Jacksonville to see the first great grandbaby. They were on their way back on a Saturday night when a drunk driver...Grandmother hated wearing her seatbelt. The police told my dad they found Granddaddy holding her in his arms when they arrived on the scene."

"He must have been devastated. Sounds like he loved her so much. Did he not get hurt?" Craig thought maybe it was the passenger side that had been hit, and her grand-mother had been flung out the front window. The grandfather must have had minor injuries.

"Oh, yes, he was. Hurt inside and out. Emotionally, he was a mess as anyone should be, but that is what baf-fled the police. His own physical injuries. Granddaddy had broken both legs, several ribs, and he had a large piece of glass protruding out of his chest. He told them he had walked to her, holding her; while waiting for the ambulance, he talked about how they met, their wedding, how wonderful of a mother she was, that God had blessed him with the best gift besides salvation-her. The last thing Grandmother said to him was she would wait for him at the gate of heaven, cause it couldn't be heaven if he wasn't with her."

They were both crying when the driver pulled the car-riage to the curb in front of Lithia's apartment. Craig jumped down and helped her onto the sidewalk. He spoke to the driver, gave him a healthy tip, and off he went. Craig came back to stand by Lithia. Taking her arm, they went into the apartment building and hit the elevator button. He kept his arm around her waist as they moved up each floor.

"Would you like a cup of coffee, Mr. O'Shay? I can make a pot, unless you want to get back to your hotel." It was not a statement, but a question. Lithia knew she was hoping he would stay, if only a little while. She didn't know how they had gotten into talking about Grandmother, but she was glad to share her memories with him, and that he had shared his own. How would she persuasively charm him into telling her more?

Plopping himself on the sofa and kicking off his shoes, Craig got comfortable. He leaned back with his arms behind his head before he spoke. "Sure, coffee sounds nice. So, tell me how your grandfather is now?" He turned his head toward the kitchen.

"Granddaddy went to be with Grandmother about three months later. Right before I left for college. There were complications from the wreck. It was hard losing them both back to back, but I can't see him living without her."

"You got a romance novel with those two, it seems. They must have been fun to be around. Were your parents like that? I mean, did they have the same type of relationship? I, well, I never saw, I never knew my father. I don't know what it would be like to have a role model of a good marriage. Not growing up, anyway. I have seen a handful in the last few years."

Lithia brought over two mugs with hot coffee. Then went back to the kitchen to retrieve a plate of cheese and crackers and ham slices. She placed it on the coffee table in front of Craig. He tossed a hunk of cheese in his mouth while rolling up a slice of ham. In two bites, the ham was gone too. "Do you have any brothers or sisters, Cinderella?"

"I have an older brother. Two years old than me, so 26. Married. Last time I saw him, he was going to be a father. He's a lot like our dad. I know he is a great parent."

"When's the baby due? Do you know if you're having a nephew or a niece? Aunt Cinderella has a nice ring to it." He teased her. "I always wanted a sibling and to be called Uncle Craig. I would spoil the kids rotten and send them home. Tell my brother or sister, 'This is for all the times you picked on me when we were little.' Revenge is sweet."

"I haven't seen the baby or have any idea what the sex is...that was five years ago. He told us they were expecting at Thanksgiving. I've never been home since. Who knows, they could have two or three kids now."

"Didn't you say you grew up only an hour or so from here? Why haven't you gone home? If I had a brother and parents that close, I would be there at least a couple times a month. We can go there one day this week. I would love to meet the man and woman that raised such a wonderful girl. Let's go on Sunday morning. Charity ball will be over, and I have plenty of time. This will be wonderful. What do you think?"

He was all excited and planning every detail, while Lithia started sweating, her stomach tightened, and she wanted to throw up. He put down his coffee and pulled out his phone. "What is the name of your hometown? I want to see the driving distance and where I could get a hotel for the night. You will stay with your parents, of course." Then he saw she wasn't getting caught up in the excitement, and he stopped. "Am I missing something?"

"Craig, I appreciate your enthusiasm, and I wish I could have the same joy, but I can't. My mother is the only one back home. Dad passed away from a heart attack a couple weeks before that last Thanksgiving. He never knew he was going to be a grandfather. Home wasn't the same. I wasn't the same; no one wanted me to stay. I doubt anyone misses me anyhow."

Lithia picked up her cup and the empty plate going into the kitchen. Craig came in behind her. *What can I say to her? I keep putting my foot in my mouth; we both seem to hit on each other's trigger issues. If I don't blow this tonight, I'll be surprised. And I still don't know how Cinderella and Daniel met. The only thing I am sure is that somewhere in her childhood she was taught about Jesus. I just want to know if she has Him in her heart. I have got to take that move.*

"Jesus can take that hurt away. You must give it to Him. The Bible tells us to take our burdens to the Lord and He will carry them. Hurts, bitterness, guilt...I know until I knelt at an altar and gave everything to Jesus, I couldn't handle all the pain from my past. But I know God had a purpose for what I went through so I could help someone else. Cinderella, from all you have told me, it sounds like at least your grandparents were God-fearing people. Did you ever pray the Sinner's Prayer?"

"God loved me a long time ago, but not now. It's too late for me. Thank you for a lovely evening, Prince Charming. Good night." She opened her door and took the coffee cup from his hand.

He had been dismissed. He walked to the elevator, praying inside he hadn't screwed up. She made him emotional, and he didn't want to leave, not yet. If he had insisted, she might have taken it a different way then he meant. It was too late; he was always too late to help the damsel in distress.

Chapter 12

January 2003

Christmas vacation was over, and Craig was happy to be back at school. He hated to be around "Uncle Jim" any more than necessary. School was always better than home alone or when Jim was there. He could think back to when he was little. His mom had to work, but he could stay at Señora Corona's after school until she came home. Sometimes he would eat before his mom came, tacos or burritos, and flan for dessert. Señora Corona would give him a small bowl of flan to take home for later. He would give it to his momma. Other times, Momma would bring supper home from the diner for him; a hamburger and fries or a BLT and chips, which they might split. That's when they were happy. They didn't have much, but he was loved.

Then Momma had to work the night shift. He didn't understand why the restaurant stayed open all night long when it didn't before. When school was over, he came home and did his homework and would wake Momma up for her to get supper and be ready for work by eight. Some days, he would still go to Señora Corona's for dinner if there wasn't anything to eat. He would go after his momma went to work. He didn't want her to know he was hungry. Craig wanted his momma to have food when she got back.

Señora Corona taught him to play the piano. She had been a music teacher and enjoyed teaching up and coming artists. She had told Mrs. O'Shay Craig was a natural musician. Since she wasn't teaching anymore, she had no problem helping Craig learn some basic elements so one day he could get real lessons on a tuned piano. He had thought of her as a grandmother he always wanted.

Craig noticed his mom didn't get dressed for work like she once did, and when he asked her about her uniform, she told him they liked her to dress at the restaurant. She had a locker assigned for her things. He believed her, for there was no reason to lie. He just didn't get leftovers from the diner after that. She was extra tired and didn't look like she was only twenty-eight. Then by the time Jim came along, even when they must have had more money, she looked forty instead of twenty-nine.

Right after Jim started hanging around, Momma had moved them into a bigger apartment. Craig had his own room, and they had gotten more furniture. He thought he was rich, and Jim was going to be his dad. But after a couple of months, Craig wasn't so sure. Then the whole birthday thing happened. He had wanted to just ask his mom for the truth, but he never got any time alone with her. She seemed guarded with any words she said to him.

He knew he was almost twelve and a half. He was already taller than his mom and had ten or more pounds on her. During the school week, he was sure to have breakfast and lunch, then supper was up in the air. His mom let him do a lot of the grocery shopping, but because he was always the one cooking and he didn't know how, he'd buy peanut butter and jelly, hot dogs, frozen pizza, and ham sandwich makings. They didn't have a microwave until recently, so he couldn't even buy those types of meals.

What made Craig angry, Jim did. Momma had an EBT card for food. Jim would use it to buy steaks and vegetables. He would have Momma make huge meals for him, but Craig wasn't always invited to eat those meals. Or they would be prepared while he was at school. If he was lucky, there were leftovers. However, when Jim figured out Saoirse was leaving her partially-eaten plate for Craig, Jim would throw away anything she couldn't eat before they left to take Momma to work.

The old routine began: teachers and school friends, home at four. Craig did his best to be quiet when he came in and would do his homework. Two or three times a week, he would go to Señora Corona's for piano lessons. If he got there at the right time, he ate dinner. But he had to be in his apartment no later than six in the evening. On the sofa, at the table, or in his room is where his mom or Jim would find him. Maybe watching television in the living room, reading a book in his room, or doing homework at the table. This evening, he had something planned.

"Craig, you need to take the trash down to the dumpster before you go to bed. We better not get back here in the morning and find it still in the kitchen. You should sweep the kitchen and clean the bathrooms too."

Jim was ordering him around like his personal slave. Jim hadn't lifted a finger to do anything in the apartment, unless it was to eat, sleep, and use the bathroom. Cleaning was a woman's job, and he was unable to lower himself to do that. Cooking, well, he wasn't doing that either. Craig should deal with that because his mother worked, and Jim worked. *You seem too lazy to work. You are either on your phone or laid up in the bed with my mother. Unless you work at night when she does, I never see you work.* Of course, Craig never said any of this out loud. It probably wouldn't go over well if he did.

When Jim and his mom had left, Craig waited until he watched them go out the door to the street, then he ran downstairs just in time to see them get into a taxi a block away. He waved down the next cab and jumped in. "Follow that taxi!"

Winding through the streets, the taxi followed Jim and his mom. But when they pulled over and got out, Craig had his driver park farther down. He turned around in the back-seat and watched his mom and Jim walk into a building that did not look anything like a restaurant to Craig.

Bright lights with flashing colors were on the roof of the building. The windows were black except for the pink lights that outlined the words on the signs hanging in them. He wasn't too sure what the words were, but assumed it was the name of the diner. Loud music was playing from inside, so there must be a dance floor, too. But he couldn't under-stand why people would want to eat there with the music so loud. It sounded more like a night club than a restaurant.

Craig noticed the wrestling-looking dude standing by the front door. He looked mean and wasn't letting anyone in, it seemed. Already a line of men was standing at the door to get a table. Some were having to show their ID to the guard dog at the door. Occasionally, there was a lady with one of the men in line. Those guys were let inside at once.

He told the taxi driver to turn the car around and take him home, but to go slow as they drove past the place the man and woman had been dropped off. It was right before they got near the building, another flashing light turned on from outside. Craig's eyes turned red with anger, just like the red lights from the sign. He read it: *ALL NUDE GIRLS*. That was on one window with the name of the place on the other: *THE JUNGLE CATS*.

"Take me home." Craig was not going to cry, well, not until he got home, he wasn't.

"So, kid, who was that in the other taxi? Your father cheating on your momma with some hooker from that strip club? You should beat the man with a baseball bat if you got one." He looked in the rearview mirror. Nope, the kid didn't look anything like the guy, but there was a resemblance to the woman. Oh, God! He done shown the kid where his mother worked. How would he feel if he been a kid and some man took his mom in a stripper club, or worse, made her work there?

"Was that your momma with that guy? You know not everyone in there does that. Maybe they're just going to grab a drink or something. Don't jump to conclusions until you know everything. Think it through before you do any-thing rash." Poor kid, what will he do with the information he just learned?

But Craig didn't think when he got back to the apartment. His anger took over and he didn't wait to talk to his mom. He went into the bedroom his mom shared with Jim and began to search through every corner for clues. Matchboxes with *The Jungle Cats* logo on it. Business cards with Jim's name listed as manager for the club.

In the closet, there were costumes. Not much mate-rial, but you could see it was supposed to be types of cats. Anything from tigers, panthers, lions, and regular house cats.

Did his momma wear this? There wasn't much to it. A bikini covered more. Men could see his momma, all of her. Did they touch her?

The more Craig thought about this, he could only rationalize that Jim was making his mom do this. Things changed after Jim came around. The business card said Jim was the manager. He got Momma to do this, whatever she did, wearing these strings. Craig didn't even think what she might do at this place, but if she was there and NOT wearing clothes, he didn't want her working there after tonight.

Jim was the bad guy. Jim had to go. Craig collected all Jim's clothes and belongings and threw them out the window of the apartment down into the street. Craig expected most of the stuff would be gone by morning from some random homeless person. He wasn't thinking what consequences could come for him or his mother. He would be leaving around the same time they came home in the morning. Jim probably wouldn't even know anything until later. He would be too tired to notice.

Craig went to bed, thinking how he was going to get his mom alone to discuss her job, and how they were to get away from Jim.

When the alarm clock went off, he got up quick, dressed and left for school. He didn't see any change in the apartment, and he could hear Jim sleeping in the other room. So far, he was safe, but who knew what was going to happen when he came home this afternoon, he had until then to get his story straight.

The bell rang, and the school day was done. Craig had no clue what he was going to do when he got home. He walked slowly back to the apartment, hoping Jim wouldn't be there when he returned, or at least be asleep. It was quiet when he opened the door, and his mom was in the kitchen. She looked tired, but she smiled when he came in.

He hugged her probably a little tighter than usual, but he didn't care. She seemed pleased and asked about his day. "I got an A on the math test I took last week and a B plus on the science test from yesterday. Uh, Momma, where's Jim?" Craig looked around like he was afraid Jim would come crawling out of the woodwork.

"Oh, he's in the shower. He said he was going to take a long hot one while I fixed some food. What is it, Craig? Did you need to talk to Jim?" She started taking some meat out of the refrigerator and began to season it in a pan.

"No, I don't have anything to say to Jim. I thought we could talk. Alone." Looking up at her and still keeping an eye out for Jim to come into the kitchen, "When is Jim moving out? I don't want him living with us anymore. He is rude to me and I don't like it when he yanks and orders us around. I want us to go back to the way it was when you worked at the diner. We spent afternoons together and ate food from the diner or went to Señora Corona's apartment for meals. You had time for me." He was doing his best not to be some little toddler begging his mommy for attention. But he had to say whatever he was planning before Jim came out of that bedroom door.

"Honey, Jim is in this apartment with us. He can't just move out. We need the money he gives me to keep the bigger apartment too. Do you want to go back to living in a one-bedroom and sleeping on a mattress on the floor? I hated that for you. Plus, you are getting to be a man, I can't have you sleeping in a bed with me. What kind of mother would I be?"

Everything she did was for her son. Things she never would do she did though, she couldn't even look in the mirror. She had gone against all her morals and ethics to give her child a bed, clothes, food, so other kids would stop bullying him. One day she would tell him; one day when he could understand.

Saoirse hugged her son one more time, and with a kiss on the cheek she turned to her cooking. A little oil in the skillet and the pan would be ready for the meat soon. "Start on your homework. There's enough steak for you, too, if I cut the biggest one in half. I know I don't need one that big. I'm going to make a tossed salad, and I already put three big potatoes in the oven to bake. It's my favorite meal."

How am I to tell her I know about The Jungle Cats? How do you tell your mother you know she works at a strip club? I must be honest. Just ask her who got her to work there. Maybe if she knows I am stupid about the job, she will understand why I want Jim to leave. "I followed you to The Jungle Cats last night."

And that's when Jim stormed in with a towel wrapped around his waist.

"Where the hell is my clothes? You, bastard. What did you do with them?" Jim was trying to hold up the towel, and swing at Craig at the same time. He kept missing.

Saoirse walked away from the stove and put her hand on her son. "What are you talking about, Jim? Craig doesn't know anything about your clothes. He has been in the kitchen with me, and before that, school. Your shirts and pants should be in the closet where I hung them, boxers and socks are in the top drawer of the chest. The only dirty clothes were what you took off last night." She opened the oven and turned over the potatoes, then threw the steaks in the skillet. The skillet was hot, so it wouldn't take long to get them to medium-rare.

Craig sat down at the kitchen table and opened his backpack. He took out a history book and a composition notebook. "Did you hear me, Momma? I followed you last night." He wasn't loud, but he knew he was loud enough. He knew this time Momma had heard him.

She made no remark, but took the salad fixings out of the fridge and placed them on the counter. When she was slicing the tomatoes, Jim came back, still wrapped in the towel. "I'm telling you, my shirts, pants, even my underwear is missing from that bedroom. What did you do with it, boy?"

He didn't give Craig a chance to reply when he started hitting him. Craig tried to get away or dodge the blows. He put up a textbook and Jim punched it, but that made him furious. Craig crawled under the table, but Jim just flipped it over. Saoirse tried to block Jim from hitting Craig, forgetting the steak and potatoes were cooking. Jim pushed, Saoirse fell but tried to catch herself before she hit the floor. The knife she had been using clanged on the tile.

Craig and Jim raced for the knife. Two swift slashes, one on the thigh and one across the back, and Craig's momma screamed as she dropped the hot skillet on Jim's back. Cursing, Jim flung it off him as he came at her with the knife and stabbed her in the abdomen. The towel had fallen to the floor, which Saoirse placed to her wound. She tried to see where Craig had hidden, then she fainted.

The commotion had caused neighbors to open their doors and check the hallways. Señora Corona had expected to see Craig after school, but he hadn't come. She had heard the bang from furniture, she assumed, but then the cursing and screaming brought the other neighbors running to the hall. She had called the police.

With help from a nice policeman, she climbed the stairs to the apartment where Craig lived. But he held her outside as his partner drew his gun and entered the apartment. There was blood on the rug in the living room and moaning coming from one bedroom. She stepped right inside the room, but didn't move when she saw so much blood on the floor. One officer moved into the kitchen while the other went toward the bedroom.

"I got a woman in the kitchen, looks like a stab to the abdomen. Dispatch, Office Pratt here, I need an ambulance at my location, woman, approximately thirty, with knife wound to lower abdomen. Seems to have fainted, pulse is weak."

"Officer Pratt, I got nude adult male with a burn mark on his back. Other than that, he seems to be okay, physically. He seems to be in a lot of pain, probably why he is unconscious." He came out into the living room and saw Señora Corona crying.

"Hey, Pratt, does the woman look like she's moved since she was stabbed? I got blood in here, but there was none in the bedroom with the guy. He hasn't any cuts, only the burn mark. This blood had to come from someone."

"Craig." She only spoke his name once and barely loud enough for Officer King to hear her.

"Who, ma'am? Did you say Craig? Who is Craig? Is that the man's name or someone else?"

Tears came as she began to speak in her native language, but with the crying and only one year of high school Spanish, Officer King was clueless. He finally picked up "niño" and "hijo." Boy and son. "Is Craig a boy that lives here, is he their son?"

Chapter 12

"Si, the son...the momma." But she looked at the blood and wondered where the sweet boy was and if he even lived.

Officer King found him under his bed with cuts across his back and a gash in his thigh. In his hand, he clutched the kitchen knife.

The EMT's were working on Mrs. O'Shay to place her on the gurney and take her to the hospital. Another group was taking down Craig. He had lost a lot of blood, his pulse was barely audible. The last to be taken to the hospital was Jim.

Both officers didn't know what to report. Who was the assailant? The boy with cuts on his back, the mother with the gut wound, or the man free of any cuts at all. Until someone could make a statement, all were victims.

Chapter 13

May 2, 2019

*O*h, why did Craig O'Shay have to bring up God? Lithia didn't need anyone to tell her about Jesus and the Cross or anything else on forgiveness. She grew up in church, went to church every time the doors were open, she even sang in the choir. But that was a long time ago when she was young and innocent. Craig could think she was pure; he knew nothing. God had left her.

It wasn't that she didn't wish all of it was true. God sent His son to die a horrible death and pay the cost of sin. Lithia knew Jesus rose again, and she believed He was coming back one day. But those happy feelings of joy weren't in her anymore. When she needed Jesus, He wasn't there, even though she never did the rebellious things others did. So if she lived a good life, worked for His kingdom, and followed His commandments to the best of her ability, why did He forsake her when she needed Him the most? Simple, He didn't love her.

God doesn't love everyone. Not that I can blame Him. I can think of some people I am not fond of at all. And if we are made in God's image, then why can't He, like us, not love everyone? Especially someone who has hurt us or forced us to do things, put us in situations where there was no way out.

God's Word says He provides a way of escape when bad things come. Did He forget my way out? He gave me none. Now, I am making my own the best way I can. As soon as Craig O'Shay is gone and I get the money from Daniel, I'm out of here. I will have the money to start over. Sure, I may never see my family again, but they haven't come looking for me either. Mom made it clear I wasn't welcome back.

Yep, Lithia felt this way, but consequently, she did remember what being in a relationship with God was like; the wholeness and fulfillment of following the will of God. When her grandparents died, it was hard, but she had the Holy Spirit to comfort her. But then, He left her too.

Maybe if it hadn't been for that one summer.

Chapter 14

July 2010

$\mathcal{A}$ nd this summer brought Harold Gibson.
Lithia had packed her suitcase before they left for Sunday School at 9:30. She would just need to change clothes, eat lunch, and slip her Bible into the bag. It shouldn't take her thirty minutes. But who knew how long Pastor Johnson would be preaching this morning? If the Spirit moved, it could be one before he would wind down.

Reverend Howard Johnson was a powerhouse preacher that had been called to Hopewell Methodist five years ago. Lithia thought about how some of the members weren't too sure on how a predominantly "white" church was going to be shepherded by a Jamaican spitfire. But it worked. He had the demeanor of Job and the courage of King David. The man preached with boldness like Peter on Pentecost in the Book of Acts. His wife, Ruth, was a source of strength for him. We all had heard the love story between them, making both a strong influence on dating and Christian responsibilities when looking for a mate. Pastor Howard and First Lady Ruth had met at youth camp. Now, twenty years later and three daughters, Sunflower, Violet, and Lily, and pastoring for eighteen, he said he was home to stay if the congregation would let him. That was five years ago, and the church has not regretted keeping him. Attendance had grown from eighty members to almost two hundred. For such a small community, that's amazing. Diversity was the key. The audience on a Sunday morning looked like a smorgasbord of paint palettes with the shades of colors on faces. Grandmother would tell some of the older members, "Guess you won't like heaven then, better get a different ticket." Lithia could just see the grin on Grandmother's face as Sister Ethel Brown would stomp off to her car after Grandmother's chaste warning.

Yep, it's going to be one of those long services today. Elder Franklin wanted to testify before he prayed for the offering. After telling his current medical prognosis and medicines his doctor wanted him to consume each day, he had finally told the Lord to heal him. He didn't have the money to waste for all those pills when he was on a fixed social security check; how he dumped all the pills down the toilet and flushed them. "That's what having faith in God is all about, young'uns."

Sister Ethel hollered a big "Amen," and then she began to sing "Leaning on Jesus" all five verses until Pastor Johnson told Sunshine to stop playing the piano. He prayed over the tithes and offerings himself. The ushers did their job. Lithia saw her dad lean over to her mom and say something; he probably was wishing for earplugs 'cause Sister Ethel did not have Beyoncé's voice.

Services wrapped up about 12:30.

Lola had Peter grab some KFC on the way home. It would be simple to make a paper plate and not mess up her kitchen with Lola having to cook for the Barnes family. Lithia quickly changed clothes as her mom got out paper plates and plastic silverware for their lunch. She threw her Bible and her journal in her suitcase, zipped it up, setting it by the front door. Now she wanted a big piece of chicken and cole-slaw. Peter liked the crispy pieces, while Lola preferred the original recipe wings. It seemed her dad had already filled his plate full.

Grace was said when Lola finally sat down after turning on the oven to get warm for the apple pie she was making for later. Peter didn't mince words, "Thank God for the food and bless it. Amen." Shoveling his mouth of mashed potatoes, "Lithia, you better be ready to go when I am. I will not wait on you. You might want to eat up because I am not stopping for anything on the way." That was her dad, all right. When traveling, you drove until he had to stop for gas. Too bad if you had to use the bathroom, you would just have to wait.

The telephone in the den rang. Lola went to get it. Lithia couldn't hear much of the conversation, but enough that Carrie, Leslie, and Renee were headed over. The look on her mom's face when she returned to the table let Lithia know her dad wasn't going to be any happier than he already was about driving to Wekiva.

"Peter, that was Brother Arnold on the phone. He must take his wife to the hospital, her mother just had a heart attack and he won't be able to drive Carrie, Leslie, and Renee to youth camp. I told him no problem, he can drop them off at our house and you would be glad to take all the girls in an hour." When Dad gave Mom the "look," Mom replied with, "When you do the least to one of my little ones," and smiled.

106

Peter Murphy was not pleased. "You have got to be kidding! I not only have to miss my baseball game, but I must drive two whole hours with four teenage girls in my car! Do you know how that's going to be? I will hear all about makeup, boys, movie stars, clothes, and the singing. They will want to listen to music of TODAY! I probably can't even get them to listen to contemporary Christian music. I'm going to need Tylenol before I even leave."

Lola was not going to listen to Peter's complaints. She could name a few of her own. "Let's not forget when I took the boys three years in a row. My minivan was stuffed with seven boys and their bags. Heading to Wekiva Springs was okay, it was the return trip from picking them back up the following weekend that killed me. The smell of stinky clothes radiating from the luggage which I couldn't get any relief. It was too hot to roll down the windows and turn off the AC. Add the burping and deadly gas leaks coming from their bodies is enough to know I am glad I don't have another son." She took another biscuit and slapped butter inside.

Lithia thought, *"I bet Mom wishes she slapped the butter on Dad. That would have been funny."*

Brother Arnold dropped the girls off promptly at one o'clock, and as Peter loaded the SUV with the extra suitcases, he told the girls to make their final trips to the bathroom. He gave Lola a kiss on the cheek, told her he should be home in time to load up her car with food to take to the Barnes, just in time to miss the entire Braves game as well. They had barely made the interstate when Peter's nightmares began: the topic of boys. He even turned up the radio so he couldn't hear the oohs and ahhs of schoolgirl love. As normal, Leslie was the dominant in the "boy" debate.

"I cannot believe you didn't want to ride up with Leo and your brother, Lithia. Two whole hours with the best-looking boys at church. I would have signed up to help with the concession stand if I knew they could have taken me. Think about it. Sitting in the cab of the truck between Sean and Leo would be heaven." Leslie sighed and closed her eyes as she imagined the college-bound guys drooling all over her.

"Seriously, Leslie, first, it is my brother, yuck! Second, Leo sees me like some little annoying sister. Always has and always will. They don't look at high school juniors anymore. We are not sophisticated enough for them. Sean says we are too immature for college freshman."

Carrie and Renee were nodding their heads, but chimed in there would be plenty of guys at youth camp to meet their own age. Plus, they were hoping the twin brothers they met last year would be coming again. Those guys would be seniors in high school this coming year, and lived in Kissimmee, near Disney World. Renee said Anthony could "kiss a mee" any time he wanted. Carrie was hung up on Allan.

Lithia wasn't going to mention any boy if her dad was in earshot. She was supposedly going to camp to increase her spiritual walk with God, not increase her knowledge of teen boys. Although, if she could have ridden with Leo Standford alone, she would have jumped at the chance. But again, he saw her like a little sister and was head over heels for Sunflower Johnson. He was going to theology college in August to be a missionary, and Sunflower was going to be studying music education. They were practically engaged already. Though, Grandmother said things could change when they saw other fish in the sea at college. Granddaddy said Leo was enchanted by Sunflower's piano playing.

Grandmother asked Granddaddy what enchanted him about her, "Not sure, Rosa, if it was your cooking or your curves!" *"Duck, Granddaddy, here comes the magazine!"*

By the time Peter pulled onto the campgrounds, the place was buzzing with teens of all shapes, sizes, and colors. He seemed to throw the suitcases at the girls, kissed Lithia bye, and told her to be good, and went to check on Sean. He said he wanted to talk to Sean about bringing his sister home next weekend. The other girls were getting a ride back with Renee's mom and dad, who were going to Renee's sister's house in Daytona Beach to see their first grandbaby. They would just swing by camp on their way back home to Hopewell.

"If my dad can pry my mother's hands off the baby," laughed Renee, though she knew her dad was overjoyed her sister and brother-in-law named the baby after his Grandpa Joe.

Lithia was going to try her best to beg her brother to let her go with Renee's parents. It was too uncomfortable in Sean's truck, all squeezed in by Leo.

The first day of camp was simple. Find your cabin, organize your stuff, and meet your bunkmates. Since all four of the girls were sharing the cabin, that was one less thing to deal with after they arrived. Luckily, they got the closest cabin to the bathrooms this year-the coveted Cabin Kindness. Each area of cabins had a biblical theme. For example, fruit of the Spirit and the twelve disciples. The boys' cabins were names after the disciples and the major prophets. The girls' cabins were the fruit of the Spirit and women of the Bible. The chapel area was in the center of the camp with the mess tent and the boys' bathrooms to the left. Next to the boys' bathrooms were the male counselors' dorms. On the other side of the chapel was the art supply craft building that also had the main offices with nurses' station and the girls' bathrooms and showers. Then there was the female counselors' dorm. Years ago, when they had a large attendance, it could be up to eight per cabin, and after one year of pranks and tricks, counselors had to sleep in the cabins with the campers. Lithia didn't have to worry this year. Seventeen and eighteen-year-old campers would only have four per room and cabin-free of counselor roomies.

Dinner was at six pm sharp each day. The camp director wanted everyone to be finished eating and able to be at chapel by seven thirty each evening. Sunday night would kick off camp with chapel. First impressions were important, so the girls wanted to look "cute" for chapel at seven. They got to the mess tent right at opening, gulped down a tuna fish sandwich and chips and Coke to have plenty of time to get makeup and hair perfect before chapel. Leslie was hoping she could get there early to see if she could sing on the praise team. It gave her the best view of the crowd, and she could see all the new guys too. Mainly, they could see her.

Everything was working according to plan, Lithia had on a sundress with pink flowers and white gladiator sandals. Carrie had French-braided her hair and she was wearing her cross necklace her parents had given her the day she was baptized two years ago. She thought she looked elegant. Leslie was completely different. Off-the-shoulder floral top with dangling hoop earrings and white capris that accented her dark tan. Leslie footed high heels that only a model would wear. Carrie had short light brown hair, usually cut like Emma Watson's in *Harry Potter*. She wore a solid red top with a red and black layered skirt, accessorized with black earrings and a necklace and bracelet to match. Her lipstick was as red as her shirt. Renee had been working at the mall since before Christmas. She had purchased a couple of new outfits for camp. This night, she wore the mint green sleeveless dress with tan heels that tied around her ankles. It was quite the head-turner, and she accented with a gold chain and small studs in her doubled pierced ears. Her hair was pulled back in a tight bun, showing her slender neck. Her ebony skin glowed. Lithia thought Renee had to be the most beautiful girl she knew.

As the girls were trying to find the best seats, Leslie had already gone on stage and flirted with the band to find out what the praise songs would be. When Lithia saw Leslie grab a mike, she didn't worry about saving Leslie a seat at all. Service started with a prayer from the camp director, and the music began. Leo was on stage playing the bass; too bad Sunflower didn't get to camp until tomorrow after the Barnes' funeral. Lithia kinda missed Sunflower's touch on the piano. Violet, her sister, was learning to accompany Sunflower on the organ, but Violet wasn't ready for this stage, maybe next year. Lithia couldn't tell who was on the drums. He had dark brown hair, and it was long compared to Leo's. He was wearing black jeans and a Jesus Freak t-shirt. Sean was at the sound booth with headphones on, making sure the music was balanced through the chapel. There were also intercoms throughout the camp so the services could be heard anywhere on the property. Some guy from Orlando Living Water Methodist Church was leading the praise and worship. He was in his thirties, and his wife was singing alto with Leslie's soprano. Carrie pointed out Anthony playing the trumpet and Allan on the electric guitar. Renee tried to wave at Anthony, then played it off like she was praising the Lord.

Lithia was singing along with her eyes closed. She knew all the songs. Then a guy started singing without music. His voice was purely angelic. Lithia expected to see some angel like Gabriel, bright lights and wings standing on stage singing, "How Great is Our God," but, no, he had dark curly auburn hair, cargo pants, and a camouflage t-shirt with the message, "I'm in the Lord's Army" printed in black. When the music begins to play along with the soloist, Lithia is captivated. There was something genuine about this guy. He was good-looking, not as cute as the drummer, but there was something about him; Lithia discerned this guy was not putting on a show. He was worshipping in spirit and in truth. This guy believed every word of the song. When the song was over, he stepped back in the shadows to continue singing with the praise team.

There were only two nights the entire camp that offering was collected, the first night and the last night, which would be Friday. Friday was the biggest night of camp. That was date night. After the final service, there was a big party with dancing and boat rides across the lake and back, food, and you could take a date. If you didn't have a date, the label loser would stick until next year when you prayed you were asked by someone. Therefore, the first night and the last night of camp were the most important to look your best. Lithia had never had a date since she started coming to teen camp. Last year, Carrie and Renee went with the twins; Leslie went with a different guy every year. Sean always had someone on his arm. Maybe this year would be Lithia's turn. She had lost ten pounds.

Wow, her mind wandered. She rambled in her own head most of the time. Offering was blessed and the musicians began to play. The brown-haired drummer was given a solo and he made the most of it. When he finished, teens all over the chapel were on their feet cheering him on. Lithia got a long look at the muscular build under the tight t-shirt. He stood up and bowed. He even stepped out into the center stage, and it seemed as he looked right into Lithia's eyes. She couldn't blink or turn away. She was bewitched by his smile. She felt her whole body go numb; he never broke his gaze until he walked behind the curtain. Lithia couldn't believe he hadn't fallen. Then the doubts came tumbling down. *"He couldn't have been looking at me at all. It had to be someone behind me. I just wished and imagined he was looking at me."*

The sermon was halfway through with Lithia hearing very little of the message. She had turned in her Bible to John 3:1-21. She had followed along. There were notes in her journal from the sermon. But when she looked down and focused on what she had written, it was just "drummer," "Mrs. Drummer," and a sketch of a guy playing the drums with long hair. Lithia had to shake herself out of this trance. "Satan will try to distract you with the pleasures of this world so you will not focus on God and the plan God has for your life. Pleasure is for a season, young people. It might feel good now, but what will the results be next week, next year, ten years from now," the minister shook his head. "I have seen too many adults regret the actions of their youth." Then he finished telling the story of Samson and Delilah.

Musicians begin to play softly in the background and teens began to pour into the altar. Adults were walking through the teens, praying for each of them. Carrie and Renee had gone up and left Lithia standing by herself. She lifted her head and looked to the stage. She didn't see the drummer at first, but she saw Leslie's back. She must be talking or praying with someone on stage. Then Lithia noticed a guy sitting at the keyboard. He began to play along with the pianist. Could the drummer be able to play the keyboard as well? That's when Lithia heard the laugh. Who in the world would be laughing that loud on stage during the altar call? She turned and saw Leslie with her hand on the shoulder of the cute drummer boy. No wonder he wasn't playing the drums; he was being distracted. What was Lithia thinking anyway? The drummer sure didn't see her. Then the keyboardist began to sing an old hymn, "He Touched Me." As he sang, the other instruments grew silent. A holy presence filled the room with as the words came from his lips. "Oh, the joy that floods my soul. Something wonderful happened, and now I know, He touched me and made me whole."

When the song was over, the minister thanked CJ for his songs of worship and allowing the Lord to use him in the service. And like that, service was over and the teens were dismissed. All were to be in their cabins by 10 and lights out by 11. The day would start at 7 am for breakfast. Lithia looked around for Leslie, but she was nowhere to be seen. Carrie and Renee had already made a bee-line for the stage to Anthony and Allan. Lithia was sitting on the bench all alone. She picked up her Bible and her clutch bag and begin walking toward the concession stand. It was usually open after chapel until 10, and she had about thirty-five minutes.

Arriving at the concession stand, she saw many of her old friends from years of camp. Sara Jenkins and Linda Jones were hanging with Nick Perez and his brother Miguel. Lithia had heard the boys would be joining the Army after high school. Miguel this October, and Nick next June. Sara was trying to talk Miguel into waiting and go to college first.

He had been called to preach, but felt his country needed him. Sara had been praying that either he would change his mind completely or would consider going in as a chaplain in four years. It seemed they had gotten engaged after they had graduated last month.

Erika Rodriguez was with her little sister Jennifer. This was Jennifer's first year to teen camp, and Erika could not shake her. Their mom even made Erika be placed in the same cabin. Lithia liked Erika. She was sweet and could sing like a bird. She loved kids, though little sisters didn't count. Her goal was to be a teacher, and plans for college were in the works for next summer. She wanted a scholarship and could possibly earn one through her singing or student government. Erika had won the student council election and would be the president for her senior year at St. Petersburg High School.

Lola and Peter had their eye on Erika for Sean. She was intelligent and loved the Lord. You could see she walked the walk. Her parents were pastoring the St. Petersburg United Methodist Church. Hopewell Methodist had been invited many times to revivals or worked on projects with the St. Petersburg church over the years since Pastor Johnson had come to Hopewell. It seems the two ministers went to theological college together. Sean wasn't blind either. He knew his parents were pushing a relationship with Erika, but she had already caught his eye at youth camp way back in seventh grade. Little did Mom and Dad know what had been going on behind the scenes.

Ed Brady and Larry England were checking out the girls coming out the bathroom. Those two boys only came because their parents made them every year. If something didn't take hold in the next two years, they would be too old to be forced to youth camp. Lithia wished they would just get Jesus or grow up. Unfortunately, Ed and Larry had younger brothers who were at camp too. They thought their brothers were OGs, and all the 13 and 14-year-old boys followed them around like puppies. Around day two of camp, most of the younger boys saw Ed and Larry weren't that idolized by the girls and bailed the following.

Lithia ordered a blue raspberry snow cone and waved to Sean, who was making snow cones for Erika and her sister. Jennifer began to talk to one of the girls her own age, and Sean gave Erika a kiss on the cheek. Of course, Jennifer turned just in time for the smooch, and the torment began. "Erika and Sean sitting in the tree, K-I-S-S-I-N-G. First comes love." Pop! Jennifer felt her sister's hand close over her mouth and not very gently. Erika dragged Jennifer, kicking and screaming, back to Cabin Rebekah. Lithia knew at that point her parents would know by the end of the week; their prayers had been answered. All it would take is for Jennifer to call home. Sister Rodriguez would be phoning Lola.

Her watch said 9:43. She had a little bit more time before she was confined to the cabin. She knew the twins would wait until the last second to say goodbye to Carrie and Renee at the cabin door, and sprint back to Cabin Matthew on the boys' side of the camp. Rules for the boys were a little bit liberal; boys were expected to walk a girl to their cabin, so they got a ten-minute leniency on lockdown. God only knew where Leslie was. She had been lucky too many times last year coming in after ten o'clock. One time, it was after eleven, but Carrie and Renee told the camp counselor Leslie had dropped her cell phone at the concession stand and went to find it. Leslie just jumped in bed, completely dressed, when the counselor came back fifteen minutes later. Lithia would take her time walking to the cabin.

With her head down and trying not to step on anything which could make her trip, Lithia made her way back to the cabin. It was right there in the distance, the moon just over the top of the trees behind the cabin roof. What a gorgeous setting! God created such a beautiful world. Then Lithia heard a noise to her right; it was coming from a clump of trees. She wasn't sure if it was just a couple getting some last-minute kisses before curfew or an animal. She shook her head; it could be someone trying to play a prank. Lithia wouldn't put it past Ed or Larry to do something to scare her. And it was at that moment, he stepped out of the shadows.

Tall and lean, Lithia figured about six foot one. His hair was pulled back in behind his ears and he had on a baseball cap. At first, she wasn't sure who this guy was standing there staring at her. Then she saw the drumsticks in his hands. Her heart skipped a beat and she held her breath. Was he waiting for her, or had she just interrupted his thoughts? The silence was deafening.

"Hey, you!" The drummer walked a couple steps closer and her heart began to race. She couldn't move toward him or toward the cabin. Any minute and the other girls would soon be strolling up. "Aren't you Sean's little sister? Didn't realize you were so grown up. Was thinking his little sister wasn't so developed and mature as I see you are." He walked a little closer as Lithia still seemed paralyzed. "Yyyes, Sean is my brother." Lithia sounded like a five-year-old little girl. Gosh, could she show any form of confidence when talking to a cute guy? "Well, I thought we might get to know each other. I've heard so much about you from Leo and

Sean the past two weeks since I'm sharing a cabin with them. Your name is Lithia, isn't it?"

She still just stood there, blinking her eyes. *Okay, big deal he knows your name from Sean and Leo. The guy probably asked about their families and Sean said he had a little sister who would be here this week. However, hadn't she seen Leslie talking to him earlier during altar service? He was probably looking for her; I'm just what he found instead.* Second place again, friend zone or little annoying sister slot is all she was good for when it came to guys. "Leslie hasn't gotten back to the cabin yet. I saw you guys talking earlier on stage. Did you want to leave her a message?" Lithia was finally able to move, and took a step toward the cabin door. It only took a second, and Mr. Drummer had his hand on her arm. She felt chills up her back from his touch. "Don't you want to know my name? It's Harold. Harold Gibson. And no, I don't want to leave a message for Leslie. I spoke with her a few minutes ago. I was hoping I could introduce myself to you."

Harold had a way with words; he was charming, with eyes that could melt an iceberg and lips that anyone would want to kiss. *What are you thinking, Lithia?! He was talking to Leslie and you do not even ponder another girl, especially a friend's crush. And I was thinking about kissing his lips...they look so soft.* Harold squeezed Lithia's arm. "Are you okay? Would you like to sit down on the steps or let me help you into the cabin?" Lithia stammered a thank you, but really didn't answer the question at all. She let him lead her to the steps of the cabin and open the door. It was when the screen door slammed shut behind them and Harold closed let go of Lithia's elbow to close the solid door, Lithia came out of her daze.

"Which bed is yours? I'll help you to it where you can relax." He took her Bible and clutch from her arms and dropped it on the desk at the left of the door. The only light in the cabin was the stars and moon coming in through the windows. Lithia pointed to her bed to the far right, and as he guided her slowly to the twin bed, Harold told her she looked beautiful in the moonlight. He stated when he had seen her coming up to the cabin he didn't want to interrupt as she mediated at the stars. The celestial lights from the heavens illuminated over her like a halo.

Lithia's stomach had butterflies. No guy had ever told her she was beautiful. This wasn't some family member or one of the boys at school playing a joke; this was a Christian man named Harold Gibson. She was beautiful.

Lifting her chin up to see into Harold's eyes, she smiled. He leaned down and whispered in her ear. His warm breath was on her neck as he called her name, "Lithia. I am going to fall asleep dreaming of you tonight. I will see you tomorrow. Get some rest. "He placed his lips right below her ear and his razor stubble from his chin touched her shoulder. She shuddered as his pressed his mouth to her skin. Harold stood straight and tipped his cap, walking out the cabin door.

Lithia was still standing in the darkness when Carrie, Renee, and Leslie came running in just as the loudspeaker announced ten o'clock. "What are you doing standing in the dark, Lithia?" Carrie was the first to speak as she picked up Lithia's purse and Bible from off her desk and sat it on Lithia's.

However, it was Leslie who would keep the conversation flowing for the next two hours. "I can't believe Harold, he's the new drummer, was waiting for me at the cabin. I hope he made it back to his cabin in time. He is so hot! He let me feel his biceps. He said he works out to build his arm muscles for playing percussion. I bet he would have kissed me tonight if the intercom hadn't bellowed right when he got his arms around me. We were standing right under one of the speakers as it went off. Poor guy jumped like he had been bitten."

Renee tried to talk about Anthony and his new car he had gotten for his birthday in May. Carrie explained Allan didn't get a car, but a truck, and they had to drive Anthony's car to Wekiva because they needed space to bring their sister Ava and her best friend. Renee was hoping at some point during the week, she could get a chance to ride in Anthony's car. He was promising to come down to Busch Gardens before the summer was over and see if she could go with him on a real date. All the while the girls debated on which twin was the cutest or had the best shoulders, muscles, or smile, Leslie went on and on about Harold.

Harold lived in Miami Beach and knew how to surf. He had a convertible, but the top won't go down right now because he had been in a car accident and it's never worked since. He had a job at this music store in Dade County Mall, and sometimes he gave drum lessons for extra money. His dad was an advertising agent and his mom worked in real estate.

Harold hadn't been to youth camp for eight years, and his grandfather insisted he go one more time before he was too old. However, when he got here, and they found out who his grandpa was, they insisted he be one of the camp musicians instead of a camp helper this week. So he pocketed the money his grandpa gave him for camp and figured he would make the best out of it. By the way, the big televangelist on Trinity Channel 42, that's his grandpa.

Blah, blah, blah...

"Leslie had to take a stop for air at some point, didn't she?" Lithia thought. What did all this mean? Was Harold waiting for Leslie in the shadow as Lithia expected, or did he really tell the truth and he was waiting to meet her? If he was with Leslie, Lithia would have to stay clear of Harold the rest of the week. She would never want to mess up her friendship of a lifetime for some guy. But if he was serious about Leslie, then why did he say those things to Lithia? She wasn't naïve; guys lie. But this was youth camp, Christian camp, where everyone here should or was expected to be a Christian. It was after one in the morning before Lithia shut her mind down and slept. But dreams of a drummer talking in her ear, with lips so soft touching her neck, filled her sleep until the alarm awakened her for the next day.

Chapter 15

May 2, 2019

Craig woke on Thursday morning, not sure what he wanted to do for the day. He knew that Friday would be filled with last minute preparations for the charity ball for Saturday night and then other meetings that morning. He probably wouldn't have time to speak with Cinderella until to the ball or a short call to verify the car's pickup time. Then he didn't see much alone time with her during the charity event, with a speech he was giving, mingling with guests and sponsors, and he would be expected to dance with some of the ladies there. He was hoping his dance card would be full of Cinderella's name.

He knew he blew his chance last night of finding out all he could of Miss Murphy's connection to Daniel. Nevertheless, he did get somewhere in his quest of learning more about her. Her grandparents, her father, all dead, and though she spoke of a mother and a brother, Cinderella didn't want to see them. He wondered why.

I do not regret telling her about Jesus. "Satan, you will not make me feel guilty for speaking of salvation and causing her to cry." He raised his fist as if to fight an enemy. As quickly as he threatened the devil, Craig kneeled at the foot of his bed and prayed, "Lord, I asked you for a door to open so I could speak freely about you to someone in need. I have felt all week Miss Murphy needed you. I walked through the door you opened. But she didn't give me much time. Let the door open again. I only have four days left in Tampa, but your timing is always perfect. And maybe I won't see the fruit of my labor, but let me have planted the seed for Cinderella to come home to you and her family."

He got dressed for the office and sent Cinderella a message he was going to spend the morning with Daniel. He assumed she needed a few hours in the office as well. Would she meet him for an early lunch? He would stop in at her office around 11. Then he wanted her to accompany him to a couple of women's shelters in the area. He wanted to observe the places he was donating funds and see how wisely those funds were being used.

Lithia read the long text message from Mr. O'Shay and replied, "That will be fine." Come on, what else could she say? If she didn't finish out this week and get that bonus from Daniel, how was she going to move on with her life?

She hadn't slept well after Craig left her. He brought up all those old memories of home and Grandmother. Then he had to discuss God again. What was his problem? Didn't he see she wasn't into God? Back in the day, when she was a teen, Craig would be the kind of man she would have prayed to have as a husband. Handsome, charming, Christ-like (as far as she had seen), successful, just an all-around nice guy; not counting the perk of being financially well off.

Why couldn't I have met this man before I stopped being loved by my family, by everyone, by God?

Ring, ring, ring! It was Daniel. Why couldn't she have met Craig before Daniel, at least?

"Yes, Daniel, what are your needs this morning? I'm getting dressed as we speak."

"Oh, really? What are you wearing, Lithia? Black lace panties and bra? Why don't we video chat so I can see, hmmm, shall we?" Lithia hung up.

Ugh!!! His voice made her convulse with vomiting. Could he just make things any worse? Of course, what was she thinking, it's Daniel. *Good grief, Lithia! Control yourself and make it through just a few more days.*

Daniel called back and on video as he had warned. But Lithia was ready for him. She had quickly slipped her dress over her shoulders, put on her ruby heart earrings, and was brushing her hair into a French twist. She hit accept but placed the phone where the camera was pointed to her ceiling fan.

"If you're calling about my tardiness to work, I could get there faster if someone would stop calling me. Unless there is something I need to do before I come into the office, can't this wait? I've got makeup and shoes to put on, and I will be headed to you."

She latched the ruby bracelet that matched the earrings around her left wrist and slipped on her red heels. She had on a white A-line dress with ruby red three-quarter sleeves, attached was a white ruffle band at the end. The hem of the dress was the same with four inches of red and then a white ruffle. She looked like a peppermint stick, or that's what the little girl in the apartment across the hall told her the last time she wore it.

Putting on her makeup, Lithia realized Daniel had been talking to her. "Are you going to answer me, Lithia? Lithia? Are you even listening to me?"

"Daniel, I'm here. But I would like to get in some work at the office since Mr. O'Shay wants me at eleven, then I have no clue when I will be back at the office afterward." She sprayed some perfume on her wrists and behind her ears, snatched her phone from off the dresser, and walked into her living room to get her purse.

Daniel hadn't seen Lithia yet until she turned the phone on her. "Wow, that's much better. You know, you should dust your bedroom fan more often. Now let's look at you. Pull the phone out so I can see what you've got on. Not bad, cute number. Sophisticated, but sexy. Craig's going to love it."

Time to get serious with her. She has got to understand the livelihood this contract was for him and for her. "Now, have you spoken to him about the proposal? Craig is only going to be around for a few days. I think his last day here is Sunday."

"Yes, Daniel, his plane leaves early Monday morning. I have to take him."

"Good, so you need to use today and tomorrow to get him to sign the deal. I need him to sell me that piece of property in Miami and to have him buy one here. I already have a buyer for the property in Miami. He will sell it to me for pennies, and I'll resell it for millions. I'm taking him to see the property here shortly. Tell him all the good qualities of the building in Temple Terrace. Craig must buy it if you want your money, do you understand me?"

His voice had changed from the playful seductive voice, wanting to know what Lithia was wearing, to the greedy man he really was. He might not be the same guy as when she first dealt with him, but his main qualities were instilled. She also knew he wasn't the kind of man that you pushed. She had some advantage, but she also remembers the old times, times she felt his frustration more than she heard it. That was almost two years ago, he hadn't touched her since then.

"Okay, okay, Daniel, I heard you and I am on it. I will do my best. You just do what you promised me. I get the money, and I can walk away for good this time. Look, I'm leaving my apartment now. I'll see you at the office."

He had better follow through with his promises. Until this week, Daniel had been keeping the agreement almost eighteen months. Then he sold out and gave her to Craig for "whatever he wanted" this week. She had been given mercy; something she never expected from an old friend of Daniel's, but Craig had been a gentleman. So far. But there were still four days. She didn't trust men, Christian-talking men either. Those liars were even worse.

Chapter 16

July 2010

The first full day of camp would be busy. Up for breakfast, with everyone trying to get a shower and brush their teeth in the girls' bathrooms. It did help that all cabins were equipped with a sink and mirror. At least not everyone had to fight for a mirror and sink for makeup purposes. The other thing that made Cabin Kindness wanted by all the female campers: it was originally a counselor's cabin. It had a walk-in closet and full-length mirror. There was a screened-in porch looking out the back facing the lake. The cabin had a small refrigerator and a microwave. A bookcase was between the desks to the right of the door and another one by the two desks by the closet. Each girl had their own chest of drawers beside their bed. Their cabin was big enough to add at least one set of bunk beds, two desks, and chests. On the porch was a table and four chairs and a swing. Under the trees was a hammock. But those were things you didn't know about unless you walked around to the back or you went inside Cabin Kindness. Lithia and her friends had the golden ticket this year for accommodations.

Breakfast was a la carte. It would be the same each morning, scrambled eggs, toast, sausage, bacon, ham, pancakes, waffles, grits, oatmeal, four different kinds of cereal, pastries, bagels and cream cheese, and if you still couldn't find something to eat, guess you were waiting until lunch. Orange, apple, or cranberry juice, or milk, and coffee were available as beverages. If you were ever hungry during the day and the concession stand wasn't open, any counselor would let you in for watermelon, an apple, or banana, or some form of fruit.

Lithia scanned the mess hall and didn't see Harold. She waved to her brother, who was sitting beside Erika. Leo was staring at his cell phone as he read a text message, probably from Sunflower. Lithia was sure the plan was for her to be here by lunch. Sunflower and Violet would be in Cabin Rebekah with Erika and her little sister. Leslie ran over to Sean, giving him a big hug. Sean rolled his eyes and Lithia knew he asked her what she wanted. Whatever Sean replied to Leslie didn't make her happy; she walked by pouty and sat down. "I asked Sean where Harold was, and he said Harold wasn't coming to breakfast, but was going to sleep until Bible study. I think I should take him a coffee and a bagel. He might get hungry later and not be able to have anything. I would hate for his stomach to growl in the middle of Bible study. I know I would be so embarrassed." Leslie proceeded to pour a coffee and toast a bagel. She grabbed a package of sour cream. A red flag of warning went off in Lithia's head, but she didn't open her mouth as Leslie sashayed toward the boy's cabins.

When breakfast was over, campers would have thirty minutes of free time before Bible study. That early, some campers liked to take a short hike, others called home, those that didn't really get dressed for the day at breakfast, showered and put on more than pajama bottoms and a t-shirt. Bible study was split in groups. Each study group comprised of two cabins of boys and two of girls. It wasn't fate that placed Cabin Rebekah and Cabin Kindness together with Cabin Matthew and Cabin James. Cabin James was Sean, Leo, and Harold's cabin. Their final roommate was CJ. Their Bible group would be studying the fruit of the Spirit this week and would be meeting at the gazebo by the waterfall.

On Friday, every group would be in the chapel and had to give a five-minute presentation about their topic. They decided most of the group was musically-inclined and the presentation should have some type of music. Ed and Larry, who were the twin bunkies in Cabin Matthew, thought they should do a rap about the fruit. Leo felt they couldn't take a vote, with Sunflower and Violet on the way, and Harold hadn't showed up yet.

It was halfway through Bible study when Harold came dragging in, with a wrinkled shirt and his hair under a baseball hat again. Leslie slid over to let him sit by her, but he squeezed Lithia's shoulder as he walked behind her. Then he winked right at her after he sat down on the opposite side of the gazebo.

Bible study was over, and the girls ran to the cabin to change into bathing suits and get their towels, sunscreen and glasses. Girls had swimming, canoeing, and snorkeling in the morning while the guys got the baseball field, tennis, and basketball courts until noon. Lunch was at twelve, then they switched. There was archery, hiking, and crafts from three in the afternoon until four thirty. Some would hang out in the music room off the chapel to practice for service that night. Either you got a bath before supper, which was scheduled for six, or you took one before chapel at 7:30 pm. Each day would be structured the same with a mix-up of who went swimming first or when they did co-ed volleyball games on the sand at the lake. There would be the big counselors verse the camper's softball game on Friday after Bible study presentations. The best part, even though it was scheduled for you, there was still some time to relax or hang with other people besides your Bible study group or roommates. You did get some free time to write letters home or nap. Lithia liked lying in the hammock under the trees. It was quiet, and no one bothered you. She could think, read, listen to iTunes, pray, or get away from everyone.

Lunch came, and somehow Lithia found herself sitting between Harold and CJ. Of course, Leslie was on Harold's right-hand side. But Lithia couldn't help thinking Harold didn't need to be so close. His arm or thigh kept rubbing against hers; was it intentional? She had no idea. CJ almost fell off the bench. Lithia realized she had been moving closer to him self-consciously each time Harold touched her. Leslie sighed, "Really, Lithia, you don't have to crowd the boy." Couldn't Leslie see it wasn't that way at all? It was she that was laying all over Harold, which pushed him into Lithia. In turn, Lithia kept scooting closer to CJ. Blood rushed to Lithia's face as she apologized to CJ as he stood up so she could slide out. She tried to gather her food tray, but she was so nervous now. Her fork dropped, and her empty milk carton. When she reached down to pick up her milk carton, Harold reached as if to help, but instead, whispered how desirable she was whenever she was frustrated. Pulling away, she bumped heads with CJ, who was leaning under the table to collect her fork and napkin she lost, too. They made eye contact. He seemed to sense her tension, taking the milk carton out of her hand, "I'll take this up for you." Lithia thought he had the kindest eyes. She nodded thanks as she briskly walked out of the mess tent.

What was it with Harold? He jolted her to the bone. She couldn't think when he was around, and her body got all tingly in places she didn't want to name. Lithia glanced back to see what was happening behind her. Everyone seemed to not even care she left; though, CJ had cleaned up her spill and was watching her leave. It almost looked like he smiled at her. *Oh, no! Did CJ hear what Harold had said to her? Is that why he was looking at her and smiling? What did CJ think of her actions or what did he make of Harold's confession? And why did it suddenly matter what this guy thought anyway? She had to get her head straight before Leslie got suspicious that something was going on between Harold and her.* Lithia washed her face with cold water as soon as she returned to the cabin. She would sit here and read a little before she went to play softball at one. Maybe reading the Psalms would be a distraction with a calming effect before she had to face Harold again at dinner.

Her Bible was set on the desk where Carrie had placed it the night before. Lithia flipped to Psalm 34:5 and read the verse aloud, "Those who look to him are radiant, and their faces shall never be ashamed." *That sure wasn't talking about Harold. I'm so embarrassed.* Turning a few pages, she came to, "He will cover you with his feathers. He will shelter you with his wings. His faithful promises are your armor and protection, Psalm 91:4." She kept searching the Scriptures. At one point, she put a piece of paper at the beginning of the Book of Psalms and one at the end; she would let the pages fall as they may, and closing her eyes, she would wiggle her index finger and point. Whatever verse her finger fell on, she believed God was trying to get a lesson across to her. "Delight yourself in the Lord, and he will give you the desires of your heart." They had a joke about that verse here at youth camp. *"I'm just delighting in what God has made, and he is hmmm, so delightful. That boy is one thing I desire, now to sit back and delight, delight, delight in God's creation until God gives me my desire."* Lithia could think back to when she told her grandparents this. Granddaddy had told her to be careful what she wished for because God can give it to you, even when He knows it isn't what you need. There are consequences to our choices, right or wrong. She didn't want to think of that; God answers prayers, and right now, she wanted Harold. Ok, she would read one more verse, go to the restroom, and head to the ball field. "I keep my eyes always on the Lord. With him at my right hand, I will not be shaken." *Well, she knew who was doing the shaking lately, and no one had to worry, it wasn't Satan. Harold was making her tremble all over; and CJ, what was that? He had a different effect on her. It had to be those eyes. They stared into your soul.*

The ball field was already beginning to see activity, and teams were being picked for the first game. Lithia would be third baseman. She would rather be outfield; most girls never could hit that far. She would be able to think more while she was bored. They lost after she dropped the ball on a foul and couldn't recover it fast enough, causing the girl on third to make it home. Leslie was in the dugout texting when Lithia flung her glove down on the bench. "Texting your mom?" "No, silly. I'm replying to Harold's text while we were on the field. He said what was the fun of swimming if he couldn't see me in my pink bikini? I let him know I could get you to take a photo of me and send it to him. Will you?

You know, take my picture later? He wants to use it as his screen saver on his cell. Isn't that sweet?" *Leslie can be so annoying. And what is this? Harold makes these comments to me, but sending these texts to Leslie? I do not get him. If I get the chance tonight, I'm going to just ask him what's the deal.* Field time was over, and a quick clean-up and the campers grabbed supper. Lithia went to take a shower. She might get to speak to Harold before chapel. Leslie would take longer to get ready than she would.

As expected, Lithia was buckling her sandals when Leslie walked in from the showers. Carrie and Renee were putting on the last of their makeup and fixing their hair. The twins were going to walk them to chapel and would be at the cabin in ten minutes. Lithia made an excuse to leave early, even though Leslie begged her to wait. She didn't think Harold would be able to escort her to the chapel because he had received a text that musicians had to arrive a few minutes early. "Allan got the same message, but he is walking with me," Carrie chimed in. Renee nodded in agreement. Leslie complained, "Harold is more important for the music program than an old trumpet player. He has more talent in his little pinky; they need him to help prepare the unskilled 'talent' on stage." With that, Lithia skipped out the door as the other girls began to argue. She passed Anthony and Allan on the way to meet the girls and waved as she went on by.

There were only a few campers in the audience when she crossed the chapel door. Sean was in the sound booth; Sunflower had made it and was practicing a song on the piano while Leo sat on the piano bench beside her. Harold was adjusting the cymbals on the drum set. His back was to her as she walked up on stage. Stepping over to the side, Lithia called his name. "Harold, could I talk to you for a minute? Over here." She moved to the side of the stage out of her brother's watchful eye. Lithia knew he couldn't see her but would be able to tell Harold was talking to someone on the sidelines. He put his drumsticks down on the snare and strolled over to her with a big grin. Harold crossed his arms and leaned on the post, looking down at her. "So, what you wanna talk about with me, cutie?" He reached out and tucked a strand of hair behind her ear. Now that she had him alone and his attention, Lithia couldn't think again. What was she going to ask him anyway? "Oh, maybe I shouldn't bother you if you are going to be practicing. I can talk to you later." He took her arm and stepped closer, "This is a perfect time."

There goes her heart again. She felt like she would lose her dinner right here. *God, give me the nerve.* "I wanted to know if you liked me or Leslie?" *There, she had said it. Now he could give her a straight answer and she could get through the rest of the week like she always did-no boys.* She tried to look him in the eye but only got to his lips when he said, "Both." Taken back, Lithia repeated Harold, "Both?" "Yes, I can like two girls at the same time, can't I? She's fun, but you are so mature and mysterious. Honey, you challenge me. I want to get to know you; we will talk later tonight after service at the hammock." He squeezed her hand and went back to the drums. Lithia stood in the wings with her mouth wide open.

"Are you wanting to sing tonight?"

She jumped as someone laid their hand on her shoulder. "Oh, I didn't mean to scare you. I figured you were up here to sing for praise and worship tonight. We are trying to have a variety of campers participate, unless you can't carry a tune in a bucket, or you are afraid of a crowd."

"Oh, hi, CJ. I wasn't really, but I do sing in my local church praise team a couple of times a month. I don't have to if there is someone else that you would prefer. Got to be more talented singers then me here at camp. Thanks for asking me." Lithia turned to walk off stage; CJ took her hand.

"Come on then, let's practice and see what you can do before it's too late. He led her to the piano, sat on the bench, and patted the bench for her to sit beside him. He played the scales several times, warming up, then played "Alleluia." CJ had her sing lead, and he came in with harmony. He changed keys and began to play "Your Great Name." When he said the words, "Every fear has no place," he turned to Lithia and nodded for her to join him. Here she added the harmony.

Leo interrupted their practice, "Wow, you two sound amazing together. You singing with us, kiddo? Because I'm thinking that's a duet for service. Why don't you ever sing like that back home for church? Stop, I know the answer-Leslie. That girl begs for all the solos unless Pastor Johnson has Sunflower or her sisters do it." He shook his head. Then he handed her a microphone. "Sean, give your sister a mike check before we begin service. Go on, sing something else. Turn on CJ's piano mike too."

CJ smiled at Lithia, "Let's go with something a little old school and fast. Can you keep up?" Fingers were flying across the ivories just like in the song, "I'll Fly Away." People that were coming into the chapel started singing along and clapping their hands with them. Harold had jumped on the drums, and the rest of the band was playing right along. Erika was playing her tambourine, and her sister pulled out a cabasa. Church had started fifteen minutes early.

Church service was the best. Lithia heard that two boys and a girl had given their hearts to the Lord during altar call and one of the college-age counselors testified they had been called to preach. She felt so elated after she gathered her purse and Bible. Maybe she would be asked again to sing before the week was over. She did have quite a few campers and counselors comment on how well she sounded singing with CJ.

The night was so joyous, and Lithia's heart was so fresh, so clean. She had forgotten about everything, she just wanted to go to her favorite spot. Dropping off her purse and Bible, she went out the back door and fell into the hammock, right on top of someone that couldn't be seen in the dark shadows.

Arms came around Lithia, although she tried to get up, she was held tight.

Whoever it was, it was male. She could smell the cologne or after-shave or whatever. He had to be lying in the hammock on his back, then she laid right down on top of him. Her back was against his chest. One of his arms was around her waist, the other across her breasts. Then his left leg wrapped over hers and kept her from moving.

His face was on her neck as he moved her hair away with his chin. He moaned as his tongue licked behind her ear and took small bites on her shoulders. Lithia wiggled; she even bent her right knee hoping she could use momentum to push her right side to flip them off the hammock. But that didn't work; it seemed to make him moan louder.

It was at that moment she knew who was beneath her. This wasn't some trick one of the boys was playing, no, this guy wanted a lot more than she was willing to give. His right leg caught her right leg and penned her down completely, but it was what he said that gave him away.

"I knew you would meet me tonight. Were you trying to make me jealous singing with Mr. CJ O'Goody? Let me teach you how to harmonize with my instrument." He moved his arm down from her waist and pulled up her skirt as he pulled her legs apart with his own.

Lithia could feel the cool breeze from the trees blowing on her bare skin. Harold was telling her something, but it was all a daze. She could only concentrate on his hands, mainly the one trying to push down her panties. His other hand was groping her breasts and had managed to rip the buttons off her top. No matter what she did, her vocal cords didn't work.

Oh, Jesus, please, don't let him. Help me. Help me speak.

"Don't think anyone is coming. All your roommates are at the afterglow bonfire with their guys and your big brother. Tonight, I am going to release all your inhibitions to the wind. You will know what the difference of being a woman and a little girl. Even your body knows what it needs, see how it moves to me. I can feel the heat from you underneath my hands and how rapid the beat of your heart races in passion."

Harold gave a thrust of his hips upward and it seemed to jolt Lithia's voice. She inhaled deeply and let it out, "JESUS!"

The sound echoed in the trees and down the pathway, but did anyone hear her? Tears began to run down her cheeks. Harold let go of the granny panties he had been struggling to pull down or tear off, which ever was easiest, and he smacked his palm over her mouth. It stung her face, but it renewed her vigor. She began to make her body sway back and forth, and right when she felt ready, her teeth went into Harold's finger. Using the force of the swinging momentum, Lithia pushed off with her right foot, leaning all her weight to the left. The hammock flipped over.

Lithia was able to pull her legs together as the hammock dumped them, Harold on top of her this time. He might have thought he still had the upper hand until the knee to his groin changed his mind. He rolled away from her, but to add to the bedlam he had caused, he hit a barrel half-full of rainwater. Now he was soaking wet and muddy. How was he going to get back to the cabin like this without an explanation?

"You'll pay for this, you wait." And he slowly walked the back way to his cabin as he held his manhood in his hands.

All Lithia could do was crawl to the back steps. Sitting huddled on them, she groaned, "Jesus, Jesus, Jesus" over and over.

Until a light came around the corner of the cabin, a flashlight beam glowed around her, but extinguished as the owner cradled her in his arms. He asked for no explanation, but she relaxed in the security he gave while rocking her to his soft baritone voice singing, *"Jesus Loves Me."*

CJ didn't know what had happened to Lithia, but seeing her torn blouse and her ripped skirt, he was pretty sure. He had wanted to be alone with the Lord, so he decided to walk away from the bonfire. The sound he heard wasn't much, but he thought maybe an animal had been caught by its prey from the moans and groans. What made him investigate was the "Jesus" from a woman in a voice of desperation. He thought it was coming in the same direction as the moans, but he wasn't going to turn on his flashlight until necessary. It was when he heard the thud, CJ had picked up his pace toward the noise.

Right before he turned on his pocket flashlight, he spotted a man's figure limping away from behind Cabin

Kindness. Waiting until the man was farther away, he turned on his light and rounded the cabin. He saw the hammock still swinging and the barrel on its side. Then he heard the weeping coming from the steps.

His singing partner, the girl with the angelic voice, Lithia, looked so fragile as she tried to hold her blouse over her breasts. Her long hair was matted with leaves and covering her face. It got worse as he walked closer. Her skirt had been torn up the middle and with one hand she was squeezing her panties to keep them on. He deciphered the animal responsible was the man in the shadows. The jerk had ripped her shirt and skirt, and from what he could tell, a piece of her underwear.

He turned off the flashlight as he sat down behind her, his arms enveloping her trembling body. He didn't know what to do, but he knew she would feel ashamed if he called out for anyone to come. Only Jesus could calm her now. As he prayed, the words came as a lullaby for her.

"Jesus loves me, this I know..."
Lord, I came too late. I didn't save her either."

Chapter 17

March 2003

Momma won't tell the investigator anything other than we had a slip in the kitchen. She made it out like it was some freak accident; we got stabbed and Jim got burnt by the skillet. I don't get it. Why is she protecting him? I don't want to be mad at Momma, but this is wrong. What if he does this again? Will we survive?

Jim had come back to the apartment within the week after the incident, as it was called. But Craig and Saoirse had a much longer vacation. Craig called it that because he had cable television and no Jim. The first few days after it happened were blurry, but when he began to stay up longer, he wanted to see his momma.

"Honey, you can't go down to ICU where your momma's at. Children gotta stay up here. When she gets in a regular room, they can bring her to you." Nurse Mabel was a big-boned woman. She was overly padded in all places, like a comfy couch, you could get lost in the pillows. All the kids liked her, and parents did too. She made you feel like you were the one patient she had. If she could, she read you stories, played games, and there were a few times she'd sit on Craig's bed and tell him about this man called Jesus.

Jim didn't visit Craig once. *No skin off my back, no pun intended. Haha.* But after ten days, Craig wanted his momma. Saoirse wasn't in ICU, but until she could push herself in the wheelchair to him or someone would bring her to pediatrics, even Nurse Mabel couldn't make it happen.

It seemed the knife had penetrated a kidney as it cut through the large and small intestines. Her kidney had to be removed and parts of both the intestines. His momma was anemic. Because of her poor diet, she didn't have the immunities to fight off infection. She would have to stay in the hospital at least three or more weeks longer than Craig. He could go home...to Jim. *Momma must not have been too quiet about that idea.*

Señora Corona, who had been visiting them both almost three times a week, was told the plan by Nurse Mabel. Officers Pratt and King came back for a visit with Craig. Between the four of them, they figured out a way Craig could stay with Señora Corona until his momma was to be released. But Nurse Mabel would be checking in every other day. The officers and Señora Corona went together to give the news to Mrs. O'Shay after Jim's daily visit.

The morning of Craig's hospital release, Officer King and Señora Corona went to Jim's apartment to pick up Craig's clothes and school supplies. Jim wasn't happy his privacy was being invaded, but he really didn't have time for the kid, he liked his longer reprieve from the smart aleck.

The last week Craig had been in the hospital, his history teacher had been bringing him work to stay caught up. He would be a week or so behind, but he was a smart boy, capable of the impossible. Even though he was going to leave the hospital, he still had a week before they were let-ting him go to school. Señora Corona was making sure all his work would be completed on her watch. He had to be ready to take the end-of-the-year tests in a couple of weeks.

Craig was wheeled to his mom's hospital room before taken to the taxi downstairs. He hadn't seen her in almost four weeks. She looked so tiny in the bed, and she still had an IV in her arm. Nurse Mabel had told him she had to have two surgeries that first week, one for the kidney and one for her intestines. That didn't even count closing the long gash in her belly. Her eyes didn't have the sparkle they once had before Jim. She was very pale, even her freckles.

They told him he had to be careful when he hugged her, he had to be easy with her wounds. But he just wanted to stay lying next to her. He knew boys that were almost thir-teen weren't supposed to think that way, but she's the only momma he had.

He whispered in her ear before he left, "Nobody is ever going to hurt you again as long as I live. Let's not go back to the apartment with Jim when you come home. We can live somewhere else. You can get a job during the day while I'm at school. Please, Momma, I don't want you to do what you're doing. It's not good."

Keep my baby safe, God. I don't have any other way to survive now. I gave my word, Jim owns me. Oh, God, just two more years. I promise I'll come back to you. I don't know what he will do to my boy if I refuse again. Saoirse watched her son leave her room; she was afraid of how soon he might walk out of her life forever.

Staying at Señora Corona's was the best. Craig always had three big meals, and he could get a snack every night before bed if he completed schoolwork before supper. She let him call his momma right before bedtime each night for ten minutes.

One night, when Señora Corona was fixing supper, Craig asked if Momma could come live there too when she got out of the hospital. He and Momma didn't take up lots of room; why they could sleep in the spare bedroom, they only needed to bring their clothes. His eyes pleaded with her heart. She only wished she could, but what would her own family say, or what if Jim decided to retaliate on her? No, she would be Craig's safe spot if he ever needed it. Everyone should have one. *Dios, don't let mi chiquito get hurt again. Find a way for them to be out of this gringo's power.*

Then his momma came home just in time for his thirteenth birthday.

Chapter 18

May 2, 2019

At precisely 11 AM, Craig O'Shay knocked on Miss Murphy's office door bearing a bouquet of yellow long-stemmed roses. He looked...dapper, if people still used the word, in his black suit, white shirt, and red tie. It almost looked as if Lithia and Craig had planned their attire together. When she stood up from her desk as he entered, he thought he had never seen someone as lovely as this woman.

For a time, Craig just stood there, a statue inside her office. Lithia wasn't even sure what to say either. The knock on her door took them out of the trance.

"Miss Murphy, will you be leaving for the day now? I wanted to know if I should forward your calls to my desk." Martha Redding was a recently divorced mother of one, that had been hired a couple of months ago. She seemed to thrive working as a secretary in the real estate office, but Lithia was worried Daniel might corrupt Martha when she left the company in a few weeks. He had already been sizing her up for Lithia's job. She hoped the young mom didn't need the money bad enough to do the things Daniel might require of his future assistant.

"Oh, thank you, Martha, that would be fine. Mr. O'Shay, have you met Mrs. Redding, our newest and brightest employee? She works directly under two personal assistants other than me. Martha does more than her share when one of us is busy on other assignments; for example, this week while I work with you, she has been doing over half of my job. She is an asset to the company."

"My, I don't know what to say with your recommendation, Miss Murphy. I am so happy to hear I am appreciated. I'll leave you to your client. Nice to meet you, Mr. O'Shay, have a blessed day." She closed the door on her way out, but the smile on her face was contagious to everyone she passed the rest of the day.

"She seems delightful." Craig handed Lithia the bouquet he had been holding. She took them, bringing them to her face. Her eyes closed as she inhaled the sweet perfume of the flowers. It took her back to her grandmother's, and the rose garden, and a boy from summer camp.

Lithia collected her purse, slipped her cell phone inside, and readjusted the flowers in her arms. Craig offered her his elbow as they walked through the corridor to the elevator. When they came to the lobby, she could see the driver and company car parked right in front of the building waiting for them. She wondered what this day would hold, and would she be able to do what Daniel required? *I have to, there is no other choice.*

"If you don't mind, Cinderella, I would like to get something light. How would a club sandwich or a grilled chicken salad be for you? If you want more, I can adjust. It's just we are going to a couple of safe houses for abused women; I just don't have an appetite right now. I don't know what we could experience."

"I don't get it. Experience? Am I going to be abused while I'm there?" She was trying to make a witty comment, but Craig was serious, and she felt foolish.

His reply came in a more formal tone, "No one is going to hurt you, but what you might see today, well, it could affect you to your core. I have gotten physically nauseated from the evidence of abuse on clients and their children. You need something in your stomach, but not a lot, just in case. Then you want to wait three or so hours afterwards to eat for the same reason."

He hoped he didn't sound rude, but she probably never had a man hit her or cut her like many of the women they would meet today. She had to get prepared to look the evil effects of domestic violence in the face. The driver pulled into a small Greek restaurant and let them out. He told them he would return in an hour.

The menu of Athens' Cuisine had a list of more bottles of wine than types of food, but finally, they were able to order a large Greek salad with pork and a loaf of bread to share. The waitress offered a bottle of wine, but Craig didn't drink, and Lithia had quit, so they opted for lemon water.

"Before we get to the shelters, I want to pray for the opportunity to show these women and their children Christ's love. The need to know they are not alone in the situation; we are there to help." Craig took Lithia's hands and prayed right there in the middle of the restaurant for their food and for women they would be visiting soon.

"My goal is that every woman that comes to our centers never feels the need to return to the abuser. Those that do, increase the risk of more physical altercations, loss of life, and violence to the children. Permanent displacement of children can occur, even complete separation of parent and child."

Lithia could see this tormented him to the bone. He didn't want any of these women to return to their husbands or the father of their children. "Don't you think the children should have a relationship with their fathers? If the abuse is towards the mothers, the kid would be fine."

"It doesn't work that way. Many of the kids may never get touched inappropriately by the adult male in the home, but that doesn't mean they are not broken by the assault. Kids see the violence and will act on it, good or bad. Some show it through actions at school or towards siblings in the home. You might see boys become disrespectful to women, from their mom to grandma to female teachers. It may not manifest itself until much later when the children become adults and treat their own spouses or children the same way."

"Craig, do you have counseling available for the clients when they leave? Those feelings won't go away in a short time. If the abuse was for years, it may be decades to combat the trust issues or nightmares from the PTSD they could contrive."

Red flag, hello, what did she just reveal to me. That sounded a little bit too casual for her to not know something about the PTSD possibilities. Many people only associated that with military personnel. I could find out more about her today than I expected.

"Well, Cinderella, most of my centers do have an excellent list of resources for the women and children to reach out to after they leave the center. We have, from churches, government-funded programs, and even private counselors, who do pro bono work on occasion. We don't look for a quick fix and a boot out the door. That makes it easy to go right back to the man or to find one just like him."

Lithia almost choked on her piece of bread. She knew the feeling; out of the pot and into the fire; she had been there and was now only caught up in the smoke.

"Another thing I want to be sure is the women have career training. You will see all types of women. Don't think just because they have come to the center, they are poor or uneducated. I will admit, the majority normally will be, but there are cases of economically successful men and women that struggle with this violence in their homes."

"What kind of training are you looking to give? College courses? What if some don't even have a high school diploma?" Lithia was intrigued by the passion in Craig's voice as he spoke about these plights of women he didn't even know.

"Here, is the thing, Cinderella. You have no idea how many dozens of these women will have to fall into the trap of selling themselves to survive. Women with high moral character from wealthy homes, even. But without the man or a family who's told her 'I told you so' or one that 'doesn't believe he is capable,' what will become of their finances? If they can find a job, if they didn't have one, can be rough. What about a place to live or food? Many times, they come to us with just the clothes on their back. This is when they become a victim again to the circumstances. First, maybe it's a waitressing job at night, then bartending, dancing, to stripping, to even more just to have enough to feed and clothe the kids."

Why did I keep talking to her? She is probably wondering why I am so passionate on this subject. Her eyes are moist, and her cheeks are tear-stained. I think she figured out why my foundation is named after my mother.

Chapter 19

April 27, 2003

I had been back to school for over two weeks when Momma told me she was finally coming home. Only three more days until I turned into a teenager. I couldn't wait. My best birthday present was having Momma back. The negative part, we would be back in the apartment upstairs with Jim. Momma told me she didn't have any money to get us our own place. I had to know she wouldn't, she hadn't worked since before the accident.

Jim had only been out of work a couple of weeks. Momma had told Craig they could come back home. But Craig didn't see a home in that place if Jim was there. Yet, even though in the few weeks Craig had been in the apartment building staying with Señora Corona, Jim never visited him. They didn't go to the hospital to visit his mom unless they knew Jim wouldn't be around.

There was only two times Craig had seen Jim since the accident. The first time was the day Señora had sent him to go get her mail from the mailboxes. Jim almost ran into him as he turned away from locking his back. Craig dropped his key just in time to miss the swing of Jim's fist when he saw who he had bumped him. Jim would have turned and kicked him if the maintenance man hadn't walked through the door and asked Craig how soon before his mom would be released from the hospital.

The other time was a couple of days ago, when Craig had gotten off the school bus and was walking with a couple of friends that lived upstairs. Jim was coming out of the elevator as they stepped through the door of the building. "Well, there's the soon-to-be birthday boy. What you want for the old birthday? A cake maybe, or balloons and candles? I know my favorite part is going to be the birthday spanking."

The grin he gave Craig was pure evil. The laugh...from the pits of hell.

Saying goodbye to his friends that lived on the fourth floor, he ran on in Señora Corona's apartment.

"I'm home! Can I get a snack? Yes, I made a B on my math test and I only have one homework assignment for tonight. When do we go get my momma?" During his rambling, he had dropped his book bag in the bedroom, kicked off his shoes, and had plopped down in a chair at the kitchen table, waiting for the routine after-school snack.

"Respira, chiquito, you got to breathe between sentences. Here's a Coke and churros; use the napkin." Señora sat down in the chair opposite of Craig and watched him swallow a whole churro in one gulp. "I think you have gained ten pounds in the weeks since you have lived with me. I think I need to start calling you my gordito." She loved this boy as if he was her own grandchild. It hurt he couldn't stay with her, but she couldn't keep him from his own mother.

Half a churro sticking out of his mouth, Craig begin the inquisition. "How soon can we pick up my mother? We need to make sure she gets some of these churros tonight for dessert, and some pollo y arroz, and a salad. I know you bought chicken at the grocery store Saturday. I'll even help with the cooking and keep Momma comfortable."

If Señora Corona can see how much he wanted to stay with her and how much help he could be with cooking and cleaning, maybe she would let his momma live here too. *She knows the truth about what happened; I know she doesn't want us with Jim.*

"Craig, I believe your momma is already upstairs. She called me from the hospital before lunch and said she was just waiting on release papers and a ride home. I asked if she wanted me to send a taxi to bring her home, but she said her boyfriend was picking her up soon." When she said the last bit, her voice softened to almost a whisper. She looked at her hands instead of Craig. His failure to speak or to eat another churro confirmed he had heard enough to spoil the day.

"I want to thank you for letting me stay with you. I appreciate all you have done for me." He pushed his chair under the table, threw his napkin away, stuck his Coke can in the recycle bag, then walked to the room to get his things. His heart had sunken as low as it could go.

Within a few minutes, he had removed his belongings from the closet and dresser drawers. He took a few plastic shopping bags from the kitchen to "pack" his items. Stepping into the bathroom, he collected his toothbrush and stuck it in his back pocket. With a double check in the room, he put on his backpack and picked up his plastic bags of clothes.

Señora Corona was standing by the sofa when he headed toward the front door; her arms opened wide to embrace him. Craig dropped everything going into her arms.

The tears fell from them both as they knew what could lie waiting for him and his mother in the future. Neither wanted to release their hold.

"Dios, I ask you to protect mi chiquito. Let him know he can call to you when he needs a friend, when he is afraid, when he is alone. Have angels surround him and keep guard over him each night and day. Make him see having bitterness toward those that try to harm him will cause him to hurt even more. May he grow up strong, willing to show others a Christ-like attitude; give him a generous heart to protect those who cannot protect themselves. Let him show love. Most of all, give him a desire to do your will and follow your Word. Amen."

A final squeeze and she turned him to the door. "Go to your momma, hijo. She needs you more than you'll ever know." With a smile, he walked out the door.

Procrastination was just going to make it worse. He had to go into the apartment. The television was on, and he could hear Jim laughing about something. Craig opened the door like everything was normal and headed to his bedroom to put his things away. Jim was in the recliner, watching some old sitcom, he didn't see his momma.

Momma must be lying down in her bedroom. I'm going to put these things away and go visit with her before starting my homework. Someone is washing dishes in the kitchen. But I can't see who it is from this angle. Guess I will find out soon enough.

The bedroom door was slightly ajar, so he bumped it with his knee to enlarge the gap. Craig never expected to see what awaited him in his room. On his bed was a girl, not much older than he was, but only wearing a see-through nightgown. The room smelled of cigarette smoke, and beer bottles were on the dresser. In the corner of the room was a tripod and camera aimed toward the bed.

The girl jumped and pulled her legs up to her chest when she saw Craig step in the room. She was ashen and thin. It was hard to cover her body, even though she did try. Craig thought she should get up and put on clothes or pull the blanket around her. Then he saw why not, the handcuffs on her wrist were attached to a chain on the headboard. She was a prisoner in his bed.

His packages dropped to the floor and he went to the bed to release her. Behind him, a chuckle, an evil laugh, caused Craig to turn to the door. There stood Jim, blocking the entrance.

"How do you like your birthday present? Figured you'd think you're a man now, so you need to learn how to be one. As soon as you're ready, I'll just turn on the camera so we can get a good birthday video to remember the day."

Jim slapped Craig on the back hard enough Craig lost his balance and fell forward on the bed, headfirst into the girl's legs. The girl began to kick and scream, while Craig was trying to push himself off her. He tried to protect his face from her kicks, but then he was sprawled back on her again. Jim had lifted him off his feet and tossed him on her.

Cloth tore so that Craig felt skin touch his arm. He knew it must be the girl's thigh. Groping to get his balance, he had caught her gown on his belt buckle, which was making the material rip. He tried to disconnect the gown, but the girl wasn't helping, and neither was Jim. He didn't want to look at the girl naked, but if he didn't look down at his belt, how could he get rid of the problem? His fastest way to solve it was to take off his belt.

Craig had noticed bruises on her legs and arms when he was trying to release the handcuffs. He wondered who gave them to her. Jim? She had a black eye, and her lips were chapped. How long had she been tied to his bed?

Smash! Jim turned his head to find Saoirse at the bedroom opening. She had been holding a coffee cup until her eyes beheld the situation.

"What is going on in here? Who is that girl? Oh, my Craig, what are you doing? Get off her now! Jim, why are you laughing?" *Dear God, there's a teenage girl almost naked in my son's bedroom. And he is taking off his pants over her? Wait a minute What is Jim doing in here too?*

Momma began walking in the room, but she was still weak from weeks in the hospital. She grabbed the belt out of Craig's hand to try and stop whatever her son was going to do to the girl. Jim had moved to the foot of the bed, and with a tilt of her head she could see he was holding a video camera. Somebody had some explaining to do.

Craig stepped back from the bed, now that he was untangled from the flimsy gown. He picked up the comforter, which had been thrown on the floor and tossed it over the girl. His momma finally saw the girl's hands and climbed on the bed to fight getting the chains from around the scared teen.

It's when Jim stopped laughing, things escalated more.

"Go get in the kitchen and make my dinner, I have this handled. Take that blanket off her, the camera's missing the good stuff."

"I am not! She's cold and doesn't have anything on. That's disgusting what you're doing!" Craig went back to working on the handcuffs and chain to loosen her. At least she had stopped screaming when she knew Craig, nor his mom, were trying to hurt her.

Whack! Down came the belt across Craig's back, with another strike immediately after hitting both Craig and the girl. Again, Craig found himself trying to regain his balance and not be on top of the teen.

Crash! Ugh! Wallop! Craig heard the lamp fly over him, hitting the wall on the opposite side. Jim wailed when the school science book knocked him in the head followed by the math text.

Jim punched Craig in the side of the face as he passed him in search of the pitcher of the books. The screams as his mother was whipped over and over with the belt buckle brought Craig bounding into the living area. With all his strength, Craig lifted the end table over his head. He let go at the precise time Officer King and Pratt came through the door, and poor Señora Corona trailing behind.

Everything was one blur for Craig. He wasn't sure exactly what came after the triumph entrance of the police, but it wasn't the homecoming he expected, nor the birthday three days later.

Señora Corona sat on the sofa, looking down at the crumbled woman at her feet. Bleeding from the rips the belt buckle had carved into her back, she moans in the fetal position. Spanish prayers are whispered as the EMT haul Jim onto the gurney and roll him out into the corridor. The prayers she speaks are for the boy sitting in handcuffs by the wall, whelps on his shoulders and back turning to colors of purple and black. DCF and another medical responder are in the back bedroom with the young girl that seems to have been imprisoned for several days. Sounds of more sirens coming, coming for Saoirse, for the teen, for her chiq-uito. *Why, God, didn't you protect him?*

Life changed for Craig more than it ever had in a matter of one week. Handcuffed and in juvenile detention on his birthday, to seeing his mother in the hospital again, to DCF placing him into a foster home.

Because the officers had seen Craig drop the end table directly over Jim's head intentionally, he was arrested for assault and battery. However, after viewing the video that Jim so expertly positioned, almost all the event was recorded. Investigators found other videos of the teenage girl with random males and Jim, which collaborated the teen's story of being kidnapped at the bus stop over two weeks ago. The girl's parents were able to reunite with their daughter that night at the hospital. Jim was going away for a long, long time.

Saoirse wasn't even home for a day to return from the beating Jim had given her. The buckle's hook had caught on her skin and ripped open the former wounds and made new ones. She would always have scars from her time with Jim, inside and out. When Jim had fallen on her from the end table bashing, two ribs had broken and her right arm from the weight. Her home would be a hospital again.

Craig was released from DCF care, and charges were dropped. It was deemed as self-defense, protecting his mom, the girl, and himself. However, DCF did not see Señora Corona as a good fit to send Craig back to live. It would be in the same building as both attacks had occurred, which might bring PTSD to the boy. She wasn't his real grand-mother either, and she was on a fixed income. Mrs. O'Shay didn't have any family to release Craig to until she became able to support him, so there was no other option but foster care. They did allow Señora Corona to keep Craig for the first few days after he was released from the JV center, but only until they found a suitable placement.

Officer Pratt retrieved the apartment keys from the landlord, and Craig was able to collect everything that was his to bring. Nurse Mabel came with her sister, LaShell, and cleaned the apartment before Craig had to venture into the crime scene again. It didn't even look battered. His momma's things were boxed up and stored in a closet at Señora Corona's. Jim's personal items, well, a thrift store got a donation.

When Officer Pratt and Officer King came to take Craig to his new home, he asked how long it would be until he was with his momma.

"Boy, I don't know. Look, she doesn't have a job, and really, nowhere to live. The apartment was in Jim's name. It's going to be a good month before she even leaves the hospital again. She's only got one kidney, and he just gave that one a beating this time. When she's physically capable to work, she'll need money for a place, food, everything. Going back to her old job is not the smart thing to do. Those people were friends of Jim."

Officer King concurred Officer Pratt's remarks, "He's right. A judge is not going to allow you to move back with your mother if she has no home, no job, and questionable ethics. The one thing she has on her side is Señora Corona and the landlord. They can vouch for her character prior to the jerk and how he controlled her with fear. School records of your attendance and grades can help show the judge she didn't neglect your education."

The DCF lady, Ms. Tindall, met the policemen and Craig outside the placement home. She had been there with the teen girl the day he had been arrested. Ms. Tindall was kind and didn't yell. He watched her wipe the tears away from the girl as her statement was given. She even stayed with Craig when he kissed his momma before the EMT took her back to the hospital. And she helped him blow his nose when his hands were behind his back.

It seemed the home he would be living in wasn't going to cause him to start at a new school. He just lived close enough to walk, not ride the bus. This was a widow who was God-fearing and didn't take disrespect and entitled attitudes. She had been a foster parent for years and a real parent as well. She knew everything, so don't try her.

I would have a foster brother who was two years older than me. He was fifteen. We didn't have to share a room unless another kid came to live with us, then it depended on if it was a boy or girl. But she never took more than three unless they were a whole family of siblings.

So, on May 5, 2003, Cinco de Mayo, I met my foster brother. Daniel Armstrong. Then my foster mother came out of the door running to me, Nurse Mabel.

Chapter 20

July 2010

*L*ithia wasn't sure how she got into her bunk, the last thing she remembered was someone singing "*Jesus Loves Me.*" She seemed to have on her daisy gown and blue underwear. *I thought I was wearing white last night.* As she lay in her bunk, everything started coming back to her. The hammock, the hands, ripping clothes, the terror...until, the voice came. The strong arms embraced her after she called out for Jesus. But the voice was CJ.

"You sure look like something the dog drug up this morning. And where did you get the bruise on your arm, Lithia?" Leslie took hold of Lithia's right arm and turned it over looking at the huge purple blotch on the forearm. "That's nasty."

Renee came over and sat on Lithia's bunk. She looked concerned for her friend. "Why don't you just sleep in a little and I'll bring you some fruit from breakfast? It won't hurt you and we don't really have anything else until Bible study." She rubbed Lithia's forehead like a mother would do, then pulled up the covers and left for the mess tent.

Leslie was still putting on her makeup when Allan came for Carrie. "I hope you feel better, Lithia. Allan and I will see you at Bible study."

Won't they just leave me alone? God, I can't be like this all week. It's only Tuesday, and I don't go home until Saturday. How I am going to function in front of everyone? Can't Leslie ever get ready on time? I'm surprised she hasn't asked any more questions.

"Where did you go last night after you came off the stage? I never saw you at the bonfire. It was really the best too. Harold sat with me and held my hand for the longest time until he got a text message from his grandfather. I don't know what was so important he needed to call him. He never got to come back to the fire at all. I'm going to make him apologize for leaving me stranded. It wasn't fair." After Leslie complained how no one has disrespected her like that before, she smacked her lips together a few times in the mirror and waved as she pounced out the cabin.

At least she never shut up long enough to realize I never answered her questions. Now if I can just think, what happened at the steps? CJ was singing and... he was rocking me in his arms, my skirt was ripped and my panties. No, he saw me. My ugly body, and I couldn't cover my bra, I couldn't button my shirt. He must think I am an awful person. If he thinks I was willing, oh, I'm dirty, so dirty.

Sobs of shame came flowing swiftly as the night replayed over and over in her mind. But when CJ came into the story, she couldn't get the rest out, she felt calm and went to sleep. She didn't even hear Renee come in with a fruit cup from breakfast or a water bottle. Sleep overtook her. Dreams of Harold and the hammock would have her tossing on the bed, but in a little bit, CJ's singing would pierce the silence, and her breathing relaxed.

It was afternoon when Lithia woke up needing to use the restroom. The alarm clock read 12:45 pm. She had missed breakfast, Bible study, swimming, and lunch. It won't be long until time for archery and other sports. Her roomies could be stopping by before they go out to the ball field, hopefully not.

Picking up the water bottle and taking a sip, she tried to get out of bed. Her body ached with pain at every joint. She had to get to the bathroom, but she had to get out of the cabin first to walk there. Lithia slipped on her bathrobe and flip flops as she headed to the girls' bathroom. No one was around, and that was good. Her reflection in the mirror let her know she did not want anyone to see her right now.

Now if she could make it back to Cabin Kindness before anyone came her way. The thought of food made her stomach have butterflies, and not the good kind. She might try a couple grapes from the fruit cup Renee had left.

Just before Lithia got to the steps of the cabin, she heard a soft voice, "Are you okay?"

Leaning on the corner of the cabin stood CJ, he didn't get any closer, but he looked as if he wanted to support her as she took the first step. "I remember you from last night; your voice calmed me."

She couldn't look at him; he had seen her like that, vulnerable and dirty. But she wanted to know what happened; it was a blank slate from the steps to waking up this morning. Who else knows about what happened? Did he dress her? Did her put her in bed? Someone had to have done it, she needed to know.

"CJ, could you tell me what happened after you sang to me? I don't remember." She lifted her head and turned to him. His eyes were so full of compassion and no judgment. She wanted to get lost in them.

He took a couple of steps closer to her before he spoke; it was just a little louder than a whisper. "I couldn't let you stay in those clothes, and you had scrapes on your arms and legs. Your hair was matted with dirt and leaves from the ground. I got you in the cabin, but I couldn't bear to leave you for anyone to see you like that. I don't know how, but I figured out what clothes were yours, I found a nightgown, panties, and a robe. I grabbed the shower bag and towel that was on the chair by the bed."

Lithia couldn't believe he had found her clothes; he even touched her unmentionables, as her Grandmother called them. But he didn't seem to think disrespectful thoughts, and she wasn't even ashamed he had gotten her clothes together. But how did she get a shower? Take the rest of her clothes off?

"Lithia, I know you are worried about how I got you into clean clothes and out of the others. I promise, I did nothing ungodly. I...I knew you wouldn't want to be seen by anyone. At this point, I only had seen you in the moonlight and with my flashlight. Everything happened as much in the dark as possible. I was able to steer you to the girl's showers. I turned on the water and had you get under the stream with your clothes on. I washed your hair and rinsed it. I stepped out of the stall and stood with my back to you as you took the rest of your clothes off and washed your body. When you turned off the water, you wrapped yourself in the towel I had placed over my shoulder. Then I turned around. I was able to put the gown over your head while you held the towel still around you. As I picked up the wet clothes you left lying on the shower floor, I guess you put on your panties. The wet clothes I placed on a high shelf right inside the showers so I could come back and get them later. I carried you back to the cabin and tucked you in bed. I brushed your hair as best I could, but when I heard the other girls coming near, I went out the back door. You had fallen asleep before I ever laid you in the bed. When the lights went out in the cabin, I slipped to the showers and grabbed your clothes. I've been waiting for a chance to check on you and return your things."

He was so sweet. He wanted her to feel comfortable but knew how some might treat her if they had seen the clothes, the marks, what they could have called her. CJ did everything he could to keep her secret safe. She didn't even know if he knew what the secret really was, but he seemed to be able to discern what happened. But did he know who did this to her? Then she fainted.

Thank God he caught her just in time before she fell backwards off the steps. He remembered how she had felt last night in his arms, on the steps, and then afterwards as he carried her to her bunk. Now, here he was holding her again. Her head on his chest with her strawberry hair on his arm. The daisies on her gown were cute and made her look like she was a little girl who had fallen asleep watching TV and needed carrying to bed. He took her flip flops off and put her feet under the covers. Then he tried to wake her.

Holding her hand, he prayed for this teenage girl that was taken advantage by someone at camp. It had to be the guy he saw limping away into the woods; he was going to find out who, and when he did, he hoped God would forgive him.

CJ was gone when Lithia came to, but her towel and toiletry bag was back in place. Hmmm, but where were her ripped clothes? She really didn't care; she didn't want them back.

When the girls came in before dinner, Lithia had fallen back to sleep. They woke her up, but she didn't feel like eating.

Renee was a mother hen. "You can't just stay in here all day. The counselors are asking about you. I told the director you weren't feeling well. You're not going to skip chapel tonight unless one of the counselors comes in and gives you the okay. I'm going to bring back a salad or something light for you."

Renee and Carrie were really bothered by Lithia's color. Her one arm was purple and black as if she had been hit or fallen. There was a red mark across her face, and one eye was blackened. They were sure her leg had scratches on it and more bruising. She must have tripped on the way back to the cabin last night and she's embarrassed. The fall is giving her some aches and pains. She'll be okay tomorrow.

"It's fine, Lithia. I can sing on stage tonight. I practiced with Harold instead of playing softball. He didn't want to go to the lake to swim, so we met up in the music room. He is such a good kisser. Things were getting hot until CJ came in and wanted to practice the piano. That's when we left. But don't worry about me, I'll be fine singing tonight. No one will miss you." And Leslie was gone.

Would Leslie be Harold's next victim, or would she willingly submit to his desires? Lithia hoped for neither.

She never made it to chapel, but she did have a visitor before the girls returned for the evening.

CJ stopped by with a single yellow rose.

Chapter 21

May 2, 2019

omen's Safe House was on the front of the building Lithia and Craig were visiting first. It was a smoky grey color and black lettering, not very hopeful by the appearance walking in. The front lobby was lined with about ten chairs of assorted types, from metal folding ones to wooden straight backs. There was even a beach sand chair. In one corner, a small table and a few plastic kid chairs were placed. A few children's books, a box of Legos, a truck, and a doll were the only distractions a child would have if one came in with their mother. The walls were bland, no paintings on the white paint.

Straight ahead was a counter. On top was a can holding a few pencils beside it, clipboards with forms to be completed by those that came in for help. And a box of tissue. The lady behind the counter-she was a different story.

Eva Cisneros was a pistol. Her raven hair was shoulder length and made her red framed glasses pop out at you. She loved to wear bright colors, so the tied dyed t-shirt dress with the wide yellow sash belt worked. And loud, her voice was as loud as her fashion fix. There was no filter, she was blunt. Eva was on the phone when Lithia and Craig walked into the empty lobby.

"No, baby, you need to get down here to the office as soon as you can, and bring the kids. That man is going to come back and hit you again. How many times has it been in a month?" Pause for a response. Eva was shaking her head and frowning. "Look, I don't care that the little one is napping right now. Get him out of the crib, grab Sissy, put them in the car, and you can be here in 15 minutes."

Eva was waving and smiling at Craig, but held up her index finger telling us to wait a minute. "Nope, if you aren't here within the next thirty minutes, I am personally calling the sheriff to go to your house. It will be a wellness check, but you don't want that riffraff of a husband to get wind you had the cops by today. Don't interrupt me! My clock is ticking. 30 minutes!" She hung up the phone and pulled a kitchen timer out of the desk drawer.

She saw Lithia's puzzled look. "Babe, you have to give out some tough love on days like today. He is going to kill her next time, and it isn't happening on my watch." Eva walked over to the counter, stuck out her hand to Craig, and shook it aggressively. "It's about time you came to visit. I expected you all week. So, what will you be wanting to discuss or see today, Mr. O'Shay?"

"Right to the point, I see, and efficient is what I have heard about you. I would like to see your filing system and the data of cases you have on average. A tour of the facility, including the rooms for short-term lodging and childcare. If any client would like to speak to me, I would be glad to lend an ear. Any suggestions or recommendations from staff or clients can be given to me before we leave. I want to be able to give a detailed account to the needs of all concerned when I speak at the charity ball Saturday evening. Ms. Cisneros, do you think this will be possible?"

"Oh, I got you! Here is a folder with all the data you will probably need. It also has an explanation of our bookkeeping-accesses and liabilities. Inside is a list of all staff members with emails, phone numbers, and job titles. There is a breakdown of clients: single, single with children, married, and married with kids, nationality, even social economic status is a category. Ages are all over the chart, as is educational background and religion. It is a sad situation."

Lithia was quite impressed with Eva. She didn't think some of the women she worked with in her office could be that thorough without a list from the boss days in advance. Then Lithia noticed a little boy, about eight, sitting in a little chair behind the counter.

He had blonde hair and glasses, and in no world could be Eva's son biologically. Quietly, he sat reading a book with monster trucks on the front cover. When he turned the page, she could see the cast on his left arm. He must feel her staring at him, and he looked up. His face was scarred, and there was a bandage under one eye.

"Well, hello there, can you tell me about the book you're reading? Looks interesting from the cover." Lithia wondered how he got the scars, but feared the worst.

The little boy looked at Eva for approval before he spoke, and when he was given the nod, he became gregarious.

Lithia and Craig had come back behind the counter, and Craig was looking over the files with Eva. What else was Lithia to do as she waited, and he was so sweet and eager to tell her everything.

"Pleasure to meet you ma'am, I'm Jenson Gibson. I'm eight years old. I'm tall for my age, they say, but I don't think so cause Bobby Dodd is much taller than a couple twelve-year-old boys. My book, oh, it's about trucks, monster trucks. Have you ever gone to a monster truck rally? I'm going to go one day. My momma's going to take me, if she gets better. See this one here on page 14, that's the kind I'm going drive one day. The name on it says, "Big Foot" cause it stomps on all the other trucks."

Jenson rattled on and on. He jumped from one topic to another with no stopping for a breath. Lithia laughed; Lithia might not be able to keep up. He had taken her hand, and she found herself being given the Jenson tour. He was quite the storyteller as they walked in and out of every room, whether they were welcomed or not, and he introduced her to as many of the staff and clients he came across.

The weirdest thing was that Lithia never told him her name. She kept thinking Jenson must have overheard Craig call her Cinderella, but she was pretty sure she had been introduced as Miss Murphy to Eva. Finally, it got the best of her, and she squatted down to Jenson.

"Jenson, why are you calling me Cinderella? Did someone tell you to call me by that name?"

"Nope, I made it up. You don't wanna be called the name of a pretty princess? Most girls I deal with think they are princesses, but really, they aren't. See, I watched the movie Cinderella, and at the ball with the prince, she wears her hair up like yours is today. And I know you will be going to a ball with that man in there on Saturday. He has money and the power to fix this place up and help kids like me and our moms. So, you're Cinderella, and he is Prince Charming. Get it?"

Boy, did he seem pleased with himself. Jenson smiled as big as he could, but it looked like it hurt the scars. Lithia reached up and caressed his cheek. He took her hand. "It doesn't hurt like it once did, Cinderella. I know I'm ugly now, but the scar will get smaller as I get older, I gotta wait the doctor said."

He led her farther away from Craig and into a room that had *Clinic* written in bold letters on the door. There were some hospital beds on one side with curtains drawn around them. A nurse in white was speaking with a woman wearing a doctor's coat. Lithia was glad to see if a woman and her children came in for help, there was some medical staff if it was needed.

"My momma is in that one, but I can't see her right now. She might have to go to the real hospital. That's what I heard the nurse tell Ms. Eva. If she does, I might have to go back to foster care again. Can you pray and ask Jesus to heal my momma? If I go away, I won't know anyone, and they may not take me to see Momma." He was trying hard not to be a baby and cry.

Lithia was heartbroken at this child's plea. She would pray for a miracle.

"Here you are, Cinderella! I see you have your own personal tour guide for today. And who do we have here, and how much is the private tour going to cost me?" Craig tussled Jenson's hair and shook his hand. "Have you swept my Cinderella off her feet, young man, or may I have her back? We have a ball to go to Saturday night, with your permission, of course." Craig bowed.

Jenson was ecstatic. "I just knew you were Prince Charming and Cinderella. She tried to tell me different, but

I didn't believe her. You don't need my permission to go to the ball, her fairy godmother will make sure she's there."

Jenson couldn't have been more entertaining and informative. He and his mother had taken refuge over two years ago at the center. With help of the staff and resources they gave, she was able to get a divorce, find a job, and rent an apartment within six months. Everything was going well, his mom even volunteered at the center a couple times a week, and then Jenson's father found them. It wasn't a grand reunion. Now they were at the center as clients once again.

Craig was touched to the core with the boy's story. Lithia could see how deeply Craig was feeling the emotion and sympathy for Jenson.

Picking Jenson up, "How would you like to go to the ball on Saturday night with Cinderella and Prince Charming? Your mom, too, if she's able."

Jenson was nodding and hugging Craig so tight Lithia thought Craig would put him on the floor, but instead, he hugged him just as tight.

"I like your name, Jenson. Do you know what it means?" Jenson shook his head no. "It means 'son.' Do you know what sons are supposed to do for their mothers? Take care of them. Will you promise me you will always do that for your mom? No matter how big you get, you love her. She may make mistakes, but we all do, so you just love her. Promise?"

With that, Craig placed Jenson down on his feet. "I promise, Prince Charming!" Jenson shook Craig's hand, then saluted him like a little soldier and trotted off to be with his mom.

Lithia was in awe of this man she was escorting. Her mouth dropped as did her heart, "Ms. Eva, order a dozen yellow long-stemmed roses for Jenson's mom. Send me the bill; you have my information. And let Jenson sign the card. Tell the boy I'm starting him on the way to be a 'Prince Charming.'" Craig took Lithia by the elbow and walked out the door.

Chapter 22

March 2004

Nurse Mabel was stern, and the rules were not to be broken in her house. Craig had no problem following them. They weren't all that bad. Everyone had chores to do each day, school was not to be skipped unless you were sick, and she checked EVERYTHING to be sure you weren't fibbing. Homework was priority after school before going off with friends, TV, video games, and bedtime was ten, except on Friday and Saturday; you can stay up until, if you're lucky, midnight. Saturday was laundry and Sunday was church.

Church was something Craig had never attended until those few weeks with Señora Corona, but she went to a Spanish church, and he didn't always understand what they were saying. But Nurse Mabel's church, well, it was LOUD.

Mt. Zion Missionary Holiness Church of Our God was a music concert in your ears. The church wasn't that big. The auditorium could seat two hundred, but over fifty were on the stage every week. You name it, somebody in the congregation played it. Organ, piano, drums, trumpet, sax, two bass guitars, and a couple of electrical ones, and tambourines. Tambourines were EVERYWHERE. On the stage, in the pews, in the choir loft, in the balcony, everywhere you looked, someone, young and old, with or without rhythm, was playing a tambourine. Add the fifty-voice choir, a praise team, and praise dancers, the music portion was louder than Nurse Mabel let him turn up the television. Then Lord knows how much it increased when the people in the pews got happy, too.

You went to church, rain or shine, as long as you lived at Nurse Mabel's. Church was every Sunday morning at ten o'clock. First, there was Sunday School. Craig was in the teen class with his foster brother Daniel. Daniel knew everyone, Craig knew a couple of the guys from school. When class was over, everyone went to the auditorium for praise and worship.

Depending on how many times the music director had them sing a song, or how many verses of *"Rock of Ages"* Sister Edna would sing, well, they might be singing and standing for over an hour. By the time Reverend Hawthorne began to preach, why, it could be near one o'clock. Why, there were Sundays there wasn't any point to going home. You had to come back for choir practice at five, and night service was at six.

Wednesday nights were youth service. After a day at school, homework, and chores, it was sandwich night. This means hot dogs or grilled cheese, or even bologna was for dinner.

Service would start at seven, so there wasn't much time for an elaborate meal. The teens would oversee all aspects of the service. From playing the instruments, singing, collecting the offering, and even preaching the sermon.

Sometimes they would perform skits or plays instead of preaching. One time, they even played Bible Trivia, parents against the teens. The Rev, as every teen called him, said kids were the church of today not of the future, and they needed to learn leadership roles before it was too late. If the church wasn't going to make them welcome, the world would.

Craig thrived. Sister Edna heard Craig playing the piano and saw the talent; said she'd give him lessons for free if he played once a month for youth service. He had now played four times. Brother Blake, the music minister, took notice of Craig's singing voice, and started him in the choir, and that wasn't the only time Craig was at the church.

Since Nurse Mabel did have to work, the hospital was nice enough to give her a schedule to work around her foster kids. Mabel had been in the career three decades; they owed her. Normally, her hours were the same as the kids. She went to the hospital at seven and came home by four or five. The longest was if she caught a 12-hour shift. It was in the afternoons the church helped her with the boys.

Mt. Zion had an afterschool program for kids. Children were able to get homework help, snack, and could be in sports programs through the city. Practices were held on church property, with a gym to play basketball or volleyball, a field for football or soccer, and a baseball diamond; the boys had plenty to keep them occupied. Craig found that he was quite talented with a baseball. He had a decent arm, but he'd rather be on first base.

Craig's schedule became very busy; church on Sunday and school and baseball on Monday, Thursday, and Friday. Tuesday was school, piano lessons, and baseball. Wednesday took him back to school, baseball, choir practice, and youth service. On Saturdays, he was to clean his room and any other chores; most times, he had a baseball game, and he saw his momma.

When he first moved in with Nurse Mabel, Craig visited his mom at the hospital twice a week. After she was released from the hospital, Señora Corona let her stay with her until she could find a job and her own place. Craig would visit on Saturday evenings for dinner. Then when his momma got a job, she moved in with a girl from work and rented a room. There wasn't a place for a boy that was almost fourteen. So, his momma resorted to coming to his baseball games on Saturdays instead. The judge had said if Momma didn't visit at least once a week, she could lose the chance of ever having him live with her again. Nurse Mabel reminded Craig his mom could also come to church anytime there were services. Those could be extra visits, and she could hear Craig play the piano or sing. Momma hadn't come to any yet.

"Momma, I was calling to tell you I would like for you to come to church this Wednesday evening. It starts at seven o'clock. I'm going to be playing the piano and singing a song. I want you to come hear me. I'm also going to get baptized too."

Craig was so excited. He just knew his mom would come this time. She wouldn't let him down.

"I don't know, dear, I'm working at a new place and picked up some night shifts. Have Nurse Mabel take pictures so I can see them later. I can try, but no promises. I do love you." And like that, she hung up.

The other aspect of living with Nurse Mabel was having a foster brother, an older brother. A brother, that, well, wasn't living with Nurse Mabel cause his momma had gotten hurt; he was there because he was the assailant.

Daniel Armstrong was just that. He could "armstrong" anyone, but Nurse Mabel. It was said that Daniel tried twice, it didn't end well. Daniel's parents had money, and most of their time was at work. Daniel spent his afternoons finding something to do. Idle hands are the devil's playground.

When Daniel became old enough stay home alone after school, the nanny was terminated, and rules were given for Daniel to comply. Since Daniel never had to deal with parents that were authoritarians, but lenient, and spoiled him rotten, now he didn't have much respect to follow orders. At school, he did well in classes where the teachers were "cool," and in those he didn't like, he skipped or acted like an idiot. He would get referrals and suspended, but his parents were usually stuck at the office or out of town, so no true punishment came.

Then Daniel turned fifteen, he been given one more chance, or he would be taken off the football team. He had been benched for the homecoming game and failed his quarter exam in biology. His dad had enough, and his mom had turned to drinking. Their marriage was falling apart, and they placed all the blame on their son. The final straw came when he stole a neighbor's truck and trailer with jet skis. He and a few of his friends went out to Miami Beach; they wrecked the jet skis and sunk the trailer. The truck was found parked in a desolate area, stripped and layered with graffiti. Daniel's fingerprints were evidence, along with the video footage on the security cameras and the social media postings of Daniel's friends.

At court, the judge gave Daniel probation until his 18th birthday, no driver's license, even a permit, until then. Mrs. Armstrong let the judge know she was at her wit's end. She didn't even think he could do the right thing for less than three years. She'd probably have a nervous breakdown by then. The judge ordered Daniel to be placed as a ward of the state, and DCF took over. Daniel found himself living with Nurse Mabel until he was to become an adult and graduate high school.

"You are going to hate it here with this big ole'..." Daniel stopped when he saw Nurse Mabel come into the bedroom. "I'm just getting acquainted with my little foster bro, Mother Mabel. I want him to know all the rules and stuff, so he won't get in any trouble."

"Why, that's mighty nice of you, Danny. It's good to see you getting along. There haven't been any kids come through here but toddlers. Now you got somebody close to your own age. Craig just turned thirteen a few days ago and will start high school in the fall. This will be good to have another person he can lean on when he gets there. Supper's in an hour; don't forget to wash up."

Nurse Mabel headed to the kitchen humming the Macarena song. Daniel turned back to Craig, "You just remember, I'm the one in charge when it comes to you and me. Do what I say and that's all that matters. We will get along fine."

Craig didn't know what it was to have a big brother; he figured that's what older brothers did.

Big brother Daniel was not innocent, to say the least. He didn't always tell the truth, and he manipulated Craig into doing his chores several times during the week. His grades were mediocre, but still high enough to play junior varsity football.

The only time Daniel saw his parents was at football games. Then the conversation with his dad was only about the plays and what he did or didn't do right on the field. Mr.

Armstrong expected Daniel to get to college on a football scholarship because he wasn't going to pay for a child that didn't have any remorse with what he had done.

"Do we have to go to church every Sunday? I mean, if God loves us so much, He is bound to let us have a Sunday or so off. It's just so boring, the same thing over and over. Jesus died on the cross, rose again, coming back. Praise Him, amen. Doesn't take me four or five hours to tell it." This would be the normal Sunday morning argument Daniel raised with Nurse Mabel.

"It seems to me we need to go so often because there are people who don't get it the first 500 hundred times. Did the people who died in the flood? No! Noah preached for 120 years, and still, only eight people made it out. Jesus told the disciples for three and a half years, then look at Judas. And if you must ask me one more time, YOU need to hear it. Get dressed." Nurse Mabel would turn on Gospel music until the time to leave. She said she was getting her heart ready to worship.

Daniel hated wearing the tie and dress shoes. He said he was going to dress like the rappers do when he moved out. He liked to show off his bling. "I'm never going to wear a monkey suit like this when I grow up; you can't make me."

"Never say never, Danny," Momma Mabel would tell him. "You never know where the good Lord will place you. Might have a job so you dress like that all day." Craig imagined Daniel as an adult in a suit and tie; who knows, one day.

Chapter 23

July 2010

C J had stayed up all night Monday after finding Lithia on the steps. He didn't know who to tell or even if he should say anything to the director. He wanted it to come from Lithia, but didn't think she even had the heart to tell anyone; she was so ashamed.

It was a little unorthodox how he got her showered, dressed, and in bed, but he didn't know any other way unless he left her to get one of the female counselors. Then there would have been tons of questions he couldn't really answer. And by the looks of things, neither could she. CJ had been worried while in the girl's shower, but knowing how long the bonfires could last, he felt he had plenty of time. He had been right.

She had felt so helpless in his arms. Lithia wasn't one of the little skinny girls, but in those moments, she was tiny and vulnerable. She was his roommate's sister, someone's daughter. He just wished he had gotten there a few minutes earlier. *I could have stopped it from happening at all, or at least before it got to...*and his thoughts trailed off.

Lithia probably wonders what happened to her personal things. I need to tell her I burned the clothes on the bonfire after everyone went to bed. I knew she wouldn't want those clothes reminding her of the night or the guy that did this to her. Why can't I figure out who it was? I didn't stay at the bonfire long enough to see who was missing. If I had, I would probably figure it out.

The guy in the shadows, the one limping away must be the assailant. He could be anyone, camper, counselor, or some transient from in the woods. What clues do I have? Wasn't at bonfire, got hurt, tall six ft. or so, slender built, wore a baseball cap, no idea of skin tone, eyes, hair. Hmmm, I wonder if Lithia bit him. If so, someone might have some visible teeth marks. I need time to talk to her alone. God, give me the opportunity. I don't even know if the man stole her virginity or not, but he stole her innocence.

All day he prayed for God to show him who it was or give him clues. Nothing came. He finally got a chance to talk to Lithia between dinner and chapel, returning her toiletries, but he forgot to tell he about her clothes. She didn't seem upset on how he got her dressed and in bed. She didn't come to chapel, but he wanted to give her something to make her feel better.

His mother's favorite was a yellow rose. She always said roses made her day brighter. Craig was pretty sure there was a shopping center a few miles up the road from the camp. He just needed permission to leave for a bit.

She was asleep when he dropped it off. Her Bible was on the nightstand by her bunk. He laid it there. No card, no note. She would know it was from a friend. A single yellow rose.

It was Wednesday of camp, and still no Lithia at break-fast or Bible study. Sean finally went by to check on her when the other girls said there was no change.

"Sis, I think maybe you should go home. I'll call Mom and Dad and see if someone can come get you. I can't take you; I have responsibilities here for the concession stand and sound booth each night. Carrie told me you haven't even been to the camp nurse. What's that about? If you at least went to her, maybe she's got something for whatever is hurting. Lithia, you can't just sulk in your bunk either."

He leaned into whisper, "Leslie said you are jealous Harold the drummer likes her, not you. I pray that isn't it. He is not the guy people think he is. Stay away from him, okay." Sean kissed his sister on the cheek. "I'll see you tonight at chapel or I call the folks."

Renee brought Lithia lunch. "Well, the redness on your face has gone down from yesterday; that's a good sign. I have some makeup that should be able to cover any other marks on your face. I told the head girls' counselor you fell down the steps to the cabin and were bruised and achy all over. She gave me some Advil for you to take. I wish I knew what to do to make you feel better."

Lunch tray was a BLT and strawberry Jell-O cup. The strawberry coolness slid down so easy, but the BLT wasn't doing the trick. Lithia was only able to eat half. It was still the most she had eaten since Monday.

No one was in the cabin with her, nor would there be for the next couple of hours. She thought she might want to get up and move around to see how bad it did hurt. Somehow, she was going to need to get to chapel. Mom and Dad couldn't get a message from Sean. Who knows if anyone else had told their parents? If they did, she'd know soon enough.

Getting a shower now might not be such a bad idea. No one would see her and the extent of her bruises or be there to ask hundred questions. She could come back and lie down until chapel.

Towel, toiletry bag, some clean underclothes and a t-shirt was all she took. With her bathrobe over her daisy gown, she made it to the bathroom. The water was warm and gave her some sense of normalcy. Clean hair, bra, and panties, she wrapped her wet locks in the towel and dawned the bathrobe, tying it tight at the waist.

"Might as well brush my teeth in this sink while I'm here." She was talking to herself, but it helped her focus. "Toiletry bag and dirty clothes, yep, that's it. I'll go back and read some Scripture and relax on my bunk. I'll have to figure out what I can wear without all my bruises exposed, though. I didn't bring jackets and long sleeves for this heat."

The alarm clock on the desk showed 2:30. She had taken a long shower. Lithia had emptied her hands and turned to sit back on her bunk to find Harold standing in front of her. She froze.

"Oooo, look at this. Clean and fresh, all for me. I think I need to unwrap the package here in the daylight this time. I can see what I'm getting."

Harold began to untie the bathrobe belt and took the towel off her head. Throwing the towel on the wooden floor, he took her wrist in his hand, while yanking the belt loose with the other.

Wet strawberry locks cascaded down her shoulders, making her shiver, but was it the wet hair or fear. He looked at her and laughed.

"What is it with you and the granny panties? Are you sixteen or sixty? Men don't like this." He popped the elastic waistband of her underwear. The noise was all it took.

"Let go of me now, Harold! Don't you touch me again! You need to get out of my cabin before I scream."

With her free hand, she tried to hold her robe together where she would be covered. But he threw her onto the bed.

Harold was going to make her pay for his humiliation from the other night. Lead him on, would she. As he reached for his button on his shorts, Lithia scooted to the other side of her bed and got up running for the door. Harold caught her arm and jerked her back, Lithia screamed as loud as she could, grasping for anything to keep her close to the cabin door. *Please God, let someone hear me.*

He couldn't pull her to the bed, get her to stop screaming, or keep his balance. He knew if she didn't shut up, this little tease would make this look like he was to blame. He stood still and got in her face.

"Shut up, slut! Don't scream again, or you'll regret it. If you tell anyone what has happened, I'll tell everyone how you threw yourself at me. I had come to leave Leslie a note, and you were waiting for me naked in the cabin. I tried to leave, and you blocked the door, rubbing your body on me. When I didn't respond, you began to scream as if I was the pervert. Remember who my family is, we have money, you'd lose. And do you want all your do-gooders to think you're not as pure as you let on?"

She was quiet; listening to what he said. *No, I can't let people know what happened. They're going to think I'm at least a part of this. CJ probably already does too. My poor parents and grandparents would never see me the same way again. People will always wonder if I'm a good girl or not.*

Harold took her off guard again as her thoughts raced through her head. His hands went under her robe and caught her waist then pulled her into his body. She could smell his breath, feel his lips brushing lightly on her cheek as he spoke one more time.

"Don't underestimate me, for it will be your downfall."

He pressed his mouth on hers till she was sure he had bruised them, then let her go, walking out the back door to the cabin into the woods.

Lithia fell to her knees on the floor.

CJ found her like this thirty minutes later.

God, not late again!

After he got her into bed, covering Lithia with the comforter, CJ found a washcloth to wet and wash her face. She opened her eyes to find him, once again, her rescuer. Singing over her with a little bit of praying incorporated too, he laid the cool cloth on her forehead.

"Are you okay? I found you crumpled by the door." He helped her lean up to take a drink from the water bottle he offered her.

"Thank you. Thank you, again. Please CJ, don't tell anyone. I can't let anyone know what happened. My parents, my family would be so hurt." She closed her eyes.

Did he think the worst? I must tell him I'm still...that I'm... hadn't been a willing...that he hadn't fulfilled his plan. Today or at the hammock.

His eyes were so sad, but there was hope in them as he looked at her. He didn't seem to be judging; he had to know. Now, before anyone else walked into the cabin.

"I didn't let him." *Did he understand me? I'm talking crazy. Rambling, with these tears and thinking gives me a headache. He needs to know.*

"I was kicking and trying to get him off me. He couldn't...I flipped the hammock. My knee, I bit his hand or finger, he was limping."

Sobs, it was hard to understand the bits and pieces she tried to tell him, but he could see she needed him; she wanted him to know the truth. Her hand took his arm to pull him closer.

"He never took...and today, he came back. Hidden in my cabin when I returned from the shower. He had me...the bed...my face, stomach. He tried to take his pants..."

Oh, God, he didn't, did he? I was on the way to her cabin. I was that close again.

"I screamed. I... almost made it to the door. I wasn't fast enough. His lips on me... hurting my mouth. He made me promise. Promise not to tell."

In desperation, "You can't tell anyone, CJ. Promise me, promise me." She shook him to get an answer.

"He said he would make sure I lost...I lost it next time. He would tell everyone I wanted it. Promise me, CJ. Keep my secret forever."

He held her in his arms once more, promising he would never tell. Promising he would keep the secret forever. Promising God, he would do whatever he needed to do to help another girl or woman from this again.

But he couldn't promise what he would do to the guy he saw walking out of the back door to the cabin minutes before he walked in the front.

Chapter 24

2006

*D*aniel had graduated high school after making up credits over summer school. He at least had his families support to persuade the university to allow him to keep the football scholarship, even though he had to graduate late. The judge had allowed Daniel to get his driver's license after he turned 18, but he had to get a part-time job as well. He couldn't move back home or anywhere else until his probation was over on August 1st. He was stuck at Nurse Mabel's for six months after becoming an adult, and he hated it.

College life was going to be the best. No Nurse Mabel, Mom and Dad, no probation, and 18 years old. This was going to be the best years ever. Oh, and the best was no more church.

Nurse Mabel had a going away party for Daniel at the last youth service. Church members gave him money, presents, and stuff for his college dorm room. He was set from the congregation without anything from his parents. It didn't matter; his dad had given him a car. So, with his college scholarship, a car, all the money, and gifts...

University of Miami, here I come! Parties every weekend, beer, girls, out-of-town games, living in a dorm with all the football team...this is the life.

Nurse Mabel told Mr. and Mrs. Armstrong she thought Daniel should live at home. He had been gone so long already, plus, he was just going to college in town anyway, why should money be wasted? Mr. Armstrong believed it was best for Daniel to bond with the team and learn to be independent. He was still close enough if he needed his parents, but not underfoot either. And if Daniel did anything stupid this time, he was an adult and would face the consequences alone.

That was not Mabel's parenting philosophies, but she couldn't teach an old dog new tricks. She just prayed Daniel would remember things she had taught him, especially about Jesus. He always rejected Christ, but God's Word never went out void. She prayed it would come to Daniel when he needed it most.

Craig was just the most compassionate teen she'd known. Sister Edna had pretty much stopped playing the piano altogether, letting Criag play all but once a month. Then "The Rev" had him teaching the fifth-grade boys Sunday School class. Nurse Mabel kept expecting him to get called to preach. But whenever it was mentioned, "I think God has something else in mind for me to do with my life." He never would say what it was, but he just smiled and went on.

With Daniel gone, Craig had more chores to do at Nurse Mabel's, but since he had done most of Daniel's anyway, there was less arguing first. He just did it. School was easy, he was on the varsity baseball team, and youth group was growing. The only thing wrong was his momma.

He saw her less and less. She had moved to another apartment, but he hadn't been allowed to move in with her. Her scheduled hours were inconsistent to plan visitation around a week in advance as DCF required. Nurse Mabel still invited Saoirse to church for Sundays, but the excuses were the same. It's the only day I have off, laundry, sleeping late, cleaning. But if Craig was brought to her house, she was never home or at least didn't answer the door. He worried about her, but Nurse Mabel got a monthly check from Saoirse for expenses for Craig, so she must be making it okay.

Occasionally, Craig would get a text message from Daniel wanting to meet up for pizza or for Craig to come to a college party. He went a few times, but he didn't really like any of the other guys Daniel was hanging with now. It wasn't that they were all bad guys, just that they were older. Even up to four years older than Daniel, so six older than Craig. They could drink, a lot, and they wanted Daniel to drink with them. They called Craig names when he refused, calling him a baby, which was tame.

Craig stopped spending time with Daniel unless he was alone. He didn't like the guy Daniel had become. The drinking and girls were getting in the way of his studies, and if he didn't watch out, he would lose his scholarship. The one thing Craig was glad; Daniel was drug tested often enough he hadn't gotten into that pit. But if he lost his football, Craig knew that could be the next rung down on the ladder Daniel was on.

During the Christmas break, Craig was to be interning at an investment brokerage, and he was excited to learn something new. He wanted to be able to think about the future and be prepared. He didn't have parents like Daniel to pay for college, and he didn't know if he could get a scholarship, though he had been told his grades and baseball could be the prize for one.

"Next summer, Craig, I would like for you to be a camp helper. If you go and help for two weeks, they will let you stay the third week as a camper for free. Do you think you might be interested? We turn in the papers in March to be sure of a spot. I'm counting on you, son." The Rev wished this kid the best of everything. God had truly blessed the boy with talent and a heart of gold.

"Hey, buddy, I want you to meet my best friend. Can you come down to the college this weekend?" Daniel wanted Craig to meet his BFF. *I thought I was his best friend.*

"I don't know Daniel, I got a game on Saturday, plus I'm going to try and see my momma before she goes to work. And you know Nurse Mabel, laundry has to be done on the weekend."

"Well, we got to connect. You're gonna like Harry. Loves music like you and plays instruments. Oh, and he has this sports car his grandfather gave him. The girls will do anything for a ride."

Harry says he has no problems getting the girls when they see him in that car. I can't wait until he lets me drive it one weekend.

Craig still tried to see his mom, but it seemed he always missed her. Then one day, he got there at just the right time. He had picked up a yellow long-stemmed rose, her favorite, and was waiting for someone to answer his knock. Right when he was going to push the elevator button to leave, his mom and a man walked out of the apartment.

They hadn't seen him, but he was close enough to see and hear everything, things he never wished he heard.

"Here you go, baby, the money I owe for last night. You took good care of me and my friends. I'll be back later with some other friends to release some stress. You'll get another payment for your services then. Make sure you're wearing that new teddy I bought you when we come. Got to show some of the goods to get the money, honey." He lit a cigar and slapped Saoirse's backside before heading to the elevator.

Saoirse was standing at the doorway of her apartment in a translucent red gown. When she heard the elevator door open, she looked up to see her son drop the flower and run down the stairwell.

Craig ran down two flights of stairs then halted. He knew if he went all the way down to the first floor, he would go after whoever that guy was. He wasn't twelve anymore. He was sixteen, his body was strong from working out, his muscles were tight. He could have given that man trouble, but what about his momma?

What had she done? No, it wasn't Jim, but it was a man just like him. This time, she wasn't dancing, she had taken it a step further. He was never going to be able to live with her again. He just didn't understand how could she go to that level? There had to be another way then to go backwards. Maybe when he was a man, he could take care of her. No woman should ever have to take this path to survive.

God, my momma needs your salvation. She needs to see she's a sinner and that you died for her sins. I don't want my momma to be this kinda woman, to sell herself to others, or to have men use her anyway they want. There must be some other way for her to survive. A job that doesn't make her lose her self-respect. She doesn't see how much her life is worth to you, to me. God, protect my momma from these men, men like Jim. Give me self-control. The anger in me to protect her to hurt men like that is so intense. Show me, Lord, when to use this strength and when to hold back.

Saoirse had closed the door and locked it. Craig had seen her dressed like this. She was sure he heard every word her pimp had told her. His face was full of hurt and disappointment. In the past, she had told him everything she did was for him. To be able to give him the necessities of life, but she couldn't say that now. He had all the things he really needed. But she would be homeless if she didn't do this each week. It was only to pay her bills. She could do it; once those hospital bills were paid off, she could go back to just waitressing or a cashier. Could she make it that long?

Chapter 25

July 2010

Lithia had to get ready for chapel. But now she had more bruises to try and hide. She had no idea what to do. When the other girls left for dinner, she tried on every outfit she had. Nothing worked. Her legs showed, her arms. People were going to stare and question. She had just about given up hope when CJ knocked.

"I can tell you're upset. He hasn't come back, has he?" He looked relieved when she said no. "Okay, then what's the issue"

"I have nothing to wear!"

"Now, finally, some normal teen girl problems."

They both laughed. The laugh was almost satisfying compared to the things they had been dealing with the past few days.

"CJ, I have nothing to cover my bruises. It's hot. All the clothes I have with me are sleeveless, tank tops, shorts, sundresses. I need something to wear to chapel, or Sean is calling my parents if I don't show up."

"Do you have jeans with you? I know you have sandals. Ok, that takes care of the bottom half. What if you wear a tank top, but you put one of my shirts over it? I have a couple of long sleeve dress shirts. You wear them over the jeans and roll up the sleeves a little. They'll be baggy, but at least it covers your arms. Two shirts, two nights of chapel. Will that at least get you through tonight until I can think of something else?"

She was smiling. Her eyes twinkled. Craig thought her dimple was cute too. He was so glad she seemed hopeful now. He ran back to his cabin and grabbed the shirts. She had already put on the jeans and sandals and her tank top. With his shirt, the outfit was completed.

"Here, put the collar up so the marks on your neck aren't noticeable. And if you want a belt, I'll give you my tie." He proceeded to untie his tie and drape it around her waist. "How's that?"

"I have two different looks. I'll wear it like this tonight, tomorrow without a belt. I just got to figure out the rest of my day. I just don't know how to thank you."

"My pleasure, as your knight in shining armor. Tonight, you sit on the platform with me by the piano, far from the drums."

He knows it's Harold. But he promised me. I trust him, but how is he going to be able to stand being in the same cabin with the jerk?

"I want us to sing a duet again. I guess I am not good enough alone now. You walk with me to and from chapel. Never are you to go alone. I have another idea for daytime clothes. If I think it will work, I'll give it to you after chapel so you can have it to wear tomorrow morning. I'll be back to get you in thirty minutes."

He did come back even sooner than he said. When the other girls saw Lithia had an escort to chapel, they tried to make something of it, but CJ didn't allow it. "Director wants us to sing a duet again tonight. We need to practice."

Lithia never left his side the entire chapel. She was standing by him to sing or sitting on the piano bench with him. During the sermon, they sat side by side in chairs by the piano, far right of the drums.

Harold kept looking over at her, but she'd turn her head so he couldn't see her face. CJ made sure he was between them.

When chapel was over, they straightened up all the music and picked up some empty water bottles the audience had left. Then CJ walked her to the concession stand for a snow cone.

Eating their snow cones CJ guided her toward his cabin. When she realized where they were headed, she questioned him. "This isn't a good idea. Harold could be there, and it doesn't look right me coming here with you alone." Lithia was nervous; what if Harold saw her? He would think she was coming to be with him, and CJ just showed up.

"It's okay. Harold was with Leslie over by the gazebo and they looked busy. You aren't coming in my cabin, but you are going to stand on the steps so I can see you. I told you I was going to try to find something you can wear tomorrow during the day. Hold my snow cone, I'll be right back."

CJ was holding a big camp t-shirt that could have swallowed Lithia. He held it up to her shoulders; it came past her knees. "I bought this for my foster mom, and she's on the larger size. I thought you could wear it over your bathing suit. It's long enough to cover your thighs where the bruising is, and looks like a lot of your arms are covered as well. Just swim with it on. In the morning, wear it with shorts to break-fast and Bible study. Dry it to wear the rest of week over the bathing suit."

He was pleased with his idea, and Lithia was smiling. "Now my other thought was for the afternoon; you need something for softball and lunch. I have my baseball uni-form. It covers your legs, and with sleeves to your forearm, it should work. I have two sets, so one for tomorrow and one for Friday. Satisfactory?"

Lithia hugged CJ around the neck, forgetting she was holding the snow cones. He felt the cold ice hit his back. His arms went around her when he jerked forward from the ice, but she didn't pull away. She felt good there, protected, safe.

Tonight would hold no nightmares for Lithia, but CJ tossed and turned with every snore coming out of Harold's mouth.

Chapter 26

2008

$\mathcal{D}$aniel was enjoying college life way too much. School was still easy, and football had gone well. He didn't get drafted by the NFL, but he was one of the best that year. He wasn't into a football career; he wanted money fast and with less risk of getting hurt. He was graduating with his whole life ahead of him.

Dad could bring Daniel into the business and teach him the ropes. He wouldn't need to start at the bottom like his dad had done. He would have a college degree, something his dad never got. That would make Daniel already far above his father's first position.

I hate asking Dad for money. And if I take a job at the company, he'll still control my finances. Harry always has cash, but I don't know where he works. It's not all from his folks either. Then, there's the girls. I see him hand hundreds to them at least once a week. I got to talk to Harry. He's gotta hook a friend up. The next chance he got...

"Harry, my man, I want to talk to you about a job. I wanna do what you do. Tell me your trick to make the money. When my dad gives me that job, I want to walk in with the big bucks. If I can show him I have made a little on my own, maybe he won't be so inclined to put me in the mailroom for my first job. I want a corner office now."

Daniel bought Harry a beer, and they sat down at a booth in the back of the sports bar which was located near the college campus. "You want to do what I do to make money?" Harry took a swig of the cold brew. "Are you sure? You don't even know what I do."

"Yea, I do. The car, the money, the girls, you flash bills all the time, you give the girls hundreds, hook me up." Daniel leaned back in the seat. "What do I need to do? Who do I talk with for the job?"

"Anything? You will do anything to make the money?" Harry leaned in close, motioning Daniel to do the same. "Anything you are asked to do?"

"I said so, didn't I? Spit it out."

"You'll need to meet Killian."

Craig hadn't heard much from Daniel in a few months. They both were getting ready to graduate, Daniel with his AA degree from college and Craig from high school. He knew it was a stressful time for them both. He missed hanging out with his "brother," but it bothered Craig how Daniel had changed. Sure, he used to say negative comments or not like to go to church, but Craig never expected Daniel to go off the deep end as it looked. Maybe they could hang out for a couple of days before Craig went to counsel elementary camp in July, and he was off to college in August.

"Hey, bro, you wanna get a room at the beach for a couple of days to catch up before I become a college nerd and you go into the big world of adulting? Two days shouldn't be too bad, and the beach, pool, boardwalk, just talking would be nice."

"Little brother, how's it hanging? You know that does sound like a plan. Do you think you might want to help me move into my apartment? Dad is renting me a place, but I must get my master's degree. I'll still be doing the college routine; however, I'm going to do some online and only a couple at school. My counselor said if I take classes online, I can finish my BA degree and master's at the same time. Then he wants me to work at the office."

"Wow, that's amazing. God sure is blessing you. Your parents have really been there. I told you they loved you. Okay, so when do you move? This is going to be a two-bed-room apartment or have a sofa bed. I am not sleeping in the same room with you and your snoring."

They hung up, planning to move Daniel in four weeks. *Now this is what it's like to have a brother.* Craig was excited.

Daniel wanted to make the money to buy furniture for his apartment. His mom was going to give him old stuff from their home and buy new for her. He had told her to donate it to charity; he was getting new. He had money from his part-time job to buy what he liked, and he would be meeting Harry's boss tonight. If that went well, he could be doubling or tripling his money.

Harry had been letting Daniel ride with him a couple of nights a week, usually on Friday and Saturday. If he did, Daniel had been earning from $75-$150 a night. That was good money for just chauffeuring a few girls around all night. If the boss liked Daniel, he would have certain chauffeuring duties, and then Harry would have others. He wouldn't have to share money with Harry. He would see Harry with a thou-sand some evenings.

If I can work three weekends before I move, I could possibly make six thousand dollars before Craig comes, and we can get furniture. I'll impress the little brother once again.

Ready to meet the boss, Daniel looked sharp, dressed in suit and tie. Harry told him he looked like a banker, not at all what was expected.

"I dress for the job I want. I want to oversee my own company one day. I dress for success."

"Oh, alrighty then, let's get you a job. Daniel Armstrong, meet Killian Shaefer. I'll get us some drinks." Harry left Daniel with Killian and went to the bar to order two beers for them and a rum and coke for Killian. Killian joined Daniel in the booth.

Killian Shaefer was not what Daniel expected at all. His hair was long and pulled back in a rubber band. He was blond with a dark tan, and was wearing sunglasses pushed up on his head. His pants were black cargo jeans, and he had on a white tank top under an opened short-sleeved dress shirt. There was a gold chain around his neck, a diamond stud in both ears, and he was wearing a Rolex watch. On each hand he wore a gold ring. Daniel was quite overdressed for the meeting.

"Harry tells me you dress for the job you want. I should be worried you want mine by the look of it, mmm?" Killian called a waitress over for a menu.

"No, I don't want your job. I meant one day I want to own a business and be the boss. Not oversee your business." Daniel did not want this guy to misunderstand him. He didn't think it would turn out well if he did.

"Good to know."

Harry comes back with their drinks and sits down by Daniel.

"You two getting along, I see. Killian, Daniel doesn't know the full story of your outfit. I thought that would be for you to tell him. Shall I leave you to it or sit right here?" Harry took a sip of his beer and waited.

"Drink up. But when you're finished, I'll take it from here. Daniel, you got your car, or did you come with Harry? Naw, it doesn't matter, if you need a ride, I got you."

Harry downed the beer, "Later." And walked out. Daniel didn't see much of Harry after that.

Graduation was one of the highlights of Craig's life; that, and salvation. He was so happy that not only his church came out to hear his valedictorian speech and hear his sing at the event. Daniel had come, and the best guest, his mom.

Craig hadn't seen her since the day in the hallway of her apartment building. He had sent her an invitation but never heard back. She seemed proud. He saw her cry and take a few photos. He hoped she would come to the party Nurse Mabel and the church was planning after the ceremony. Maybe someone from there would try to get her to come to church on Sunday. If she would only give her heart to the Lord before he went to Gainesville to college.

"I'm so proud of you, son. You have grown into a wonderfully handsome man. I just can't believe how my little boy is so big now. I bought you a present, well, two presents. One is for graduation. The other..." Saoirse began to choke from the tears. "This is for your birthday I missed."

Craig wrapped his arms around his mother and let her cry. She was so small compared to him. He remembered when she held him as a kid when he was sick or had a nightmare. She held him sometimes when Jim wasn't home.

Everything about his momma wasn't bad. He knew there was a hold on her heart. The hold was not a man, but sin.

Sin bound her with situations, people, shame, hurt, and guilt. She didn't think she was good enough or worthy. Only God could prove she was, if she would just let Him.

"Your momma is still a looker, Craig. If she liked younger men, I would be kicking her door down." Daniel was giving Saoirse a total examination, one that made her blush and made Craig rage.

"Don't you talk about my momma that way! Show some respect for your bro, geesh. What is wrong with you?" Craig punched Daniel in the arm hard enough, he winced.

"Hey, you didn't have to hit me! I get your point. Sorry, Mrs. O'Shay, I wasn't trying to be rude, just, you're hot for a momma. And if you like younger guys…"

Whack!

"OKAY! I get it. What's your problem? Man, Craig, the same spot? I didn't realize baseball jocks can pack a punch."

Daniel rubbed his bicep to get the sting out of Craig's double whammy punch. That was going to leave a bruise. He had really pushed the wrong button with Craig. What's the big deal? Wasn't like he was going be his daddy or anything. He was twenty and Craig's momma was like thirty-five or thirty –six. If it wasn't for Craig, oh, he would be all over that woman.

"Look, congrats, bro. I gotta run; meeting up with my boss in a couple of hours, then I got work. Now I will see you in two weeks. I'll send you the text of my address. Goodbye, Mrs. O'Shay."

Daniel stepped over to Nurse Mabel to speak to her before he left. If he didn't, she would have run after him. He checked his watch and was gone.

He was going to have a busy night ahead of him. Graduation parties were all over the area, and entertainment would be needed. Time to get the girls and see where Killian would need them for the night. He was going to rake in the money this weekend.

Chapter 27

August 2008

"I'm so glad that Ms. Tindall and DCF let you go ahead and stay with me until you left for college. I don't know what I'm going to do when you're gone. I told her I don't want any more foster children. It just about kills me when you leave. Did I ever tell you, I had you and Danny the longest? It's like you're my own flesh and blood."

Nurse Mabel had written several letters to the judge and to the Department of Children and Families, begging them to not take Craig away from her. She understood he was already eighteen, but he would be leaving for college the first week in August, and they needed to remember he had lived with her for almost six years. By the way, he had known her even longer.

"They had better let you stay. After all the children I raised for them, and some weren't well-behaved when I got them either. I'm going to leave your room alone, Craig. I want you to be able to have a place to come home to when it's Christmas and spring break. Now, don't go giving me that look. I won't hear another word. When summer comes, well, we will deal with it then."

Craig knew there wasn't any reason to argue. He would always be welcome at Nurse Mabel's. Summer was a long way off. Maybe he could crash a few days, even at Daniel's. He was already scheduled to work at camp for three weeks, so he wouldn't be around that much then either.

Brother Blake had taken it upon himself to drive Craig up to the university. After a big send-off from Mt. Zion Missionary on Sunday night, they loaded the car early Monday to head to Gator country. Since the music minister had family in the Orlando area, they would be stopping there for lunch.

Craig got to see how musical Brother Blake's family really was, with most playing two or three different instruments each. And sing. Oh, the voices were from heaven. From parents to siblings to nieces, nephews, and cousins, this family knew how to worship the Lord through song.

By the time they reached the dormitory, it was late. Brother Blake helped unload the car and get Craig situated in his dorm room. Craig didn't have a roommate yet, but before the week was over, he should.

Brother Blake gave him a phone number to a music professor who was expecting his call. "I've already got you on the list for voice and piano lessons. He's a great man of God and wonderful musician. The number on the back is to my sister in Orlando. If you ever need something fast, one of my family will get here quicker than anyone in Miami."

"I think I might know some of the teens in your family. Do any of them go to Wekiva youth camp during the summer? If so, I probably know them from there."

"Yep, most of them do. You're right. Good, then you will see them again next summer or sooner. I'm praying for you;

all the church members are. Stay focused on your school-work and Jesus and baseball, don't forget baseball."

They hugged bye. "Brother, could you do one more thing for me? It's not for college, it's down in Miami. Look after my momma for me. I just have this awful premonition something bad is going to happen. Pray for protection around her."

Brother Blake promised he would, and he headed back to Orlando to spend the night at his sister's house. But before he went to sleep, he said a little prayer for Mrs. O'Shay.

It was a good thing he did because Jim had been paroled.

Chapter 28

May 2, 2019

"Look at the time. We are going to need to wait until tomorrow to review the other center. You up to that in the morning, or do you have a million things to do for the charity ball? If you can't, I'll go solo."

Craig wasn't sure if Miss Murphy would even want to go with him, but he hoped she still would. She had been so compassionate with the little boy. One day, Cinderella was going to be a great mother. She seemed to have a lot of patience; she had to, with Daniel for a boss.

"Mr. O'Shay, I do want to go with you tomorrow. I can be ready whenever you say. Jenson was so adorable, wasn't he? I just kept thinking what kind of person would hurt their own kid or let it happen? I had this desire to protect him in whatever way was necessary. Children and woman like these need knights in shining armor. That's what you are to them; you protect them from the evil lurking in their own homes."

"Do you like Chinese takeout?" Craig pulled out his cell and started to Google Chinese restaurants nearby. "It's almost six, and we haven't eaten since before noon. I know I'm hungry. You?"

Lithia was nodding her head as her stomach made a big grumble. "It would seem I am very hungry."

"I've had four missed calls and too many text messages to count. Can we pick up some Chinese and go back to your apartment to eat? I can return the calls and texts while we relax and have some supper. Game?" He didn't want the day to end yet, and they did need to eat.

"Yummy, sounds good. I know a little place a few blocks from the apartment; we could call and pick it up. No problem having it delivered cold with us able to drive right by."

Lithia called in an order of Kung Pau chicken and General Tso's beef, fried rice, wonton soup, and egg rolls. When they were back in her apartment, she changed into yoga pants, a t-shirt, and socks, so her feet wouldn't get cold.

Craig was searching the kitchen for plates and forks when she emerged from her room. She noticed he had taken off his suit jacket, tie, and rolled up his sleeves to his dress shirt. A couple of top buttons were undone, and he had untucked it from his pants. His shoes were off by the front door.

"You seem to be comfortable," Lithia was leaning on the counter, looking into the kitchen. "Hand me the plates and silverware, I can put it on the table." Taking them, she turned her back to Craig, "Did you get a chance to reply to any of the texts while I was gone, or did you just take your liberties with my kitchen cabinets?"

"Funny, haha. I was trying to hurry before the Kung Pau got cold. I hate cold Chinese food, and it's gross if you warm it in the microwave." He made a face like he was spitting out the food. "I wish I was as relaxed as you are." He had just noticed her clothes were different, and those yoga pants, well, they hugged her in all the right places.

"That's the best part of coming back here to eat. I get to take off the heels." Lithia lifted one foot up so he could see and wiggled her toes. "See here, I can do this too." And with that Craig stuck his foot from under the table to wiggle his toes at her.

They started laughing until Craig dropped sauce and chicken all down his shirt. "Great, a stain has been created." He tried wiping it off, but it made it worse. Now he had spread the sauce all over half his shirt.

"Take off your shirt. You're never going to get it off doing that, and it will stain. Come on, I'll put some degreaser on it and let it set. I can wash it while we discuss tomorrow's center visit."

She really wasn't thinking bad thoughts at all. She knew what it could cost to clean if an expensive outfit was the wearer of food. Sometimes if not dealt with, the whole outfit was ruined. It was when she returned to the table, the bare chest in front of her made her heart pound and her thoughts of hunger went a different direction.

Trying to take her mind off his bare chest, Lithia said, "I know why you ruined your shirt." He looked at her puzzled. "You didn't pray for our meal."

"Cinderella, my deepest apologies. Let me amend for my sins." He took her hand and prayed for the food, for Jenson and his mother, and for the woman who sat before him. She rubbed his hand and smiled before she let go.

They ate in silence while Craig replied to the text messages and made a couple of call backs. Lithia left him alone, and when he pushed his plate away, she cleaned up the table, putting the leftovers in the refrigerator. She was washing the last dish when Craig took the dishtowel and started drying the plates in the dish drain.

Did he not know what his bare chest was doing to her? Thank God the washer pinged to tell her the shirt was ready for the dryer.

He was holding a photo when she came back into the living room. *Please don't let him see me in that photo. I don't want him to know the fat girl was me.*

"Hey, you know this looks like the camp I went to when I was a teen. I even was a counselor my first two years of college. I really enjoyed making friends, helping people. Was this a Christian camp because mine was. I learned what God wanted me to do with my life while I was there."

He didn't ask me who anyone was in the photo. I'm so glad. I must have been fourteen in that one.

"Yes, it was a church camp. I went every year from eight years old. I was probably about fourteen that year. I went for two more years, then I quit going when my brother stopped. I took a part-time job and couldn't take time off work. I have fond memories of most years." *But not the year with Harold.*

"I had good memories of camp as well. I wasn't as blessed to go as many years as you did, but I am glad of the experiences I had. My last year attending was the worst year." He could see the camper's face in his mind.

"Why do you say that? Rainy weather and all activities cancelled?" Lithia hated being stuck inside the whole week, but they found other things to do and it turned out great.

"It wasn't really a 'me' thing, one of the campers had a rough week and I felt like I couldn't help. It has always haunted me. I pray everything worked out."

Craig seems to be sincere. He must love people he cares about unconditionally. That's got to be why he loves Daniel.

Either he doesn't know all there is to know, or he loves him, not what his choices have been.

"Are you going to tell me about how Daniel is your foster brother? I have met his parents. When did this 'foster' thing happen?" Lithia sat crisscross applesauce on the rug, looking at Craig, sprawled out on the couch.

Craig wanted to tell her. He didn't give her all the details, but the short form. Single mom with son, she could barely keep a roof over their head and food in his stomach. She worked double shifts at the diner, mostly nights, and he was alone often. There was a boyfriend who wasn't everything he seemed to be, and after beating Craig and his mom more than once, Craig moved into foster care. The boyfriend was to have gone to prison with fifteen years for attempted murder and other charges.

"That's good he went to prison. I am sure he is rotting in there. Serves him right to treat a woman and her child like that." Lithia could see now why Craig was so adamant for the woman's shelter.

He continued. His mom never could get from under all the hospital bills, and returned to the only way she had been taught to make money quickly.

Jenson's story really hits home with Craig then, poor man.

"I was told I would continue to live with Nurse Mabel until I was eighteen. Daniel was living there too because he had been giving his parents a hard time and gotten in trouble with the law. Nurse Mabel took us to church all the time, that's how I met Jesus and gave my heart to the Lord. Daniel, well, he wasn't all into church. He went; she made him. But as soon as he graduated high school and got off probation, he was gone. Daniel found new friends in college, and because he was older than me, we didn't see each other as much. When we did, I didn't want to do the things his friends did."

"Now don't give me that face. Daniel and I are still brothers. But he knows not to do anything Jesus would disapprove around me. He has a conscience, but when he got with this guy in college, the influence was too much. He thinks I'm old fashioned in my beliefs, but he stopped teasing me long ago. Really, he is a great guy. I pray for him daily to find peace through Jesus."

Ping!

"The dryer has stopped. Let me get your shirt." *Hmm, this does give me a different side of Daniel, but Craig doesn't know my story.*

She handed Craig his clean shirt, warm from the dryer. He noticed she was watching him button it up. He smiled; she blushed.

"I didn't know Cinderella did the wash for Prince Charming, I thought it was only for the wicked stepmother." He took her chin in his hand and made her face him. "You know, you're cute when you blush."

He picked up his coat and tie, stuffed the tie in his pocket, and slipped his shoes back on.

"I'll be by at 8:30 with bagels and cream cheese. Have the coffee ready. When we finish at the center, I'm going to have work to do. I can drop you off at the office. You need to get as much as you can done because we are going to see the lions, and tigers, and bears, oh my, in the afternoon."

"You want to go to the zoo?"

"You heard me. They feed them in the late afternoon. I want to see that."

He turned to go as Lithia was laughing at him. Then he stopped and turned around, "Will you be my date to the charity ball Saturday night? I know you are going already, but go with me, as a date, not as my tour guide or as a favor for Daniel. We can pretend it is prom. I'll let you in on a secret, I didn't go to mine. Say you'll be my date? Is that a yes, or a no answer?"

Lithia hadn't gone to the prom, and always wanted a guy to ask her. Here she was, being asked to a ball by Prince Charming. "Of Course, I would be honored to go, my prince."

She curtsied; he bowed. He kissed her cheek and left. They both were on cloud nine.

Chapter 29

July 2010

The clothes CJ had given Lithia worked perfectly. She survived Wednesday night chapel and had used the big t-shirt Thursday morning for breakfast, Bible study, and over her suit at the lake. His baseball uniform was long on her, and the pants were odd, but her body was covered all afternoon. Her roommates questioned her fashion choice, but she told them she had spilled coffee on her some of her clothes and didn't have a choice but to get the counselors to help her out.

Only Leslie, "Seems to me there's only one counselor that's helping you out and his name is on your back."

Lithia didn't even think about that at all, but who cares, she had clothes to wear, and the bruises were covered.

Chapel worked the same as the night before, with CJ picking her up from the mess tent and going over to the chapel for practice before service. He never left her alone if able. She went to the breakfast with her roommates, the lake, even the bathroom, but she never dressed in front of them anymore. Her clothes came off in the bathroom stall only.

CJ didn't walk her all the way to the cabin after chapel Thursday night. He saw Renee and Carrie with the twins already there. One couple on the hammock and the other on the front steps. He told her both doors were covered, and she would be fine. He squeezed her hand and left.

Friday came and Lithia followed the same pattern of dress from Thursday; however, the closer it came for chapel, she got nervous. She had nothing to wear. She had skirts to cover her legs or capris, but the arms were going to be the problem. Even if she could have worn something of the other girls, she was at least two sizes bigger than they were.

When she came to the mess tent for dinner in the base-ball uniform, CJ questioned her.

"Why aren't you dressed for chapel?"

"I don't have a long sleeve shirt to wear. I have some-thing to cover my legs but not my arms. It's not even both arms anymore, just my left. If I had a shirt, that matched a black skirt or tan capris, I'd be okay. None of my roommates wear my size."

CJ looked around the mess tent and spotted the direc-tor's wife. She was an endowed woman. He would just ask her. CJ got up and walked away.

Much to Lithia's amazement, he went to directly over to Sister Lisa. Oh, dear heavens, what is he going to do?

She watched him go out of the mess tent, following Sister Lisa. If he breaks his promise!!!

Lithia kept watching the door he walked out through; he wasn't gone too long. Sister Lisa came back and sat down where she had been eating dinner with her husband and other older counselors. Then CJ peered in. When he caught her eye, he gestured her to meet him outside.

"Over here, Lithia." CJ was standing near the concession stand. He handed her a plastic bag.

"You promised me you wouldn't say anything. I trusted you." She wanted to cry. She felt betrayed.

"Please hold up your head and look me in the eyes. Do you think that all this week and all I have done for you, I would break my promise today? Shake your head no because I didn't. Sister Lisa was told you had a wardrobe malfunction. You didn't have shirts to fit you, and the girls in the cabin didn't wear your size. When she asked me why you didn't come, I told her you were embarrassed. I didn't lie, did I?"

Lithia investigated the bag. She could see a flowered black and white blouse. It would be perfect with the black skirt. Moving the flowered shirt, she found a turquoise and cream billowy top that would work as a match for her tan capris. CJ had just given her clothes to get her through until the dance Saturday evening.

"You are the best friend a girl could have. Why, you're better than a big brother, and I got a good one of those."

She was jumping up and down until CJ stopped her.

"You need to bathe and get out of my baseball jersey. I need both sets of uniforms for tomorrow. I got to wear one for the staff and camper game. Go on, get yourself ready. I will be back to your cabin in forty-five minutes. You can be ready by then?"

She was nodding her head. *Forty-five minutes, I will be ready.*

And she was.

Things had gone a little differently the last couple of days for Harold. When Lithia had stayed in her cabin, he had been worried, but after she showed up to chapel with CJ, Harold started sweating.

He was sure they had been alone at the hammock, and he didn't think anyone had seen him walk away. Sean couldn't have known because any brother would have come after him; Sean treated him the same. No one was in the cabin on Wednesday when he had hidden behind the desk, waiting for her to come back from the shower. Did she tell anyone? He couldn't read her like most girls.

She's too scared. Virgin girl doesn't want anyone to know she liked it. I know I would have enjoyed every minute of those soft curves. The spitfire is Leslie. Cute and sassy. She has been eating out of my hand every night. I have been wheeling and dealing that one. Tonight, I will have it all. By the time I'm through, she will be begging me for it.

CJ...why does he keep glaring at me?

"Isn't that a cute outfit, Carrie? Lithia, I don't know where you are getting your wardrobe perks, but these misfit clothes are fashion worthy." Renee was honest and blunt, so Lithia knew she was sincere.

Lithia even felt prettier, though when she remembered Harold, she wanted to take a shower and scrub his hands off her again. But she could always count on Leslie for a negative statement.

"Personally, I would never wear just anyone's clothes. I would have gotten my boyfriend, or you could have had Sean take you, well, I would have gotten my boyfriend Harold to drive me to the nearest mall and buy more. And how could you wear CJ's baseball pants? They had grass and clay stains; were they clean when he gave them to you?"

Leslie had annoyed CJ one time too many this week. "They were clean, Leslie. Grass and clay stains are very difficult to remove. I had no problem with Lithia borrowing my uniforms, or my shirts. I'm glad I could help her out. Oh, and by the way, you are not allowed off the campgrounds with a counselor unless it is a family member. You're not related to Harold Gibson, are you?"

"I will be one day. He loves me, you know. He is going to wait for me until I graduate high school, and then we will be married. CJ, you are invited, if you wanna come. Renee, Carrie, and Lithia will be my bridesmaids. I have it all planned out."

CJ was not too thrilled to hear this piece of news. "Leslie, please be careful. Your heart is a precious thing. Don't give it to anyone. You are worthy of a man that loves you as Christ loved the Church. Someone who will protect you and treat you like a queen. Don't settle for any Tom, Dick, or Harry."

"Somebody call me?"

Harold stepped into the cabin, but CJ blocked him for walking in further.

"Nope. Your name never came up. Lithia, if you're ready, we need to get to the chapel. I promised the director we would sing 'I can only Imagine.' Renee, Carrie, the twins are here. See you guys shortly."

Turning toward Lithia, "Let's just walk out the back door. There's already a crowd by the front."

Harold popped down on Leslie's bed. "What's his problem? He upset 'cause he got the fat girl and not a hot girl like I do? Yep, you are looking good tonight, baby."

He laid on down on the bed. "Comfy, and I'm sure there's room for two. Want to see?"

Harold reached out to Leslie and pulled her on to the bed with him.

"Oh, let me up. You are being so silly. This is a twin bed. One person. We can get married and have a king size bed for us to have plenty of room to be happy." She winked at him.

He reluctantly followed them to the chapel.

Leslie decided she needed to sing in service with Lithia and CJ. It was really a ploy to stay near Harold. She pulled a chair over by the drums and sat by him through the entire service. Lithia was fine with it. Leslie made sure he was never alone, so less possibilities he would try to corner her.

At some point during the altar service, Lithia noticed Harold and Leslie weren't on the stage. There were too many down at the altar to be able to see if they were praying, plus Lithia was preparing to sing another song with CJ.

The director came and asked CJ if he knew where Harold had gone, CJ said he hadn't seen him walk down. Maybe in the crowd at the altar *(he sure needed it)*, or could have went to the bathroom. Lithia told him she hadn't seen him leave either, but Leslie was missing too.

Red flags were flying in CJ's mind. Was Leslie going to be the next Harold victim? He hoped not, but this didn't look good. It didn't feel right in his spirit. What could he do? If he said anything, he would be questioned on why he would think Harold was dangerous. Then he would have to explain what he saw and with whom Harold had victimized.

I won't break my promise, Lithia. Secret forever.

When chapel was completed, all of them went to the concession stand for ice cream. Anthony and Allan chose butter pecan, Renee liked rocky road, Carrie, Sunflower, and Sean had chocolate chip, everyone else did plain old vanilla. But Lithia and CJ-strawberry shortcake.

No one thought about Leslie and Harold. They hadn't been hanging out with the crowd the past couple of nights after chapel anyway. They had gone off on their own, even though they had been warned by the directors.

The intercom said time for the campers to go to their cabins, the guys left the girls at Cabin Kindness and Cabin Rebekah, then raced back to their own cabin before final curfew check.

When 11 o'clock came, Leslie and Harold hadn't showed up. By midnight, the director checked again, this time he looked in the parking area. Harold's car was gone.

It was four in the morning when the girls woke up to find Leslie in bed crying. They could see she was shaken up.

Leslie told them Harold had wanted to show her the falls in the moonlight over by the bridge. They had driven his car and parked on the overpass. It was beautiful and romantic.

He told her he loved her, and if she loved him, prove it. They were going to get married anyway, they might as well be sure they were compatible. There in the moonlight, they became one like a man and woman should be.

Lithia wanted to throw up. *How could this have happened? Leslie let him. She was a willing participate. Oh, God, I should have told someone what kind of man he is. It's my fault.* Guilt for being silent ate at her insides, at her heart.

"I fell asleep exhausted from our loving. Time just got away with us. We wanted to hold each other, never to let go. Then some police officer tapped at the window. Seems somebody told the camp director I was a missing sixteen-year old and out with a 22-year-old. They almost arrested Harold. Then he mentioned his grandfather, and they let us go. I don't know where they took Harold when we pulled up at camp, but Sister Lisa escorted me here and told me we would have a serious talk in the morning. I can't even ride back with you guys tomorrow night. My parents have to come get me."

Chapter 29

"What were you thinking, Leslie? You are only sixteen. Harold is six years older than you. That's rape." Renee was so upset. She couldn't believe what was coming out of Leslie's mouth.

This was going to be a long night.

Chapter 30

May 3, 2019

et's see what I can wear this morning, hmmm. Thinking I might have been overdressed for the center yesterday, business informal could be appropriate for the visit. I don't want to seem uppity to anyone.

Lithia searched in her clothes rack for an hour, so it felt. Having to represent the company, Mr. O'Shay, go back to the office, please Daniel, tough order. She pulled a hanger holding a tan dress.

Boring! I will be as dreary as the building. Colors make me feel happy, and I want to make one of the ladies or a child happy to be alive. White walls mean hospital, sterile, sickness, and pain. I should wear something fun!

It was like she had an epiphany. She was ravaging through boxes, garment bags, and dresser drawers to find the exact look she was imagining. In the back of her closet, hanging between two garment bags, she found the ultimate dress.

Yellow, it's yellow like his roses.

Lithia didn't wear this dress because yellow wasn't the best color for her pale skin, but she had forgotten it wasn't predominately a yellow dress. Turquoise was scattered in small quantities on the cream background. If she accented with the turquoise, it would do nicely.

She clicked on the morning news and started the coffee as she finished putting on makeup and did her hair. Craig would be bringing bagels and cream cheese; she could just taste a blueberry one.

"This is WRXU reporting live from..."

Ring, Ring, Ring!

"Good Morning, Mr. Armstrong, and what will you be needing from me today? I'm sorta busy right now."

"Found women ages ranging from fourteen up to thirty-six in an apartment..."

"Lithia, when are you getting into the office? I have a caterer issue for the charity ball, and I have a massage at one. You are going to have to help me out." *Daniel could be so overdramatic.*

"Biggest prostitution sting in over a decade."

"I can cancel your massage appointment right now if that's it. Gives you more time to work on the caterer problem. How's that?" She had a grin on her face; she knew he wanted her to handle it. Daniel would force her to give him the massage and more if she would, but he knew not to go there again.

"One of the men arrested was the grandson of..."

"No, don't you dare! I need my massage. I have so much tension right now. You don't know the pressure I'm under for this contract, then I got a call."

"All evidence proves this began while in college..."

Daniel sounded scared, not worried about business. She'd seen him concerned for a deal, but there was more to the tension in his voice then he was letting on.

"Shaefer was the brains behind the business. Manipulated guys and girls..."

"Daniel, I will be in later this morning. Mr. O'Shay and I were unable to complete our plans from yesterday, and I'm expecting him any minute. He said last night he wanted to be at the office no later than eleven. I will deal with it then."

"Wife of Gibson has been working with police collecting lists..."

"Hey, Lithia, you haven't slept with Craig, have you? Like I told you to do?"

Okay, that was a weird question even for Daniel. He always assumed, or the client told him the horrid details.

"Police from Dade County and Hillsborough are working together to find all others linked to the prostitution ring. Former prostitutes will not be charged for crimes in lieu of testimony and information in the arrest and prosecution of the men and women exploiting the sale of others."

"OH, GOD, Lithia, answer me! I take it back; if you haven't, don't. I promised you almost two years ago I would never make you again."

"Yes, Daniel, you did promise, but you broke that this week. Be glad you have a friend who hasn't been nothing but a true gentleman, even when he has had the opportunity to have what you told me to offer."

"Shots fired! Shots fired! Someone's hit! I can't see exactly what just happened; the police have me behind some barricade, but I can see the huddle of officers. Paramedics are leaving some of the women to rush to the wounded. Officer, can you tell me who was hit?"

"Daniel. do you have on the television? We must be on the same channel. It's echoing through the phone line. Look, he is going to be here, and I have got to finish my makeup. Calm down, Daniel. It has been over two years since you sold me to a 'john.' I will pretend this week's demands were never said. But you know the deal, I walk, and I will give all my information to 'Dad and Mom' if you refuse."

"I signed the contract you made. I never want to do that to anyone again. I was so wrong."

"Confirmed two dead and one injured. Officer Smith is on the way to the Tampa Medical Center with a gunshot to the thigh when Shaefer grabbed for Smith's holstered pistol. There was a struggle with Smith and Shaefer to retain the weapon when the 357 went off into the crowd. A stray bullet hit handcuffed Gibson in the chest; it was fatal. Lieutenant Dorn was given the opening, he disarmed Shaefer with a final shot.

The line went dead, and Lithia's doorbell rang. Turning off the news, which hadn't given her the weather for the day yet, she opened the door to yellow roses and bagels.

Craig's breath was taken away. She was as gorgeous as ever. The sundress with yellow and turquoise daisies was stunning on her. Cinderella looked like a meadow full of scattered flowers. She wore her hair down with a white hairband, and tiny daisy earrings sat on her lobes. He saw she was wearing a cross necklace. Miss Murphy hadn't put on her shoes yet, but he assumed the white pumps and turquoise crop jacket laying across the back of the sofa was the finishing touches. Slipping on the shoes would be all she needed to do.

"Good morning, sunshine! My, you look beautiful today. I love how cheerful you are. Don't get me wrong, you have looked amazing every day, but this, this look...my favorite. You look like a girl I once knew; she had this dress or something with little daisies all over. You are going to brighten up the center when you enter."

Digging in the bagel bag, "OOO, you got blueberry ones, my favorite. Shall I put cream cheese on yours, Mr. O'Shay?"

"There are only blueberry bagels, and yes, you may. I'll pour the coffee; where are the mugs?"

I'm going to miss him when he is gone. I've never had anything like this, and I don't want it to go away, but it is just business, or is it? Sometimes when he looks at me, I know there's more in his eyes. I can't put my finger on it.

They had finished eating and were on mug number two, "We got to get out of here if I'm going to have you at the office by eleven. Daniel texted me to demand I get you there no later than that. Is he worried about tomorrow night?"

"Oh, he called this morning. From what I can remember, the caterers have backed out at the last minute. I'm going to have to find someone to do it, and fast." Lithia was a little concerned over who she could schedule on such short notice.

"I might be able to help with that. I have an idea. I'll send some text messages, and we could have that settled before you even get to the office. Let me help with your glass slippers, and we're out of here."

With her hands on his shoulders for balance, he slid her feet into her white pumps, then held her jacket as she put her arms in.

"Do you mind if I take the roses you brought this morning to the center? They might bring cheer to more people that way." She was afraid he would think she was ungrateful for the gift, but he picked up the bouquet as he held the front door.

"That's a good idea; I'll even order a bouquet for Mrs. Eva. She can have it on her desk to brighten up that center, too."

Once again, Lithia thought the women's center was too sterile. No art on the walls in the lobby, just some posters with resource information for the clients. The only difference here: the chairs matched. All of them were mud-stained brown. Depressing. At least yesterday, the woman at the front counter was lively, but this one looked like she had been crying and no makeup. The clothes she was wearing, grey pants and shirt, made it seem even more of a gloomy place.

While Craig and the grey woman went over files, Lithia found a kitchen. Checking all the cabinets, she came across a vase, poured water, and arranged the roses for the front counter.

A woman around Lithia's age walked into the kitchen as Lithia was walking out. She was pregnant, ready to explode. She waddled to the refrigerator for a bottled water.

"Hello, I'm Lithia Murphy. Do you work here at the center?"

When the pregnant girl turned around, Lithia could see that was not the case. Her face was bruised, and she had stitches over her eye.

"No, I'm here to be safe for my baby." She was tearing up but smiling as she caressed her swollen belly.

"How much longer?" Lithia wasn't sure what else to say. Most people she had been around pregnant in the last few years, well, they didn't stay pregnant long.

"My daughter will be here at any time. The doctors were concerned after my boyfriend did this, but it all looks okay on the sonogram." She touched her face carefully.

"A girl. Have you picked out a name yet? My grandmother said a child's name means something. You want them to have a name that is strong, and it will help define them. For instance, my name means "flower." I don't know, but when I was a toddler, they said I brightened the day like a golden flower. I just always thought that was nice."

Great! Here I go rattling on about some stupid thing my grandmother used to say, while this girl is about to have a baby alone in a woman's center. And then the bruises and cut on her face. I can be so self-centered.

"I hadn't thought of any names. My boyfriend wanted a boy, and to call him Jr., but when he found out it was a girl, he blamed me. He had thought I had an abortion, but when he saw me after several weeks, he did this."

The baby kicked, and instinctively the woman placed her hand on her abdomen. "Do you want to feel her? She's listening to us talk."

Lithia allowed the woman to guide her hand over her huge belly as the baby continued to move underneath. She was in awe of the gift of life this woman was able to carry.

"She's a blessing, a precious gift from heaven. I wish you all the best for you and the new life forming inside." Lithia pulled a rose from the vase and gave it to the girl. "Here, a rose for your precious baby."

Craig was ready to leave when Lithia returned from the kitchen and sat the vase on the counter. She was glad to return to the office, but she would be buying some baby clothes to take back to the center later today.

At the office, Lithia went straight to her desk. She would need to find out what was going on with the caterers, and hopefully, fix the issue. It was going to be impossible to find another caterer with right over twenty-four hours to plan, prepare, and cook for three hundred guests.

Let's see what miracle I can do.

Nothing Lithia could say would change the mind of the head chef at Pierre's Restaurant to recommitting the food for the ball. The clock was ticking, and she had tried four other well-known chefs in town. All she heard was excuses; head on her desk, she sat up to Craig's voice.

"It's not the time for sleeping, Cinderella. I need to know the head count for tomorrow evening. The caterer needs the number."

She saw he was in the business mood, and was talking on his cell phone. Instead of speaking, she held up a paper with a list of names; she had circled the number at the bottom.

"Got the total, Chef LeeAnn. It's 289, but I would prepare for 325. Then there will be enough for last minute donations, and all those working at the ball will get a meal as well."

Lithia was sitting with her mouth wide open; he had done it. Saved her from Daniel's wrath again.

"Yeppers, I am sending over the contract with all the details. Let me recap the menu now that I am sitting with Miss Murphy. You will start us with jumbo mushroom caps sautéed in garlic butter, and a house salad with oil and vinegar. There are two entrees to pick: jerk spice-crusted salmon grilled on mixed greens with red pepper jelly glaze and crispy fried onions, or roasted half duckling, marinated in a blackberry brandy sauce. I believe seasonal vegetables and mashed potatoes with a crescent roll will be delicious."

Craig was patting himself on the back and grinning like he was the cat that ate the canary. Until he saw Lithia mouthed, "*What about dessert?*"

"Oops, I wasn't thinking, dessert. What do you recommend?" He would rather the cooks make whatever is their best dish. "Angel food cake with strawberries and whipped crème on top is perfect. I appreciate you coming through for me. I will need to call Leonard and tell him thanks for hooking me up the second time in a week."

"You did it! Was that Captain Fred's LeeAnn? She's a chef? This is nothing short of a miracle."

"Was that everything on your office agenda? If so, I need to rent a tux for tomorrow, and I believe you need a dress. Let's tell Daniel we have a caterer and he can chill out. I haven't seen him so uptight since he went to court as a teenager."

It was almost one, Daniel would be leaving for his spa treatment if they didn't hurry. With Daniel getting the good news, some of the frown lines disappeared. He still would be getting his massage. Martha was left to handle any slack on Lithia's desk; and she and Craig were headed to "She said Yes Bridal and Tux Shop."

Craig was handsome in each tux he tried on, but the one he decided to purchase made Lithia get tremors to the pit of her stomach. She didn't know how her body was going to react to dancing or sitting with him all Saturday evening.

"Yummy!"

"OH, really? I'll take this one, sir. It seems Cinderella likes me in the black and white."

I said yummy out loud. Oh, boy. I have got to be beet red. I feel my face all flushed.

Lithia got up to look at dresses, anything, so Craig could not see her face. But there were so many to pick from, and she didn't know the budget Daniel would expect her to stay in. She knew if it was coming out of her pocket, Macy's at the mall would be her go-to store.

"Mr. O'Shay, did you call the lady, Cinderella? Why not this elegant gown? It would fit her name. If she wore her hair up, with pearls and heels dyed to match the dress, she would fit the part.

Lithia could hear the tailor saying something about Cinderella and dyed shoes. Walking back to the two men, she saw the most dazzling ball gown. It draped off the shoulders and the back, but not too low in the front. The bodice hugged the body to the waist, then flowed down to the floor. It was baby blue with shimmers in the material. If she had white gloves and glass slippers, she would be Cinderella.

"She'll take it. Can you make any alternations by four tomorrow? Here's my credit card."

He had bought her the most expensive and beautiful dress she had ever owned.

Craig dropped her at the apartment, with plans for zoo and pizza later. Well, she had two hours of her time and she was going to use it.

Jumping in her car, she went the mall in search for baby clothes. It wasn't hard to find a store that screamed baby girls. Lithia picked up two pink blankets and a teddy bear that played *Jesus Loves Me*. Three adorable pajamas, one with a duck, one a ballerina, and the other a sunflower. Included in her purchase was a onesie with "Mommy is my hero," and a pack of assorted colored socks. But her favorite was the pale green lace dress. There was a headband to match and socks.

Lithia had the items gifted-wrapped and headed to the woman's center she had been earlier. The grey woman was at the counter and recognized Lithia. "Can I help you?"

"I'm looking for a pregnant lady. I met her when Mr. O'Shay and I came this morning. I wanted to give her some presents for her little girl. Could you tell her I'm here? I don't remember her name, but she was about to bust. Oh, she had bruises on her face and stitches over her eye."

"That would be Linda Woods. She went into labor right after you left. She's at Tampa Medical Center. Baby was born healthy and momma doing fine. I'm sure she would love to see you."

Lithia looked at her watch. *I'm going to see a baby.*

Craig saw Lithia waiting for the car when the driver pulled up. Her arms were loaded with gifts, and she was still wearing the outfit from this morning. He had changed into cargo shorts and a t-shirt. He took the packages and sent her back upstairs to at least change to flats. He didn't want her walking around at the zoo in heels.

She had put on white sandals and pulled her hair up into a ponytail when she got in the car. It didn't even look like she had been wearing those clothes all day.

He was observing her clothes and she knew it. "It's just the zoo. I'm not going to be getting in the cages with the animals. See, I pulled my hair back and switched to sandals. I will take off the jacket when we get there. Happy?"

"Fine. I just don't want to hear anything if a monkey decides he likes you and throws feces."

"Funny, real funny."

"What's with all the presents? Are they for me? I don't think I can wear these socks." He held up a lacey pair of white socks and gave her a quizzical grin.

"I would like to go to the hospital after we leave the zoo. I bought presents for the woman I spoke with at the center today. I had gone back to drop them off, but the lady at the counter said she had gone into labor after we left and already had the baby. I want to see the baby."

"Whatever your heart desires. Driver did you hear that? Miss Murphy would like to go to the hospital when we finish at the zoo."

"Yes, sir, Mr. O'Shay. Then you will need to leave the zoo by seven this evening to get into the hospital before visiting hours are closed."

Craig hadn't been to a zoo in almost a decade. It was interesting to watch the animals interact with people and other animals. He thought about what the Garden of Eden must have been like for Adam and Eve. Talking to God and the animals. Animals had to talk, why else would Eve not think twice when the snake had a conversation with her in the garden?

His favorite was the monkeys, even though the lions were enthralling. They were able to feed the giraffes lettuce and the elephants peanuts. The tigers roared when rare steaks were dropped into the den.

"I like the monkeys best, and you? Which animal is your favorite?"

"The elephant. The elephant never forgets. It marries for life, elephants protect each other, family first, then the rest of the herd. If only people would be the same way."

"I'm not going to let you outdo me. I need baby gifts. Something from the zoo for this precious baby."

Craig's choices were from a different mindset than Lithia's. He picked the biggest stuffed elephant in the gift shop.

"She's gonna be five before she can lift it."

"I don't care. I also want the baby t-shirt with the zoo name on it and the sunhat. Oh, and this little stuffed turtle that rattles."

The presents and elephant filled half the backseat of the car.

I can't wait to see how he plans to carry all this into the hospital. If he did all this for a stranger, imagine what he will do for his own daughter."

Linda was humbled by the gifts she received and handed the itty-bitty girl to Lithia. Her tiny hand curled around Lithia's pinky.

Craig asked Linda if he could pray a blessing over the baby. He put his arm around Lithia and laid his hand on the baby's head. He prayed for the precious baby God had given Linda and asked for her protection; that angels would guide her to the love of Christ.

"That's her name. Precious Rose Woods. Precious- because that's all I could think of yesterday after you said my baby was a precious gift of God. And the rose you gave me. You told me your name meant "flower," and flowers were ways of brightening the world."

"Welcome to the world, Precious Rose." Lithia kissed the soft pink cheek, then Craig kissed Precious's forehead. Lithia placed Precious in her mother's arms, then they left mother and daughter to bond.

Clasping hands just happened. They never released the hold until the apartment.

Craig ordered pizza to be delivered after he kicked off his shoes and got a bottled water from Cinderella's fridge. He found the TV control and clicked it on.

Lithia went to change into shorts and an oversized T. She could hear that Craig turned on the television and the news was on. The bathroom fan muffled the reporter's words, so she didn't hear what had happened. But when she came back into the room, Craig had turned the TV off, and his face was white.

"What's up, your stock market crash?" Lithia laughed.

He didn't think it was funny. It had taken him a second to registered what he had just heard.

"Someone I knew was shot and killed today. I wonder if he had time to make his peace with God."

Knock, Knock! "Pizza Delivery!"

Chapter 31

July 2010

*L*ithia was right. It was a long, long night. No one slept in Cabin Kindness. Sunflower and Erika had stayed with them too.

Leslie didn't let them sleep. It was a night she would never forget.

Well, I would love to forget it. I did not want to know that much about sex from what Leslie and Harold did in the car. TMI, the mental picture is too much!

Saturday, the last day of camp, was always the best. Competitions between cabins, and the big baseball game between the staff and the campers. Many parents came early to pick up their kids and participate in the activities of the day. Anyone who had given their heart to the Lord this week was able to get baptized in the lake after the game. The preaching would be at the lake as well. It was the big banquet and dance that evening everybody wanted to attend. However, this day would be exciting in a whole new way.

First, Harold was not at breakfast; the boys said he never came into the cabin all night. Leslie was summoned in the middle of breakfast to the camp director's office. She didn't return until lunch. She wasn't very chipper after that.

A police car was parked outside the main entrance by lunchtime, and so was a BMW with PTL on the front plate. During the ballgame, a news van pulled up and a reporter began interviewing people, but that didn't last long. Since most campers didn't know about the escapades of Leslie and Harold, they couldn't get any gossip.

Lithia noticed Leslie's parents during the end of baptism at the lake, and when the girls returned to the cabin before the banquet, Leslie was packing her bags. Her aggressive behavior told them; she wasn't happy about leaving before the dance.

"Leslie, calm down or all your clothes will be wrinkled. My parents are going to give us time to pack up after the dance; take your time." Renee tried to refold the mess in Leslie's suitcase, but Leslie wasn't helping.

"I can't stay. Because of last night, my parents have to take me home before the banquet and dance. The best part of the whole week and I have to miss it because of your boyfriend."

Leslie got right in Lithia's face and poked her in the breastbone.

"My boyfriend? I don't have a boyfriend." Lithia was confused. She really didn't understand why anything was her fault when it came to this. She didn't make Leslie go out all night with Harold, and she sure didn't tell her to have sex with him.

But was it my fault it happened? If I had told what happened with me, maybe he would have never been able to get Leslie in the position she's in now?

"Yes, Lithia, your boyfriend, Mr. CJ O'Goody. He was the one that told them we were probably together, and that the car was gone. It was CJ and Sean that was told to pack Harold's stuff and take it to the office. I heard that this morning. Harold was held at the jail until earlier. It took his grandfather to come to town to stop my parents from pressing charges. I don't get why no one understands we love each other."

"Leslie, are you listening to what you are saying? Why don't you see what happened between the two of you was wrong? It was a sin and illegal. Then on top of that, you want to broadcast your actions all over the camp like it's right. People don't need to know what you did; take it to God. However, you're blaming the wrong person for the out-come of your situation." Carrie had her rant, then headed to the showers. She prayed Leslie would be gone before she returned to the cabin to finishing dressing.

Leslie was embarrassed, hurt, and her friends weren't on her side. They told her she was in the wrong.

"You aren't even my friend. I know all about the hammock, Leslie. Always trying to play the innocent girl. Harold told me how you came on to him one night after chapel. Then when he told you he liked me, you kicked him in the privates. When he fell, he got bruises."

"That's not what happened at all, Leslie."

"I'm not listening to you. The whole sad, crazy wardrobe this week was just your way of sulking with the unrequited love. You're pathetic!"

Smack!

Leslie was slapped across the face so hard she lugged forward and hit her mouth on the corner of the desk. He had hit her so hard, the cut on her lip was deep, and blood was pouring rapidly from the three-inch gnash.

Renee and Lithia were so intensely watching Leslie, Harold had slithered in the back door. He had grabbed her arm, spinning her around, slapping her before anyone could move.

"I told you not to say anything about that. You fool! I thought you were a little smarter than this. Telling every-thing we did; how does that help me? Everyone back in your little hick town will be calling you the church slut by tomorrow. And you, Miss Tease, because of Leslie's mouth, you're going to be right there with her. When you grow up, Leslie, call me."

Just like that, Harold was gone out the back, as CJ came in the front.

Renee helped Leslie control the bleeding with a wet towel while walking her to the office to meet her parents.

I was left to explain what CJ had walked in on. CJ wanted to go after Harold, but I wouldn't let him. I didn't want a fight, nor anything to blemish CJ's character.

He had come in, holding some white shawl across his arm, and dropped it on Lithia's bed to go after Harold, when she grabbed his arm.

"When we were going through your clothes on Wednesday, I thought I saw a pastel blue sundress hanging in the closet. Do you think a thin white shawl tied over your shoulders would cover the last of the bruises for the banquet?"

He opened the shawl up for Lithia to examine, wrapped it around her shoulders for effect. He stepped back and gave her two thumbs up.

"I should be a fashion designer for a living."

"CJ, helping damsels in distress is your what you're good at doing."

"Then, m' lady, I will see you at the banquet."

It was odd without Leslie. This is the first time she wasn't with me at the banquet. CJ didn't stay by me all night; why should he? Harold was gone. I didn't need protecting. He did sing a couple of songs, and I was even asked to sing a duet with him later.

CJ asked me to dance after our duet. It was the first time I had ever danced with a guy other than my brother or another family member. It was a slow dance, and I was a princess for the first time in my life. I wished the night would never end.

Sean and Leo told Erika and Sunflower goodbye and had been kissing until I was ready to throw up. I went to wait behind the cabin on the hammock. I wanted to prove I could be there without shaking and freaking out.

CJ came around the corner of the cabin then handed me a yellow rose.

"Yellow roses are for friendship. I'm your friend; Jesus is and should be your best friend. When thoughts of those days come, pray to your best friend. He will hold you in His arms and cradle you better than I did here on the steps. He is always on time. You'll make it with His help. I'll keep your secret forever. I won't break my promise. Remember, you're worthy of so much more than a guy like Harold."

CJ had looked in Lithia's eyes the entire speech. She soaked in all he said. It was the soft kiss on the nose that made her wonder what a kiss on the lips from him would have felt like.

"I'll see you next summer."

But Lithia didn't know, she would never be back.

240

Chapter 32

Sept 2010

*E*ver since his momma had attended his graduation party, she would visit Nurse Mabel's church on occasion. Other times, she would attend with Señora Corona. Her waitressing job wasn't forcing her to work on Sundays as often, and since she has promised her son, she tried to go at least once a month with each lady. Saoirse hadn't given her life to the Lord, but Craig was hopeful for results.

When Saoirse's rent increased, she was afraid of not being able to stay at her apartment. Craig told her to pray about it; maybe she did, Craig never was told. Others were praying for her anyway.

Not long after his mother got notice of rent increase, Señora Corona fell and broke her hip. Nurse Mabel said this was an answer to prayer. Now Señora Corona didn't think so, but it was a solution. The señora contacted Craig, asking if Saoirse had found a new place to live. She thought it would be perfect if his mother moved in with her; instead of rent, do the cleaning, cooking, and other helpful activities that she was unable to do for herself.

During spring break, Craig had helped his mom move into their old apartment building, and even into the old bedroom he had once used many years ago. Craig had faith, the miracle of salvation for his mom, would happen living here. His momma was doing well. She didn't need to go back to that old way of life.

After four months of living with Señora Corona, Craig was convinced God was doing a great work in his mother's life and his.

A lot had occurred at camp that summer; he felt God calling him more and more to outreach ministry. He had met lifelong friends in his roommates, Leo and Sean, and learned what damage a fake Christian man could have on a woman's heart. He felt that he was slowly learning what it must be for his mother. How her heart and mind was crushed, manipulated for love, like Leslie, then how the distrust and fear had grown in Lithia's after Harold's lust had tried to take her over.

But when he returned from camp, Señora Corona had been placed in a nursing home. She had a stroke the day Craig left for camp. Thank God Saoirse had found her in a clump in the bathroom when she returned home from work. The doctors didn't see how Saoirse would be able to take care of Señora Corona and still work. There would need to be round-the-clock care.

God was still taking care and protecting Saoirse. The señora was able to communicate with the landlord for Saoirse to continue living at the apartment until she came home, or the lease could be switched into Mrs. O'Shay's name. Craig was even told to take the old keyboard of Señora Corona back to college with him so he could practice in the dorms.

It had barely been six weeks since camp, and so much had changed.

Craig had returned for his third year of college, and life was looking up. His roommates from camp, Sean and Leo, had started at UF, and were in his dorm. Leo and Craig were together often with music classes, plus both boys had joined the Gospel choir. Craig was vice president of the Jesus Rocks Christian club on campus, and the other boys had joined too.

"For He makes His sun rise on evil and good, and He sends rain on righteous ... He lets rain fall on them whether they are just or unjust..." Matthew 5:45.

And the rain fell.

Señora Corona passed in her sleep on September 21. Craig was able to get permission from his professors to travel home for the funeral services. Leo drove him down in his truck.

It was a solemn weekend, with visits from Nurse Mabel and The Rev, along with others at Mt. Zion Missionary Holiness Church of Our God. Señora's church, Mother Mary's Catholic Church was standing room only, with so many in attendance to celebrate her life. Almost every tenant at the apartment complex had come.

The repast at the apartment wasn't any better. There was enough food from the Mt. Zion ladies to open a restaurant. People were having to fix a plate and sit in any place they could find. There were guests sitting on the stairwell with plates on their laps. The woman was loved.

As the day ended, an older gentleman in a suit handed Craig a large envelope and a business card. The card read: Gabriel Luis Valencia, Attorney at Law. His number and address were below his name.

"Mr. O'Shay, please read the documents enclosed at your earliest convenience. If you have any questions, call my office and I will explain. I was Señora Corona's lawyer for many years. She thought of you as her grandson and loved you more. Accept my condolences." Mr. Valencia shook Craig's hand, nodded his head to Saoirse, and departed.

The apartment was empty except Momma, Nurse Mabel , Leo and me. I had cried until there were no more tears to fall. I opened the envelope, spreading the contents on the coffee table.

"She left me with $25,000. Momma, how? Where did she get all that money? This is a bank statement with my name on it. Craig J. O'Shay Trust Fund."

I was flabbergasted. Never would I believe this was true if I hadn't seen it myself. It was real. The papers attached stated when I turned twenty-five years old, I would have access to the entire amount, plus interest occurred. She had been placing money into the account for fifteen years. Since she met me when I was five and had moved into the building. There was a letter in her handwriting, dated from the day I graduated high school, where she told me to use the money for what God had called me to do for Him.

Handing the papers to my momma and Nurse Mabel, I could only say a prayer of thanks to God for all He had done in my life.

"Oh, Lord, you have saved me more than once. Let me use this to save others one day."

"The Lord is good, and His mercy endures to all generations! I just feel a Holy Ghost praise coming on this old body." Nurse Mabel got up and did a little jig.

"Honey, there's more in the envelope; son, look." Saoirse took out a folded paper. She read the heading on top. It listed the apartment complex and address. But the letter was addressed to her.

"She left the apartment lease in my name. I can't believe she cared about me. I mean, I get it, she loved you, but me?"

"Don't you get it, Mrs. O'Shay? God is showing you how much He forgives and loves you. He wants to give you a home and safety. This is God blessing you through Señora Corona. God wants you to lean on Him. Because when you do, He will bring you through any fire the devil throws at you." Nurse Mabel hugged her long and hard. She kissed Craig on the cheek, gave Leo a hug, and left.

Leo and Craig left the following morning for Gainesville, not knowing Jim was knocking on Saoirse's apartment that night.

Meanwhile in Hopewell...

Lithia had returned home from camp with a heart full of guilt and shame. She couldn't get the hammock event out of her mind. Nightmares were fluent, along with stomachaches. She slept in her clothes some nights, afraid to be in just a small gown or PJs. The only time she changed clothes was behind locked bathroom doors. Her bedroom door and windows were checked and locked each night before bed. Closet doors were left open, and she poked under her bed with a broom handle often to see if anyone was hiding beneath.

Lola saw the change in Lithia's appetite. She ate all the time. Snacks were her friend. Pounds were adding up, and clothes were getting smaller. Lithia stayed in her room when it wasn't school or church. When Lola would say anything about her eating habits, Peter would tell Lola to lay off.

Without Sean at home, Lithia had her mom's full interest. It just stressed Lithia even more.

"Hey Mother Murphy, how are you and Pops doing? We heard rumors you could be a great grandmother in a year."

Lola loved to get the gossip.

"I know they are trying. Course, I just think they're making an excuse for having fun more often. I know we'd say that every time my parents wanted us to come for a visit. Daddy would say he didn't want to hear none of that in his guest room. Little did he know that's exactly where I conceived Peter. Well, Daddy's in heaven, guess he knows now."

"Not what I wanted to know Mother Murphy. I did want to talk to you about Lithia. You two are very close, and I think something is bothering her. She's been different since she came back from camp. I thought, well, maybe this weekend she could stay with you. She doesn't confide in me, but has always seemed to find your ears more inviting then mine."

"Don't say another word, Lola. You know right well; I want her to come visit. Sure, we see you guys at church, but it's not the same. Tell her I will pick her up after school on Friday, and if you want, I'll just take her to school Monday morning. I'll try to get to the bottom of all this mess."

They hung up, and Grandmother prayed.

Lord, I knew something in my spirit was going on with my grandbaby. The time she was at camp, I could only pray for protection. I didn't know why, but your Spirit gives discernment. I felt evil around her some nights, and others, safety. Let me know what to say and do while she's here.

Friday afternoon came, and Lithia was happy to be going to her grandmother's. It was always a place she felt safe from worry or despair. She didn't have to be concerned with nightmares or unlocked doors. Grandmother's house was the closest thing to heaven.

"Honey, I want to talk to you about camp." Grandmother had sat down on the bed next to Lithia. She knew it was going to be one of those heart to heart talks. Grandmother's eyes and tone of voice gave it away.

"The Lord, He talks to me just like I am talking to you now. He told me something bad happened at camp. Now you don't have to tell your ole' grandmother, but if you need to talk to me, I'm ready to listen. No judgment, no chastisement. And through the grapevine of a few 'church sisters,' I'm hearing some other things that disappoint me."

Did God tell my grandmother I was almost raped by Harold? Or that he touched me? God did that kind of thing in the Bible, telling prophets and disciples what people did in secret. I can't have anyone know this.

So, she lied to her grandmother for the first time Friday night.

On Saturday, Granddaddy seemed to ask questions too. And when he prayed for the meal at dinner, he asked God to let things that happened in secret to be brought to light. Then by Sunday morning, Lithia felt like everyone was staring at her in church. Pastor Johnson and First Lady. Her Sunday School teacher.

Why are people looking at me like I'm the slut from camp? I didn't try to do anything with Harold. Leslie is walking around like gold. She admitted to sleeping with Harold, bragged about it over and over. Has even told people at school, but I'm the one people are shunning.

Lithia sat in the back row. She didn't want anyone to look at her. It was like Harold examining her body and laughing. Her heart became heavier as she was reminded of that night.

Sunday night, Lithia was asked to sing a solo, but before she was able to answer, Leslie's mom piped in, "Oh, no, not her, Leslie can do it."

It was the look on the woman's face that made Lithia cringe. *She's been told something by Leslie. What lie has been weaved?*

Lithia's grandmother came into her room that night and sat on the bed. This time she brought her Bible.

"Lithia, I overheard some talk tonight. I want to know the truth. The Lord keeps bringing me back to a story in the Bible in John about a woman that was brought to Jesus. You know the story; they had caught her in adultery."

Grandmother is pausing; to make a point or to see if I'm going to say anything.

"Now I have always had a problem with this story. Why would they bring the woman and not the man? It takes two to tango. By the law, there had to be two or more men that had to witness the act. I'm rambling, but you get my annoyance. So, she's at the feet of Jesus expecting to be stoned. Instead, He writes in the sand. There's never been an account of what He wrote, it's what He said. 'He who hasn't sin, cast the first stone.' You remember the story, don't you?"

Yes, Grandmother, see I'm nodding my head, but why are you doing this to me? Would she just go away?

"We should all be like Jesus and forgive people who have said things about us, true or not. I don't want to hear that you have hard feelings toward someone. Don't let a lie, an unkind word, don't let anything keep you from a relationship with God. Jesus forgave her. He forgives if you just ask Him. What is it that you feel can't be forgiven?"

She knew. I told her everything. From Harold in the hammock, and later his hiding in my room. My ripped clothes

248

and panties and bruises. About Leslie and Harold leaving the campgrounds. How Leslie got the huge cut on her face. I also told her about the young man with auburn hair and soul-calming eyes; his voice singing to me; his arms carrying me, and the yellow rose.

"CJ, huh? Sounds like God put him in your path for a reason. I like a God-fearing man, and he plays the piano and sings. If I ever meet him one day, I want to tell him thank you for being a rock for you to lean on."

Monday at school, Renee and Carrie came running up to me all out of breath. "Did you hear what happened last night? I can't believe she did it."

"He came here to get her. Packed her bags and everything."

"Did the police or her parents call you? We both got calls."

"What are you talking about, and I was at my grandparents' house all weekend except when you saw me at church. So, stop talking at once and tell me, slowly. One at a time."

"Leslie came up missing last night. Her mom called my house to see if she had come over. It was like 11 pm." Carrie looked over at Renee.

"I got the same call too, right after. No one knew where she was. I told them to call your house. I'm sure they did; your folks probably told them you were at your grandmother's."

"Okay, so what? Leslie has gone AWOL before."

"No, Lithia, this is different. Way different. Harold picked her up."

Both Carrie and Renee looked at me like the end of the world was coming. Harold had come to Hopewell. For Leslie.

"All right call the police. Harold is still twenty-two and Leslie is sixteen. Kidnapping. Whatever it's called. They pick them up, and Harold goes to jail this time."

"Renee, you tell her. I'm still not believing this whole mess. It gets me so angry."

"Well, Renee, get on with it. I would like to finish my lunch."

"By the time Leslie's parents contacted the police, Harold and Leslie had over a four-hour head start. Her parents received a phone call around six this morning from the police. They had been found in Jacksonville."

"Fine, she's okay and should be home by supper." *She didn't want to hear any more about Harold and Leslie.*

"No, the police couldn't bring her back." Renee whispered. "They had a marriage certificate and a letter from a doctor. Leslie is pregnant."

Chapter 33

September 2011

I didn't go to camp this past July; didn't feel the same. No Sean, no Leslie, even Renee and Carrie didn't go. We had all gotten summer jobs to earn money. I wanted to get a car. My plan was to go away for college. I was not going to be a Gator like my brother; I wanted to be a Hurricane. I told my parents I always felt like I was walking in my brother's shadow, and I wanted to be my own person. Learn to be independent.

"I think you are making a big mistake, but hopefully, you will change your mind before next summer. If we're lucky, they won't accept you. Tampa is closer anyway, and you won't be at the same campus as your brother." Lola was doing her best to persuade Lithia not to go far from home.

There had been some talk at school and church after the upset with Leslie, Harold, and the pregnancy, but most people were trying to keep it quiet so her parents wouldn't be upset. Leslie had showed up to Sunday service months ago, bursting at the seams. She didn't really talk to Lithia, but she showed off the big diamond wedding ring, bragging how

Harold's parents got them an apartment and were helping set up the nursery. His parents and grandfather would foot the bills as long as Harold would go back to college and finish his college degree. Leslie's parents had made her get a GED a couple of months ago because she wouldn't have time after the baby came. The whole thing was one big cover-up. Precious Grandpa didn't want his television ministry to fail. Anything to make it look like a youth camp love story.

Well, it was nothing like the romance of Pastor Johnson and his wife. I can't believe people at the church are seriously taking this hogwash. The grandpa isn't any better than Harold.

Lithia had just walked in the door from working the morning shift at Panera's to find an irate mother.

"Do you want to explain to me what happened at camp with Harold? I got a call today from Leslie's mother. She claimed you slept with her son-in-law."

"No way! I never slept with Harold. I haven't slept with anyone."

"What about this redhead guy from camp? I heard he was around a lot too."

"Mother, where are you getting this information? I did not do anything with a boy last summer."

"Oh, you're right. You did nothing with boys...they were grown men! SLUT!! Acting all pure and innocent with all this talk going on about Leslie getting pregnant, at least she married him. You just jump around like a whore!"

"Momma, it's not true! I'm a virgin."

I can't tell her anything. She will not listen. Even if I told her the whole story, she already has in her head I did something wrong. God, what if she finds out CJ's name. She's going to think he is a terrible person.

"Harold is a disgusting guy that preys on young girls. He made passes at almost every girl at camp. Ask Renee, or Sunflower, even Violet, no one was safe from his remarks. And the redhead, he was the sweetest, kindest, gentlest guy ever. He is a good Christian guy. If it wasn't for him...just believe me, Harold was the bad one."

"You are a liar!" *WHAM!*

Lola's hand slapped Lithia's face as hard as possible. You could see the handprint across her cheek.

"You will go to school, church, and your job. Nothing else. I hope you can get your grades up and win a scholarship. My money won't pay for college. I'm glad you want to go somewhere away from us and your brother. I don't want anyone to know what kind of daughter you turned out to be. Graduate. Then get out. You won't live here afterward. You best pray your father never gets wind of this."

Then the phone rang. Grandmother was dead.

Granddaddy and Grandmother had driven up to North Florida to see their first great grandbaby. My cousin and her husband had been trying for over a year to get pregnant, so when they announced the big news in March, the entire family had been counting down to delivery. There was Facebook and parties and gender reveal videos. The whole world would know the Murphys were going to be great grandparents.

Susan had delivered a bouncing baby boy, Elijah Murphy Edwards, the last week in August. The plan was to dedicate the baby to the Lord on Grandparent's Day on Sunday. The G-grands had arrived on Saturday, spent an entire week with the exhausted new parents, spoiling Elijah so he didn't want to sleep in his cradle, and left right after lunch to return home. They had church duties that couldn't be passed off to another two weeks in a row.

It seemed a drunk driver had lost control of his vehicle on the Interstate 95, hitting Granddaddy from behind. Grandmother hated wearing a seatbelt, and had flown out of the car. The paramedic found her dead in Granddaddy's arms. They had no idea how he even got out of the car and made it to her with all the damage he had to his own body.

"We didn't even want to bother him. He was just holding her in his arms, singing to her when we arrived. It was the most tender moment as he kissed her lips and told her he loved her. When we took her out of his arms, it was then he fainted."

The television reporter was crying as she listened to the EMT tell the story. The reporter was live at the wreckage.

Lithia's safe place was gone. Grandmother had known her secret and kept it. But now, her mother knew something, but not the truth. She couldn't go to Grandmother and get her to confirm the whole story to Lola. How could she make her mother understand?

I can't even tell my dad. What do you say when he is grieving over his mother's death? Granddaddy isn't even out trouble yet. There's so much wrong. Internal injuries, broken bones, He already had a bad heart. I must pray my mother will change her mind. That she will see I am being truthful.

Three months later, Granddaddy died.

Chapter 34

May 2012

Craig had turned twenty-two only two weeks before his college graduation. He hadn't been able to come home since Christmas, so he didn't know exactly what to expect when he called to see if his mom was coming up with Nurse Mabel for his ceremony. His mom hadn't been returning his calls lately, and Nurse Mabel had told him Saoirse hadn't been to church for over a year.

Any phone conversations were blunt. It always sounded like someone else was in the background, or she was trying to get off the phone. Craig even called a couple of times at her job; she was never there. He had to get tickets for graduation; he was desperate.

"Hello, I'm Craig O'Shay. Saoirse O'Shay is my mother. I was trying to reach her. I'm sorry to call her at work, but it is important."

"Did you say your name was O'Shay? There's no one working here with that last name. I recall a woman with the last name, but she was fired last year after her boyfriend pulled a fast one. I think it was October or something. She was a nice looking 40ish lady."

"No, you must have her mistaken for someone else. She doesn't have a boyfriend. Momma has reddish-brown medium length hair. She's not very tall, just a little over five foot. She does have a scar on her forehead and one on her arm."

"Nope, I got the right lady. She was very nice and bright. Hard worker when she first began working here, but her boyfriend, he was nuts. Came in one day and snatched her up. Said she owed him money, and she didn't need to waste her time here making minimum wage. When a couple of the guys tried to step in, he pulled a gun. Boss told her to get her things and leave. He didn't want trouble."

"Thanks for your help. Could you tell me one more thing? What did the boyfriend look like?"

Craig was speechless and dropped his cell phone.

Dear Jesus! He described Jim.

Saoirse didn't come to Craig's graduation, but Nurse Mabel and some of the others from Mt. Zion made the drive. Even Daniel took time off his busy schedule to fly up for a day. Craig told everyone at their dinner celebration he was going to go home for a couple of weeks, but would be coming back in the middle of June for a mission's trip with his Christian club. They would be gone until the first week in August. He had also decided to get his master's degree, following in his friend Daniel's footsteps, to increase his employment opportunities.

"Your room is available, son. We can't wait for you to be home and worship in song this Sunday. I know Brother Blake could use some good music for a change."

256

"You're so right, Sister Mabel. Anything is better than the soloist last Sunday."

He was laughing, even after she hit him.

"What did you hit him for, Nurse Mabel?" Craig did not see it coming.

"Because I was the soloist last Sunday."

Three days later, Craig pulled into his mother's apartment parking lot. He hadn't reached her on the phone, but did leave her several messages. The last one was short.

"I'll be in town in a couple of days. I want to talk to you. I know you don't have your job and it's been months. I also know Jim is back in your life. I love you, but what were you thinking?"

Craig had purchased a dozen yellow long-stemmed roses, and as he got off the elevator, he thought of the last time he brought her flowers. He prayed he was wrong, but everything in him cried evil with each step to Señora Corona's old apartment.

Lord, please let me be wrong in this. Let me find Momma well and happy. I really don't know how I will react if Jim is here. Jesus, keep me calm.

The television was playing inside the apartment and by the sound coming from inside, there was more than his momma behind that door. He had come straight to his momma's before taking his suitcase to Nurse Mabel. Earlier, he had called to say he would be there for dinner after visiting with his mother.

Drawing the courage, Craig knocked on the door. He had to knock a couple of times before anyone even heard him.

The door was opened by a blonde woman in her mid-twenties. She was cute, but barely clothed. Another girl was sitting on the sofa with only her bra and panties, watching a soap opera.

"Can I help you, handsome?" The blonde put her hand on Craig's chest and pulled at his tie. "Or maybe you can help me?" She licked her lips and moved in close.

He stepped back, putting the bouquet of roses between them.

"I'm here to see my mother, Mrs. O'Shay. She should be expecting me."

"Oh, here I thought you might want someone your own age. Have a seat, honey, she's working right now. When she's through, she'll come out and get you. Nice touch bringing flowers. Hey, Jimbo, get a load out of this one."

The door opened to the bedroom, and out walked two men and another woman. Craig didn't recognize the one man or the woman, but he knew Jim.

"What the …? What are you doing in my apartment? You got some nerve showing up here. No one wants you, haven't you figured that out yet?"

"I wouldn't mind have a chance at this one." The blonde started rubbing her body up and down Craig's back.

"Look, Jim, I'm not here to talk to you, I'm here to speak with my mother. Where is she?"

"Saoirse is busy working right now. She can't be bothered with you. Now if you want to see your mom, I can hold you a spot for an hour or two. It will cost you the normal price." Jim laughed, as did the other guy. The man handed a couple of bills to Jim and left the apartment.

"She's in the other bedroom, isn't she? I'm not waiting for an invitation. I'm seeing my mother."

"I wouldn't go in there if I was you. It might not be the best mother/son reunion if you go through that door. You get she's not alone, kid? Most kids don't want to think of their mommas doing what is going on behind that door. But hey, you're grown. You can handle it."

As Craig moves to open the door, Jim pulls a gun. "Boy, you better stop right there. If you interrupt your mother making me money, I swear, I'll shoot you right now."

The blonde and the other girl jumped, screaming, while running into the empty bedroom and locking the door. The screams brought the door to Saoirse's room open. A man in boxers came out to see what the commotion was; Craig's mother was sitting naked on the end of the bed.

When Saoirse saw Craig standing there, she grabbed the sheet from the bed and draped it around her. She began to cry as she searched the floor for her clothes.

Boxer man was getting vexed. He had paid for his turn, and now it was interrupted. He didn't see any other girls, and the one he had been with was getting dressed. Then the guy he had paid was pointing a gun in his direction. And who was this boy with suit and tie and a big bouquet of yellow roses?

"Take your clothes off, I'm not through with you yet." The boxer guy ordered Craig's momma around like a slave.

When she told him no, he was finished, he hit her with his fist. She fell backwards onto the floor. Craig started to go after the man, but Jim pulled the trigger. The bullet grazed his shoulder and Craig staggered back.

"You leave your momma alone, I said. She's working. And you, don't go beating her like you did the last time; I had to take her for stitches. I can't get money if she has too many scars. Gosh, she isn't making me what she used to haul in. Whore's getting too old."

Craig didn't know if he wanted to go after Jim, who had a gun and already fired at him. Or did he want to go into the bedroom for the man who had just punched his mother? He couldn't hesitate, for any second, Jim could take a shot again, and he was pretty sure the other man had hit his momma another time.

Craig flew into the bedroom and shut the door behind him.

Bang! Bang!

Jim sent two more bullets in the direction of Craig, but this time, they lodged in the door.

Craig jumped on the guy still wailing on his mother, but didn't expect him to turn and have a weapon. He barely had time to move away from the switchblade when another bullet came flying over his head.

Jim had come into the room. He aimed this time at Saoirse. Craig tried to jump in front of the gun, but the boxer guy sliced him across his back. It wasn't deep, just a nick, but enough to make him drop to his knees.

Two shots and a scream came from the other side of the room where his momma stood. Craig saw blood and his momma fall behind the bed.

"No, Momma!" Craig gave a right hook to the man who had cut him and started to climb over the bed.

"Not this time, little boy. You can't save her or yourself."

Craig didn't care, he was going to his mother.

Bang! Bang!

His was holding his mother as he blacked out.

Nurse Mabel was working for a few more hours, then she would be going home to get dinner, for Craig was coming in this evening. He would expect dinner on the table at six o'clock. She hard sirens pulling up at the emergency entrance.

Sounds like a long night for someone. Now who would be paging me to go to the ER knowing I get off in a couple of hours?

When she walked out of the elevator into the ER, she never thought she would see the chaos. Three gurneys: one headed to emergency surgery, one was covered in blood, and the other carrying a body bag. She heard there were more ambulances on the way.

"You need to go with that patient, Nurse Mabel. He is going to need you the most."

Mabel thought it odd a doctor would tell her something like that, but who was she to argue? She went to get towels to get rid of some of the blood on the man's face. She didn't know what needed to be stapled or stitched.

Oh, no, it's Craig.

"Jesus!"

Nurse Mabel's cry could be heard all throughout the emergency unit. But she didn't care. She became so hysterical they had to physically remove her from the room. The seasoned nurse became useless. Coworkers were trying to calm her down as others were working around her. Calling out to God was all she could do.

A police deputy had sat down beside Nurse Mabel and taken her hand in his. When he handed her Kleenex, she focused on his hands as he began to speak.

"Nurse Mabel, it's me, Officer Pratt. I'm here with you. My partner King and I were the ones who got the call on the shooting. We found them."

"Shooting? My baby was shot. Who? Where?"

"I don't think Craig has anything but a graze from the bullet, but..."

"Did you say, 'found them?' Who was with him?"

"As I came into the apartment, his back was to me. I saw his reflection in the mirror, and the gun in his hand. We weren't given a choice. That's when, I guess, I saw Craig crawling across the bed. Officer King gave a warning cry first, but he didn't even hear us come into the apartment. I had already pulled my gun; it's just how you are trained."

Nurse Mabel could tell Officer Pratt was having a difficult time with his description. She tried to give him encouragement to finish by a smile and nod.

"I aimed my gun and fired. So did King. I've never killed anyone before in all my years in the force. Now one lies dead, and two more lives in the balance. We don't even know which one of us made the fatal shot."

He slumped his head; the demons were toying with his mind replaying the scene.

King came up to his partner, tapping him on the shoulder.

"Body count is two. Haven't gotten any information on the one in surgery, but by the looks on scene, I'm not getting my hopes up. The chief is going to want to talk to us downtown." Addressing Nurse Mabel, "I never thought I would see you again for the same thing. The boy was cradling his momma when we got to her."

It was another hour later before the surgeon came to speak with them.

"I did my best; it's in God's hands now. Mrs. O'Shay has been through a lot, hasn't she? This is going to be a hard battle to fight. She'll need round-the-clock nursing for some time, unless God intervenes. She's not out of the woods yet. Officers, I'd like to speak with her son. I was told he was asking about his mother."

"I'll come with you, Doctor. I'm Officer King; I was one of the men who found her." He paused. "Was it a police bullet you found in her?"

"No, not at all. I understand the one who did this got what he deserved."

Craig wasn't looking the best, but he was awake when the doctor and Officer King entered the room. After giving Craig an update on his mother, he asked about the others who had been at the apartment.

"The two girls were arrested for prostitution, but have written a confession. They both wrote in their statements that your mother was always kind to them; she never wanted them to be involved. Seems your mother wasn't given much of a choice not to participate in Jim's dealings. When she argued, he dealt fiercely, and let his clients do whatever they wanted. Saoirse never let the girls get treated the same. She'd always take the punishment, so Jim left them alone."

"And Jim? The other guy? What about them? The one man was beating my mother."

"Why, Craig, Pratt and I shot them. They're dead."

When Momma came home from the hospital, it wasn't back to the apartment. She would need lots of care. Momma moved in with Nurse Mabel. I could finally not be afraid of the dangers that could happen to Momma. She was in a safe place; she'd learn more about Jesus; and she was alive.

Chapter 35

December 2012

The first semester of college was nerve-racking for Lithia. She had no one from home attending the University of Miami with her. She had never felt all alone in her life. With her grandparents gone and her brother off at the University of Florida, she only called home occasionally. She knew better then to call when only her mother would be home; if Lola answered, Lithia just hung up.

Lithia hadn't found a church to go to as Pastor Johnson suggested. She studied all the time. When Thanksgiving had come, she didn't go home. Sean had called to tell her he had proposed to Erika, and they were getting married after college graduation in June. Erika was going to call her about the details, for Lithia was expected to be a bridesmaid. She was happy for them but didn't know how that was going to work with Lola. At least the wedding wasn't in Hopewell.

When it was close to Christmas break, Lithia sent gifts home through FedEx. Her dad called upset she wasn't coming home. She reminded him her school scholarship was only for a year and she needed to get a part-time job to earn money toward next fall.

"Lithia, there is no need for you to work. I have money put aside for your college tuition. God will provide."

"Daddy, you need money to help pay for Sean's wedding. That's huge. Save the money for you and Mom. Go on a vacation after the wedding, a second honeymoon. I'll be fine."

But he knew she wasn't fine. She hadn't been fine since camp. He just didn't know why.

Christmas parties had begun, semester exams over, and many of the students were headed home for the holidays. It was very few that would stay. Lithia being one of them. She had been looking for work for over a month, hoping to at least find some seasonal assignment through the holidays. Her plan was to show them an outstanding work ethic and get hired on permanently. Nothing came.

Then she was asked to a party that would take her to the top, or so she was told.

A couple of girls in her dorm asked Lithia to come to a Christmas party with them, it was sure to be a blast. It was Miami, so a green and white sundress in December was fine. She brought a red sweater just in case.

The party was at a former Hurricane football player's home. The house was huge. Lithia heard that the guy's parents had money, and he was working on getting loaded himself. She never met him to thank him for the invitation or that his home was lovely. She would later, but not tonight.

"Is that the guy hosting the party?" Lithia saw him from across the room. He was tall, with thick hair that any girl would be jealous to have. He was wearing low riding, black dress pants and an unbuttoned red shirt. His tanned chest was hairless, and in the center of his chest was a gold cross necklace.

"Ooo, I want to know, too. Let's go find out." Her dorm mate pulled her arm and walked over to this Greek god standing in front of them. He had observed them staring, he was just waiting to see how long it would take.

"I was wondering how long it would be until you came over and introduced yourselves. If you hadn't, I don't think I would have thought this party was any good. The hottest women here are now talking to me."

Bigger girl isn't saying much, but she can't keep staring at my chest. Nor I hers. Wonder what they look like without hindrance of clothing? These other two, they'll be easy. This one with the rack, she's going to be a challenge, but one I'd like to take.

"Is this your place? I love it! Wanna show us around? I mean, you do want us to have a fun time at your party?"

Did she really do the pouty face? Lithia rolled her eyes. Can she just tone it down? Why are these two asking so many questions and touching all on him? He says he likes us, so maybe you should back off, see which one of us he likes the most. It won be me; I'm boring compared to them.

"This isn't my place. Dan, my employee lives here. Not a bad spread, but my place is better. You'll have to come to the New Year's Eve party at my house. Plenty to do, hot tub, pool, drinks, anything you desire."

"Yes, I'll be there. Put your number in my phone so I can get the information." She flashed a big smile and handed him her phone. He was so yummy. Dina wasn't going to give the phone number to Lithia or her own roommate; she had her own agenda for New Year's Eve.

"Would you like my number, baby? I can place it in your contacts for you." He was looking down at Lithia with his palm out to take the phone. She just stood there.

No one has ever asked for my number. He must be doing this to be nice and not make it as obvious I am not his type. I'll let him put his number in; what could it hurt? I'm not going to call him; he's not going to call me.

She gave him the phone. He popped the number in and then took a selfie. He reached out to hand it back. "My photo and my digits. I will be in anticipation, waiting for your call."

Lithia blushed as their hands touched as she took her phone. It was when she scanned her phone later, she found what he had done. Her screen saver was a photo of his chest; his ID pic was him licking his lips. Her face was red again.

Where is his name? Killian Shaefer, oh, what you do to me. My temperature is rising just watching him, parts of me are tingling where they shouldn't be.

The party progressed late into the early morning. The host who she hadn't met seemed more like Killian then anyone because he was the one you saw mingling with the guests. He spoke to all the women, but many there were men. Each man shook Killian's hand or congratulated him for a "new one" or "exotic piece."

Lithia assumed Killian was an art dealer or collector. She thought about asking if she would be able to view his collection when she came New Year's Eve. Then she changed her mind; *don't want him to think I'm overeager.*

Her friends were constantly chatting from one guy after another. Lithia lost sight of Dina and Tori more than once. They hadn't neglected her; she wasn't alone, for somebody would sit with her or offer a drink. It was nice without worrying about school, her family, bills, studying or finding a job. Plus, it appeared Killian was on hand whenever the other girls were gone.

Around 2 AM, Lithia knew Dina and Tori hadn't been seen for an hour. She was getting sleepy and was wanting to go back to the dorms. She tried to cover a yawn.

"Don't tell me you're bored of me; why, I would be sad." Killian had a drink in his hand, but slipped his arm around Lithia's shoulder. "If you're tired, I could take you home if you don't have a ride. I haven't seen your energetic friends in quite a while, and I'm thinking they are having a different kind of party. A party of two."

There she goes blushing again. She is going to be one I can sell. An innocent, next-door girl that men are always asking me for. The virgin they can teach to do their will. But first, I'm going to conquer this one. And I'm going to take my time.

"Ugh! I don't want to impose, Killian, but I am very tired. I would appreciate the gesture. Do you mind if I look around one more time before we go? I don't want them to find me gone and get angry."

"Oh, sure. I'm going to find the kitchen; see about a cup of coffee to balance the liquor I've had. I'm not drunk, but would rather be a little less intoxicated before zipping on the road." *That should make her think I'm the good guy.*

Lithia searched the house, well, everywhere except the bedrooms. She refused to walk in, just thinking she might find Dina or Tori in a situation, or anyone else for that matter. She had heard enough of the gossip in the dorm and other common areas on campus to know there was promiscuity running rampant at parties. This was first real party she had attended, and she had been invited by her ride.

With no sign of Dina and Tori, she came into the kitchen as Killian poured a cup of coffee. "You want a cup? Black, cream, sugar?"

"Yes, that would be nice, black with sugar, please."

Perfect! I'll drop a touch of powder along with the sugar, she won't have a clue. "Here you are. Soon as you finish, we will go to the car. I'm parked right out front."

Before Killian had driven a mile, Lithia was passed out in the car.

She woke up not sure where. The bed was soft and warm, with satin sheets and lots of pillows. The sheets felt so smooth on her skin.

On my skin! I'm naked! Dear, God, where am I? My clothes are missing. My purse, I see is on the chair, and my shoes are beside it. My clothes are missing. I can't even get out of bed. What am I to put on? I need to think. What was the last thing I remember from last night? Calm down. Breath. Last thing I remember was Killian was going to take me to the dorms. Dina and Tori were AWOL. I was sleepy. I couldn't find them, but Killian was in the kitchen with coffee. I left with Killian. I'm sure of it, or not. Was he driving me, or someone else?

Wrapping the sheet around her, she started pacing the room, searching frantically for her clothes. They weren't there. She was afraid to open the door; who would be on the other side? There were three doors. Probably one for the closet, bathroom, and to leave the room. She tried the first door-bathroom. Huge walk-in shower, garden tub, double sink, a bathroom to die for, but her clothes were not there.

Alright, door number two. Closet with clothes. Men's clothes. Oh, this is getting so much worse. Look on the bright side. My clothes may not be here, but there's got to be something in here I can put on. It doesn't matter if fits properly; it covers me, and that's what matters.

Finding a pair of jogging pants and a big t-shirt, she slid into her sandals and picked up her purse.

I have to get the courage to open door number three. It would seem to be the way out. I don't hear anyone, maybe they are asleep. If so, I just want to sneak out the door. I'll use my cell to call a cab or something to take me back to the dorms. You have to figure out where you are, Lithia. Can't call a cab without an address to pick you up.

Lithia took a peek out the bedroom door into a hallway. Deciding to go left, she followed the corridor until it opened into a great room. From here she could see a kitchen, dining room, and a large living area. Through French doors, she could see a patio with a pool. She jumped when a cuckoo clock chimed eleven. Carefully, she crossed the room to get another perspective of the house. She could step out on the patio to be outside, but she needed to be in the front where it would be easier to get help and a ride to the dorm.

"Hey, don't you think someone should check on the girl in Killian's bedroom? I haven't seen her yet this morning. She's been passed out long enough." Lithia didn't recognize the man's voice, but she didn't think she was going to like him.

"Send one of the girls. I don't want her freaking out if you walk in. Or see if Killian even wants us to intercede. He's out in the pool, swimming laps." Another man's voice, and she didn't like it either.

Okay, I'm at Killian's house. Wherever that is. I was in his bed naked. How did I do that? Did he sleep with me? Or did he SLEEP with me? Nothing in that area feels strange, but I wouldn't know what that felt like anyway. He is out in the pool, where I could go to get some questions asked or get the heck out of here before those guys find me. I'm not alone, two other guys at least, and they said girls-plural. Leave. "Flee from all appearances of evil" her grandmother used to say. This is on that level.

By using her GPS on her cell, Lithia was able to find her exact location and call for a cab. When the men had went out to the pool, she quietly went out the front door and down the street. The cab was there within fifteen minutes.

In her room, she dug through her purse for traces of clues about last night. She had to find out what happened in that bedroom. Her mind kept thinking back to camp; she didn't want to remember. She took a long hot bath, put on her own clothes, and washed Killian's. He would get his clothes back; she wasn't a thief. Then she went to find Dina and Tori.

"Well, look who the dog dug up! Have a good evening, I see?" Tori was still in her clothes from the night before.

"We got to meet the host of the party; kinda had a party all on our own, didn't we? By the time we came back downstairs, you were gone. No one seemed to know when, with whom, or where."

"I was tired and called a cab. Been in my room, guess I didn't hear you if you came to the door. Sorry. Sorry about last night too. I didn't want to disturb you, so I left." *Dina and Tori were clueless. What was the point to talk to them anyhow?*

Her cell was beeping when she came back to her room; it showed Killian was calling. There was a voicemail. *He's probably ticked I stole his clothes or wonders why I left. I was naked in his bed.*

"Lithia, Killian here. Where did you go? I was letting you sleep after our long night. You said you were tired; just didn't think you'd fall asleep on me on the way back to the dorm. I'm sure you are wondering where your clothes were when

you woke up. Simple answer-you threw up on them. You passed out, then halfway to the campus, you sat up and vomited all over the car, you, your clothes. I didn't want you to be in trouble, so I brought you to my house. We got you cleaned up and put you to bed. I washed your clothes. Can you call me back?"

Why can't I remember throwing up and being undressed? He has more explaining to do than that.

The jogging pants and the t-shirt were dry and folded when Lithia called Killian. "We need to talk and exchange clothes. I took some pants and a shirt out of your closet when I found myself without any. I've washed them for you. I'll meet you at the university's park in an hour. Goodbye."

Hmmm, she was a little spitfire. Did not see that coming. I pull this off, I will be through with step one.

"Lithia, I am so glad you are feeling much better this morning. I didn't have the best night myself. I'm thinking it was that coffee we had. It was the only thing that made us sick."

"You were sick, too?"

"Yes, I didn't throw up until I got home, but I don't think I was as bad as you. My stomach was rumbling, but I over-looked it. You were sick, so I drove home. Come on. What would have happened if I had carried you passed out and covered in puke into the dormitory at two in the morning? I couldn't have you humiliated, embarrassed."

Lithia was trying to figure this out. If she could only remember the vomiting, or how she got naked.

"So, if your stomach is bubbling, I'm passed out with puke all over me and your car, how did I get in the house, undressed, cleaned up, and naked in your bed? Answer that." *This better be good, mister.*

"I got you in the house. My stepsisters were visiting with their boyfriends, so they took over from when I left you in the bathroom. They got you undressed and cleaned up. During your clean-up, I was getting sick in the hall bath and getting all your explosion off me. I felt better after it got out of my system. You must have as well. All I had to do was carry you into my bed. Had the car cleaned this afternoon by mobile detailers before I came here. Does that answer everything?'

"No. You saw me naked. And where did you sleep?" He didn't know if she was going to hit him or cry.

"I didn't see you completely naked; they had wrapped you somewhat with a beach towel, which I took off from under the covers. I slept in my bed on top of the covers with my pajama bottoms on. You were underneath. Perfect gentleman. Satisfied? I can get them to collaborate my story."

Her arms went around him before he could say another word. *Where did this come from?*

"What a knight in shining armor! Only one other guy did something like this for me. You are just the sweetest man ever. A true gentleman. I do apologize for my attitude, but I have had some one in my past that tried to take advantage of a situation, I don't trust men very well."

Lithia kissed Killian on the check, but then he held her tight against him. "Oh, I would never take advantage of you."

Then as she felt his lips overtake her own, she allowed her body to mold into his arms.

The trust had come. The attraction had come. Now to play this along until he had her fully. It would take some time after that, but he had a gut instinct. Lithia was going to be well worth the wait. Alone at Christmas, the timing couldn't be better.

The best thing about New Year's Eve for Lithia: Killian said he loved her, and then he showed her how much.

The best thing about New Year's Eve for Craig: his momma found Jesus.

Since the shooting, Saoirse had to face many challenges. She was already a woman that had lost one kidney by Jim's attack, but now she was losing the other one. The first bullet had penetrated her only kidney and went out her abdomen. Her kidney didn't always want to function, and they didn't know how long it would last without a transplant. The doctors weren't very optimistic; she was given six months without the donor kidney.

With the second bullet, he had hit her spinal code. She was paralyzed from the waist down. They had prayed the doctors were wrong and feeling would return, but it had been seven weeks, and nothing changed.

Craig was needed to help care for his mother, although Nurse Mabel could take care of it alone, Craig believed it was his responsibility. He transferred to online classes so he could stay at home. With the master's degree courses online, and his mother's care, his only outlet was church.

When Saoirse was brought from the rehabilitation center to Mabel's house, the rules were discussed. Chores every day, no cussing, bed at ten, and everyone goes to church when the doors were open. Everyone. Saoirse had no choice. Sunday morning, evening, and Wednesday night; she was in her wheelchair by the fourth row at Mt. Zion Missionary Holiness Church of Our God.

Nurse Mabel had started to see an attitude change soon after Thanksgiving. She had stopped being a Daniel, complaining about having to attend services. By Christmas, she was asking questions in Sunday School and at the ladies' Bible study every Tuesday morning.

"Nurse Mabel, why didn't we go to Bible study on Tuesdays since we went to every other study, meeting, service, revival there ever was?" Craig couldn't remember Nurse Mabel going.

"Child, think about it. Ladies' Bible study. Why would you ever go? I also worked during the day. I don't work now, I'm retired. I get to go."

He leaned over to his mother, "Surprised she didn't take us anyway. Dress us like girls and go." They were giggling over his comment when Nurse Mabel knocked Craig over the head with a wooden spoon.

"I heard that!"

Mt. Zion planned to have a New Year's Eve service. It was going to be full of praise and worship in song and dance. The teens were putting on a short skit, and there would be light refreshments, which meant "dinner on the grounds" with everyone's best dishes to eat. At 11:50 pm, prayer would start. The entire congregation was to be praying in the New Year as the clock struck midnight. It would be close to 12:30 am before anyone thought about leaving.

The Rev wasn't a man that minced words when it came to salvation. He quoted the words of the Gospel of John 3:16. He read from Romans, "all have sinned and come short of the glory of God." He described the rich man in purgatory, wishing for just a drop of water.

"'Today is the day of salvation.' We are not promised tomorrow. There may be some of us in this room who will not see another New Year. Where do you want to end? God doesn't hate you for the things you have done. He hates the sin, not you. Stop punishing yourself for going back to what you may only know. Take the step of faith, let God guide you so you won't make those same choices again and again. No matter what you have done, God will come and love you anyway. He only wants you to love Him back."

That's when Saoirse pushed her wheelchair up to the altar and accepted Jesus as her king. A harlot's heart had been cleaned of sin, guilt, shame, and fear. She was a child of God.

Chapter 36

October 2013

Though battle-worn, Saoirse's life wasn't worthless as she had been told countless times. She had a son that loved her, even knowing the things she had done. She now had a church family who didn't see her as some piece of trash hooker on the corner. They saw her as a sister in Christ.

I have been forgiven; my old life has been washed away; I'm clean. Why did I keep going back every time God had given me a way out? Fear-that was it. Fear of losing my child growing inside me, of hunger, of cold, of loneliness, of Jim. No more fear.

That's how she had felt since last New Year's Eve. The revelation of Christ's love and forgiveness had grown even more relevant when The Rev and her son had baptized her.

Craig got goose bumps whenever his momma would testify in church now about her conversion. She told of how even in the middle of her former life, she could hear a song in her head from when she was a toddler. And she would close her eyes and forget what was happening in the present, concentrating on that one song and the comfort it would bring.

Saoirse would explain how God had given her opportunities to let Him take charge, but she didn't want to lose control. Then she allowed others to take control instead. When her own child was hurt, she knew the only way to save him was to let him go.

"It was heartbreaking to see the one reason I gave up everything become the one reason I had to let him go. Watching him become a man under someone else's care and nurturing increased my thoughts of worthlessness. Thoughts of suicide entered my head more than I can count. Even after this, I wanted to be left alone to die. But God said, 'Not yet.' Again, the song would come. The only one I sang to my tiny baby, taught him to sing when he was afraid in the dark, the one I still sing in my soul today, 'Jesus Loves Me.' The simplest words, but oh, how true."

"Today, on our sister's physical birthday, we want to celebrate instead, of the beginning of that life, we want to celebrate her rebirth in Jesus Christ our Lord as her Redeemer. Now, with your blessings, members of Mt. Zion, and the help of Sister O'Shay's own son, Craig, I baptize you, my sister, as a symbol of your sins...Hallelujah! Being forgiven, washed away, a clean, pure heart through Jesus' blood... Praise the Lord! And that your name, Saoirse O'Shay, is written in the Lamb's Book of Life...then in the name of the Father, of the Son, and of the Holy Ghost...the church said... AMEN and AMEN! HALLELUJAH!!!!"

That had been in February. Saoirse became radiant with her newfound joy in the Lord. Her disabilities didn't hold her down. She had a beautiful voice, probably where Craig got it from, and they built a ramp for her wheelchair so she could sing in the choir. She was a greeter before services, and went once a week with the First Lady to the woman's prison to tell her life-changing story of a harlot's heart. When her health would allow, she helped in any capacity she could to spread the news of God's heart-changing experience.

Until a couple of months ago.

"Thank you, Doctor, I understand." Craig had taken the news like a champ; now to tell Momma. "Momma, that was your doctor on the phone. It wasn't the right match for your kidney like he thought. You're going to have to wait a little longer for the transplant."

"She's becoming weaker, but she won't say anything. She doesn't want you to worry or miss turning in school-work deadlines. Craig, I know she is proud of you. She just hates you gave up being away at college to be here with her. Online is not the same. She knows you miss your friends. When was the last time you saw them, Leo and Sunny's wedding, no, you didn't even get to go? It was the weekend Sean and Leo met you at the beach. Two days. That's what a twenty-three-year-old should be doing. Spending some time with his friends. Why Craig, you haven't gone to lunch with Daniel in a month of Sundays."

Nurse Mabel was still her old self, though she, too, wasn't as spry as she once was. She always was saying seventy is just a number.

By the beginning of October, Saoirse was barely holding on. It was just a matter of keeping her comfortable. She'd asked to be at Nurse Mabel's, not the hospital, for her final days. She said it was the home her son had met Jesus and where she had as well. She wanted it to be the place Jesus took her to heaven.

On October 10, 2013, Jesus and the angels carried Momma home.

Chapter 37

May 4, 2019

Good morning, world! I will be organized today. Hmm, no office, anything about the ball, Martha is on it. Not seeing Mr. O'Shay today until he picks me up for the ball. On my own to swing by the bridal shop, grab my dress and dyed shoes. I can do my own hair and makeup, but do I want to get a mani-pedi? Yes. I'll do that, then get my dress.

"Good morning, Mr. O'Shay. Is your offer to take Jenson Gibson to the charity ball still standing?"

"And good morning to you as well, Cinderella. Of course, it is. Why do you ask?"

"I am thinking he might not have the expected outfit for tonight's event. I would like to purchase it for him."

"You are right. Don't want the kid to feel embarrassed in jeans and a t-shirt. I think that is very commendable of you. I don't know how his mom is doing, but I'll would be willing to pay for her dress if you can find out."

"Not a problem. I have some errands to do, then I will run to the center. I can find out about the mom, get his sizes, and pick up my dress. Hopefully, I can get his suit from there, too."

"You are a sweetheart, Cinderella. I will see you later. Let Jenson's mom know we can pick them up in our limo."

Nails and toes painted in the classy French tip were stylish for the ball. They went with anything. Getting an eight-year-old boy to wear a tux may not be as quick as the mani-pedi had been. Then there's the mom. Would Lithia have to pick out a dress for her? She hadn't even met the woman.

"Good Morning, Ms. Eva. I don't know if you remember me, but I was here Thursday with Mr. O'Shay from the Saoirse's Heart of Hope Foundation."

"Yes, yes, Miss Murphy, wasn't it? What can I do for you this morning?"

"I was wanting to find out how Jenson's mother was doing. Mr. O'Shay had invited Jenson and his mother to come tonight as his guest to the charity ball."

"No, Mrs. Gibson is not doing well at all. She's been back to the hospital, but at this point, only God knows. I will say she is in good spirits. Not sure how I could do it. Her faith is stronger than most women I meet here."

"That's horrible. I had no idea. I just thought it wasn't so bad if she was here and not at the hospital. What's going to become of Jenson if his mother, God forbid?"

Lithia couldn't think of being eight and losing her mother. They had never been close as she wanted, but at one time, at eight years old, her mother was the most beautiful woman in the world. In Lithia's mind, Lola still was.

"I would assume he would go to DCF. His father is dead. I understand his grandparents haven't seen him since he was a baby. I'm not sure if his paternal grandparents are alive. I know his mother has given us information on her family. She hasn't spoken to them since Jenson was two. Her hope is they will take him. I believe they live in Florida."

"Would it be alright if I speak with her? I would like to get permission to take Jenson to the dress shop to be fitted for a tux. It would be nice to give her time to rest and for him to feel special."

"He would love that. Yes, sounds like a wonderful plan. Do you remember how to get back to the clinic from when Jenson gave you the tour? She's there. Mrs. Gibson is the only patient, so you won't miss her. Jenson is probably there too. He lives in there with her."

With a nod, and grabbing a handful of tissues, just in case, Lithia headed to see Mrs. Gibson.

Jenson was watching Saturday morning cartoons while sitting in a chair by his mother's bed. He was eating a Pop Tart. Then he saw her hovering at the doorway.

"Momma, Cinderella's here. You got to meet her. She's pretty, not as beautiful as you, though. It's the lady I told you about from the other day. She was with Prince Charming, and they are going to a ball. And he said I could go with them."

"Jenson, that is the reason I am here. I wanted to speak with your mother to see if she will permit you to attend. If you can, you need a tux for tonight."

Lithia had only stepped in the doorway. She could see the small body lying in the bed, but wasn't close enough to see her face. An oxygen tank was beside the bed, and a catheter bag was connected to the bed railing. Jenson was leaning over the railing on the opposite side, trying to hear the hushed voice of his mother.

The closer Lithia came to the hospital bed, her heartbeat grew louder. She was almost afraid of what she would see. She stopped at the foot of the bed. The woman's face was bruised purple with fresh cuts. Out of her nostrils was the oxygen hose. Her one arm was in a cast, the other had a bandage wrapped around the forearm. Lithia didn't want to think what other horrors were hidden under the covers. Her husband was some piece of work. To hurt his wife and his kid just unforgiveable.

"Jenson, can you sit mommy up to speak with the lady?"

"Her name is Cinderella. Remember?" He pushed the button to make the head of the bed rise a little more.

The first thing Lithia noticed as her face became more visible was an eye was swollen shut. However, it was the scar which caused her to move closer and speak.

"Leslie, oh, Leslie."

Lithia couldn't hold back the tears as she looked at the mangled woman who was once her best friend. And Jenson. This adorable boy was Leslie and Harold's baby. It was her fault Harold had done this to her. All the guilt from camp, keeping Harold's actions a secret, if she only hadn't been so scared and ashamed.

"What's the matter, Cinderella? You don't have to cry. Mommy doesn't feel a lot of the pain because we give her medicine. I cried when I first saw Mommy after the bad man did this, but Mommy said if your heart is clean from Jesus, you are beautiful on the outside too. Come stand here by me if you're scared. It's also easier to hear her."

He took Lithia's hand and brought her to the side of the bed. Leslie's one good eye had followed Lithia as she came with Jenson. Leslie tried to cover her face with her hands.

"Thank you, God. You have given me the chance I have prayed."

What do I say to Lithia? We were best friends, until I let lust and pride get in my way. I became jealous over a guy. I spread lies about her at school, at church. How do I apologize for these things?

Lithia gently took Leslie's hand, "I'm sorry this happened to you and to this sweet boy. I can't forgive myself for not telling you how Harold really was. I blame myself for it all."

Leslie was taken off guard with Lithia's apology. "No, you have nothing to be sorry for at all. I am the one to blame. I was so naïve to his ways. Then when he told me you made a pass at him, I knew you. I knew you would never do that. What he told me about you and him in the hammock was true, wasn't it? But he was the aggressor. Did he...did he?"

"No, he never did. But he tried twice. I am not sure what would have happened if not for CJ. He came in, and Harold ran. I swore him to secrecy. I was so embarrassed."

"Oh, it makes so much sense now. That's why the odd clothes and CJ with you everywhere. He became your bodyguard. Then when my parents caught me sneaking out at night, I threw you under the bus again. I took the story Harold told me about you and told my mother. Anything to take the blame off me. Then she told Lola."

"Mommy, do you know Cinderella?"

"Oh, we have known each other a long time. We were BFFs before you were born."

"So, you were like Sleeping Beauty and Cinderella?"

"I would agree. Beautiful in our own ways. Cinderella never realizes how beautiful she is until Prince Charming. Sleeping Beauty knows she's pretty but ignores the temptation and still touches the spinning wheel. I'm like her. It took me closing my eyes to sin and opening them to Jesus so I could live again."

"Then do I have permission to go to the ball? We got to get my tux, Cinderella. Can we go now?"

"Yes, go. Lithia, we should continue our conversation later. Have fun and behave."

Wow, Leslie has changed. Not by looks, which is obvious, but her personality. She's not haughty or sarcastic. The fact she apologized and took the blame. That is not the Leslie she once knew. If only I had a relationship with the people back home. Her mom and dad should be here. I can't believe they wouldn't want to see their only child and grandson. I will find a way to send word to them soon.

Jenson was a delight trying on the suits. He asked to see a suit for Prince Charming. The tailor assumed Jenson wanted one like Craig's. When Jenson found out Craig had a tux just like it, he was sold. He wanted to show it to his mother when they returned, but she was sleeping. Lithia left a message with Eva that Mr. O'Shay would be by to help Jenson dress at 5:30. She went home with a lighter heart.

Chapter 38

May 2014

For Craig's final semester, he returned to the college campus. He didn't realize how much he missed it. His friends were gone. They moved on with their lives with wives. Leo and Sunny had a baby girl, Valentine Rose, appropriately named for her birthday, and had moved back to their hometown to head the music ministry for Sunflower's father, Rev. Johnson. Sean and Erika were "trying" to catch up, but they had moved to the Central Florida area where Erika was teaching elementary school, and Sean was working in sound and audio for a Christian television station. But here, he was alone.

His momma had been in heaven exactly seven months when he received his master's degree in business finance. His professors raved at graduation on his natural abilities to choose stock, which would sell, or not. He saw potential to save money in business and how to increase profits and quality of service. The internship program he had been in since undergrad did nothing but brag on his entrepreneurship and the incentives Craig had integrated at the company.

"Your momma would be so proud of you, baby. I bet Señora Corona and your momma had front row seats in heaven today for graduation. Now for a job offer at a national investment company...God has given you favor in the eyes of man. 'If you exalt me, I will exalt you in front of men.' God has blessings for you. His hand is on your life."

I know Nurse Mabel's right, but what if I can't do it? I will be going far away. I've never really been many places; Gainesville to Miami, not a big world traveler. One or two mission trips does not count. I don't know if I want to move to North Carolina.

"I don't want to leave you. My adopted grandmother is gone, my mother, most of my friends are at least within a couple of hours' drive to visit. What if you need me?"

"Craig O'Shay, I am a grown woman who has taken care of herself for longer than she cares to admit. I raised children that needed love and showed them God's way of salvation. I am never alone with Him in my heart. If I would need you, I know how to use a cell phone. Buy me one of those computers and teach me how to do that Skype thing. You and I will be fine."

"The thing is, I know what God wants me to do with my life. I want to build or have a center for women who are in abusive relationships. I want to help women with children trying to get out of situations so they aren't dependent on a way of life, one which makes them feel unworthy of love."

"Why, that is a beautiful dream! You want a place for women who might be like your momma, turn to a life of shame because she didn't know where to go."

"Yes, Nurse Murphy, I want to get them off the streets, and help them not go back. But we need one here. That is my dream. For momma and little kids like me."

Tears came, and he poured his vision from God out to Nurse Mabel until he fell asleep on the sofa, and she rested in her recliner.

Time was up to give his decision about taking the associate's position in Raleigh, North Carolina. He asked if he could work in the branch in Miami until summer was over, and they accepted his terms. He was to report to their main branch in Raleigh by August 31st. He would need to secure an apartment and settle in to start work on Tuesday after Labor Day.

I have a little over three months to clean clutter out of my room in Nurse Mabel's, hang out with as many friends from church, and try to see Daniel a few times before I leave. I'd also like to get with Sean for a day before I head up north, and Leo.

"Hey Leo, How's fatherhood? Uncle CJ needs a photo."

"It's great! She's crawling already, saying 'Dada' to her momma's dismay. What's happening to you, Mister master's degree?"

"I got quite a lot to tell you. One, I accepted an associate's position for the finance company, but I will be moving to North Carolina end of August. I was thinking you, Sean, and I could get one more visit before I go. You think you guys will be up for it?"

"Sure, we will, but I got a better idea. A couple of weeks together where we first met. Wekiva Youth Camp. Sunny and I are leaving Valentine with her parents while we co-direct camp this year with none other than Sean and Erika. Why not come and be head counselor? See if your new company will give you those weeks in July and we got us a fun vacation."

"That would be an adventure, two old married guys and the third wheel. Where do I sign up? No, in all seriousness, I'm there for you. I'll get back to you in a couple of weeks with the final okay, but don't tell Sean until it's definite."

"No problem, glad to hear from you. I'll wait for your answer."

"Tell Sunflower hello from me and to keep posting baby pictures on Facebook. Kiss my Rose for me. God willing, I'll see you in July."

Now I need to set a couple of dinners with Daniel. I should invite him to supper with Nurse Mabel and me. I know she prays for him every day to see him give his heart to the Lord. We could take her to a fancy restaurant, she won't have to cook. But if I know her, she's going to want to fix Daniel's favorites.

"Daniel, it's me your little brother. I got some big news."

"Hey kid, let's hear it. Tell me something good."

"You are talking to the newest associate investor of Wise Men's Financial, Inc. I want to go celebrate."

"Wow, congratulations! When and where? I'm game. Strip club and drinking, I'm there for you."

"And no."

"I'm kidding, Craig. Don't get all holier than thou on me. What do you want to do?"

"Well, the job is going to send me to the head office in Raleigh at the end of August. I was hoping we could get together for dinner a few times before that."

"Yep, that works. We got plenty of time to try do dinner once a month before you go. Just don't forget me when you get all rich and famous in the stock market."

"How would this Sunday be for our first dinner? Go to church with me and Nurse Mabel; when it's over, we take her out to lunch. She loves you, Daniel. She thinks of you like her own kid. You know you love her, church and rules and all. You will make an old lady happy."

"I don't know. I could do lunch, but church can be soooo long."

"We can surprise her. You can just walk in late and sit down beside her. She'll probably faint if she doesn't have a Holy Ghost fit right then."

It was like when they were kids, thinking of ways to surprise Nurse Mabel.

"This Sunday, for church service, NOT Sunday School. And I'm not going to evening service, so don't try persuading me into that."

Sunday came, and just as Craig predicted, Nurse Mabel did a jig when Daniel slipped in the pew beside her. All she could do was brag about her two boys. Master's degrees, good jobs, how they needed Proverbs 31 wives, and a houseful of babies for her to love on. When Daniel helped her in his sports car, she thought she was a movie star.

"Do you think I could get you to put the top down on your convertible? I want to feel like Angelina Jolie with the wind blowing in my hair." Of course, she complained that he was going too fast and she might lose some of her weave.

"What are we doing here? I got plenty of food I can make at my house. Won't take me any time to get some butter beans and cornbread going. I can do rice and collards. Throw some pork chops in the skillet. Mac and cheese. Why, I can even cook your favorite coconut cake for dessert."

"Nope, we are taking you out. You deserve someone to wait on you for a change. Craig and I have planned this all week. You don't want to be one of those ungrateful people you taught us about in the Bible, now?"

"I appreciate it. It is about time you guys started showing some love for me. I mean, all the tom foolery you did. Especially you, Danny Armstrong. but when I get home, I'm making you that coconut cake. Promise you will come by and pick it up after work tomorrow."

"I promise."

"What about me? I don't like coconut cake."

"Craig, stop being so jealous. I made you a cake last week."

"That was for my birthday. It doesn't count."

"Good Lord, I'll make you a chocolate one, too. What I have to do to get a free meal."

Precious Jesus. Oh, my boys for a whole Sunday, and at church too. Then to see Daniel tomorrow, even for a little while. Lord, thank you for one more time to let your Word be sown into Daniel's heart. It never goes forth void. Let Daniel see his world would be so much better with a relationship with Jesus.

Both cakes were baked and iced, placed in cake storage tins, and sitting on the table when Nurse Mabel had said her bedtime prayer. But she never was able to enjoy a piece with the boys on Monday afternoon; she was feasting with the Lord.

Craig came home from work early to see if Nurse Mabel wanted any help with dinner. If he knew her, she would be sure to have made every item she had mentioned the day before. It would be her way to get Daniel to stay for supper.

He was surprised when he didn't smell butterbeans or cornbread cooking on the stove. When he walked into the kitchen, she hadn't even started preparing for dinner. The television was on in low in the living room, and the lamp was on by Nurse Mabel's recliner.

On her lap, an old photo taken of the boys on Easter 2004 was lying on the open page of her Bible. Nurse Mabel had gone to meet Jesus.

A funeral was not how Daniel and Craig expected their next visit, but since most of her family had passed away, they were left in charge of the arrangements. Daniel oversaw her life insurance policy. He found she had more than one. Going through her files, Craig also found her will and plans for her death. Her plot, gravestone, coffin, all of it, had been prepaid. The boys had little to do. She left a list of songs, singers, Scriptures, and who had HER permission to speak at her funeral.

"She's dead and still bossy. But this is making a hard thing easier." Daniel was talking it harder than he was letting on. He covered up sadness with sarcasm.

There was a photograph of the outfit she wanted the boys to bury her in. Another for the spray of flowers to top the casket. The craziest list: the food to have at her repast. AND WHO WAS ALLOWED TO COOK IT.

"Hey, what she don't know, won't hurt her." And Daniel wadded it up and threw it in the wastebasket.

A week after the funeral, Daniel, Craig, and The Rev came together at Nurse Mabel's to read the will. The Rev was the executor. One life insurance policy had Mt. Zion Missionary Holiness Church of Our God as the beneficiary. In the other policy, Daniel Armstrong was listed as beneficiary of $100,000. Daniel was also given Nurse Mabel's Bible.

The mortgage on the house had been paid off years ago. The deed was listed in Craig's name. The date was October 11, 2013. The day after Saoirse had died. A letter was included for each "son." Daniel's letter was in the Bible. Craig's was with the house deed.

The final piece was a stock market portfolio. Enclosed was all the companies she had invested in during her life. It wasn't many, but she had been an intelligent woman. She had invested wisely. In the last five years, she had invested in businesses Craig had been sure were goldmines. He had been right. She had tripled her investments. Those stocks were now Craig's. The others were co-owned by Daniel and Craig.

Instructions were left that Craig must use his inheritance to open a woman's shelter. To follow his call from God. But he must consult Daniel in all real estate purchases, since he was the real estate guy.

With the money Craig had now from Señora Corona's trust fund and Nurse Mabel's smart money management, Craig could see his vision unfolding soon.

Chapter 39

November 2014

S ean hadn't heard from Lithia since his birthday in August. It had been a quick call from an unknown number, but he had gotten used to it. They had always been somewhat close until he had left for college. At one time, they talked or texted every week, then it just dwindled. Once in Gainesville, he dove into the life. Studying and more time with Erika, he knew he had neglected his little sister. But he needed her to come home this Thanksgiving; he wanted to give the big news while everyone was together. He had to persuade her to be home for the holidays. Sean started praying she would call again.

Not the holidays, God, no, not today. Killian promised I wouldn't have to go with him. And today, it's my dad's birthday. I want to get a chance to call. I got to figure a way to reach him without Killian or my mother interfering. If Killian would let me have a phone; he is so jealous other guys will call me. Well, that's what I used to perceive. Now I know better.

"I have a paper to complete for business ethics and semester exams are coming. Killian, I don't want to be a part of this "busy season" as you call it. You promised I didn't have to do this anymore."

"I told you I would think about it. I never promised you anything. You need to understand, you do as I tell you and I'll let you keep taking classes. I need you on campus anyway. You're like a walking advertisement. Maybe you should ask to take your exams early. Gives me more investment opportunities for you to be available to my clientele."

"Killian, I love you, don't you know that by now? How much longer until you believe me?"

"Yea, yea, I love you. Look, I'm giving you a month's reprieve. Get your damn course work finished, so I have a solid month of employment from you. If you pay for your keep, I'll let you take courses next semester."

Lithia had relished their first months of dating. She thought she was beautiful for the first time in her life. Killian doted over her, lavished her with gifts, and had romantic candlelight dinners. He wanted to teach her the art of love-making. Her body was an open canvas, and only he could bring out the beauty. He instructed her on the masterpiece of a man's body, and how she could enjoy the intertwining of the two. Nights in his bed took her body and soul to heights she'd never flown. But it wasn't the same, not anymore.

Those days had begun to vanish at end of her second semester. Killian and Lithia had been dating seriously, close to six months. College kids had gone home for the summer or were partying from graduation or just hanging around the bay area for vacation. He had told her May through August were his busiest months out of the whole year, other than the Christmas-New Year's holidays. This was when he depended on her the most. She was needed.

Lithia had become putty in my hands at the mention of love from me. Then she submitted herself totally; I knew it was only a matter of time. I maneuvered her into accepting my lifestyle as free and open. Convinced her this is what men want, and I had her questioning her old-fashioned theology. Whenever she balks to do what I want, I drop a little in her drink. But lately, she's been trying my patience.

"Oh, thank you! I'm going to the media center on campus then, I can work on my paper. I'll give you a taste of my gratitude later." She knew if she offered him sexual exploits, he would be more agreeable.

"I'll take that 'thank you' now."

And on demand, she obliged.

Killian had perfected his talents; then, he would teach others. For example, Harry was a spoiled kid looking for some fun. He wanted to make money that Mommy and Daddy didn't know about and couldn't question his spending. Killian would get a kid like this from the college campus and train him.

Harry was handsome, dressed fashionably, and was pliable. Girls followed him around like puppy dogs, oohing and awing over his muscles. With his high school graduation sports car Daddy had gifted, Harry was the perfect choice. Add that he had access to all the football team and other guys on campus, Killian's wallet would stay full of Benjamins.

Harry would find girls on campus that seemed eager to please. He would be interested, and quickly checked out the merchandise. Between drugs and liquor, or just manipulating the females, Harry persuaded them to do whatever he wanted. Only time that had backfired was when he got the girl pregnant and married her. Killian let him play Daddy for a while, then they added the wifey into the game.

College kids had parties, lots of them. Host a party and invite tons of guys and girls. But you have other girls available. To have a "fun night," pick a girl and Harry would make sure the evening ended well. Time limits were negotiable as were various activities allowed. Prices were established, depending on what girl was chosen too.

Killian was always at the party, keeping an eye out for new recruits, both guys and girls. He needed more guys to help "guard" his harem, and more girls to add to it. Killian was willing to give a cut to any guy who brought him new merchandise. If you could add five girls to the group, you could branch out on your own. Killian still got his cut. It was like a pyramid scam.

Harry had gotten to that point. Now he had even added his own lower levels. His first one was his college buddy, Daniel Armstrong, a football player. He was almost ready to step out on his own, but Killian and Harry weren't too sure yet. Daniel was bringing in a different scene. He had connections to the business world, top dollar clientele, with plenty of money to spend, compared to the college boys. He still worked the colleges for girls and "guards," but Daniel was pulling in more money with the business types he was associated with through work and his parents. Killian didn't want to lose the money Daniel was pulling in every weekend, convention, holiday, and summer.

It had been at one of Daniel's party's he had met Lithia. Funny, Daniel had no clue who she was when he was asked about her. She had just shown up with Dina and Tori, who he had invited. Lithia was NOT his type.

"God, no, Killian, I would never invite a chunky girl to my party or think once on putting her in the 'harem.' That would be a game changer." He had told Harry about the 'fat' girl Killian thought he should include, but Harry agreed with Killian.

"There are more guys out there then you think that like a big girl. I have seen a few in my life that I wanted. Think, just another type for those men who have fetishes." But neither Harry nor Killian could convince Daniel.

Lithia had used a random girl's cell phone to call her dad for his birthday. She was glad she didn't hang up when her mother answered. It surprised her when Lola put her dad on the phone. He sounded tired at first, but he perked up at her voice.

"Happy birthday, Daddy! It's your little girl. I miss you. What are you doing for your special day?"

"Wishing my children were with me. How are you, and when will you be home? I would love to have a birthday Thanksgiving celebration. You think you can make it next week?"

"I don't know, Daddy. I really would like to come and see you. It depends on exams and everything. I'm trying to take my semester exams early; I've been guaranteed more hours if I can work during the holidays."

"Then you must come for Thanksgiving. It's only one day. If you come then, I won't push Christmas. We haven't seen you in over two years. Please, for me."

"Can I bring my boyfriend?"

"Boyfriend? Well, sure, I would love to meet him. If you want, spend the night. He can sleep on the sofa bed in the den. Now, if you don't come, I'll be driving down to you instead. I'm serious about seeing my girl."

"I'll talk with Killian and ask him. I gotta go, Daddy. Love you!"

"I love you, too."

Now how can I approach Killian about driving to Hopewell for Thanksgiving? I need to use tactics. Maybe a little trick he taught me for clientele could do it. If I can promise him we will be back by Friday night, I might win this battle. And I can't have Daddy showing up. He has no idea I moved in with Killian.

After a wild toss in the bedroom, Lithia decided she was ready to breach the subject of Thanksgiving.

"Killian, I've been thinking. Since I have already spoken to my professors about taking the exams a week early, do you think we could drive up to my folks for Thanksgiving Day? I haven't seen them in over two years."

"No can do. Got a big party at Daniel's on Friday and Saturday nights. I want to be there. He is wanting to branch out on his own, and I'm not ready for that yet. I got to keep an eye on him."

"Look, I spoke to my dad for only a bit. It was his birthday. He asked for me to come. I told him I would talk to you about it. He said my boyfriend was welcome too."

"You did what?! I tell you when you can talk to anyone! That's funny! Your daddy wants to meet me, the man that took his little girl's virginity."

"Killian, you don't understand. He said if we don't come, he is coming here. Is that what you want?"

Please God, let me see my parents one more time.

"You know, I will take you home. But here's the condition: you work for the party Friday and Saturday night for however much time we are there. Do you understand?"

She nodded her head. For every hour they would be at her parents', she must be working for him on her back.

Lithia and Killian got to Peter and Lola's Thursday morning. Lola was in the kitchen with Erika as Sean let them in the front door. He had been so thankful to hear his sister had called home, he was elated when she showed up at the door.

Sean wasn't too keen on Killian. He was too handsy with his sister. The amount of touchy-feely was not appropriate in front of others or with someone that wasn't your wife. He didn't trust him, but he wasn't going to ruin the day by saying anything.

Peter cried when he saw Lithia. He didn't want to let go when he hugged her. He observed the young man with her. Killian was not the type he wished for his daughter; however, first impressions can be deceiving.

"Lithia, I'm so happy you are here. Come and meet your niece or nephew. Can you believe it? Sean, going to be a daddy?"

Erika took Lithia's hand and placed it on her small baby bump. There was a tiny movement under her hand.

"It moved!"

"Yep, he has been doing that recently. But every time Sean tries to feel him kick, nothing. Baby Murphy is already showing a preference for his Titi Lithia. I find out the sex right before Christmas. We are going to do a big gender reveal Christmas Eve. You have got to be here."

"Hello, Lithia. Nice to meet you, Killian. Dinner will be ready in an hour."

Lola had graced them with her presence and retreated to the kitchen.

Lithia has lost lots of weight. She is smaller than I've seen her since middle school. For a minute, I didn't recognize my own daughter. Boyfriend of hers might be exactly what she needed to get off the pounds. I think I'm going to like him. From what I see, he is quite handsome; and the car, he has money.

"Mrs. Murphy, the food was magnificent! I haven't eaten home cooking in a while. Lithia is not the best cook. Now I see why she was so hefty when I met her. I like my girl thick, but she must have been eating second helpings. Now that I have her working out, all that plump is in the right places."

"Why thank you, Killian. I can see you are perfect for my daughter. I've been putting her on diets for ages. Should have known all it would take is the right boy. I am surprised you bribed her to go to a gym. I could never get her to do that or jog or even ride the exercise bike."

"Oh, no ma'am. The only place she works out is in the bedroom. Sometimes for hours. Ain't that right, babe?"

"Lithia Murphy, is what this boy's saying the truth? Are you married and didn't tell us? Or are you living in sin? You are going to make me the center of gossip. Lola's daughter fornicating. Look at your daddy; you did this to him. You should be ashamed of yourself."

Daddy, dear Daddy. What have I done? You are as white as a ghost. I'm so sorry; I should never come home. Momma was right when she told me I was nothing but a whore. I might not have been one then, but I can't deny it now.

"Daddy, I'm sorry. I'm...I love you, Daddy!"

"I think it is best you leave now, for all concerned, Killian. You can see yourself to the door."

"Something's wrong with your dad, Sean! Call 911. I think he is having a heart attack. Momma Lola, you need to stay calm and help me with Poppa Peter." Erika was starting to get nervous.

"I've got Daddy, Erika." Lithia had tried to hug her dad, but her mom knocked her hands away.

"Get your harlot's hands off my husband and remove yourself out of my house. I told you once to never come back, now heed my warning."

"But Momma, Daddy, I love him. And Daddy needs me."

"Lithia, we are leaving, get in the car now."

Peter's eyes were fixed on Lithia as Killian pulled her out the door. Her wails of "I'm sorry and I love you, Daddy" were the last things he heard as his heart beat for the last time.

In the car ride to Miami, Killian reminded her of the promise she made: *If you take me home to see my daddy, I will work for you Friday and Saturday night.* She better make good to her promise, or she would regret it for a long time.

Chapter 40

May 2016

The opening of Saoirse's Heart of Hope was on Mother's Day. Craig was ecstatic as people from all over came to dedicate the women's center. Sean and Erika had come with the twins, Gabriela and Gideon. Leo and Sunflower were toting Valentine and her little brother Patrick, with baby number three coming in early November. The running joke was if Sunflower had a baby boy on Halloween, they couldn't name him Freddy or Jason. Other guests at the ball were members of Mt. Zion -only a few, but they remembered Saoirse and Señora Corona and Nurse Mabel that made Craig's dream a reality.

Daniel had been there. He had come up a few months earlier to help with locating a building to purchase. They had found something in a centralized location at a reasonable price. Craig, with his financial brains, and Daniel with his knowledge of architectural structures, they had a deal in no time and were renovating. By Craig's birthday, furniture and office supplies were being purchased, and while the last of the painting was completed. The final touch was the bouquet of yellow roses placed on the table in the lobby under the framed portrait of his mother. A portrait of Nurse Mabel was in the clinic, and Señora Corona had one in the children's playroom.

Craig knew it was the right thing to do. Now he wanted to make Nurse Mabel's house into a smaller version back home. He had seen too much in his hometown, and he wanted to give back. He could start with a small one in her home and advance it later to one like in Raleigh.

Daniel had other ideas. Sell Nurse Mabel's and make some money. If Craig wanted to open another shelter, buy something else. Or let Daniel see what he could find in Tampa. He had been looking to move there in a few months, let him scope out the real estate for a while. Why not wait a couple of years to let the market settle? Let him do his magic in the real estate game and Craig in the stock market. Think about what they could do in two or three years.

Now Daniel had more going on in his life than just the real-estate market. The college "harem" scene was making him a rich man on its own. He had finally cut from Harry when Killian sent the best girls to Daniel's parties, not Harry's. Why, he didn't even associate with Harry anymore after what he seen.

There had been a party at Harry's one night, and Daniel had noticed one female who was very sexy. He had thought he might "check out Harry's merchandise."

"Hey, Harry, who's the busty one over by the bay window? I'll take a spin in her. What's the going price, and we are friends, that should be a discount."

"Huh, her? That's my ball and chain. You can have her for a dollar. I don't get much out of her at home, but she's been a goldmine at parties. Hey, Les, come here."

Daniel watched as Harry's wife swayed over. He knew it had been a forced action for her husband's benefit. She was quite pretty, maybe more so when she was younger. Now she had a worn look on her face. One that gave a presumption of wrong choices from the wearer. He wondered how she received the scar on her lip. It was the only flaw he saw, but her meekness made him deduce she had scars in other areas besides her body. She reminded him of Craig's mother. He thought what Craig would do if he was in my shoes. Craig would never be in his shoes.

"Look, Les, this here is my friend Daniel. He likes what he sees, so take him on back in our bedroom and give him the full treatment. Why, Daniel, I am so generous, you can have her all night long."

Without lifting her head, "If I do, can I see Jenson tomorrow? I haven't seen him in three weeks."

"Daniel, if the whore does a good job, let me know. She's been begging to see our kid every day. You hear that, Leslie? If he doesn't give you a good report, no baby for three more weeks."

Harry pushed her into Daniel's arms.

Nothing happened that night in Harry's bed, but Leslie told Daniel about her little boy. In the morning, Harry was nowhere around. Daniel left Leslie with five thousand dollars and told her of a woman's shelter in Tampa. He got an anonymous call a few days later, "Thank you, my son and I are safe."

Daniel wasn't a Christian man, but he wasn't going to physically abuse his "harem" like Harry. And to put his own wife in the party? What was that about anyway? He swore he would get more girls out; he would not put any more into the harem.

Killian had finally let Daniel go out on his own. Daniel was relocating to Tampa by the holidays. He was contemplating going totally legitimate, but he would take a couple of his girls with him. He could use them for special events or to help persuade clientele to purchase his property. Killian asked for a payout. Daniel agreed to twelve of his girls. He never told Killian he had "released" all the rest, but two, who were going to be secretaries in his office.

At Killian's summer kickoff party Daniel made sure all the girls were present. He would be moving at the end of August. Doing this change now made sense. These next few months would be spent making trips back and forth from Miami to Tampa; he didn't have time to worry with it. This was going to be his last party until Tampa holidays.

"Man, you got to have a good time before you leave Miami. This is a Killian Shaefer party. No friend of mine is going to not have a bang of a last night. You have a preference? Blondes, brunettes, redheads, raven...Asian, Spanish, what's your pleasure? I got it all."

"Killian, I got to talk to you."

This voluptuous strawberry blonde with a string bikini came over to them. She had smooth skin with a little bit of freckles in places, and it made you wonder where else they might be. Daniel had never seen this girl before. He figured she must be new to Killian's collection. New girls weren't always the best to choose. Unfortunately, Daniel's body was thinking otherwise, and it showed. The blonde didn't look impressed.

"What now, Lithia? Don't you see I'm busy? You are supposed to be in the room with Tiffany and that CEO from whatever that company. Take photos. I'm thinking I could blackmail a few for more profits."

"That man's an issue. He has already hit Tiffany several times; she's got bruises coming up on her face. Her eye is black and swollen. I barely made it out. We need you to get him. I couldn't find any of the guards."

"Get back in there. If you start taking photos, he will be too scared to hit anyone anymore. He paid over a thousand for both of you. Do your job; I'll do mine."

"No, I won't. The only thing I am going to do is get Tiffany out of that room now!"

Lithia turned and Killian grabbed her arm. He pulled her closer to him, "If you even try to stop him from having what he considers a good time, I'll give you what punishment I desire."

"I don't care." She snatched her hand away, but not before Killian sliced the back of her hand with his switch-blade. Lithia screamed in pain, grasping her hand to stop the bleeding. Her eyes searched Daniel's for help.

"Killian, I'll take the girls. This one can't work now anyway. She'll probably need stitches. Who knows about the other one? I'll take them both, right now. Here, two thousand. They just made you three thousand tonight. Lithia, is it, take me to the other girl."

Daniel took off his shirt to wrap around Lithia's bleeding hand, threw the money at Killian, and helped get the other girl from the room. These girls were going with him to Tampa. He was getting more girls out.

Chapter 41

May 4, 2019

When Daniel Armstrong had woken up this morning, his only thoughts were of the charity ball and how many days he had left to make Craig sell the property. What Craig didn't see was the potential in all the sale. Nurse Mabel's house needed a major re-haul. They had put a lot of work into it for sentimental values.

Exercise made him think, so he jumped on the cross-trainer while he pondered his next move. The house was sitting on a large block that was being rezoned. Most of the other homes had sold already and were being torn down to start construction. Nurse Mabel's property was one of the last to sell. Daniel had been offered an extravagant amount.

I just want Craig to sell me his portion of the property. Nurse Mabel put me in charge of real estate for a reason; if he would stop being so dang sentimental and let me do what she wanted. I can't tell Craig the entire proposal, but I want to leave a legacy, too. If Craig finds out what I'm planning, he is going to go all Jesus crazy on me. I'll do the God thing when I'm old, like fifty. I have time.

Ring! Ring! What now on a Saturday morning before 9 AM?
"Yep, Daniel Armstrong here!"

"This is Captain Justice of the sheriff's department. I'm in charge of the prostitution ring investigation and your name has been brought to our attention. I'd like you to come down to the precinct to answer a few questions. I have an officer in route to escort you."

"I'll need to shower and dress, but I will be expecting him."

I'm trying to get my life right and obstacles keep standing in my way. No way can I be like Craig, all Christian-goody, but God wants you to give to others, help the widows and orphans and the hopeless. I can do that. I'm trying to do that. Nurse Mabel would probably quote the verse about 'reaping what you sowed.' Guess I'm going to be paying the consequences.

As Daniel showered and dressed in trepidation of the impending interrogation at police headquarters, he thought back to the night with Leslie Gibson. How brokenhearted she was from a man who vowed to love and protect her. How Harry had blackmailed her with his own child to force her to perform vulgar acts for his pleasure and others. Leslie had reminded him of Craig's mother. The hopelessness in the eyes was the same. He never knew what had become of her after the phone call stating she and the boy were safe until the reporter mentioned the wife was testifying as a witness.

The back of a police car was not where Daniel ever imagined to ride, but as he took this journey, he knew he deserved to be there. Big deal he helped Leslie get away from a horrible marriage and slavery. So what he had gotten Lithia and Amy from under Killian's thumb. But he hadn't been any better. Had he not tricked girls into working for him, doing the same thing? Did he really think he was the good guy because he didn't beat them, or let them get abused by the clientele? He had sold women. Why even the day he 'saved' Leslie, he had physically wanted her more than any female he had ever seen. Then after talking to her all night, he only wanted to protect her.

Lithia, too, had brought on a strange emotion in Daniel that first meeting. There was a beauty like Lithia, but different. His body had a mind of its own, but his heart saw a girl needing a big brother. He had taken her away, placed her in an apartment, and gave her a job, and she excelled. There was a time or two in the first few months, he intimidated her into entertaining a few clients. Guilt had racked his dreams for weeks until he promised her never again. Was it really three years ago, today, he had bought her from Killian?

"Thank you for coming in to speak with me, Mr. Armstrong. I'm hoping you can clear up a few items on this prostitution scandal we have uncovered. I'm assuming you have seen reports on the news. From the beginning of our investigation over three years ago, we have been working with Sheriff King in Miami on a filtration of college formed 'harems' for parties and such. These last three years, it has shown up a little in Tampa. The head of the organization was killed a couple of days ago, along with one of his right-hand man. Have you heard any of this from the news, Mr. Armstrong?"

"Yes, sir, I am aware of the outcome of the sting operation via the nightly news. But what does this have to do with me?"

"Aww, then you heard how we were asking for information from anyone that might know about these men or others who might have worked under them. We even asked for former 'employees' to speak up. One of the gentlemen who died, Harold 'Harry" Gibson, his wife has been very influential to the case. Your name was mentioned when she gave her statement; a few other 'harem' girls have given us your name as well."

Daniel's arms had been crossed on the table in front of him. With this, he laid his head down and covered his face.

I'm doomed; Oh God, I'm doomed. Nurse Mabel taught me the path to follow; why didn't I listen? Over three years trying to sit things right, and it has been for naught. Craig says that God knows your heart. Then God see my heart; I've been trying to make up for the mistakes I made. I'm sorry. Jesus, I need you.

"Mr. Armstrong, are you okay? Would you like some water?"

"I know my rights; may I speak with my attorney?"

"Excuse me, but Mr. Armstrong, did you think you were under arrest? Far from it. Mrs. Gibson listed you for helping her get away from her husband. She said you gave her five thousand dollars to take her son here to Tampa. You told her of a woman's center for abuse, and since then, she has been living right under your nose. Why, Harry only found her this week after she was televised on the news, speaking on behalf of the charity ball, which I believe you are helping host? Did you not realize who she was?"

Daniel had sat up and his mouth was wide open. Was this really happening?

"I've had at least five women from the 'harem' of Killian Shaefer who collaborated Mrs. Gibson's story with similar events. An 'Amy' applauded you and dubbed you the 'Harlot's Hero.' Her tale included a girl with a bleeding hand wrapped in your shirt, a knock-out punch to the man that was beating her, two thousand dollars thrown at Killian, and carrying her out of his house with the other girl following behind. You didn't stop there, but gave them an apartment to share in Tampa and clerical jobs in your real estate company. Amy worked there until she married. I understand the bleeding hand girl, a Miss Lithia Murphy, is still in your employment. I'm going to need to speak with her. Other women state you gave them money, bus tickets, and paid Killian for the night so they could use the opportunity to get away. Got them to go back to college or get their GED or some other training. Mr. Armstrong, you have been a savior to many of these women."

"There's only one Savior, the one who died on a cross."

When Daniel was brought home, it was noon. He couldn't believe how the morning had went. There was no doubt it was God. It was a miracle they hadn't put him behind bars and locked the doors for good. He didn't just feel relieved, he felt alive. He knew what sinless felt like. And he wanted to tell someone.

I want to tell Craig. In person. No too much to do, I'll have to do it over the phone. But first, I want to call The Rev. I need to get baptized tomorrow.

With The Rev on board and thoroughly joyous of Daniel's repentance, it was time to call Craig.

"Craig, brother, we need to talk. I would rather do this in person, but times been wasted long enough. We are true brothers. As of today, no one can say that stupid foster brother stuff again. We have the same Father; do you understand, Craig? Through Christ, who has set me free, we are brothers!"

"Hallelujah! Thank you, Jesus! It's about time! I bet Nurse Mabel is having a good Holy Ghost jig on the golden streets about now. Tell me when and where and how did your devil-living self finally give God a chance?"

"I'll explain all that in due time. Look, Craig, I know you really don't want to sell Nurse Mabel's home. But she had me in charge of the real estate portion of all this for a reason. This is what I have been working on. I have someone who wants to buy the property at triple the price. I wasn't telling you because I wanted to do this on my own. I was going to buy you out, then sell to them. Not to cheat you, but to purchase the six acres adjunct to Mt. Zion Missionary Church. I want to build a women's center for your foundation, a daycare facility with the ability to bring senior citizens in to interact with the children, and a small walk-in clinic named after Nurse Mabel. There's going to be enough money to remodel the church gym and add to the after-school building after relocating the CJ O'Shay's baseball and the Armstrong football fields."

"That's what you have planned? Why didn't you tell me? I would have said yes in a heartbeat. Nurse Mabel would have loved every bit of it. How about The Rev? Have you discussed this with him? I would want the church on board before we start rearranging their buildings."

"You can ask them yourself tomorrow. I'm getting baptized in the evening service, and you're coming with me. Now, if I have your permission, I'm going to confirm our sell of the house and the purchase of the six acres. I will see you tonight; I've got errands to do and a lady who needs to be thanked."

Thank you, Jesus. My prayers are answered. The rejoicing in heaven must be great today. This week has been one of the biggest blessings in my life. Everything in business is well; and the foundation is growing larger, all miracles from you. I finally have a brother who has given his heart to you; now maybe he will open his heart for you to fill it with the woman of his desires.

Since you seem to be in the mood for prayer requests filled, I need help, Lord. Cinderella, there's something about her I can't explain. At her very presence, my body rages with a fire I've never experienced. The physical desire is so over-whelming, I fight to keep my body in control. The chemistry between us is apparent; however, I am not sure our feelings are as pure as they should be. I sense she's not innocent of physical relations, but here I am, completely naïve. How do I even compete? She will think I am a silly teenage boy.

I believe she once knew you, had faith, and walked with you, but something happened. Her flesh was weak, she was tempted, she disappointed you and her family. I don't know what, but there are guilt and shame, even hopelessness sometimes in her eyes. All week I have asked for opportunities to speak to her about your love and mercy. Some days I boldly spoke; others I pray my actions showed a Christ-like spirit of love. I wish I could pursue a relationship with her, but it would be pointless without your blessing. I ask that one day, she comes back to you.

Daniel felt like a new man. With Jesus in his heart, life took on a different meaning. He was fearless of tomorrow and joyous of today. He had found hope.

He finished with the call to The Rev, and Craig dialed the real estate agency to confirm the sale of Nurse Mabel's home, asking to close within a week. Then contacted the owner of the acreage by Mt. Zion and gave an offer on the land. It was accepted with closing on the same day as Nurse Mabel's. It was going to be another adventure traveling between Tampa and Miami, and adding that Craig needed to be included in flying down from Raleigh.

Ok, Big Guy, I got another one of those requests. I need to tell someone thank you. I am not sure how, but I need to explain who I really am. May she accept me as willing today as she once did. Amen.

"Wow, those are gorgeous blue flowers. Don't think I've ever seen anything like it. Oh, and a present, too, I see. You're not a reporter, are you? I can't let you in, if you are."

"I'm Daniel Armstrong, CEO of Armstrong Corporation. We are cohosting with the Saoirse's Heart of Hope Foundation for the charity ball tonight. I was here to see if Mrs. Leslie Gibson was available to have visitors."

"Why, I am sure she would love to have another visitor. I'm glad it isn't a police officer again. Those stress her out. You will make her second guest of the day. I'm Eva by the way, at your service. Just come on through those doors and follow the hallway to the back. You can't miss the clinic. She's the only patient right now. Leslie is going to love those flowers."

"Did you say she was in the clinic? She's a patient? I thought she worked here."

"She does, but after she went on the television to promote the charity ball, her husband found her and the boy locking up the center a few days later. He messed her up and the boy. Jenson is getting better. His bumps and bruises are minimal to what his momma received. She isn't out of the woods yet."

Thanks, God. I got her from Harry to deal with him one more time, years later. How I wish she had never spoken on camera. She's got to be a strong woman for her son. Heal her for his sake."

"Hi there, Mister. Who's the present for, and that's a lot of blue flowers! Are you a prince, too? Prince Charming always comes with flowers for Momma. So, are you a prince, too?"

"Nope, kiddo, never been classified as a prince, but I have been told I'm a hero. I'm Mr. Armstrong; I'm looking for Wonder Woman. Do you know where I can find her?"

"My momma is Sleeping Beauty, Cinderella said so. But she could be Wonder Woman. She's in the clinic resting. Do you want to see her?"

"Why, yes, I would. I presume you are her son, Jenson Gibson? Happy to make your acquaintance. Then this gift bag is for you, but you have to open it with your momma."

Spunky kid there. Broken arm must be a gift from old Daddy Harry. Poor guy, he needs a real dad. I always thought my dad didn't love me or have time for me, but I still remember fishing and catch with the football and baseball. Dad was even coach for Pop Warner football. I'd never gotten a football scholarship if he hadn't taught me how to play.

"Momma, you got another visitor, and this one is a hero. He brought me a present. Can I open it? Oh, you got some blue flowers. Come on and sit down by Momma. Her eye doesn't look too good, but they took the bandage off after Cinderella left. Things get a little blurry, so you got to sit close."

"Jenson, why don't you sit down on the end of my bed and open your present. Let me see what the nice 'hero' gave you." Leslie was trying to see clearly who this man was at the foot of her bed.

"It's a football! Thank you! Wanna play catch with me?"

"I just might do that, but why don't you let me talk to your momma for a bit, and I know you are going to a ball tonight. You are going to have to get ready for that soon. I will, too."

"You're going? Did you hear, Momma? I'm going to a ball that has a hero, Cinderella, and Prince Charming. This night

316

is going to be awesome!" Sobering, "Only thing missing is Wonder Woman."

"Wonder Woman? Who are you calling Wonder Woman?"

"Armstrong the Hero did. He said you were strong like Wonder Woman."

Leslie finally turned and focused her eyes on the man sitting at the chair to her left. When she realized who it was, tears began to stream down her face.

"Jenson, you were right. This is what a hero looks like. He's my hero and yours." But softly whispering as she reached for his hand, "Daniel Armstrong, the harlot's hero, I've prayed you'd come."

Daniel left in high spirits. He had never felt so carefree. Jenson was the best kid ever. Smart and quite good at catching a football, even with a broken arm. He had promised to come back and work with him, especially after his cast was off. Maybe in the fall, if Wonder Woman would let him, he could sign him up for Pop Warner football. Shoot, he might even investigate coaching the team.

He had given her the flowers, the forget-me-nots. She said how could she ever forget him. Leslie, she amazed him. She had taken even more abuse from a man that once claimed to love her, and she stood strong. But this time, she didn't look heartbroken. Physically broken, but the hope in her eyes, the glow around her face, even the tone of her voice, was full of faith and joy of tomorrow. He thought she was still beautiful. She told him of how she had prayed that night years ago for God to bring her a way of escape. He had met her request with Daniel, her hero.

God let her body heal so, I might show her how a hero can love.

Chapter 42

May 4, 2019

I can't believe Leslie apologized to me. All these years I felt responsible for what happened to her, and bitter towards her, at times, for the lies she fabricated. That was not the Leslie I once knew. She's changed; not from being with Harold and the horrible experience, but she's humble and mellow. Her face was glowing with love and hope. Who does she remind me of...my grandmother! Leslie gave her heart to the Lord. There is no other reason I can fathom than God.

"Excuse me, Miss Murphy, Miss Lithia Murphy? I'm Officer Pratt with the Tampa Police Department, and I need you to come with me to the station."

What now?

Revelations were abundant today. Leslie has been forgiven and has forgiven others. Then Harold and Killian are dead and punished for all the hell they put so many girls through. The icing on the cake was to hear of the Harlot's Hero as Daniel was being called at the police station. Lithia wasn't even comprehending half of the conversation. Daniel and Lithia had been named as former associates of Killian Shaefer, but the informant had been Amy. It had been confirmed Daniel had rescued not just Amy and Lithia, but prior to them, Leslie. Since Daniel's move to Tampa, he had been able to 'free' over twenty girls that police were aware so far. All which had given him the name of Harlot's Hero.

Wait? Daniel Armstrong. My boss? The man that told me a week ago to give Craig 'whatever he wants,' he is the hero, the good guy? I guess, I mean, maybe he is. He didn't know me or Amy when he took us that night. Gave us jobs and an apartment. I've seen some of the other girls from the harem at the office, but I assumed he still did a little business. He isn't Killian; I have never seen him raise a hand to strike one. Daniel hasn't even tried to sleep with me, or any of the women in the office. This day can't get any weirder.

Ding!

Cinderella, did u get Jenson his tux? I thought I would help him get ready. Pick u up at 6:15. Can't wait 2 C U in that dress! PC

Oh, Craig, my Prince Charming, I can't wait to see you either.

Craig O'Shay had showered and shaved, but wanted Jenson to feel how it was for "the guys to get ready together." He had brought along his tux to dress with Jenson. He had picked up both tuxes an hour before; the tailor had sewed the alterations for Jenson's tux Miss Murphy had purchased that morning. He stopped for two boutonnieres and a wrist corsage. A white rose and some baby's breath would give them a debonair look. Craig was getting nervous with anticipation for the night to begin.

Jenson had been told by Mrs. Eva to stay clean after his scrubbing. She had supervised his showering attempt, and today he was cleaning behind those ears. The boy's neck was still beet red when Craig walked into the center, holding the garment bags.

"Well, did a bee sting you?" Craig was smiling as he patted Jenson on the head.

"No," as he cut his ears to Mrs. Eva. "She made me take a bath like a baby!"

"I don't think you can fit in one of those baby bathtubs, or can you?" Craig started examining around Jenson's ears. "But you are spic and span."

"Aww, Mrs. Eva thinks I gotta be scrubbed like a heathen. I told her I can do it myself, but she didn't believe me. Now, look at me. I am a sunburnt piece of toast."

"Well, Mr. Sassy Pants had been playing football outside with Mr. Armstrong and gotten sweaty with grandma dirty beads on his neck and behind the ears. Wouldn't want him to be at a charity ball looking like a hooligan, would we?"

"Come on, Prince Charming, we got to get ready, or she's gonna try to scrub your ears too. Momma wants to meet you and see me in my tux before we go."

"Did I hear correctly from Mrs. Eva, Mr. Armstrong was playing football with you today?"

"Yep, he is Momma's hero. She said so. He brought me a football and Momma some blue...forget-me-not flowers. He called Momma 'Wonder Woman' just like you call Miss Murphy Cinderella. That's how we got away from the bad man. Momma's hero did it. I think he likes Momma; they held hands the whole time he sat by her bed. He said she was a strong woman, like Wonder Woman, and pretty too. Even with the bandages and bruises. She's been smiling ever since. Do you want to meet Momma now or after we get dressed?"

"Oh, is it my turn to talk now?"

"Why, sure, I'm done for now." He titled his head up to Craig and gave a sheepish smile.

"Then, dressed first. That way your momma sees us both looking our best. Lead the way to the dressing room."

Leslie was speechless when she saw her son strutting into her room. He was so grown up with his white jacket and black pants. In his lapel, a white rose with the blue baby's breath made her cry. Jenson was a mini version of Mr. O'Shay, minus the red hair. She felt so much better since Daniel's visit; she was sitting in the chair beside the bed. When she finally acknowledged Craig standing beside her son, she thought he looked familiar.

"How do you do, Mr. O'Shay; I'm Leslie Gibson, Jenson's mother, as you well know. I am so grateful for everything your foundation has been doing to promote advocacy for abused women. I wouldn't even be here if it wasn't for Daniel Armstrong or for your center. God has blessed me tremendously. I want to thank you as well for tonight. Jenson has been so excited since you came to the center. Now, today has just been one miracle after another. To reunite with my best friend and to see the man who helped me escape from Harold, I just don't know what else God could do make today better."

"Harold was your husband?"

"Yes, my husband. Some people knew him by Harry. You see, we met nine years ago, when I was just sixteen. I thought I was in love. I lost my friends, family, lost everything I valued...like my self-worth. I'm surprised I'm alive. The world has changed since that year at summer youth camp."

"I used to go to youth camp as a teen and even as an adult. I was a camp counselor. Haven't been in years. It was there I met my best friends, Leo and Sean. They're even going to be at the charity ball with their wives. Christian friends are a gift from God in times of trouble."

"I grew up with a Leo and Sean; why we went to church together. They were older than me, though. I had the biggest crush on Leo, but he didn't notice me at all. He was all about the preacher's daughter. Wouldn't it be funny if we were talking about the same Leo? What camp did you go to?"

"We went to Wekiva Springs Campgrounds for about three weeks in July. And Leo, he married a preacher's daughter. She has an unusual name, Sunflower."

"Sunflower Johnson? With two sisters, Violet and Lily? God is doing it again. Another miracle. Wait, so you went to the same camp I did and know Leo. But I don't remember any Craig O'Shay. Last time I went was 2010. When I met Harold."

"Hold on, I'm so stupid. You said Harold Gibson was your husband? That was the name of my roommate at camp. It was the four of us, Harold, Sean, Leo, and me that year. It was the only year Harold had come as a counselor, then he left with a girl in the middle of the night. I stayed up all night searching for her. The girls were a mess. I never saw Harold or the girl again."

"I was that girl. But the only guy that was their roommate that I knew of was named CJ. He was red-headed and could play the piano. He could sing, and when my friend Lithia joined him, the whole congregation felt God's presence."

"Craig Jenson O'Shay, or better known as CJ in my college years and at youth camp, at your service."

"God has been good to me today. Now I completely understand the Prince Charming and Cinderella reference.

You have a good time tonight and, Jenson, you better be on your best behavior."

"I will, Momma. I love you. I'll tell you everything about the ball when I get home."

Lithia and CJ. Cinderella and Prince Charming. I can't believe what God has done.

Did she mention Lithia? I haven't heard about her in so long. Sean doesn't say much about her since she went missing on Thanksgiving, the day their father died. I haven't dared to ask him either. He did know she had graduated from the University of Miami; the university had sent a letter to his mom. Maybe I will ask him tonight. Tell him who Jenson's mother is and that when he speaks with Lithia again, let her know Leslie is fine.

"This is where Miss Murphy lives, Jenson. It is proper for the gentleman to go up to the door to help her to the car. We open the door for them and pull out chairs."

"And say nice things to a lady about her hair and clothes. And you have to ask her to dance. Momma said the man leads. Oh, and if the guy is really nice, she might kiss him good night. I think that is gross, but Momma says I won't think that in a few years. Do you want Cinderella to kiss you cause you're going to have to be nice tonight?"

"I think, I got this, Jenson. Cinderella may not want to kiss me, and some girls don't, but that's okay. You just remember to always treat them like you want a man to treat your mom or your sister."

At least Jenson will be somewhat of a distraction. I don't want to scare Cinderella off; I'd be like the real Prince, scouring the city, looking for the girl with the glass slipper. I want her to meet Leo and Sean. I need godly wisdom to taper these emotions Cinderella arouses. The temptation has only strengthened no matter how much I pray "whatsoever things are pure, whatsoever things are lovely..." I get to lovely and I think of EVERYTHING lovely about her.

Then Miss Murphy opened her door.

Cinderella is enchanting. How can you make such beauty in one woman? And tonight, she's on my arm.

"WOW, Cinderella is really a princess! Prince Charming, you're going to have to be kind tonight for her to give you a kiss." Trying to whisper, but failing miserably, "You're not complimenting her, Mr. O'Shay, say something or close your mouth."

Lithia couldn't speak. Craig O'Shay was elegant. His eyes were so clear and blue she could drown in them. He revealed Lithia's deep desire for human touch, this need Craig awakened, she had never felt before. There was an intimacy she was finding with this man without sex. It gave a new meaning to what she once preconceived about the passions between a man and woman.

"Why, I have the most handsome men as my dates tonight. I am a lucky woman. You are so distinguished and charming, Jenson, I just don't know if I can ever find another dapper gentleman like you."

"I'm sorry, Cinderella, but you're too old for me. Prince Charming is gonna have to be the next best thing." Lithia stifled her amusement.

Jenson had no idea. Having that kid along, it was like having a matchmaker in the same room, same limo, same everything all night. Craig just shook his head.

The hotel Lithia had found for the charity ball was impressive. The decorator and an event planner had outdone themselves. Translucent veils were draped around the columns of the ballroom while clustered with twinkling lights. The tables, which wrapped the outer portion of the dance floor, were covered in white linen coverings, crystal glasses, and silver utensils. The centerpieces were mixed bouquets of carnations and roses, bringing an extraordinary splash of color to the room. On the stage, an orchestra played softly, welcoming the guests. To the right were French doors to the adjunct gardens and gazebo overlooking out to Apollo Beach. The entire space was staggering with ambience.

"Mr. O'Shay, could you meet with the cater in the kitchen? She has something to discuss with you." The event planner must have been waiting for them to arrive; he seemed nervous.

"I'll be back shortly, Cinderella. Mr. Gibson, would you be so kind to escort Miss Murphy to her seat? I believe we should be in the front." Handing Lithia's arm to Jenson, he bowed and followed the planner.

In the kitchen to greet Craig were his buddies, Leo and Sean. They were leaning on the counter, discreetly sticking their fingers in the icing bowl. LeeAnn slapped their hands with the wooden spoon.

"Hey, CJ, this place looks marvelous. Tell me we didn't just donate to pay this bill off? If so, I want an all-you-can-eat buffet." Leo was still the jokester.

"Leonard, leave the boy alone. He's probably already on pins and needles about the event. I'm just glad I was able to come through for you, CJ, after that other chef bailed on poor Cinderella. I want to be sure to say hello to her before the night's over."

"Cinderella? Who's that?" Leo and Sean said it in unison. Sunflower and Erika came walking in from being in the garden with Captain Fred.

"Why, she's a looker, that Cinderella. CJ here brought her on the sailboat Tuesday. Wonderful girl. Headful of stunning strawberry blonde hair, sorta like yours, Sean. Did you bring her as your date, Prince Charming?" Captain Fred popped CJ on his back.

"I did. She's at the table with Jenson. Stop. Wait I have to tell you all about this one. Remember back at camp, our roomie, Harold?" He waited until the four younger ones nodded. "Then you also remember the girl?"

"Of course, Leslie was so in love with him. She left everything to be with him. Married him too and was pregnant; last her folks heard from her. Mom and Dad couldn't comfort her parents enough. Mom said Leslie's mother would have horrible dreams about her." Sunflower couldn't hold back the tears.

"Yes, she was the same age as Sean's sister, Lithia. They had been friends, but after the Harold thing and the gossip Leslie told about Lithia, Leslie had dug her own hole." Erika stopped speaking when she saw Sean's demeanor change. He still hurt from missing his sister.

"Jenson, the little boy that is sitting at our table with Cinderella, he is the son of Harold and Leslie. Harold was killed this week by the police. Leslie has been hiding from him with the boy for several years. She was rescued from Harold's clutches by my friend Daniel. He found her in Miami and sent her with Jenson here to one of the women's center here in Tampa. She's been working at the center. Leslie went on the local news last weekend to support the ball. She was even going to speak tonight, but Harold found her after the broadcast. She's in bad condition. He even broke the boy's arm."

"Dear Lord, CJ. How awful! Do her parents know? Of course, they don't. I'm calling Mom and Dad. Her folks are going to need their pastor to tell them all of this. Give me the name of the center. I can have Mom and Dad give all this information to her parents within the hour. By the time you get Jenson back to his momma, he will get to meet his grandparents for the first time." Sunflower walked out into the garden to call her parents as Erika called Sean's.

Erika related the same message to Lola. Since Lola had their kids, Sean thought maybe she would be willing to stay at the Johnson's to watch Leo and Sunflower's kids while the Johnson's went to Leslie's house. Lola had been on the way to the church parsonage anyway. She and Ruth had planned on letting the grandkids keep Pappy Johnson, aka Pastor, entertained as they cooked pies for the bake sale after church. Lola told her this was an answer to a prayer and would work out perfectly.

With the two wives dealing with the next reunion for Leslie, Craig took this time to talk to his friends. "Guys, I need some advice. Advice on women." Leo was about to make a joke and Sean was doing everything not to laugh. "Seriously, I need some godly direction. Cinderella, she's Daniel's personal assistant, the one your dad mentioned, Leo, it's her. I can't explain it. You both know, I didn't really date in college. One here or there, but never seemed to find one girl that interested me. But this woman, what can I say? She makes my heart pound with those sultry eyes; when I look into them, it's like I'm connected to her in some profound way. When I am with her, nothing is forced, I'm calm and relaxed, I want to be adventurous and sponta-neous. God, how can I fall for this woman so hard, so fast?

I had to hold on to control my fleshly urges more than once this week."

Leo and Sean were astounded. CJ had fallen in love. They had been a little worried, his studies and work had always taken priority above anything other than God. "CJ, is she a Christian? If she isn't, the devil is just getting you distracted. Back away. But if she isn't, you and I know, it will be possible that she pulls you into temptation."

"I don't know. I never asked her point blank. God and church have been brought up in conversation. I believe she grew up in church, but something happened when she was a teen. I need you to pray for clarity on my heart and hers. Ask for discernment when you are around her. Maybe you could dance with her. Get the chance to talk to her one on one. I don't know. I'm going to the table and ask her to dance. I'll see you out there."

Daniel was introducing Jenson to a few guests, and the little boy was getting full attention from everyone. Cinderella was standing by the French doors, looking out into the garden as Craig came from the kitchen area. How he was going to hold her in his arms to dance was going to be another temptation, but one he was going to master.

"Care to dance, Cinderella?" He was so gallant. His hand reached out to take hers, and he even bowed. She placed her hand in his and he led her to the center of the ballroom. Craig pulled her in close as his arm went around her waist.

Lithia couldn't look at him. She was afraid all the emotions built up inside were going to explode. Then he spoke, "Cinderella, my best friends are here from college. Captain Fred's son and his wife, and my other friend is here with his wife. I've told them all about you, and they are eager to make

328

your acquaintance. They will be sitting at our table. I wanted to warn you, Leo loves to play tricks and joke around."

"Oh, I'm pleased you want me to meet your friends. It will be nice learning more about you from them. Don't worry about Leo; if I could put up with my brother and his friend Leo teasing me for years, I've got this guy."

"Thank you, Cinderella. Now let me hold you before someone else tries to snatch you from my arms. I may never get another night like this with you. I'm going to cherish every moment." She laid her head on his shoulder and let him glide her over the floor. She fit like a glove in his arms.

"May I cut in, so, I, too, may have a dance with Cinderella?"

Sean bowed low as Craig placed Cinderella's hand in Sean's. Craig took Sunflower's arm and twirled her away by Leo and Erika, who were by the stage. "I've delivered your wife back to you, Leo. However, I didn't expect you guys would cut in to dance with Cinderella this early."

"She's gorgeous, CJ, from what we can see from here. She had her head on your shoulder, so it was difficult to see her face. Wait, what's going on with her and my husband? Sunflower, why is she hanging on Sean? CJ, you better contain her, or my sanctification might get lost."

When Sean had placed his arm around CJ's Cinderella, he hadn't gotten a full look at her face. As he gave her the first spin on the dance floor, he introduced himself. "It's truly nice to finally meet the woman that has my buddy so happy. I'm Sean Murphy, and my wife Erika is over at the table."

Lithia stopped dancing. She couldn't believe it. She refused to look up at the man who had his arm still around her. "Are you okay, miss? Should I take you back to CJ? Are you not feeling well?"

She lifted her head up to gaze into her brother's face. "Sean, it's me." And he took her into his arms and wept.

When Sean picked his head up, he saw the displeased look from Erika and the others. They didn't realize who he was dancing. He was also confused at CJ's confession of love for Lithia, but he almost seemed as if CJ didn't even know her. Sean just picked her up and carried her to the table. He really didn't want to let her go. His little sister was alive and well. Why, she really did look like Cinderella.

"Sean Murphy, put that woman down and explain yourself right now!" Erika only knew that her husband was holding another woman, and she wasn't going to wait much longer to lose her mind on Sean or the woman. It was when he let Lithia down and she turned towards Erika, Leo, and Sunflower, she was able to speak.

"I didn't know you were here. I've missed you all so much. I'm so sorry for everything, Sean. I tried to come back, I tried to call, then Killian and mother. Then I didn't think you even wanted to see me anymore. I was so ashamed. I couldn't face you. It's been this week you've all been on my mind so much. Then I saw Leslie. Do you know she's here in Tampa at one of Mr. O'Shay's centers? She forgave me. Where is Mr. O'Shay? You must meet him."

"This is only a God thing. Hallelujah! Not one but two of our hometown girls have been found in one day. Lithia, why are you calling CJ, Mr. O'Shay? That's so weird."

"What are you talking about, Leo? Craig O'Shay is the man who runs the foundation for the women's centers we are here to support tonight. I've been working with him all week."

"Are you telling me, little sister, you don't know that Craig and CJ from youth camp, our old cabin mate, are the same man? All week you have been with him? If you don't know he is CJ, then he doesn't know she's Lithia?"

Leo's face had that mischievous grin, and the light bulb had come on over his head. "Oh, Sean, this is just too good. As much as CJ talked about your little sister after that year at camp. Then he never came home with us for breaks, then she was gone. He never stopped asking about you until after your dad passed. Sean told him you were with that creep. I take it he isn't around?"

"Killian hasn't been around since Daniel, my boss, bought me from Killian over three years ago. Gave him $1,000 and brought me here to Tampa. He gave him the same amount for another girl. Daniel put us in an apartment, gave us a job at his office, and Thursday, the police were in the middle of arresting Killian, and he was killed. That might not be the best way to have told you my life, but it's the truth. I'm not the girl you once knew. I'm sorry, Sean."

"He bought you? I'm not...No, my sister, who we didn't know if she was dead or alive, is here and well. You're gorgeous. I understand why CJ calls you Cinderella. Mother is going to be so thrilled to get this call. She'll probably faint. Erika already told her an hour ago that Leslie was here. Now to let her know her own daughter is alive; she's being praying for your return for so long."

Craig had host duties to fulfill and was glad to see every time he looked at the main table Cinderella was jabbering with his friends as if they had known each other for years. Each time he thought he might go back over and get a dance or even eat his meal, which was probably getting cold, he was pulled away. He noticed Daniel was coddling Jenson. The boy had tricked LeeAnn into three slices of her coconut cake. Now it was time for his speech, and he didn't want to mess it up with Cinderella on his mind. He would have plenty of time for dancing after the speech.

His speech was over, but he wanted to express his gratitude to Daniel's company and to Cinderella for all she did prior to him coming to Tampa and this past week. Craig asked Daniel to come to the stage and gave a little background on how they met. Daniel spoke of their new project, which would be starting in a month in Miami. There was a whooping and hollering that most would not think would ever happen at such a grand ball.

When the guests quieted, Craig told Daniel he was grateful for not only what he had done, but for allowing him to have the pleasure of working with the lovely Cinderella. Daniel was confused.

"The who?"

"Cinderella, would you please stand up? I want to personally and publicly, thank you for the work you have done behind the scenes for this charity ball. She has been a delight as a Tampa tour guide as well. As all of you can see, she is lovely as a princess. I haven't even called her by her real name all week. Oh, yes, Miss Murphy, Miss..."

Lithia had stood up, and everyone was looking at her. Those at her table were waiting. It was time for her to tell this man she had confided in nine years ago, the man who had promised he would keep her secret forever, this man she was falling for now, who made her heart pound with excitement just to have him near; it was time she told him who she was. In front of three hundred people, he was going to know it was the chunky girl from camp, the one he cradled on the steps, helped to shower, gave his clothes, that he sang with, her knight in shining armor. He was the man that hadn't changed. Lithia took a couple of steps forward.

"Lithia. My name is Lithia Murphy."

Craig just stood there. Comatose. Staring at this woman, this Cinderella, then he saw it. He didn't see this sophisticated Cinderella. CJ looked into the eyes of the girl he held after Harold had tried to defile her, the girl with the voice from heaven, the girl in the baby blue sundress with the white shawl covering her bruises, the girl he danced with at youth camp so long ago. His Cinderella, innocent and vulnerable in his arms by the hammock, was the same one he rode roller coasters with at Busch Gardens, the same one who rubbed suntan lotion on his back, the same one in the horse-drawn carriage, the same one who ate Chinese takeout and pizza, the one who looked like a princess in that flowing blue gown, looking up at him with those trusting eyes. Lithia was his Cinderella.

The audience was holding their breath. No one knew why, but something miraculous was taking place. In the silence, Craig had begun to walk off the stage toward Lithia. Sunflower and Erika were crying as they were being held by their husbands. Captain Fred and LeeAnn were smiling at the side; they had been praying for these two all week. Now they knew why God had laid them both on their hearts.

Directly in front of her now, Craig took her hand, and with his other hand, he cupped her chin lifting it gently for her to look at him. She was blushing, just like at youth camp, just like the other night when he almost kissed her at the apartment. "Lithia, my Cinderella. You were beautiful in youth camp just as much as you are right now. I have never forgotten you. I pray you want me to be your Prince Charming."

"You always have been."

He leaned down, his patience to devour her mouth was tremendous, he swallowed, and kissed her nose. The front table clapped louder than anyone.

The orchestra began to play, and other couples came to the dance floor. Lithia and Craig saw only each other. And at the stroke of midnight, Cinderella didn't have to leave Prince Charming, this man of faith and integrity.

So, at the last stroke of midnight, she asked this knight, this Prince Charming, "I want to feel pure love again. I want to be clean. The kind that only God can give."

There in the gazebo, Cinderella and Prince Charming prayed forgiveness, for compassion, for love, for understanding, for restoration and reconciliation.

With the joy of the Lord illuminating from her face, Prince Charming took possession of those lips for the first time. Cinderella knew it wouldn't be the last.

God had restored more than she had ever hoped.

He had restored a harlot's heart.

Character Names and Meanings

(Some characters' names not listed for obvious reasons)
Craig-Rock
Lithia-Flower
Saoirse-Liberty and Freedom
Thomas-Friendly
Peter-Stone
Lola-Sorrows
Sean-God is gracious
Erika-Powerful
Harold-Army Leader
Daniel-God is my judge
Leslie-Garden
Mabel-Loving
Señora Corona-Queen's crown
Jenson- Jehovah has been gracious
Killian-War/strife
Jim (James)- a supplanter is something or someone who wrongfully takes the place of another.
Eva-Full of life
Martha-The lady
Renee-Born again
Carrie-Warm-hearted
Leo-Lion
Officer Pratt-Cunning
Amy-Beloved

CPSIA information can be obtained
at www.ICGtesting.com
Printed in the USA
LVHW05052526I1120
672646LV00002B/217